As much as he hated the idea, Harry knew the creature had to be destroyed, but where was he?

When they returned to the Animal Care Unit, Millie wasn't there. They found Siscom in the small lab, working.

"How'd it go with Dr. Pauling?" he said after they entered the lab.

Harry ignored the question. "Where's Millie, Gerald? Have you seen her?" he demanded, his tone terse, his spine stiff.

"Not since you all left here earlier. She may have gone to say goodbye to Roku. She had become very close to that creature. I was going to euthanize it later this afternoon. Funny thing though, I feel I'd be killing Millie in the process. It carries her genome."

"Millie's been terminated, Gerald. As of now. I need to tell her. You have no idea where she is?"

"Like I said she might be at Tika's cage saying goodbye to Roku. Let's go see. I'd like to be with her when you tell her."

"Fine," Harry said, and the trio walked to the cage area.

Millie wasn't there.

Neither was Roku.

"Okay, Gerald," Harry said, irritation rising in his voice. "Where is she? She's gone and taken the chimera with her."

"I have no idea, Harry, honest."

Harry strode through the Animal Care Unit, searching the area. "Gerald," he continued, "it won't look good on your record if I learn you have abetted her in this travesty and in taking Roku."

They stopped at the airlock.

"Harry, I swear I knew nothing of Millie's plan until

shortly before delivery, and, by then, it was too late. She never took me into her confidence prior to that. You've got to believe me."

"We do," Dixie said. "Harry's just upset. This is a lot to fathom in one afternoon."

"And deal with," Harry added.

As much as he hated the idea, Harry knew the creature had to be destroyed, but where was he?

When they returned to the Animal Care Unit, Millie wasn't there. They found Siscom in the small lab, working.

"How'd it go with Dr. Pauling?" he said after they entered the lab.

Harry ignored the question. "Where's Millie, Gerald? Have you seen her?" he demanded, his tone terse, his spine stiff.

"Not since you all left here earlier. She may have gone to say goodbye to Roku. She had become very close to that creature. I was going to euthanize it later this afternoon. Funny thing though, I feel I'd be killing Millie in the process. It carries her genome."

"Millie's been terminated, Gerald. As of now. I need to tell her. You have no idea where she is?"

"Like I said she might be at Tika's cage saying goodbye to Roku. Let's go see. I'd like to be with her when you tell her."

"Fine," Harry said, and the trio walked to the cage area.

Millie wasn't there.

Neither was Roku.

"Okay, Gerald," Harry said, irritation rising in his voice. "Where is she? She's gone and taken the chimera with her."

"I have no idea, Harry, honest."

Harry strode through the Animal Care Unit, searching the area. "Gerald," he continued, "it won't look good on your record if I learn you have abetted her in this travesty and in taking Roku."

They stopped at the airlock.

"Harry, I swear I knew nothing of Millie's plan until

shortly before delivery, and, by then, it was too late. She never took me into her confidence prior to that. You've got to believe me."

"We do," Dixie said. "Harry's just upset. This is a lot to fathom in one afternoon."

"And deal with," Harry added.

After the two Yeti—that Dr. Harry Olson, an American paleoanthropologist, and his wife, Dixie, brought home from the mountains of Mongolia—escaped from the Cinder Mountain Research Facility and were killed by police, one of the scientists in Harry's anthropology department at California Pacific University, Dr. Millie Harbaum, uses sperm and an egg, taken from the two Yeti before they escaped, to create a baby Yeti and implants the embryo into a female chimp. But unbeknownst to Harry, Millie has added human DNA to the embryo, actually creating a chimera. When the baby, Roku, is born, he is clearly not a full Yeti, and Millie is forced to confess what she has done. Horrified, the university demands that the infant be destroyed immediately. But Millie flees before they can act, taking Roku with her and unleashing a chain of events that may have deadly consequences, not only for Roku and Millie, but for humanity as well…

KUDOS for *Yeti Reborn*

In *Yeti Reborn* by Richard Eddie, Dr. Millie Harbaum, a scientist in Dr. Harry's Olsen's anthropology department at Cal Pacific University, takes Yeti DNA and mixes it with human DNA at the Cinder Mountain Research Facility, creating a chimera named Roku. When the university president discovers what she has done, he demands that Millie be fired and Roku destroyed. But before Harry can carry out the president's orders, Millie flees the facility, taking Roku with her. Now the hunt is on to find Millie and Roku before the public discovers what has happened. Little does Millie know that her actions will have far-reaching effects. The book is both thrilling and educational, giving you a glimpse into the complex world of scientific research while keeping you glued to the edge of your seat. ~ *Taylor Jones, The Review Team of Taylor Jones & Regan Murphy*

Yeti Reborn by Richard Edde is the story of a scientist with a dream. Millie Harbaum is a scientist in the anthropology department of Cal Pacific University, working at the university's research facility in Nevada on the top of Cinder Mountain. After the two Yeti that Harry Olson and his wife Dixie brought back from Mongolia escaped and were killed by police, Millie is brokenhearted. The death of the two creatures has put her research, on mapping the genome of the Yeti, on hold. But Millie has frozen sperm and eggs taken from the Yeti before they escaped. She convinces Harry to let her implant an embryo into one of the female chimps at the research facility. But what Millie doesn't tell Harry is that she has added human DNA to the embryo, and the creature will be a chimera. When the baby is born, Millie's secret is exposed, and the university is outraged. They order Millie to destroy it, but she refuses. She takes the infant and flees. Now Harry's job is on the line, as well as the safety of humans if the chimera becomes too much for Millie to handle. Filled with endearing characters, plenty of tension, and fast-paced action, as well as a wealth of fascinating scientific information, *Yeti Reborn* will catch and hold your interest from beginning to end. ~ *Regan Murphy, The Review Team of Taylor Jones & Regan Murphy*

Yeti
Reborn

Richard Edde

A Black Opal Books Publication

GENRE: PARANORMAL THRILLER/SUSPENSE

YETI REBORN
Copyright © 2018 by Richard Edde
Cover Design by Jackson Cover Designs
All cover art copyright © 2018
All Rights Reserved
Print ISBN: 978-1-626949-15-7

First Publication: MAY 2018

Published by Black Opal Books **http://www.blackopalbooks.com**

To my brother, David

"Science is dangerous. There is no question but that poison gas, genetic engineering, and nuclear weapons and power stations are terrifying. It may be that civilization is falling apart and the world we know is coming to an end. In that case, why not turn to religion and look forward to the Day of Judgment...[being] lifted into eternal bliss...[and] watching the scoffers and disbelievers writhe forever in torment." ~ *Isaac Asimov*

"Germline therapy...will force us to re-examine even the very notion of what it means to be human [as] we become subject to the same process of conscious design that has so dramatically altered the world around us...Through this technology, we will seize control of our own evolution." ~ *Gregory Stock*

"When people began to multiply on the face of the ground, and daughters were born to them, the sons of God saw that they were fair; and they took wives for themselves of all that they chose. Then the Lord said, "My spirit shall not abide in mortals forever, for they are flesh; their days shall be one hundred twenty years." The Nephilim were on the earth in those days—and also afterward—when the sons of God went in to the daughters of humans, who bore children to them. These were the heroes that were of old, warriors of renown. The Lord saw that the wickedness of humankind was great in the earth, and that every inclination of the thoughts of their hearts was only evil continually. And the Lord was sorry that he had made humankind on the earth, and it grieved him to his heart." *Genesis 6:1-6*

Prologue

The clock on the wall read three a.m.

A small LED lamp, directed at the area in front of Dr. Millie Harbaum, was the only illumination for the laboratory workspace. The lab was quiet, only the soft purring of air conditioning broke the silence. Alone in the lab, Millie's heart raced. Huddled over the desk, she peered at the monitor of the dissecting microscope and adjusted the focus. As the small glistening mass of cells came into sharp relief she caught her breath and thought again of what she was about to do. Was she doing the right thing? she wondered. Or was she about to journey across a line that for years science had been forbidden to broach?

Millie pushed back from the desk, took a deep breath, tried to calm herself, and wiped her moist palms on her lab coat. What she once thought a brilliant idea now loomed perilously close to an ethical blunder. But, upon closer reflection, she knew her hand had been forced—forced by a scientific community that did not condone such breakthroughs. Down through history, progress in the sciences had been made by those few men and women who dared to dream the impossible.

Millie dreamed such a dream.

The lab in which she worked was located in the Primate Research Facility on top of a Nevada mountain and was part of the Anthropology Department of California Pacific University. Funded through private donations, the university was located in San Francisco. Millie's boss, Dr. Miles Radner directed the Primate Research Facility. The facility as a whole and its activities were under the ultimate supervision of the chairman of the department, Dr. Harry Olson. It was Dr. Olson and his team who managed to secure two specimens from Mongolia, the Yeti—a creature once thought only to exist in legends. Dr. Olson and his team of scientists brought the animals to the research facility where, over the following year, they sequenced their entire DNA genome. The work had been difficult and demanding but Millie, who was a graduate research assistant at the time, put her whole life into the project.

Then, there had been a tragic accident. Through a miscalculation of her coworker, both Yeti escaped, killing the coworker in the process. The creatures managed to get off the mountain and terrorized the surrounding countryside, killing a number of people. They were eventually hunted down and destroyed by law enforcement. Everyone, including Dr. Olson, thought it was the end of the Yeti research. Until Millie conceived her experiment.

Now she had her doctorate and was a full-time facility scientist.

And she had a few tricks up her sleeve.

After the deaths of the animals, Dr. Olson gave her the assignment to try and find a way to use the Yeti's genome. She knew that through the PCR process there was an ample supply of the animal's DNA. In addition, she and her fellow graduate student collected and stored many Yeti eggs and sperm that were now stored in a freezer down the hallway, waiting to be put to use. Prior to the animal's escape, Millie injected the female Yeti with HCG, Human Chorionic Gonadotropin, forcing the animal to super-ovulate, and with Dr. Siscom's help, she collected hundreds of ovum. Sperm was recovered by aspirating the male's testicle while under sedation. The eggs and sperm now sat frozen, without being utilized for the advancement of science. It was such a waste of good material.

During Millie's sojourn at the research facility she had became emotionally close to the female Yeti whom she named Sasha. When Sasha and her male counterpart, Bentu, were killed, a part of Millie's soul died along with the animals. But now, she was on the verge of rekindling that emotional tie. On the cusp of recreating the physical presence of Sasha.

But this time it would be different.

Startlingly different.

The air conditioner whirred, its quiet purring sounding like a sleeping kitten. Millie wiped a strand of hair away from her face, took a deep breath, and said a silent prayer.

She picked up the micropipette that lay on a tray beside the Olympus inverted phase contrast microscope workstation and video monitor. The microscope, suitable for viewing colorless and transparent specimens and live cells, was equipped with a pressure injector connected to a micromanipulator. She stared at it for a moment. Earlier, she had filled the pipette with her own DNA, her exclusive human genome, genetic material that made her unique of all women.

Millie Harbaum's DNA.

Millie sat back from the video monitor, blinked, then rubbed her face with bare hands. She was tired, nearly exhausted. Glancing around the laboratory, she waited for her eyes to adjust. As they rested, the walls and shelves slowly sharpened in her vision. She took a deep breath then returned to her work. After adjusting again the focusing knob and the diaphragm lever, she squinted at the monitor. Her hand trembled slightly as she fixed the micropipette to the capillary holder and, observing the video monitor, brought it to the edge of the cell membrane. Sasha's egg cell glimmered in its nutrient solution as she set the injection time and pressure.

Her head swirled with the thought of what she was about to do. She hesitated, momentarily unsure if she wished to proceed, then tried to will her rapid pulse to slow.

Holding her breath, Millie adjusted the scope's focus one last time then pierced the cell membrane with the micropipette. Using a slow deliberate movement with the micromanipulator, she guided the needle into the cell's nucleus, pushed the injector and watched the DNA material flow into it. The nucleus bulged briefly then returned to its original shape. After retracting the pipette, Millie took a few moments to observe the cell. Like all cells throughout the animal kingdom it appeared as nothing more than an indistinct sphere under the phase contrast microscope. Satisfied the procedure had gone well, she sat back and took another deep breath.

The clock on the wall read three-twenty a.m.

Millie knew she was embarking on a journey from which there would be no return. Creating another Sasha with her own DNA implanted in its genome was dangerously close to crossing an ethical line never done before. It was one thing to attempt to reproduce a Yeti but to attempt to incorporate her own human DNA into the resulting animal was something never before attempted. It was her hope to create a chimera—DNA from two different species in one organism.

A chimera.

The ethical and moral implications were astronomical.

After receiving her PhD, Millie took Dr. Olson's offer and became the associate director at the research facility, a position Dr. Radner used to complete all the drudgery work he had no interest in doing. She had a myriad of administrative chores, leaving precious little time to devote to her research. Her genetic engineering project was done solely by her without the help of any other scientists at the facility and certainly without Radner or Dr. Olson's knowledge. She knew what they would say if they knew. Shut it down. And she couldn't have that.

Millie had no idea what to expect if her experiment succeeded. She had just fertilized this egg with her own DNA. Now, it was time to incubate the zygote until such time when she would implant it into one of the facility's chimps. Later, and she had yet to work out all the details, she would force delivery of a newborn Yeti.

Hopefully.

A newborn Yeti that had her genes in its genome.

What would it look like, she wondered? It would be half Yeti, half human. Was she unleashing a scientific monster in the legacy of golden age horror movies?

She took the Petri dish from the dissecting scope, covered it, and placed it in the thermal convection incubator. Returning to her chair at the workstation, she turned off the light and sat in the dark contemplating what she had done. It was not too late. She could destroy the cell. She knew at some point she would have to tell Dr. Radner and Dr. Olson of her experiment but she decided to wait until she was forced to do so. Once the embryo was successfully implanted into a chimp.

She was aware that several bioethicists called for a ban on species-altering technologies that would be enforced by an international tribunal. Part of the rationale for this ban was the concern that such technologies could be used to create a slave race, that is, a race of subhumans that could be exploited. Earlier in the decade, two scientists who were both opposed to genetically modified organisms applied for a patent for a humanzee—part human and part chimpanzee—to intentionally fuel debate on the issues and draw attention to potential abuses. The United States Patent and Trademark Office denied the patent on the grounds that it violated the Thirteenth Amendment of the Constitution of the United States, which explicitly prohibited slavery.

The prospect of bioengineered life forms raised important questions about how a person was defined in both legal and ethical terms.

Although the USPTO permitted the extensive patenting of bioengineered life forms, the question raised by the scientists' application was one that could easily be resolved by answering a simple question. What constitutes a person? A genetic definition was not very helpful, given the variability of gene sequences between individuals. And a species definition could be controversial. When experts looked to specific characteristics for a definition, they were faced with the fact that humans shared many characteristics with primates and other animals, so where could they draw the line?

If science created a being that had the ability to speak and perhaps even reason, but looked like a dog or a chimp, should that creation be given all the rights and protection traditionally bestowed upon a person? Some bioethicists argued that the definition of human being should be more expansive and protective, rather than more restrictive. Others argued that more expansive definitions could minimize humanity's status and create a financial disincentive to patenting creations that could be of potential use.

The question of whether the definition should be more expansive or restrictive would ultimately be considered as courts, legislatures, and institutions address laws regarding genetic discrimination.

Opponents of genetic manipulation feared the prospect of creating a race of super-humans, while proponents supported the right to give children every advantage.

In a similar vein, the medical director of the International Olympic Committee expressed concern that athletes employ genetic engineering to get an edge over their competition. If individuals were willing to genetically manipulate their children to make them better athletes, then it was likely that individuals would be willing to manipulate their children to better looking, more musically inclined, or whatever else might give them an advantage. Opponents of genetic manipulation argue that, by allowing this, we run the risk of creating a race of superhumans, changing what it means to be normal and increasing the ever-widening gap between the haves and the have-nots. Proponents argue that currently parents can and do give their children advantages by sending them to better schools or giving them growth hormones, and that banning genetic manipulation is a denial of individual liberties. Finally, Millie realized, these arguments reflected the opposing philosophies regarding how scarce resources would and should be allocated in the future.

But she was a scientist and not an ethicist or moralist. She knew she would proceed and go wherever the science took her.

Chapter 1

It had not been an easy year for the Anthropology Department of California Pacific University and its chairman, Dr. Harry Olson. Funding shortfalls, budget constraints, and a hiring freeze, coupled with a downturn in the economy, left Harry's department thin in faculty members and research money.

He tried to relax in his chair as he gazed out the large window toward San Francisco Bay. It was an overcast day with low clouds rolling in off the Pacific. Now and then, a weak sun managed to shine through the cloud bank sending golden rays that dappled the water's surface like diamonds. Below his office window, the trees that lined the university faculty parking lot wavered in a stiff breeze.

He spent the morning working on the yearly allocation of funds entrusted to his department, budgeting how much money each faculty member would receive for their research projects. As usual, there were always more requests than available funds. A few of the scientists in his department had obtained their own federal funding, but most relied on the allotments Harry granted them. Allotments that came through the generosity of private donors. Since his own pet project, the Yeti at the Primate Research Facility, had been scrubbed with the animal's deaths, the big contributors had gone elsewhere. As long as the pair of animals was alive and making news, money flowed into the university coffers like a never-ending river. But when law enforcement exterminated Bentu and Sasha after they killed a graduate assistant and escaped into the Nevada Mountains, Cal Pacific became just another small university, struggling to make ends meet.

Glancing at the clock, he realized it was time for lunch with his wife. Dixie was his former graduate assistant on the Mongolia expedition when he first discovered the Yeti. After returning home, she finished her PhD dissertation, and they were married. Now she held a faculty position in his department. She was popular among the students, and her classes were always the first to fill up each semester. Harry donned his sport coat and hurried to the faculty dining room where he found Dixie pacing at its entrance.

"Sorry I'm late, hon," he said, "but I was in the middle of the budget."

Dixie rolled her eyes but flashed him an easy smile. She looked especially beautiful today, he thought. A perky blonde with a turned-up nose and startling blue eyes, Dixie met his gaze with an enigmatic look.

"Your favorite chore, I know," she said. She took him by an arm and led him into the dining room. "Come on, I'm starved. They're having clam chowder today."

After getting their food, they found a table in a corner next to a bank of windows. The dining room was only half full of faculty members, most of whom were liberal arts professors. The carpeted floor muffled the sound of the chatter. Dixie talked while Harry sipped his iced tea.

"I think all my students will turn out to be dunces this semester," she said, spooning up a mouthful of chowder. "It's going to be a long term, I'm afraid."

Harry smiled. Her green eyes sparkled, causing his heart to skip a beat.

"Well, you can't expect every semester to have students like your last one."

"I suppose not," Dixie said. "That was an unusual group to be sure. They all worked extremely hard. I was very proud of them."

"Pauling wants to meet with me later this afternoon."

"What about?"

"The usual, in all likelihood," Harry said. "This time of year it can only mean the budget. Maybe issues with notable alums."

"Is he still reeling from the Yeti incident?" Dixie took a bite of her roll followed by more chowder.

"I dunno. I think he's pretty much over that fiasco. At least the papers have stopped hounding him. You know, dear, the deaths of those animals hit me harder than I expected. I was really invested in them and the research our team was doing."

"I know," Dixie said. "I don't think I'm over it all yet, either. Were you and the other scientists able to salvage anything from the project?"

"Millie Harbaum is working on that as we speak. Earlier, we sequenced the animal's genome in its entirety, so that is a great step forward. Hopefully, Millie can point us in a new direction with materials we saved from the many months spent working with the creatures."

"I still have bad dreams about those last few days, especially when we were trying to track them before the sheriff's helicopter discovered them. Sometimes I wake up after seeing the animals standing there, just looking at what was about to befall them. Then the sheriff and the strike force cut them down like sitting ducks. Torching their bodies. It still makes me sick, Harry."

"I know, dear, I know. I don't think I'm cut out for

running a department as large and varied as ours." Harry took several bites of his chowder as his wife waited for him to continue. "I'm much more a field research anthropologist. I miss the excitement of the search and eventual discovery."

"We need a vacation, honey," Dixie said. "Maybe after you're through with the budget we can get away for a few days. I would like that."

"Yeah. Good idea. Maybe Hawaii or something like that."

"Oh, Hawaii, Harry?" Dixie said, her eyes noticeably brighter. "How wonderful. I'll go online and check on some possibilities. Just the two of us. It sounds divine."

Finished with his soup, Harry started on his pie. He worried that his wife still had problems dealing with the loss of the Yeti, but it was a fact he could not change. It had been almost two years since their expedition to Mongolia where they first discovered evidence of the Yeti's actual existence and located them high in the Altai Mountains. In a bizarre turn of events, Dixie was kidnapped by the creatures and kept prisoner in a deep cave system before Harry and the Mongolian police rescued her. If he had not been there to witness it, he would never have believed they were capable of such human-like actions. It was his first realization that these animals were highly intelligent. After the team had a chance to study the animal's genetics, they turned out to be distantly related to humans in a similar way the Neanderthals were related.

Then, during a return expedition, two of the Yeti were captured and brought back to the research facility in Nevada, where they were subjected to closer investigation.

Harry and Dixie both invested a tremendous amount of time, money, and personal commitment to the study of the Yeti.

Now they were gone.

Dixie wiped her mouth with a napkin then finished her tea. "I have papers to grade, so I'll come by your office later this afternoon." She shot him a quick smile and left the dining room, leaving Harry to continue mulling over past events.

When he came to Cal Pacific University to study anthropology, his first professor was Dr. Julius Kesler. It wasn't long before the man assumed the role of Harry's surrogate father and took the young graduate student under his wing. A bond formed between the two men, with the Professor, as he was affectionately called, inviting Harry to his home on a regular basis. It was Professor Kesler who put together the initial expedition to Mongolia in search of hominid fossils, and he selected Harry to be his expedition leader.

Shortly after the return expedition to Mongolia brought two Yeti back to the research center, Professor Kesler died from a sudden, unexpected heart attack. The loss left Harry disconnected from his anchor, his mentor, the only man who ever mattered to him. But it was Kesler's wish that Harry succeed him as departmental chairman, so with Dixie's support, he managed to lead his fellow faculty members through the intervening difficult months. Initially, after the loss of the Yeti, he wanted to organize another expedition to Mongolia to replace them but finding the necessary funding proved difficult. Especially since innocent people had been killed by the creatures.

Through the difficult and arduous work by Dr. Harbaum, the Yeti's complete genome was now known. And their genetics revealed a startling fact—the Yeti were more closely related to Homo sapiens than the Neanderthals. Millie, by analyzing endogenous retroviruses in the genome, determined the Yeti line split off the evolutionary bush only about 25,000 years ago.

Endogenous retroviruses were endogenous viral elements in the genome that closely resembled and could be derived from retroviruses. They were abundant in the genomes of jawed vertebrates, and they occupied up to eight percent of the human genome. Endogenous retroviruses provided yet another example of molecular sequence evidence for universal common descent. Endogenous retroviruses were molecular remnants of a past parasitic viral infection.

Occasionally, copies of a retrovirus genome were found in its host's genome, and these retroviral gene copies were called endogenous retroviral sequences. Retroviruses, like the AIDS virus or HTLV1, which caused a form of leukemia, made a DNA copy of their own viral genome and inserted it into their host's genome. If this happens to a germ line cell, for example, the sperm or egg cells, the retroviral DNA would be inherited by descendants of the host. Again, this process was rare and fairly random, so finding retrogenes in identical chromosomal positions of two different species indicated common ancestry.

Harry wandered back to his office. Along the way, he decided to stop and see Dr. Chloe Rawlings, director of Cal Pacific's DNA lab. He opened the door and was greeted by the soft whirring of a multitude of electronic machines at work. A woman in a white lab coat stood with her back to him at the lab's far end.

"Knock, knock," Harry said.

The woman turned and, upon seeing Harry, waved and approached him. She was tall, had straw-colored hair that fell loosely on her shoulders, and she wore wire-rimmed glasses.

"Out slumming the halls, Harry?" the woman said.

They both laughed.

"As a matter of fact, Chloe, I just had lunch with Dixie," he said. "I thought I'd stop and see how you were doing."

"How is your wife?" Chloe said, a broad smile on her face.

"She's fine. Struggling with her classes, however."

"Tell her welcome to the club. Want to talk in my office?"

Harry nodded, and Dr. Rawlings led the way to a small cramped office in a corner of the lab. There were books and journals piled high on a table at the side of Rawling's desk. She indicated a chair. Harry dropped into it and sighed.

"You look as though you lost your last friend, Harry," she said. "What's the matter?"

"Oh, nothing really. I just needed to get away from the office for a while. The phone rings constantly, my secretary has all sorts of questions that need answering, and the budget looms ever-present on my desk."

Chloe poured two cups of coffee and handed one to Harry. Her eyes sparkled as he took it then leaned back in his chair.

"Poor Harry," she said. "The chairmanship getting you down?"

"I guess. I do miss the classroom. But most of all I miss the field. Digging in the earth. Looking for skeletons. I was just saying that very thing to Dixie. I'm not sure I was cut out to be an administrator."

"I can relate to that," Chloe said. "Doing most of the forensic DNA analysis for the county has left me with precious little time for my own research. Pauling has me working overtime for the San Francisco Police Department."

"Good ole Dr. Pauling. The administrator's administrator. Good grief, the man actually likes all that paper shuffling." He took a sip of his coffee.

"How is the primate facility doing these days, Harry? By the way, I never did extend my sympathies for what happened to your Yeti."

"Thanks, Chloe. The facility is still going strong, although the work generated by the Yeti is now in limbo. Since their deaths, nothing is moving forward. There's data to be analyzed but..." His voice trailed off as he attempted to organize his thoughts.

"I can imagine how hard it must be without actual specimens."

"We need to return to Mongolia and obtain more animals," Harry said, his pulse quickening. "It's that simple. But there's no grant money available, and, since the tragedy, no private investors want their name on such a project."

"I do understand, Harry," Chloe said.

"You, Chloe, on the other hand, are a money maker for the university. Pauling probably gives you anything you want."

"You'd be surprised."

"I'm sorry," Harry said, standing. He set his cup down. "I must sound like I'm whining. Thanks for the coffee."

He ambled to Rawling's office door. In the doorway, he paused. Chloe smiled broadly.

"Cheer up, Harry. Go home, mix yourself a drink, take Dixie to dinner, and forget today. Things will get better."

"Thanks for listening," he said.

Chapter 2

Millie sat in her crowded office and reviewed what she was going to say to Dr. Gerald Siscom, the facility's veterinarian. Earlier, she had stopped by the incubator and checked on her experiment. The growing zygote, now called an embryo, in which she had implanted her own DNA, was about the size of a sunflower seed and ready for implantation into a chimp. For that, she needed to enlist Siscom's help. The veterinarian was in charge of the health and well-being of the animals and had access to the anesthetics necessary to carry out the procedure. The chimp would need to be well sedated while she placed the growing embryo into her uterus. The process she had earlier used was known as intracytoplasmic injection, and now the fertilized egg had divided a number of times and had begun its transformation from a ball of cells into an organized being. The chimp she selected was in her estrus cycle so implantation should occur without much difficulty.

If she could procure Siscom's assistance.

She would need to convince him.

Millie's mother was Italian, while her father came from English stock. John Harbaum was a dentist in Toledo and had wanted Millie to follow his career path. But spending all day in someone's mouth didn't seem much of a way to occupy one's time, even if the income was satisfactory. Seeing the Indiana Jones movies convinced her she wanted to become an archeologist, so she enrolled in college with that as her plan. But a professor talked her out of it, maintaining there were no jobs and the pay was dismal. So, she got her degree in history and worked for a while for the State of California. But the dream of an archeologist's life didn't die, and she was able to obtain a scholarship at California Pacific University, studying first under Dr. Kesler then Dr. Harry Olson. When the Yeti were captured and shipped to Nevada, the university announced that two graduate assistant fellowships had been created and the students would live at the Primate Research Facility for a year. They would assist in the study of the creatures. She applied and was accepted and soon found herself atop Cinder Mountain and face to face with the Yeti.

She had the usual love affairs of high school and college girls, but no one boy ever made it the top of her list of requirements for a long term relationship. Once at Cal Pacific she devoted her time to her studies with only an occasional date, usually with an undergraduate she met in the lab. Now at the research facility, there were no eligible men, which didn't matter, for she was consumed by her work.

Millie found Dr. Siscom and several technicians in the Animal Care Unit, examining the chimps and other animals. They closed a cage door, and the veterinarian smiled upon seeing Millie. The odor of the unit was a mix of animal smells and pellet food. The overhead fluorescent lights bathed the area with a cool bluish hue.

"Good morning, Millie," he said after dismissing the technicians. He ran a hand through his graying hair. "Have you had a busy morning?"

Millie nodded.

"I'd like a word with you, Dr. Siscom, if you can spare me a few minutes." She smiled and felt her heart begin to pound in her ears. She said a silent prayer, hoping to find the right words that would sound convincing.

"Gerald, please, Millie. You are a full-fledged faculty member now."

Millie felt the blood rush to her cheeks. She nodded.

"Fine, Gerald," she said.

"Well, come to the office," Siscom said. "The inner sanctum. Had your morning coffee?"

"I'd love some, thanks."

Siscom led her to a sparse office at the end of a hallway in the Animal Care Unit. It was brightly lit, and there were charts of various animal anatomies hanging on the walls. A small bookcase was full of what Millie surmised were veterinary medicine textbooks. She took a seat in a worn chair next to the bookcase. Siscom poured two mugs of coffee from a well-used drip coffeemaker and handed one to her.

"Did you see the sunrise this morning?" Siscom said. "It was beautiful."

Millie shook her head.

"Are you kidding, Gerald? I never get up that early."

The veterinarian chuckled, took a sip of his coffee.

"The view of the plains from up here on the mountain is spectacular at dawn. You ought to see it sometime. Now, what can I do for you?"

Millie cleared her throat, blew steam from her mug, took a gulp, and began.

"I'm here, Gerald," she said, "to enlist your support and help."

"I'll do what I can," Siscom interrupted. "Within reason, of course."

"When the Yeti were killed months ago, I thought my

research on them ended. I was devastated." Siscom nodded his understanding. Millie sighed. "But then I realized how fortunate we were—I was. Because we had had the foresight to store frozen sperm from Bentu. And I had super-ovulated Sasha and retrieved her ova and stored them as well."

She paused, waiting for signs from Siscom that he understood. He sat in his chair, looking at her, silent, his steel-gray eyes not betraying his thoughts, so she continued.

"I developed a plan to restore our very necessary research. I want to impregnate one of our chimps with a fertilized egg from our Yeti. That way—"

Siscom sat forward in his chair, placed his cup on the desk. His eyes widened. "*What*?" he said. "Are you kidding?" His forehead developed deep furrows as he frowned at Mille.

"Please," she said, "hear me out. Without another specimen, all the many hours and months of work we did on the Yeti project will have been for nothing. The chances of putting together another expedition to obtain an animal are remote. I heard Dr. Olson say so himself. We have successfully sequenced the Yeti's complete genome. It would be a shame and such a loss to the scientific community if we let all our efforts wither away. This would be an opportunity to build on what we have achieved so far."

"Wait a minute," Siscom said. "You have fertilized a Yeti egg with a Yeti sperm. Is that what you are saying, Millie?"

"That's correct, Gerald."

"And now you wish to implant that fertilized egg into one of our chimps?"

Millie saw the sudden look of concern on Siscom's face. Her heart sank with the realization that this was not going to be an easy sell. "The zygote has been growing in the incubator for the past several weeks," she said, trying to control the tone of her voice. "In fact, it's an embryo by now. If I could get it implanted in one of our chimps, she could carry it until birth. We would then have replaced a valuable Yeti specimen that was lost to us."

Siscom held up a hand, cleared his throat.

"You're proposing a primate IVF, an in vitro fertilization, correct?"

"Yes, I am. I am asking you to sedate a chimp to allow me to inject an embryo into her uterus then asking you to follow her pregnancy to assure all goes well."

"Well, Millie—" Siscom began.

"Please, Gerald. This means everything to me. I have devoted so much of my life to these Yeti, I can't bear to see it all go down the drain just because we have no animals."

Siscom smiled and reclined in his chair. "Does Dr. Radner and Dr. Olson know of this plan of yours?"

"Not yet. I thought I would enlist your help before getting their approval."

"It's been done in cows for sure," the veterinarian said, stroking his cheek. He strummed his fingers on his desk. "I don't know about chimpanzees. We might be in new territory here."

"It might be a contribution to veterinary medicine as well, Gerald." Millie's eyes implored the man to see things her way.

Siscom rubbed his chin while he pondered her proposal. There was an uncomfortable silence while Millie waited for the man to speak.

She realized that he was just the first of three hurdles to overcome, that even if she secured his assistance, she would still need to convince Dr. Radner and Dr. Olson of the wisdom of her project. And Radner might be the toughest of all to convince. The man was a pompous jerk, and Mille didn't relish being his assistant. He had her doing the most mundane tasks, ones that could easily be done by his secretary, but ones he seemed delighted in heaping upon her. It didn't leave her much time for research. Maybe if she got this project going, he would slack up and allow her the time she needed.

"What about embryos?" Siscom finally said. "You say you've already got them?"

"Yes. Already done." She nodded. "I have directly fertilized an ovum from Sasha, and it is a few weeks old and ready for implantation. All I need is your cooperation, Gerald. I'm imploring you to see the value in what I'm asking."

"Well," he said, "if we could pull it off, it would be a great scientific achievement. Almost like Jurassic Park for real." He continued to rub his chin for a few moments then leaned forward again, elbows on the desk. "Okay, Millie, if you can secure Radner and Olson's approval, you've got my help. With one requirement. That my name goes on any publications that come out of this. Agreed?"

Millie jumped out of her chair and reached across Siscom's desk, hand extended. She felt like giving the veterinarian a big kiss. "Agreed, Gerald."

After shaking the veterinarian's hand, she collapsed back in her chair and sighed a long sigh of relief.

"I can't tell you how thankful I am," she said.

Siscom laughed. "I was easy," he said. "You're greatest challenges may yet face you in Radner and Olson. Harry should go for it as the Yeti were his baby, but Radner—that man is a hard one to read."

"Maybe you could be with me when I talked to them. I need all the moral support I can get."

"Of course, my dear. Why don't you see if you can arrange a teleconference with the four of us, and I will be happy to help any way I can."

"Thanks, Gerald. I'll keep in touch."

Millie left and headed directly to Radner's office.

❧❧❧

The oak paneled conference room at the Primate Research Facility contained a long polished mahogany table surrounded by leather chairs. One wall of the room housed a bank of large windows that allowed a commanding view of the plains of northern Nevada. The facility sat atop Cinder Mountain and offered unparalleled views in all directions. The opposite wall of the conference room housed a large flat screen television used for videoconferencing with Cal Pacific in San Francisco. Otherwise, the room held few accouterments except for a large painting of the university on the wall next to the windows.

Millie sat to one side of the overstuffed chair at the head if the table, the one designated for Radner, and waited. She managed to convince him that a conference call with Dr. Olson would be the best way to discuss her project. Radner, to his credit she thought, had not nixed her idea out of hand. So she waited, her heart in her throat for Radner to appear and place the call to Cal Pacific.

Gerald Siscom breezed into the conference room and took a seat opposite Millie. In his hand, he carried a sheaf of papers that he placed on the table. He nodded. "I brought the information and results of the literature review we did," he said. "Might help if I had the data at hand in case Harry has questions."

"Good idea," Millie said. "Did you see Dr. Radner in the hallway?"

"As a matter of fact, he was talking to his secretary

right outside so he should be here shortly."

"I hope this goes well, Gerald," she said, drumming her fingers on the polished surface of the table.

"I think it will. Radner didn't reject the idea straight away, and Harry has always been ready to listen to new ideas from his staff. Try not to worry. Just state your case with a calm voice, and I'll chip in my two cents' worth."

The door opened, and Miles Radner strolled into the room, dressed impeccably in a dark suit and maroon tie. He nodded to Millie and Siscom and took a seat at the head of the table. A hint of sweet cologne accompanied his arrival. A thin, balding man Radner possessed a nervous manner, a quality Millie found irritating. His secretary followed, switched on the television, and dialed a phone number.

"Afternoon all," Radner said as he retrieved a pen from his shirt pocket and set it beside the legal pad in front of him. "As soon as Helen gets Dr. Olson called up, we will start. I will say hello to Harry, then Millie you can begin. He knows briefly what the call concerns."

The television flickered to life, and Harry's face appeared on the screen. The secretary adjusted the camera to Radner's satisfaction and left the room.

"Good afternoon, Harry," Radner said. "You're looking well. How's the weather there?"

"Raining, Miles. Hello Millie and Gerald. I trust all is well with both of you."

"We are both fine, Harry," Siscom said.

"Great," Harry said. "Now, Millie, what is this project idea of yours? Miles really didn't say much when we talked on the phone."

The TV flickered a few times, and Millie sat straight in her chair. Looking at her notes, she began.

"Dr. Olson, since the deaths of our Yeti, Bentu and Sasha, my research is at a stalemate. Although we were able to sequence the Yeti's genome, not much else has been accomplished to date, due to the fact we have no animals. My project proposes to rectify that situation." Millie paused for a moment, allowing her words to be understood. There being no questions, she swallowed hard and proceeded. "Fortunately, before the animals' demise, we were able to retrieve, freeze, and store sperm and ova from the two animals. We still have those specimens. And they are quite useable.

"My proposal is quite simple, actually. Dr. Olson, I want to impregnate one of our chimps with an embryo gained from fertilizing one of Sasha's eggs with sperm from Bentu. Dr. Siscom, our veterinarian here, will help with the procedure and oversee the resulting pregnancy. If the chimp manages to carry the pregnancy to term or near term, he will assist in the delivery of a new Yeti. We then would have a new animal on which we could continue our research. Pretty straightforward as you can see."

Harry chuckled.

"But Millie," he said, "the devil is in the details, as always. You know that. Gerald, you're talking in vitro fertilization, correct?"

"Yes, Harry. Nonhuman IVF."

"Has this been done successfully before?" Harry said.

Siscom consulted the papers he brought with him. After arranging them in a certain order, he nodded. "Yes, it has. Recently, the delivery of the world's first rhesus monkey twins following the in vitro fertilization of oocytes and subsequent freezing, thawing, and transfer of embryos to the oviducts of synchronized foster mothers was described last year in the veterinary journal. The cryopreservation of mammalian embryos was first described in 1972. Since that time, mouse, rabbit, and cattle embryos have been successfully stored in the frozen state, and thousands of normal offspring have resulted, following transfer to foster mothers. Trounson and Mohr reported the establishment of a human pregnancy following the transfer of an eight-cell frozen-thawed embryo, but the pregnancy was not carried to term. After several years of experience, embryo cryopreservation is now standard medical practice in the clinical application of the assisted reproductive technologies. In nonhuman primates, Pope and his co-workers reported the first baboon birth following cryopreservation and transfer of an embryo to a foster mother.

"So yes, Harry, It has been done, and I believe we could do it here, if given the go-ahead."

"Miles, what are your thoughts?" Harry said when he finished his note-taking.

"Scientifically," Radner said, "I must admit the idea is intriguing. From a political or public perception point of view, I'm not so sure."

"How so?" asked Millie.

"To start with, the public always views these things as ghoulish tinkering. For another, the public isn't completely on board with the idea of cloning."

"This isn't cloning, Miles," Siscom said. "Nothing is being done in this project that hasn't been done thousands of times in humans. And even in other primates, other animals."

A foul-tasting acidic bile shot into Millie's mouth. She knew she wasn't being totally truthful and forthcoming with her colleagues, and the thought sent a cold shiver down her spine. The embryo that was growing in the incubator contained her DNA—it was half Yeti and half Millie. It was not what she purported it to be, and the fact that she was deceiving her colleagues made her sick to her stomach.

In her heart, she knew she should tell them what she had done, what that embryo contained. That embryo was

Millie's future, her chance at becoming a world-renown scientist. Something deep inside told her she couldn't lay it all on the table. Maybe sometime in the future, but not now.

Harry was speaking, so she focused her attention on his comments.

"Science has always led the way—in fact, it has been way ahead of the masses on these sorts of things. I worry less about that than I do about the chances of creating some sort of monster or another Yeti that terrorizes the public. Especially so soon on the heels of what happened recently."

"I believe we learned a lot about security from housing these sorts of creatures," Siscom said. "Putting those observations into place would markedly reduce the likelihood of a repeat scenario."

"The immediate downside, I guess," Harry said, "would simply be that the pregnancy didn't take or that the chimp aborted later. Right, Gerald?"

"Correct," the veterinarian said. "It would be later, after birth, that things could get more complicated."

"I can't say at the moment," Radner replied. "It's hard to predict the future, but something unexpected could turn up. It usually does. But, barring any fiasco such as happened before, I believe we are well-equipped to handle anything that might develop. At least here at the facility."

"Miles, any last thoughts?"

"None, Harry."

"Okay, I'm giving my tentative approval for this project. Pending a complete written outline and proposal. Hear that, Millie? Fine. Have it on my desk by the end of the week. I'll call you and Dr. Radner for a final decision after I have read it. Have a nice day, everyone."

The videoconference concluded, Millie headed back to her office. A small voice inside nagged at her. She knew she should have been more forthcoming.

Chapter 3

D
r. Dixie Olson unlocked the door to her office and tossed her purse on her desk along with the morning paper. On her way to the university, she had stopped at Starbucks and purchased a large caramel macchiato, her big indulgence for the day. It had been a beautiful drive in from her and Harry's home in San Mateo, and the clear bright sunshine made the bay sparkle like dazzling jewels. She was in a good mood.

Dixie reclined in her chair and sipped her coffee as she thumbed through the San Francisco *Chronicle*. Not much newsworthy, she thought. She turned the pages only half attentive until her eyes riveted on a small headline buried in the back part of the paper.

Cal Pacific Professor Forged Data

She quickly scanned the article until she found the name of the accused—Dr. Harry Olson. The article was brief and to the point. It outright accused her husband of forging data for a research paper he published years ago, long before they were married and while he was still a fledgling faculty member under Dr. Kesler's tutelage. While they were dating, Harry confided in her, relating the entire affair and how the Professor came to his aid. How the man had written a letter to the journal editor explaining the unfortunate mistake. And how Harry, while in Mongolia, made peace with his mistake and reconciled with Kesler, the man he viewed as a father.

But how did the paper get the story? Dixie folded it and gulped her coffee. After all these years, how and why did the *Chronicle* run the story? For what purpose? To discredit her husband? Harry's mistake was not well known in academic circles, so it didn't make any sense that the paper should be running it now.

Then Dixie remembered.

Bernard Wickingham. Dr. Bernard Wickingham.

That bastard, thought Dixie. It had to be him that leaked the story to the *Chronicle*. But why?

Dr. Pauling fired Dr. Wickingham from Cal Pacific earlier in the year for attempting to extort lab space from Harry by threatening to reveal what he had discovered regarding the journal data. How and where he uncovered the information, he never divulged, but, in any event, when he threatened Dixie with exposure, she went to Pauling who summarily dismissed the man.

Now, for some reason, the story was out—made public—and Wickingham surely was to blame. Probably in revenge for his firing.

The bastard.

She phoned Harry's office and left word with his secretary that she needed to see him as soon as he got in. *Damn that Wickingham*, she thought, as she finished her coffee.

❧❦❧

"What's the emergency?" Harry said as Dixie plopped into a chair next to his desk. His carpeted office was lined with bookshelves, and a small round table with chairs occupied the far wall. His doctorate diploma and a photograph of the Yeti hung on a wall to the side of his desk. "Mary said when you called you sounded frantic."

Dixie tossed the newspaper on the desk and pointed to it. "Turn to page twenty-eight, Harry. And look at the headlines near the bottom of the page."

Harry did as his wife requested and, when he had the page in view, he read for a few moments then folded the paper and shook his head.

"How—how did this get in here?" he said. He suddenly had a gnawing pain in the back of his head.

"How should I know?" Dixie said. "But if I was going to hazard a guess I would say Bernard Wickingham."

"But why?" Harry knew his voice sounded shaky. He tried to not look as irritated as he felt.

"Again, I would assume it is in revenge for his firing. His way of getting even."

"This article is pretty damning in its tone, as well as what it claims as the facts. Of course, it doesn't mention Dr. Kesler coming to my defense. But the man did save my career."

"That and finding the Yeti," Dixie said. "Listen, sweetheart, this isn't the end of the world. Whatever is the fallout, we will deal with it and handle it together."

"Sure, we will. But I feel I need to respond to this idiotic article, Dixie. My reputation is on the line."

"Respond how? Get a lawyer and sue them? What is said in the article is the truth, after all. The paper doesn't slander or libel you that I can see."

"It really makes me angry," Harry said. "That creep is lower than low. I'd sure like to get even in some way."

"It'll blow over, I'm sure of it. I just wanted you to be aware of the article. Now, I have to get to my lab."

She rose, kissed Harry on the cheek, and sauntered out

the door, leaving him to call Dr. Pauling, the university president.

Within an hour, Harry was in Pauling's office, paper in hand, acid bile pumping into his throat. Pauling greeted him with a weak smile and offered a chair.

"By the look on your face," Harry said, "you've seen this morning's paper." Pauling nodded. Harry sighed. "So, what now?"

"Harry, this is beyond the pale and could be grounds for a libel suit," Pauling said. He was a middle-aged man, with a smooth face and a nose slightly askew. He wore a navy suit and dark tie.

"Not if I'm guilty, which I am. Even Dixie knows that much."

"Your offense occurred years ago," Pauling said, "and your record since has absolved you of your past wrongdoing. I don't think anyone would find much fault with a mistake made early in one's career, especially if that person made amends as you have."

"However, it's embarrassing. A blow to my ego, for sure."

"Understood," Pauling said.

"So what do we do?" Harry said. "You want me to resign?"

"Absolutely not. You have my unqualified support. I plan on ignoring the article, and I suggest you try and do the same. You've got plenty of other things to worry about."

"I sure do. Like the budget, for starters. By the way, I have given my tentative approval to an in vitro fertilization procedure at the primate facility. Thought you ought to know."

"In vitro fertilization?" Pauling's eyebrows rose, and his eyes turned dark. "You mean like IVF? What's done for couples who can't have babies?"

"The very same."

"With what?"

Harry used his hand to animate his description.

"Sperm and ova from our Yeti. They have been saved and stored in a freezer. Dr. Harbaum wants to fertilize the egg and implant the resulting embryo into a chimp. In seven months, we could have another Yeti at the facility."

"Brother," Pauling said. "Here we go again."

Harry stood, sauntered to the door, turned, and smiled. "My," he said. "Those were Dixie's exact words."

e/9e/9

IVF was used successfully for the first time in the United States in 1981. More than four million babies have been born worldwide as a result of using the in vitro fertilization technique. IVF offers infertile couples a chance to have a child who is biologically related to them. Today, over one percent of infants born in the US are a result of a pregnancy conceived by assisted reproductive technologies.

With IVF, a method of assisted reproduction, a male sperm and s female egg were combined in a laboratory dish, where fertilization occurred. The resulting embryo was then transferred to the female's uterus to implant and develop naturally. Usually, two to four embryos were placed in the woman's uterus at one time. The term test tube baby had been used in the past to refer to children conceived with this technique. The first so-called test tube baby was born in England in 1978.

Techniques used for IVF were initially perfected in nonhuman primates then transferred and used on their human counterparts. Millie took the embryo and used standard freezing techniques to preserve it. In 1972, pre-implantation mammalian embryos were first successfully cryopreserved. The method was very time consuming. Slow cooling was used, one degree/minute to about minus eighty degrees Centigrade. Then the embryos were placed in liquid nitrogen. The embryos also needed to be thawed slowly and a cryoprotectant added and removed in many gradual steps. The solution was an extracellular non-penetrating sucrose mixture.

As the day for embryo transfer approached, Millie called on Siscom to review the protocol he had devised. She sat nervous and tense in his office one afternoon.

"The embryo is ready, Millie?" he said, bending over a legal pad with his pen.

"Four weeks old," she said. "Tomorrow it will need to be thawed and injected into a chimp. You think the prospective mother is ready?"

"Perfect," Siscom said. "And yes, the chimp's progesterone level has peaked, so her uterus is ripe for implantation. Once I have her sedated, I'll load a catheter with saline and the embryo then insert it into the uterus and inject the embryo into it. I'll need to check the catheter afterward to be sure the embryo was injected and doesn't still remain in it. You can do the procedure if you so desire. Once that's done, we'll monitor the progress of pregnancy by way of progesterone levels and later, ultrasound."

"That is if there is successful implantation on the lining of the uterus," Millie said.

"Of course. If the progesterone level falls, then there's no pregnancy, and we try again with another embryo."

"I should have fertilized more eggs then frozen the embryos. If this attempt fails, that is what I'll do the next time."

"In a uterus that is ready to accept an embryo," Siscom said, "the odds are pretty good in favor of successful implantation." He stopped scribbling on the legal pad and sat back in his chair. The hum of the air conditioners droned overhead.

"Once the chimp is pregnant, then what?"

"We monitor the course of the pregnancy with ultrasound just like in humans. The gestation period is about seven months. Since your Yeti are significantly larger than chimps, we may do a cesarean prior to her going into labor. We have an incubator here, so we will put the newborn in it."

"Now that we are about to do this, I'm getting nervous," Millie said, her heart pounding in her throat.

"We are on the frontier of animal science. In vitro fertilization and embryo transfer have been done in nonhuman primates for quite some time but this will make scientific history. We should be nervous. Nothing like this has ever been done before."

You don't know the half of it, Millie thought.

"So, Millie," Siscom continued, "what do you plan to do if and when we have an infant Yeti on our hands?"

Siscom's easy demeanor began to put Millie at ease. "Study it, of course. What a unique opportunity to study the development of a creature thought only to exist in legends. I'm excited but nervous at the same time."

"A lifetime's storehouse of potential journal articles, eh?"

"Well, Gerald—"

"Don't worry, young lady. You're secret is safe with me." Siscom chuckled as if pleased with his joke.

Millie rose and started to leave.

"Seriously though," Siscom said, "you need to spend the gestation period putting together some sort of plan as to how you will proceed after birth. Dr. Olson and Pauling will probably insist on it."

"You're right, Gerald. I will."

"Have you heard from Harry? Has he given us the green light to proceed?"

Millie nodded. "He emailed me yesterday with the go-ahead. He said he found my proposal thought-provoking and insightful. I was very flattered. What time tomorrow do you want to start?"

"Not too early, say ten o'clock? Can you have the embryo ready by then?

"Absolutely. See you then, Gerald."

"Right," Siscom said.

Chapter 4

Dixie spent thirty minutes listening to her husband describe Millie's plan to birth another Yeti and was excited at the news. It seemed to her such a bizarre, impossible project that, at first, she didn't believe Harry as he described what Millie intended to do. He had waited until after dinner and they were having coffee on the patio of their San Mateo home. The softening shadows that blanketed San Francisco Bay in the distance rendered its surface smooth as glass, like a velvet blanket. The evening air was warm, and the faint scent of early spring flowers wafted on a gentle breeze.

"Do you think she can do it?" Dixie asked Harry, setting her cup on a small table next to her chair.

"With Siscom's help, probably," Harry said. "The technology is there. It's never been tried at our facility before, but they have the know-how and all the necessary equipment. So the odds are with them."

"Wow," said Dixie, going to stand at the patio railing. Harry's eyes sparkled as he related the news. It was a quality that attracted her to her husband. "Another Yeti at our primate facility. I never thought I would see the day. And an infant one at that. It'll be interesting to watch it develop. What with all the budget problems and difficulty raising donations, I figured our chances of ever bringing another animal back from Mongolia was slim to none."

"Well, Millie is a driven woman. If anyone can pull this off, she certainly can. She sorta reminds me of someone." He shot Dixie a faint smile and winked.

"Oh, hush. You're not an impartial witness. But I love your opinions."

They both laughed and finished their coffee. The dark shadows over the bay had dissipated leaving a black void out beyond the city.

"When will she try and do the embryo transfer?" Dixie said.

"Tomorrow morning. I have a feeling that when she first approached me with the project, she had already done a tremendous amount of background research and had obtained Siscom's assistance. When I gave her my approval to proceed she was able to put everything into motion rather quickly."

"I like that about her, Harry. She does her homework first before she speaks. It's an admirable trait."

"Yes, it is. I don't think she has ever done an IVF procedure, but we have the appropriate microscope, micropipettes, and injectors. It may have been more luck that she succeeded in getting the egg fertilized on her first attempt. From what I know, that is a rather complicated job, in and of itself. Millie was an excellent choice as one if our graduate students and, in the immediate aftermath of the Yeti's escape, she proved herself to be calm, collected, and resourceful. I was happy to offer a faculty position afterward."

"I don't know anything about the freezing of embryos, Harry. Do you?"

"A little from a zoology class. Previously, embryos were cryopreserved using a slow freeze method. Embryos were run through different solutions of media to dehydrate the cells of water and replace it with cryoprotectant. Then the cryoprotected embryos were individually labeled and stored in cryopreservation straws, which were put in special freezers. These freezers slowly cooled the embryos to minus thirty-five degrees Celsius using liquid nitrogen. They were then stored in liquid nitrogen at minus one-hundred-ninety-six degrees Celsius. At that extremely cold temperature, cellular activity is essentially brought to a halt, allowing the embryos to remain viable indefinitely.

"When cryopreserved embryos are used, they are removed from the liquid nitrogen, warmed and run through solutions of media to remove the cryoprotectant and rehydrate the cells with water. During cryopreservation, the formation of intracellular ice crystals can damage the cells of the embryo, decreasing future viability. Because of that, new methods were developed to improve cryopreservation techniques."

"Like what?" Dixie said.

"Vitrification is a new process for cryopreserving embryos. Through vitrification, the water molecules in an embryo are removed and replaced with a higher concentration of cryoprotectant than in the slow freeze method. This is to eliminate ice crystals forming. The embryos are then plunged directly into liquid nitrogen. This drastic freezing reduces the chance for intercellular ice crystals to be formed, thus decreasing the degeneration of cells upon thawing for embryo transfer.

"I know many studies show survival rates of vitrified embryos to be far higher than survival rates of slow freeze embryos."

"You think she did all that?" Dixie said, impressed with Harry's fund of knowledge.

"She and Siscom," Harry said, a large grin on his face. "They seem to be spending a lot of time together."

"Any men in her life?" Dixie said. "Besides Gerald?"

"Not that I am aware. I don't really know that they are a number. But you would know something of that before I would. I know she respects you immensely."

"We don't talk all that much, Harry, although we did when she was a graduate student. Now she has her work out at the facility, and I have mine here. It's been over a month since I talked to her."

"I need to go out to the place sometime soon," Harry said. He picked up his coffee cup and headed inside the house. "I thought I would wait until the embryo transfer was completed first. Maybe next week."

"I wanna come, too," Dixie said, following him inside.

Harry laughed. "Don't you always?"

oৈৄ৺ৄ

Millie tossed and turned, unable to sleep. She glanced at her bedside clock that read one a.m. She rose, turned on a light, and wandered down the hall to the dormitory kitchen. There was no one about, the place was quiet and dark. She fixed herself a sandwich, grabbed a soda, and headed back to her room.

Most of the Primate Research Facility staff was housed in the two-story dormitory. The scientific, administrative, and security staff had their own small apartments, each with their own private bath, sitting room, computer workstation, and bedroom. Millie liked the arrangement. The housekeeping personnel provided household chores, and they did her laundry as well. The communal dining room on the main floor served all employees and ran almost continuously from dawn to eight at night. Dr. Radner had his personal quarters in the main building, but he ate his meals with his staff in the dorm dining room.

The Primate Research Facility was an extensive compound located in the East Humbolt Mountain Range in Elko County, Nevada. It was an isolated part of the state, far from any major roads or highways, towns, or other conveniences. The nearest town was Grant, thirty miles to the south. The facility itself—perched atop Cinder Mountain, and reached by a one-lane dirt road, consisted of several buildings containing research laboratories and living quarters. The Primate Research Facility was Professor Kesler's crowning achievement—his last erection, Harry loved to joke. Initially, the facility, built as a place where scientists could process their archeological and paleontological specimens, had grown and become a state-of-the-art hominid research laboratory doing genome and DNA sequencing projects on all sorts of primates and hominid fossils.

Primate Research Facility scientists possessed unique expertise in gamete biology, reproductive toxicology, lifespan health, regenerative medicine and gene therapy, the application of in vivo imaging tools and technologies for translational research. Investigation of the genetic basis of human diseases had been a major focus of effort at the Primate Research Facility since its inception. Nonhuman primates made outstanding models for the study of the genetics of disease because they were so similar to humans in their biochemistry, physiology, anatomy, and behavior. As researchers in many areas of biomedical research focused greater attention on the genetic basis of disease susceptibility and rates of progression, the use of nonhuman primates as animal models for these genetic processes became standard procedure. The value of nonhuman primates as models for human genetics and genomics, and as tools for comparative genetic analysis, was now widely recognized. This was one reason why the National Human Genome Research Institute had already approved the complete whole genome DNA sequencing of nine species of nonhuman primates—chimpanzee, rhesus macaque, marmoset, baboon, squirrel monkey, tarsier, mouse lemur, and galago—and was considering others.

The facility dormitory and conference center provided a large space for year-round housing and conferences. This building had two floors, in which all rooms were fully furnished. The first floor contained an apartment for the facility director along with a kitchen and dining area. It also contained a large TV/conference room with a capacity for twenty-four, a poolroom, laundry facilities, and storage space. The second floor contained numerous bedrooms and bathrooms.

The Animal Care Unit held caging, bedding change stations, and sinks and was organized as individual rooms accessed from a corridor system. The Procedure Rooms were located next to the housing rooms and were a primary setting for research activity within the unit. The animal care area contained barrier elements - airlocks, lockers, pass-through autoclaves - that provided the primary barrier and access control that separated the controlled animal care environment from external influences. The cage washing area was the hub for all cleaning, sanitizing, and husbandry activities, duties that were performed by the animal care technicians. These areas were dominated by equipment-generated heat and moisture. The major equipment items included pass-through rack washers, pass-through autoclaves, bedding dispensers and dump stations, and bottle washing and filling stations. A quarantine room for suspect and incoming animals that could be a source of infection was located in this area as well. Down the hall and isolated from all clean areas was the necropsy/perfusion room—a critical support function used for post mortem procedures on sacrificed animals.

There were containment facilities - facilities for working with potentially infectious biological agents that operated under negative pressure to prevent the escape of air to the general environment. Wastes and effluents were separately contained and decontaminated. Sophisticated control and monitoring systems and equipment were employed to achieve closely controlled and regulated air pressurizations and flows. Air flow and air exchanges along with temperatures were alarmed and monitored. Finally, there was a veterinary care clinic that provided lab and care functions such as surgery, clinical chemistry, and histology.

Animal Care Unit technicians provided routine daily care for all laboratory animals housed in the facility along with daily observation and provision of food and water. Environmental conditions for each species were maintained as temperature, humidity and light cycles modified as required by experimental design.

Millie slouched in an easy chair and munched her sandwich. The sitting room was dim, illuminated only by the soft glow from her bedroom light. The upcoming morning weighed heavy on her mind.

It wasn't too late to back out.

Millie always thought of herself as a moral and ethical person, one who tried to do the right thing. Her father, John, always said that character was how one acted when no one was watching. She grew up not wanting to disappoint the man she idolized. Maybe that was why she never had many suitors. Sex before marriage was frowned upon in the Harbaum household.

The heart of her conundrum was the fact that she knew she was being dishonest. Dishonest with Gerald Siscom and Dr. Olson, not to mention her university president, Dr. Pauling. And that knowledge made Mille uncomfortable. Dishonesty was not one of her core character traits.

It was why sleep would not come. More than the dishonesty was the act itself. Inserting her own genes into the Yeti ovum, an animal egg cell, was something not done much before. Especially a nonhuman primate. Sure, she remembered, various human genes had been inserted into mice, guinea pigs, flies, bacteria—lesser species but never a complete human genome into a primate. And one that lived thousands of years ago.

And Siscom and Dr. Olson had no idea what they were getting themselves into.

When she thought about it in this darkened room and attempted to reflect on its total ramifications, what she was about to do was like something out of a sci-fi movie. Her scientific mind said if the technology was available, go ahead and try it. Her ethical brain said hold on, not so fast, think about it.

What had she created? Possibly, an experimental chimera in the lab. One that contained approximately equal numbers of human and chimpanzee cells. Millie had read of chimeras of human and mouse cells that were now constructed in the laboratory as a matter of course, but they didn't survive to term. Another example of the ethics debate was the fuss now made about mouse embryos containing some proportion of human cells. How human must a chimera be before more stringent research rules should kick in? To date, the question was merely theological, since the chimeras didn't come anywhere near being born and there was nothing resembling a human brain. But to venture down the slippery slope so beloved by ethicists, what if we were to fashion a chimera of fifty percent human and fifty percent chimpanzee cells and grow it to adulthood? That would change everything.

In essence, wasn't that what she was about to do?

Ethics and our politics assumed, largely without question or serious discussion, that the division between human and animal was absolute. Pro-life was a potent polit-ical badge, associated with a gamut of ethical issues, such as opposition to abortion and euthanasia.

What it really meant was pro-human-life. Abortion clinic bombers were not known for their veganism, nor did Roman Catholics show any particular reluctance to have their suffering pets put to sleep. In the minds of many people, a single-celled human zygote, which had no nerves and could not suffer, was infinitely sacred, simply because they believed it was human. No other cells en-joyed this exalted status.

Was it immoral to create an organism whose status one could not determine? Millie knew it would result in an irresolvable dilemma about how to treat this animal. More specifically, didn't this research disregard the wel-fare of higher primates involved? Higher primates, espe-cially chimpanzees, were closely related to humans and, thus, might be seen as ideal research subjects in chimera experiments. A famous biologist and noted biotechnology activist opposed chimera research because it crossed spe-cies boundaries. In his view, animals had the right to exist without being tampered with, especially because he found that other research methods could lead to the same medi-cal advances.

Wouldn't the creation of novel beings that were part human and part nonhuman animal be sufficiently threat-ening to the social order that, for many, this was suffi-cient reason to prohibit any crossing of species bounda-ries involving human beings?

Millie sauntered into her bedroom and looked at the clock. Two a.m. She collapsed on the bed, her mind worn out from the battle that raged within her soul.

Chapter 5

Millie arrived in the Animal Care Unit promptly at ten o'clock, beleaguered from lack of sleep and the ethical arguments battling in her head. Just before dawn, she made peace with what she was doing, the scientific arguments winning out over ethical constraints. There was something in her, call it curiosity, that drove her to see the project's completion.

It all boiled down to the fact she wanted another Yeti for her research, and she was determined to see what such an animal with human genes would be like. She knew if the pregnancy were successful, she would have to own up to the gene insertion and take the consequences. Maybe then, she could convince Radner and Dr. Olson to not destroy the creature. But this morning, she needed to implant the embryo.

She sauntered down the tiled hallway to Gerald Siscom's office, but he wasn't there. She turned the corner and went down another short hallway, pushed the button that opened a door into the unit's airlock. In the room, she donned sterile coveralls, hat, and mask then punched the button on the far wall that opened the door into the wing that housed the chimps, operating room, and laboratory.

She found Siscom in the small operating room, checking items on a table.

He turned and greeted her. "Good morning, Millie," he said. "Ready to begin?"

"Good morning, Gerald. Yes, I'm ready and eager. How can I help?"

"I've already sedated our chimp in the next room, so she's ready to go. We'll bring her in here, place her on the operating table, do the transfer, then move her back to her cage. Should go smoothly."

"Fine," Millie said.

The previous night, Millie removed the embryo from the liquid nitrogen, with the container, then plunged it directly into warming media that was controlled at room temperature. This was to prevent intracellular ice crystals from forming. Once the embryo was thawed and warmed, the cryoprotectants that replaced the water in the cells were removed and balanced solutions infused back into the cells. This was accomplished by bathing the embryo with varying concentrations of water. As the cryoprotectants were removed, the cells filled with water containing the nutrients and growth factors needed for cellular recovery. The embryo was finally placed in an incubator in supporting culture media for the twelve hours needed to allow its cells to continue equilibration prior to transfer.

The operating room was lit with bright fluorescent lights and was completely tiled with a drain in the middle of the floor. Next to a standard operating table stood a rack of monitors and Millie noticed an oscilloscope, respirator, oximeter, and a tray with various syringes containing medications.

Siscom left the room and returned with a technician who pushed a cart containing the chimp. The animal breathed in a slow regular rhythm. Millie helped the veterinarian and technician move the animal onto the operating table. After pushing the carrier aside, the technician began applying electrodes to the animal's extremities and connected them to an electrocardiograph monitor. He placed the oximeter on one of her fingers, and an automated blood pressure cuff about her arm. Satisfied the animal's condition was satisfactory, Siscom spread the chimp's legs and lifted them onto the stirrups.

"Very familiar, Gerald," Millie said, chuckling. "I've been in that position a time or two myself."

"I can imagine," Siscom said, the corners of his eyes wrinkling as if he was smiling under his mask. "Some things are universal."

Siscom took an instrument an inserted it into the chimp's uterus. Sedated, the animal didn't move.

"Do you have the embryo?" he said, as he adjusted the instrument.

"Right here," Millie said. She took a test tube from a rack and handed it to him.

"I need you to hold it while I suck the solution with the embryo into this tube."

Millie complied. Siscom took a polyethylene pipette, stuck it into the solution, and using the bulb, withdrew the solution containing the embryo into it.

"Fine, thanks," he said.

Siscom inserted the tube through the instrument and into the chimp's uterus. He took a deep breath.

"Here goes," he said.

Millie's heart skipped a beat and began racing.

The moment of truth, she thought. *No turning back.*

Siscom injected the solution into the uterus and relaxed. Millie could tell he had been tense because, now that the procedure was over, his shoulder and neck muscles relaxed.

"We'll leave her in this position for an hour," he said, "then move her. We can go back to my office if you want. Jake here will watch her until time to put her in her cage."

Millie nodded in silence, somewhat awed by what had transpired. Back in Siscom's office, she tried to unwind.

"Well, we've crossed the Rubicon, so to speak," Siscom said. "The hard part is over. All we do now is check the chimp's progesterone level to make sure she is pregnant and remains pregnant until the embryo is large enough to see on ultrasound. Care for some coffee?"

"I'd love some, thanks. And thanks, Gerald, for doing this for me."

"Well, I must say I had some second thoughts," he said.

"How so?"

"The obvious ethical ones for starters. But all we are doing is an IVF procedure with a surrogate mother. Done before many times. So think we are on firm ground here. Dr. Olson must agree as well."

"You remember, Gerald, when we were hunting the Yeti out on the plains? We had formed a small search party and were trying to locate them before the state police strike force did?"

"Of course. How can I forget?"

"It was out there I realized for the first time just how priceless our Yeti were. And if they were killed, what a tremendous loss to science and history it would be."

"Yes, it was certainly unfortunate. But they had killed a number of people. In the end, they had to go."

"I disagree. That's my point. We could have recaptured them and brought them back here. Beefed up our security, sure, but they would still be alive today. No. Gerald, vengeance is a terrible thing, and that is what got them killed. Vengeance."

"You're right, of course, Millie."

"And I'll never forget. Or forgive them for it."

"I can understand," Siscom said.

"All Dr. Olson and Dixie went through to get those creatures back here. Dixie taken by them on their first trip to Mongolia, a team member killed on the return trip. It must be heartbreaking to the Olsons and the rest of the team to have seen their precious specimens gunned down like they were. But more than the emotional toll, it must have taken on the people involved, think of the scientific loss. According to their genome, those creatures are closer to humans in their evolution than Neanderthals. What an astounding fact! And the Neanderthals are now known to have interbred with modern humans. What if the Yeti did the same thousands of years ago? What if we search our own genome and find bits of Yeti DNA? Wow! Just think of it, Gerald."

"I have thought about it. And it's mind blowing."

જા૭૯ઝ

Dr. Bernard Wickingham sat in his small, Spartan apartment in Modesto with a broad smile and a sense of smugness. He was reading the article in the San Francisco *Chronicle* about his old departmental chairman, Dr. Harry Olson, and how, after many years, the doctor's fraud finally surfaced and was public. *Now let the bastard squirm a little*, he thought.

Wickingham always felt he was wrongfully terminated from his faculty position at Cal Pacific. He had played his cards wrong and got himself fired, so now he was living hand to mouth while he tried to rejuvenate his career in the field of anthropology and paleontology. Being a junior faculty member again at the University of California, Merced, rankled him to the point that it was difficult getting up each morning and facing the freshman in his Biology 101 class. They were such idiots, not one of them cared to learn. He had a burning sensation in the pit of his stomach, and Harry Olson was the cause of it.

He threw the paper on the coffee table, poured himself a glass of cheap bourbon, and tried to push his headache away. Remembering Harry's wife got his pulse racing, his palms sweaty. She was a hot number to be sure. Given enough time, he could have lured her away from the hotshot scientist. He could still remember her perfume, the way the tops of her breasts peeked out above her blouse.

From his first day at Cal Pacific, he felt Harry treated him like a second-class citizen, forcing him to work in an isolated section of the paleontology lab, in spite of his begging for his own, larger space. Not enough money, the man said. Work your way up the seniority ladder. Publish more. Didn't the bastard know with whom he was dealing? Bernard Wickingham, top graduate student. He had obtained his doctorate with honors.

He took a long pull on the liquor and winced at the burn in his throat. In his frazzled mind, he couldn't remember exactly how he had found out about Harry's forging of data, but he used the knowledge to try and force Dixie to persuade her husband to give him more space. He threatened to expose Harry to the world, and it got him fired.

But now, the tables were turned. The whole world knew about Harry Olson. *Harry O.*

After leaving Cal Pacific, Wickingham left San Francisco altogether, wandering down the coast to first one small village then another. Finally, he settled in Russell City, working the fishing docks unloading herring trawlers. But he hated fish, so during the summer, he donned his suit and went in search of a teaching job, eventually finding one at UC Merced. It wasn't a glamorous job, but he didn't smell of fish at the end of the day.

The article in the *Chronicle* stated the reporter would attempt to get a reply from Dr. Linus Pauling, Cal Pacific's president, and Dr. Olson himself. Wickingham was looking forward to the reporter's future articles.

Finishing the bourbon, he stretched out on his sofa and turned on the television. The Giants were playing at home in their stadium next to the Bay, so he was soon engrossed in the game and forgot about Harry Olson.

◑◒◑

It was the end of the day as Gerald Siscom made his rounds through the Animal Care Unit. The smell of dry animal chow greeted him as he stepped into the bright light. Dinner had just been served to the animals, he thought. He met Bruce Drayton, the facility's chief of security at the unit's doorway. The chief, whose slight limp was more exaggerated at quitting time, was also making his rounds before heading to the dining hall.

"Well, Bruce," Siscom said, "I haven't seen you in several days. How is the state of security?"

"About the same," Drayton said. "Just checking on the new procedures we installed since the escape. Have the new digital locks on the cages given any of the staff problems?" The chief of security was tall and lean with long arms and oversized hands. His limp was from an old gunshot wound he suffered while a police officer.

"Not at all. In fact, I think they are going to work better and provide safer access for authorized personnel. Especially since you've been changing the lock's combination every month."

"Yeah, but I remember Jimmy Winkleman was an authorized person. One of the scientists."

"True," said Siscom. "It was he who allowed Bentu to escape his cage. But the animal learned to work the locks and managed to let Sasha out of her cage. So these new locks might prevent a similar occurrence in the future."

The air conditioning switched on to begin the cycle of lowering the unit's temperature to a chilly fifty-five degrees for the night. Its whirring sound filtered through the unit as Siscom finished his duties. Drayton checked the airlocks and disappeared down the far hallway.

"See you tomorrow," Siscom called after him. The security chief waved a hand without looking back.

As soon as Siscom finished checking on the chimp, he turned off the light and left the unit. The impregnated chimp's vital signs were stable, the pulse oximeter beeping softly read ninety-eight percent, and she was sleeping off the sedation, apparently free of effects from the procedure earlier in the day. He made sure she had food and water in her cage. Then he went to the dining hall to give Millie an update.

Chapter 6

Millie was in the Animal Care Unit early the morning after the embryo transfer. She let herself into the airlock, donned sterile coveralls, and entered the cage area. The room was cold, the temperature still at the lower level before warming for the day. There were four large animal cages occupying the room, two on each side of a narrow walkway. All were occupied by young chimps who, upon her arrival, began excited chattering and moving around their cages. The one she was interested in sat on the floor and ate from a bowl of food. When Millie approached the front of her cage, the animal stopped eating, looked up, and sauntered over, as if to greet her.

The chimp's large dark eyes sparkled as she continued to chew the last remnants of her food. Millie took a step closer. Siscom must have already made rounds for all the monitoring devices had been removed from her. The animal appeared to be without obvious serious sequelae from her procedure the day before. No blood or fluid on the floor of her cage that might indicate a miscarriage. The chimp grasped the bars of the cage and hopped up and down. Millie thought she seemed happy.

"I'll name you Tika," she said, half out loud. "And I

ought to dream up a name for the baby you're carrying."

Millie left the cage area and walked to her small work-room, where her computer and research records were housed. She sat, switched on the computer, and waited for the Cal Pacific network login to appear on the screen. She typed in her username and password and soon navigated to the research facility scientist's area. After locating her page, she began typing, entering her latest observations into her log which she renamed Project Tika.

0610 ~ Tika seems fine this AM. No worse for the procedure yesterday. Up and around in her cage. Eating. Eyes bright. Greeted me when I arrived in the unit. Will await Dr. Siscom's assessment.

She typed an email to her father then left the unit and headed to the dormitory for breakfast. Leaving the main building, Millie noticed the sun rising over the eastern edge of the plains creating an orange glow on the horizon. Gerald was right, she thought. Sunrise was spectacular. Atop Cinder Mountain, the morning air was clean, crisp and invigorating.

Millie found Siscom eating his breakfast and joined him after going through the line and selecting eggs, bacon, grits, toast, and coffee. When she slid into her chair opposite the veterinarian, he raised his eyebrows and whistled.

"Hungry?" he said.

"I could eat a horse this morning," Millie said, diving into her eggs.

"Must have had a good night's sleep then."

Millie nodded, her mouth full.

"I did," she said after swallowing, "and I just checked on Tika. She seems to be doing fine."

"Tika?" Siscom said, taking a gulp of coffee.

"That's what I have named her, our chimp. I couldn't very well go on without naming her. Couldn't continue calling her the chimp."

Siscom chuckled. "Don't look now, but your feminine side is showing, Millie."

"I've been worried I didn't have a feminine side, Gerald. It's good to know I do."

Dr. Gerald Siscom was single, having been divorced from his wife for a number of years. Millie heard talk that the woman had taken him to the cleaners and that Siscom came to the facility to escape his previous life and his ex-wife. The other men at the facility, except for Radner, had wives and families who lived in the nearby town of Grant. They usually went home at night or on the weekends. She frequently saw the two single men, Radner and Siscom, in the game room playing chess in the evenings.

The veterinarian was tall, somewhat heavyset, wore wire-framed glasses, and sported a graying mustache. He was a good ten years older than Millie, but there was something in his easy manner that drew Millie to him. He was always calm, never rattled when things got hectic in the unit, and spoke a kind word to all the technicians. He possessed an unusual softness, something Millie rarely saw in most male scientists.

"Actually, Millie, you're very attractive," Siscom said. Saying that, he ducked his head as if embarrassed, finished his coffee, and stood. "I'll see you in the unit shortly."

Mille watched him replace his tray and leave the dining hall. *Wow*, she thought. *He thinks I'm attractive.*

All that morning they worked alongside each other, their conversation focused on the work at hand. The first thing Siscom wanted to do was draw a blood sample for progesterone analysis.

"The placenta becomes a significant source of progesterone by approximately week six of chimp pregnancy. Serum progesterone concentrations rise in a linear fashion with advancing gestation, ultimately attaining values more than twofold greater than prior to pregnancy. By the end of pregnancy, the placental production rate of progesterone is a value more than ten-fold greater than at any time in the animal's estrus cycle. Progesterone levels are also predictive of pregnancy outcome. Abortion ultimately results in more than eighty percent of primates with very low levels of progesterone. Progesterone concentrations are also typically low in primates with ectopic pregnancies. So these first samples should reflect low progesterone levels and, as the pregnancy progresses the levels should rise."

"And if they don't?" Millie said.

"Then there's no pregnancy. The embryo either didn't implant or she aborted it."

"There was no blood or fluid in her cage this morning," she said.

"And that's a hopeful sign," Siscom said.

They moved to a small enclosure next to Tika's cage into which a technician rolled an animal squeeze cage. He then left and returned, leading Tika by the hand and ushered her into the squeeze cage. She squawked a few times but settled into the routine she obviously knew well. The technician began rotating the lever that moved one wall of the cage against the other until Tika was immobilized.

"She doesn't mind it?" Millie said. "Being treated that way?"

"Our animals have been trained, or rather conditioned, to accept the squeeze cage as part of their existence. Overcoming their fear is our big hurdle. Positive reinforcement training is based on giving pleasurable rewards for the desired behavioral response, so we give them plenty of treats. It's like training your dog. We give the animal a choice: it chooses to cooperate or not, rather than being made to comply with a procedure. The training allows desensitization of the animal to frightening and even painful events, thereby reducing the stress associated with such events."

"So your training uses a target or goal-defined behavior," Millie said.

Siscom nodded. "Yes. And it must be selected and clearly defined. Once the overall aim is selected, then a series of small steps is used to progress to the behavioral goal. Correct responses or approximations toward the goal are reinforced, while incorrect responses are ignored."

"They learn quickly?"

"These chimps are smart, so yes, they learn and adapt very quickly."

Siscom moved the side of the squeeze cage and approached Tika who stared at him with large dark eyes.

"There now, girl," he said softly, "you've done this many times before. We'll be through in a moment, and you can have your treat."

He reached into the cage, plunged the needle into Tika's groin, and withdrew a sample of blood. The animal didn't flinch or make a sound, she just watched Siscom work. Once she shot a glance toward Millie, whose heart skipped a beat. Soon, Siscom was finished. The technician released Tika, and the two ambled back to her main cage.

"She gets a treat now for being such a good patient," Siscom said, smiling. He injected the blood into a blood specimen tube, labeled it, and placed it in the refrigerator in the small lab. "It goes to a laboratory in Las Vegas."

Much later, Millie sat alone at her workstation, reflecting on the day's activities. She was pleased with the work to date and hoped the progesterone level would indicate

Tika was pregnant. When her thoughts drifted to Siscom, a smile formed on her face. He said I *was attractive*, she mused. She thought back to when they were on the desert searching for the escaped Yeti. Gerald listened to her, and she began to see him in a different light. No longer just a veterinarian. He wasn't exactly handsome, but he certainly wasn't bad looking either.

She was beginning to really like Gerald Siscom.

ొచెౕ

Harry sat in Pauling's office, having received a summons to an important meeting. He ensconced himself in a leather chair at a small round table next to Pauling's desk. Also at the table were his president and a man Pauling introduced as chairman of Cal Pacific's Board of Trustees, Alistair Forester. The look on each man's face was somber, and Harry sensed that this meeting might not end well. The newspaper article weighed heavy on his mind, and he rubbed one temple with an index finger.

"Harry," Pauling started, "Mr. Forester here requested a face-to-face meeting with you and me to discuss the latest developments outlined in the *Chronicle*. I want to assure you this is not a witch-hunt, nor are we looking for a scapegoat. Right, Mr. Forester?"

The silver-haired man nodded. Forester was immaculately groomed in a tailored blue wool suit and plain green silk tie. He didn't smile.

"So, to begin, Harry, why don't you give us the particulars of what happened years ago that led to the newspaper story."

Harry shifted his weight in his chair and cleared his throat. With heart pounding in his temples and bile burning his stomach, he began. He didn't relish rehashing his past mistakes.

"A number of years ago, right after I finished grad school, Professor Kesler hired me here at Cal Pacific, and I continued the research I did for my doctorate. That work led to a publication in which, in a naive and childish attempt to bolster my reputation, I used data that I knew weren't correct, that I made up. Fortunately, and to my astonishment, the Professor discovered what I had done, but not before the article appeared in print. He was devastated by my actions and left me feeling as if I had betrayed my own father. That's what he had become to me. I would have sooner cut off my right arm than see the look in his eyes when he confronted me with his suspicions.

"Of course I owned up to what I had done, and the Professor graciously used his influence to make it right. He wrote a letter that was printed in the journal, saying that he was responsible for the inadvertent mistake, and I subsequently corrected everything in a paper that followed six months later.

"In all the years I was the Professor's assistant, he never mentioned the incident and, as embarrassed as I was, neither did I. That is until one evening in Mongolia when he visited our team after the Yeti discovery." Harry's voice trembled as he continued to talk. His eyes sought some evidence of understanding from Forester but saw none. "That evening I broke down, apologized. Dr. Kesler put a hand on my shoulder and forgave me. He told me that we would never speak of it again, that I had done my penance, and that he was as proud of me as if I was the son he never had."

Harry paused, struggling to gain control of his emotions. Pauling and Forester sat still as statues, a pensive look on their faces.

"That's it, gentlemen. I owe everything I am to Dr. Kesler's kindness, and I can never repay him. I carry his memory with me every day. Dr. Pauling here was fully aware of the incident, and I never attempted to hide anything from him. However, no one but my wife knew of our reconciliation in Mongolia. The fault rests solely with me, no one else. I have no excuse, except that I was young and eager to make a name for myself. To my great relief and with my undying gratitude, Dr. Kesler forgave my mistake, and together we moved on. I believe everyone has moved on from the incident."

Pauling cleared his throat and sat forward in his chair.

"And nothing was heard about this until the other day when the article in the *Chronicle* appeared. Personally, I think it is much ado about something that happened years ago. It was handled internally and resolved to my satisfaction."

Forester adjusted his tie.

"Well," he said in a baritone voice reminiscent of an opera singer, "unfortunately, I don't think the trustees will see it quite that way. Dr. Olson's actions, even though occurring years ago, reflect poorly on the university. It is my feeling that there ought to be a formal investigation into this affair and, if warranted, a reprimand placed in Dr. Olson's personnel file."

"Mr. Forester," Pauling said, "I really don't believe that is necessary. I handled the matter as part of my administrative responsibility. I stake my professional reputation on Dr. Olson's integrity. He has brought academic acclaim to our university, which was much needed as we begged for donations."

"If I remember correctly," Forester said, "the escape of those Yetis and the subsequent slaughter of innocent people happened on Dr. Olson's watch as well. We might need to include those items in our investigation."

Oh brother, thought Harry. *This man is after my hide.*

Forester stood. "Dr. Pauling, I think I've heard enough

for now." He held out his hand. "Dr. Olson, you'll be hearing from the board in the near future."

Pauling escorted the man to the door and asked his secretary to accompany him to his car. Upon returning to the office, Pauling put a hand on Harry's shoulder. "Gird your loins, Harry," he said. "That's all I can say. Gird your loins."

Chapter 7

Over dinner, Dixie listened to Harry relate the details of his meeting with Pauling and Alistair Forester that afternoon. She was appalled that, after several years and thinking this issue had been put to rest, now it would be drudged up again. As she and Harry ate, he recounted the meeting. His description caused her stomach slowly contract into tight knots, and anger boiled in her veins. No one was going to threaten her husband.

"So," Harry concluded, "I guess I must wait until I hear from the board of trustees and whatever investigation they decide upon. I'm kinda in limbo right now."

"The bastard," Dixie seethed, spitting the word out like venom. "Can you count on Pauling for support?"

"I think so. He said as much at the meeting, but he answers to the board. I'm sure he'll protect his own interests if it comes down to the nitty-gritty. Right now, I feel I'm out on that proverbial limb, and Forester is sawing."

"I'm for locating that bastard Wickingham and suing his ass off," Dixie said, her voice still hot with rancor.

"Honey, I'm guilty as charged, remember? I admitted my crime. There's no libel in that."

"But it's over and done with. Years ago. Finished. Even Pauling agreed with that. The only motive Wickingham could have now is character assassination. If the university president is satisfied with you, why can't the trustees be?"

"It's all politics. Forester is afraid the university will suffer a downturn in public perception. And that means money. Fewer donations from the big money types."

"So this is all going to boil down to money?" Dixie's tone sounded incredulous. "They're going to throw you under the bus simply for financial reasons?"

"Maybe. We'll have to wait and see," Harry said.

"All the same, if Pauling doesn't support you a hundred percent, I'll never forgive him."

"And Professor Kesler," Harry added, "don't forget about him."

"He gave you a second chance. Doesn't everyone deserve a second chance? His support and recommendation as his successor should count for something. I hope Pauling makes that point clear to the trustees. Harry, have you thought about just resigning?"

"You mean now? Before the investigation?"

"Yes. Now. You can find another position, what with your reputation. I'll go wherever you want to go."

"I need to stay and see this through, sweetheart. If I left, this issue would just follow me wherever I went, now that it's out in the public domain. So I believe now is the time to face this down, once and for all."

"Wickingham was always such a creep," Dixie said, her tone somewhat calmer. "He was always leering at the ladies and trying to sneak a peek down our blouses. I had the jitters when he was around."

"Yeah, even Chloe Rawlings had similar feelings, and you know if she didn't like someone, they must really be something."

"I still think we need to consult a lawyer."

Harry shook his head. "Let's wait and see how this

plays out. Who knows, the trustees may decide in my favor. Forester is only one voice."

Dixie began clearing the dishes from the table. "And if
the investigation goes against you and you get a formal
reprimand?"

"Then so be it. I will have done my best."

❧❧❧

Two weeks after the embryo transfer, Millie and Siscom reviewed Tika's latest progesterone blood levels. As
they looked over the results a smile formed on Millie's
face.

"The level," she said, "it's rising. She's pregnant!"

"She sure is," Siscom said. "Now if she can just main-
tain the pregnancy. That's the next hurdle."

"So the progesterone is what maintains the pregnancy?" Millie said. The two were sitting in Siscom's office.

"Yes," Siscom said. "It's the modulating effects of
progesterone on endometrial structure and function that
are essential to the success of reproduction. After ovula-
tion, progesterone produced by the corpus luteum induces
maturation of the endometrium, involving a cascade of
molecular events that ultimately renders the endometrium
receptive to implantation of the embryo. After that and
with continued progesterone stimulation, driven by rapidly increasing concentrations of chorionic gonadotropin,
the endometrium is reconfigured to support early embry-
onic development."

"What if there's not enough progesterone?" Millie
asked.

"Considering the important role that progesterone
plays in reproduction, it is not surprising that exogenous
supplemental progesterone is a common element of

treatment regimens in infertility, particularly those relating to the assisted reproductive technologies."

"How so?" Millie said.

"A classic series of studies, conducted more than three decades ago, demonstrated that progesterone secretion by the corpus luteum is absolutely required for the success of early human pregnancy. Surgical excision of the corpus luteum, or luteectomy, before seven weeks' gestation uniformly precipitated an abrupt decrease in serum progesterone concentrations, followed by miscarriage. When luteectomy was performed more than twenty-seven days after the missed menstrual period, progesterone levels decreased only slightly and transiently, and pregnancy continued. Finally, exogenous progesterone replacement after early luteectomy prevented otherwise inevitable miscarriage."

Millie shook her head and smiled.

"All very complex, I see, Gerald. I'm glad I have you to help with this project. Without it, I could never do it. Not alone."

"It's been interesting to me as well. Given me a chance to review things I learned in vet school. Let's go see how Tika is faring this morning."

When they had finished their walk through the Animal Care Unit and checking on Tika, Millie and Siscom returned to Millie's small workspace where she poured each of them a cup of coffee. Sitting across the table from Siscom, she sipped the hot liquid. Finally, she asked a question. "What are you thinking, Gerald? You looked deep in thought."

"I was just wondering about something you said a few weeks ago before we started this venture."

"Yeah, what's that?"

Gerald set his cup on the table. "You mentioned that the Yeti and modern humans were somehow related in their evolutionary development, but you never mentioned the specifics. Care to elaborate?"

Millie nodded and thought for a moment. Sorting out how she was going to answer.

"Humans have twenty-three chromosome pairs in each of their cells. Chimpanzees, gorillas, and orangutans, by contrast, have twenty-four chromosome pairs. So if we are distantly related, evolution needs to explain: How did we end up with one fewer chromosome pair than them?

"As it turns out, modern genetic science has provided the answer. We need to look closely at chromosome two. In chimpanzees, gorillas, and orangutans, chromosome two is actually made up of two smaller chromosomes, two p and two q. But in humans, there is just one.

"The reason for this is the ancestral equivalents of chromosomes two p and two q fused together over the course of evolution and became the single human chromosome two."

"How do we know that this fusion occurred?" Siscom said.

Millie smiled. "The proof is written, indelibly, in the genetic material itself. Chromosomes have different regions, including two telomeres, structures at the end of each chromosome that contain repetitive DNA and serve as a protective cap, and one centromere, a region that binds together chromosome pairs during cell division. So if the ancestral equivalents of chromosomes two p and two q fused together, end to end, to become human chromosome two, then there should be genetic proof of this evolutionary event. More specifically, that chromosome should be a bit odd—it should have telomere DNA in its middle as well as on its ends, and two centromeres, or at least, their genetic remnants, rather than one."

Siscom leaned forward, obviously intrigued by Millie's story. "So does human chromosome two have the telltale DNA evidence of a fusion event?" He waited pensively for her to continue the dialogue.

"Yes, it does," Millie said. "The authors of the original 1982 *Science* paper had no hesitancy in declaring that the telomeric fusion of chromosomes two p and two q accounts for the reduction of the twenty-four pairs of chromosomes of the great apes to twenty-three in modern man. But they could not confirm this with the high-powered techniques of modern genetics. However, two decades later, in a study published in *Nature*, the precise fusion site was located on human chromosome two. The paper noted the presence of multiple subtelomeric duplications in this location, as in the expected telomere DNA, and also the vestiges of a second centromere on the chromosome that has since been inactivated. In other words—"

"In other words," Siscom interrupted, "the genetic evidence is precisely what you would expect to see if evolution is true."

"Yes, exactly," Millie said. "Gerald, you understand perfectly. And that speaks volumes about the power of the theory to explain what we actually observe in the natural world."

"It makes perfect sense when you think about it," the veterinarian said, seemingly proud of himself.

Millie felt warmed by Siscom's genuine interest and honored by his quick understanding of a complex idea. She was beginning to feel something more than mere professional friendship with the man. Something more personal. Her breath quickened as she continued.

"As a famous biologist said, 'Evolution makes testable predictions. When it comes to chromosomes, the prediction of evolution is that if we have forty-six chromosomes and our closest cousins have forty-eight, then somewhere in our genome should be a chromosome formed by a recent fusion, and that chromosome should have telomere DNA, and it should have two centromeres.' That is a prediction made by evolution, and bingo, you look, and there it is."

"Wow," Siscom said. "Quite a story. Any others?"

"Yes, and not nearly so involved. A retrovirus is a virus that is composed not of DNA but of RNA. Retroviruses have an enzyme, called reverse transcriptase, which gives them the unique property of transcribing their RNA into DNA after entering a cell. The retroviral DNA can then integrate into the chromosomal DNA of the host cell, to be expressed there. HIV is a retrovirus. This is a unique mechanism in the retrovirus. But it gets even more interesting. The viral DNA gets inserted into the host organism DNA. The cell then uses the viral DNA as a template for viral proteins. Instead of being co-opted, producing new viruses, and then dying, the cell lives it's full life making new viral bodies along with everything else it's supposed to do. This how an HIV infection works.

"If the virus attacks a gamete, then that viral genome can appear in every cell in the offspring's body and be passed on to future generations. It sounds like a great deal for the virus. However, the viruses are very sensitive. Viral genomes are often very tight, very compact, and very susceptible to mutation. Humans and other plants and animals and other species as well have multiple copies of each gene.

"So, if one of those alleles is broken by mutation, there is a spare. Viruses and bacteria don't have this feature. A mutation that damages the virus's ability to perform any of the functions it must perform, such as invade a host cell, reverse transcribe the RNA, build the protein coat, means that the virus is no longer effective. The entire genome is broken, the virus can no longer function, but the DNA is still there, in the host organism. That is called an endogenous retrovirus or ERV for short."

"But," Siscom said, "how can this be evidence for evolution?"

Millie smiled. She was having fun explaining this to her colleague.

"Good question. Let's say an organism gets one of these ERVs in its gametes and passes that gene onto its offspring. Except the offspring ends up with a mutation that breaks the viral gene. Now, that organism has a gene that doesn't affect anything, but it's there. All of that organism's offspring will have a copy of that gene and, more telling, that gene will be in the same relative place. As time goes on and the species diverges, speciation events occur, and mutations happen, a pattern will emerge. That pattern is the same as what is predicted for the idea of common descent. That is, organisms will share a common ancestor, and those organisms that are more closely related will have a more recent common ancestor.

"A recent study of primates shows this very well. All monkeys contain two particular ERVs. All monkeys except new world monkeys share another two ERVs. Three more are shared only by gibbons, orangutans. Another two are only shared between chimps, gorillas, and humans. And three more appear only in humans. This is but a tiny bit of the thirty thousand plus ERVs in our genome. A similar situation appears in cats. If common descent were not correct, then we would not expect to see dozens of species with the exact same viral remnant in the exact same genomic position. For example, it would be highly unlikely to find a cat with the same two ERVs shared by humans, chimps, and gorillas.

"If common descent were not correct, then we would not see a relationship between shared ERVs and the closeness of two species. The more closely related the organisms, the more ERVs they share."

"You certainly know this stuff, Millie. So the Yeti and modern humans share identical ERVs?"

"Absolutely. And none of the shared ones are shared with Neanderthals. That is how we know the Yeti diverged later than them."

Siscom sat back and relaxed, and the two were silent for a long moment. Millie contemplated this man across from her. The depths of his ability to quickly understand complex scientific ideas amazed her. And he had a soft, quiet, unassuming nature as well. One that she found charming and engaging.

It was a thought quite new to her.

Chapter 8

Long after dinner was completed, Siscom sat alone in his darkened room, thinking of Millie. Now that he had time to reflect, Siscom found himself mildly aroused after spending a most enjoyable day working alongside the woman on Project Tika. Knowing Millie for the past year, he had not taken the time to get to know her, although while they were out on the plains searching for the Yeti, he saw a side of her that intrigued him.

When Siscom graduated from veterinary medicine school, he opened a small animal clinic in northern Arizona, hoping to become part of the community and put down roots. His prospects began looking up when he began dating Jennifer, a woman he met while vacationing one summer at the Grand Canyon. She lived in Phoenix, so they began a long -distance relationship with them emailing and calling each other during the week and Gerald driving to see Jennifer on the weekends.

From the outset, he realized that Jennifer was different, her sights set on something usually out of reach to a simple dog-and-cat veterinarian. She never came right out and said that he could never afford her, but her constant allusions to wanting expensive clothes, jewelry, and travel left him wondering if she even cared about him. He was surprised then when she accepted his marriage proposal. After a brief honeymoon to Acapulco, Siscom relocated his veterinary practice to Phoenix, and the couple bought a house in Scottsdale.

Jennifer was true to her word and soon spent money beyond Siscom's ability to keep up with her. Within two years, they racked up a huge credit card debt, and Jennifer found a rich boyfriend. Eventually, she dumped Siscom, saddling him with the debt. He never saw or talked to her again.

Devastated, he threw himself into his work, struggling to pay off the debt, never doing much more that eating, sleeping, and working. It was a difficult two years. He loved Jennifer. Her desertion and betrayal left him reeling and out of focus, except for his practice, which he attacked with an unusual vigor. Once he was out of debt, he sold his condo, and left Phoenix, spending most of his time hidden away in the Rocky Mountains.

His psyche hit bottom.

After a long and arduous process of putting his life in order, he answered an ad seeking a vet for the newly built Primate Research Facility in Nevada. Following his interview, Dr. Radner called and informed him of his acceptance. Soon after, Siscom moved atop Cinder Mountain near the town of Grant. He excelled in the work and enjoyed the staff.

And that included Millie.

He hadn't looked at another woman since his divorce. But he was beginning to see things in a new light. Today, he saw Millie differently. He saw her as a woman.

An attractive woman.

ఎనఎ

Bernard Wickingham lounged in a far corner of a dim

restaurant, waiting on the *Chronicle* reporter to arrive. It was no longer filled with the lunch hour crowd, and the noise was at a tolerable level. The open door of the restaurant, located off a busy corner on Market Street close to the wharf, allowed for the clang of the cable cars to drift inside. Wickingham looked up and noticed a young man enter. He was dressed in business attire and waved at Wickingham. After making his way to the scientist, he took a chair.

"Sorry I'm late," he said. "The traffic was horrible."

"I just finished my lunch," Wickingham said. "What did you need to see me about?"

"I've had some pushback from my editor about the article I wrote on Dr. Olson. On the information provided by you."

"I don't understand."

"Well, for starters, I had to answer a grueling on why this was news, at this time, years after the fact. When, by all accounts, it was handled internally to the apparent satisfaction of all concerned. It seems I might have been a bit premature in writing that article."

Wickingham stiffened.

"You think I wasn't entirely truthful? I can assure you I was."

"No, it's not that. Some of Dr. Olson's colleagues have called the paper, complaining."

"Let them complain," Wickingham seethed. "The bastard ruined my career." He stared out at the bay and noticed a few gulls venturing over the Wharf. "I provided you with all the pertinent details," he continued. "Can't your bosses at the paper see that?"

"Well, it's not just that the facts, in and of themselves, are correct," the reporter said, "it's the timeliness of the news that has caused the uneasiness. You weren't totally truthful, Doctor. Dr. Olson has an admirable reputation, due to his discovery of those animals in Mongolia. He has authored a number of highly acclaimed articles."

"What has that to do with the fact that he lied? Published false data. His boss had to save his bacon. Like I said, the bastard ruined my career."

The reported shifted awkwardly in his chair.

"I do not wish to be involved in a personal vendetta, Dr. Wickingham. However, I do have some information to impart you might find interesting. I have learned that Cal Pacific's Board of Trustees will conduct a formal investigation into this affair and Dr. Olson's actions. There may be some repercussions following that."

Wickingham relaxed and smiled. *Wonderful news*, he thought. *Things are looking up.*

ᕔᕚᕔ

It was late morning, and Millie was in the Animal Care Unit, helping Siscom examine Tika.

The veterinarian rolled an ultrasound machine next to the squeeze cage while a technician led the chimp into the exam room.

As she had done on previous occasions, Tika climbed into the squeeze cage without resisting and stared at Millie and Siscom with wide unblinking eyes. Once secured, Siscom approached her, ultrasound transducer in one hand and gel in the other.

"Here we go again, Tika," he said in a calm, reassuring voice. This won't take long, and it won't hurt."

"Do you think she understands you?" Millie said as she stood on the opposite side of the cage.

"I think she responds to the tone of my voice," Siscom said. "Let's see what we have. She should be about two months along now. The ultrasound will tell for sure."

He squirted a large amount of gel on the transducer,

placed it on Tika's abdomen, and began moving it around. The chimp flinched slightly at the probe's touch.

Millie watched the monitor with eager anticipation, her heart racing in her chest. Then something popped onto the screen, and Siscom sighed.

"There it is, Millie. There's the embryo. We can call it a fetus now."

Millie stared at the monitor, captivated by what she saw. The eyes were large and ears were well formed as well as arms and legs. She thought she could barely make out fingers and toes. "Wow, Gerald. It's awesome. I've never seen anything like this before."

"Yes, quite magical, it is."

Siscom studied the monitor for a minute, taking time to pour over the numbers indicated on the side of the screen.

"The fetus measures a little over an inch in length. A little more than two months gestation, I should think."

"Can you tell the sex?" Millie said.

"Not yet. Still too early. Maybe in another month."

Finished with the examination, the pair headed back to Siscom's office so he could type the results into Tika's medical record, leaving the technician to attend the chimp. Millie sat watching Siscom type. She couldn't get the picture of the small fetus out of her mind. In a way, she felt exuberant, joyful over what they had accomplished. That little fetus carried her genes. Now, if all would continue to proceed normally. She heard Siscom speak.

"I'll print a copy of the ultrasound and put in Tika's record," he said.

"Oh, Gerald, could I have a copy, please? I have my own notes, you know."

"Of course. By the way, Millie, would you care to drive into Grant this evening and have dinner with me? I have my car here at the facility. It might be a nice diversion."

Millie's heart skipped a beat.

"I'd love to," she said. "You're right, it would be nice to get off the mountain for a while. I haven't done so since we searched for Bentu and Sasha."

⇔⇔⇔

Siscom called for Millie as the sun was on its downward arc and near the western horizon. She had changed her clothes and wore khaki slacks and a pearlescent blue blouse. A faint hint of perfume accompanied her as they drove down Cinder Mountain.

"This was a wonderful idea, Gerald," she said when they reached the plains of northern Nevada. "I'm glad you thought of it."

Large cumulus clouds tinged with magenta and orange hues dotted the sky creating a gorgeous evening. With the heat of the day dissipating, they rolled down the car's windows and breathed the fresh, fragrant air.

"I don't know why I didn't think of it earlier," he said. "Involved with work, I guess."

They made the ten-mile drive into Grant in twenty minutes and arrived as the sun was on the cusp of the distant mountains. Siscom parked in front of a small diner, the town's only eatery. It was a busy night in the diner, but they found a booth at the rear and had no sooner seated themselves than a waitress with a pad and pencil arrived with water. She smiled as she handed them menus.

"Special tonight is roast beef," she said. Served with mashed potatoes and pinto beans." She left, and Siscom took a sip of his water.

"I hope this diner is acceptable," he said. "It's the only place for miles around."

"It's fine, Gerald. It's just good to get away for a while."

"It wouldn't have been fine for my ex-wife. She required the finer things in life like expensive restaurants." He hoped that Millie wouldn't notice his pained expression.

"You've been hurting for quite a while, haven't you?

"I admit I was deeply in love with her, but I have put it all behind me. It's over. Finished."

"Any children?" Millie said.

"No, thankfully."

The waitress returned, and they both ordered the special. After she left, Gerald continued.

"Our primate facility saved my life, literally. And my career. How about you?"

Siscom was fascinated with Millie's eyes as she talked, bright and inviting. She wore a deep red lipstick that accentuated the graceful curve of her mouth. He found it difficult to concentrate on what she was saying.

"I was devastated by Bentu's and Sasha's killing," she said. "Jimmy's death didn't help either. At first, I felt guilty for grieving more over the lost Yeti than Jimmy. But he was such a jerk and treated Bentu in such a horrible fashion. Many times, I thought about reporting him to Radner."

"I noticed the same behavior in Jimmy," Siscom said.

"After their deaths, I really didn't know what direction my life should take. I thought about dropping out of my doctoral program, but good ole Dr. Olson talked me out of it."

"Yeah," Siscom nodded. "Harry's first rate."

"Anyway," Millie continued, "Dr. Olson asked me to be Radner's assistant here when I completed my studies. It felt like home, I guess, so I accepted. The first few months without the Yeti, I just floundered. So when I remembered we had sperm and ova stored, I couldn't resist trying IVF. I never felt I was contributing to the facility's mission until now, Gerald. Thanks to you."

"I think we're at the point where we need to give Radner and Dr. Olson an update on our progress. They will want to know."

Their food arrived, and they began eating. The diner was still crowded, but they managed to converse over the noise.

"Did you hear about Dr. Olson?" Millie said.

"What?"

"The rumor is that he is being investigated by the university's trustees. Something about forged data in a scientific paper he published."

"I don't believe it. If it's true, it's never good for a scientist to have done something like that. Careers have been ruined. I hope it's not true. Dr. Olson has been good for the university."

"Myself, I don't believe it. I just don't."

Finished with dinner, they drove back to the facility, Siscom taking a different route. The stars were out and shone brightly, illuminating the plain in a faint silver glow. The air was cool. Millie's perfume mixed with the scent of sage and filled the car.

When they arrived back at the facility, Siscom escorted Millie to her room, and the pair stood outside her door. He felt awkward, wondering, what next.

"Gerald, it was wonderful, thanks. I enjoyed it very much. We'll have to do it again."

She came close, reached up, taking his arm, and kissed him gently on the cheek. Then she disappeared into her room.

As the scent of her perfume lingered in the air, Siscom touched his cheek where Millie had kissed it.

It felt good.

Chapter 9

Harry sat at one end of the long mahogany conference table in a room adjacent to Dr. Pauling's office. At the other end was Alistair Forester, chairman of Cal Pacific's Board of Trustees. Dr. Pauling sat, unperturbed, in the middle of one side of the table. The other trustees occupied the rest of the chairs. The mood was somber, none of the men were smiling. Several thermal pitchers sat on the table along with a number of crystal glasses.

Earlier, Dixie consoled him with upbeat chatter, telling him not to worry, that everything would work out. That the trustees couldn't be so stupid as to get rid of a man like her husband. He had smiled at her and caressed her face. She was his rock.

Harry's head pounded, and his stomach was in knots. His palms were damp. *This is the moment of truth*, he thought. *My opportunity to speak to the trustees. Please, God, help me find the right words*. His head jerked when Forester's baritone voice filled the room.

"Gentlemen," he said, "we'll come to order. This meeting of the board of trustees is to consider action on the matter of Dr. Olson. Members of the trustees have interviewed the involved parties, with the exception of

Dr. Julius Kesler, recently deceased. As we all are aware, Dr. Olson stands accused of forging scientific data in a journal article in an effort to further his career. Before I allow Dr. Olson to speak on his own behalf is there anyone present who would like to say something on the record?"

Harry was surprised when Dr. Pauling raised his hand.

"Yes, Dr. Pauling. We are eager to hear you. Please go ahead."

Pauling looked around the table, smiled at each trustee, and nodded at Harry.

"As I mentioned in my interview, and I would like to reaffirm now," he began, "my faith in Dr. Olson has not diminished one iota since this unfortunate incident. I have seen many young faculty members come and go during my career, and Dr. Olson is a rising star in his field. Actually, his star is at its zenith, and Cal Pacific is indeed fortunate to have him as a member of our faculty. Because of his courage and diligent work, he has brought both fame and fortune to our university, no small feat in these times of dwindling support.

"Our Primate Research Facility, forged into reality under his supervision, routinely adds much needed scientific discoveries in the fields of biology, genetics, and anthropology. His tireless efforts in the teaching area cannot be discounted either. Hundreds of students can attest to Dr. Olson's caring attitude in the classroom. His department has the fewest complaints from students and faculty alike, almost nil. What occurred years ago is best forgotten, in light of his continued service to our university. If Dr. Kesler, a brilliant scholar and distinguished leader in the field of paleoanthropology, could manage to deal with this situation and put it behind him, even look upon Dr. Olson with genuine fondness, can we do no less? I beseech the members of the board to not ruin a young man's career. Thank you."

Bless you, Dr. Pauling, Harry thought.

"Thank you, Dr. Pauling. Now, Dr. Olson," Forester said from the far end of the conference table, "you have the floor and our undivided attention."

With his head pounding and his stomach reeling, Harry stood and faced the trustees.

"I want to thank the board for the opportunity to address this issue," he began. "In no way do I wish to diminish the gravity or enormity of my actions. They were deplorable. There was no excuse. However, as a way of explanation, let me say they were the actions of a naive young man, motivated by what all young scientists are motivated by—tenure and acclaim. I looked upon Dr. Kesler, my professor and mentor, with jealous eyes, wanting what had taken him a lifetime to achieve. And I wanted it without putting in the years of work. In my misguided attempt to circumvent years of arduous work, I chose to falsify data in an article I published. For that, I stand guilty as charged.

"My actions hurt Dr. Kesler deeply. No one knows that better than I. But to his credit and my continued shame, he rallied to my aid and corrected the problem. Even though he never mentioned it, and we became extremely close, I knew how deeply I hurt him. And it wasn't until shortly before his death that we reconciled. Not only was the man my mentor, he was like the father I never had. I know how much I disappointed him. However, I do believe he moved beyond that, and I redeemed myself in his eyes. In fact, he told me so while we were together in Mongolia. In a tearful embrace, the man I had hurt forgave me. From that moment on, to Dr. Kesler it was as if my mistake had never happened.

"Having said this, I wish the trustees to know that

since that unfortunate incident, I have worked tirelessly to redeem myself and bring credit and honor to this university. I will accept the decision of this board, whatever it may be."

Harry sat in his chair, head still in a whirl.

"Thank you, Dr. Olson," Forester said. "And now you may excuse yourself to allow the board to deliberate in private."

∽⹁∽

Dixie caught up with Harry on his way to the faculty dining room. He looked as if he had lost his best friend. She took his arm as they entered the dining room.

"So, honey, how'd it go? You don't look well."

"Stressful," Harry said as they made their way through the lunch line. "I think they're going to hang me."

"That bad, huh?"

"Pauling gave an impassioned speech on my behalf. I'm grateful for that. We'll just have to wait and see."

"If it doesn't turn out in our favor, we can always go elsewhere. I am sure there are universities out there who would love to have you."

"*Our* favor? I'm the one being hung here."

Dixie squeezed his arm as they arrived at the serving line. "Remember," she said. "We're a team. We're in this together, whatever happens."

They sat at a table and ate their lunch in silence. Dixie's heart poured out for her husband who was clearly hurting, traumatized by the morning's events.

"I guess I can tell you now," she said finally. "A member of the trustees called me last week and asked me questions. He told me I was not to mention his call to you under pain of repercussions."

Harry looked up from his food. "Oh?" he said.

"He asked me what I knew of the journal article and Kesler's actions. If I had first hand information. I'm sorry I didn't say anything, but he told me I could be fired if I did."

Harry smiled at her. "It's fine, sweetheart. Don't worry about it."

"I told him I knew for a fact that the Professor had forgiven you and wished the matter forgotten. I pray it helped."

"I dunno, Dixie. Remember public opinion and donor money are at stake."

છ૭છ૭

Back in his office, Harry received word through his secretary that Dr. Radner desired a videoconference with him, Dr. Siscom, and Dr. Harbaum. An update on Millie's IVF project.

Harry didn't feel much like discussing a science project. His head was still pounding. He grabbed some aspirin and swallowed them with a gulp of water. Then he sat and massaged his temples, hoping to will away the throbbing pain.

When everyone was online, he sauntered into the adjoining room where the three smiling faces were on the screen.

"Good afternoon, all," he said. "You're a motley looking threesome. A pretty scraggly looking group, I must say."

Everyone laughed at Harry's humor. He slouched in a chair and tried to give his faculty members his undivided attention.

"Dr. Olson," Radner began, "Gerald and Millie wanted to give you an update on the IVF project underway here. I'll let Dr. Siscom go first."

Harry settled in his chair and tried to relax. He was finally back in his element. The aspirin was beginning to work.

"Yes, Dr. Olson," Siscom said, "we are well underway. The chimp, Tika, as Millie has opted to call her, is now five months along in her pregnancy. All is fine. She is beginning to act like a pregnant chimp. At this point, the ultrasounds show no problems with the fetus. Which happens to be a male, I might add."

"Good to hear, Gerald," Harry said. "How about you, Millie? Pleased with the project to date?"

"I am, Dr. Olson. The waiting has been rather nerve-racking, but, so far, we are scheduled for a delivery in a few months."

"Millie, you're on the faculty now, so please call me Harry."

"I'll try," was Millie's reply.

"Miles," Harry said, "do you have everything you need up there? For this delivery and subsequent care of the infant Yeti?"

"I believe so, Harry. Gerald gave me a list a month ago. We have most of the items here, and the rest are due to be delivered shortly."

"Fine," Harry said. "Keep me posted. I'll try and come up there after the delivery for a firsthand look."

After signing off, Harry sat and contemplated the meaning of Millie's project.

He would never have thought of it and felt proud that a former graduate student of his was on the forefront of this marvelous project.

After the Yeti's birth, maybe the facility could get back on track with their investigation into its place in the evolution family tree.

Millie and Siscom would certainly deserve a raise.

ოოო

So it's a male, Millie thought. *Now for a name.*

"Roku," she said aloud. "I'll call you Roku."

She was alone in her office at the far end of the Animal Care Unit. All the technicians and Siscom had gone home for the day, leaving her with her thoughts. The air conditioning had ramped up, starting its cycle to lower the temperature in the unit. As the temperature began to fall, Millie donned her fleece jacket she kept for such times when she worked late. Down the hall, the chimps were quieting down for the evening. The unit was dark except for her small office.

Tika's pregnancy forced Millie to contemplate if or when she would divulge the injection of her DNA into the growing fetus. The sooner, the better, she knew. But with each sunrise, she postponed the inevitable discussion one day further. If she waited until Roku was born to tell Radner and Dr. Olson, she knew she would find herself in deep trouble. But coming clean now might mean the end of her project. Dr. Olson might order the pregnancy's termination. After birth, he still might order the newborn creature destroyed, but it was a gamble worth taking.

What was the creature exactly? She knew it was to be a chimera, a creature with its DNA supplied by two different species. Simple enough. Technically speaking, a hybrid contained genetic information from two individuals of the same species. A chimera was different. But what would it be like? Look like? Would it spend its infancy like other primates? Millie allowed her mind to wander over the possibilities for a few moments before deciding she would just wait and see. She couldn't control her excitement and anticipation.

And what about Gerald? What would he have to say? Things were taking a turn for the romantic, and she didn't want to screw it up. No, she thought, the risks of saying anything before Roku was born were too great. She would wait until she had no other alternative. And when she let Gerald in on her secret, she hoped he would understand.

She hoped everyone would understand.

She logged into the facility network and then found her file on the Tika Project. She typed a current note.

1750 ~ Just found out that Tika's fetus is a male. I have named him Roku. He is a chimera, part Yeti DNA, part human. I don't know where this will lead and I am somewhat fearful that it will not end well for the little fella. What have I created? What does the future hold for Roku and me? Only time will tell.

Millie turned off her computer and headed to the dining hall, where she was to have dinner with Gerald. After dinner, they would stroll around the facility grounds and look at the stars, talk. It had become their favorite pastime. Last evening, he had even ventured to kiss her, a fumbling gesture at first, but when she kissed him back, he regained his composure, and his repeat attempt was entirely satisfactory.

Then, during Roku's sixth month of gestation, a disturbing crisis developed.

Chapter 10

I need to show you something, Millie," Siscom said as they walked toward the Animal Care Unit.

They had finished eating breakfast together, a time normally filled with smiles after a night apart, but this morning he was not his usual self. He hadn't spoken more than a few sentences, and he knew Millie was wondering what was the matter with him.

When they entered the unit, they strolled past Tika's cage. Siscom watched Millie pause, take notice of her large abdomen. Delivery was imminent, he knew. Tika ambled to the front of her cage and rattled the bars in obvious recognition of her and the veterinarian.

"Yes, good morning, Tika," Millie called over the animals' hooting. "You're going to be a mother pretty soon."

In Siscom's office, they sat while he retrieved a folder and set it in the table in front of him.

"What did you want to show me, Gerald?" Millie said. "You've been awful quiet this morning."

"Look at this," he said, handing her a photo. "It's the latest ultrasound on Roku. Look at it closely. I didn't notice it before this but tell me what you see."

Millie studied the photo for a few minutes. Siscom

watched her until he was satisfied she understood his concern. He watched as a look he could only describe as panic, possibly dismay, formed on her face.

"Now," he said, "I want to know why. But first I want to know exactly what it is."

"Gerald—"

"I'm not kidding, Millie. What is this and how did it happen? This is ludicrous."

"Gerald—"

"Stop with the Gerald. Start with some explanations."

She passed the photo back to Siscom. He noticed her eyes filling with tears. His heart skipped a beat, for he suddenly knew she was stressed beyond measure.

"This is not the ultrasound of a normal Yeti," he continued. "So what the hell is this?"

"Gerald—I—I—Oh God, how can I tell you? I know I should have been honest with you from the start."

"What do you mean by that?" he said, his voice beginning to show anger. "Millie, I have to know the truth. What is going on here?"

Millie lowered her head and stared at her hands that were folded in her lap. "I—I injected my own DNA into Sasha's ovum before the IVF procedure. Before fertilization."

"You *what*?" he said, now with an incredulous tone in his voice. "You did *what*?"

"I extracted my own DNA from a blood sample then injected it into the fertilized ovum of Sasha. The one I earlier fertilized with Bentu's sperm."

Siscom couldn't believe what he heard. He stared at Millie for a long moment.

"Millie, tell me you didn't really do this," he said.

"But I did. I truly did." Her voice nearly cracked, and he could see she was on the verge of tears.

"So Roku is a…a…"

"A chimera, Gerald. A chimera."

"A what?"

Millie wiped her eyes and smiled.

"An organism that has the DNA of two different species in its genome."

"My God," Siscom said. "Millie, you can't do this. You can't be serious."

"Why not? It's my own DNA. What law have I violated?"

"Christ! You simply can't do this," Siscom repeated. "It doesn't look like a Yeti on the ultrasound, and it certainly doesn't look human. It is the worst looking primate fetus I have ever seen. Like something out of a horror movie. We're going to have to destroy it before Radner or Olson finds out what we've done. The sooner, the better."

"No!" Millie said. "Gerald, you can't. This can be history, don't you see? Listen to me."

"We have no choice."

"Listen," Millie said, "we now have mice with human brain cells and pigs with human blood flowing in their veins. Chimeras are no longer something of science fiction. They certainly can be useful to medical science. This Yeti-human chimera offers us an unparalleled opportunity to push the frontiers of science light-years ahead. Roku will become famous as he leads us forward."

Siscom was so flustered he was having difficulty organizing his thoughts and speaking. He was stunned, blindsided by Millie's deceitfulness. And he was a party to it. Struggling to overcome his shock, he continued his questions.

"What do you plan to do with him, Millie?"

"Study him, of course."

"How? Where? In what way?"

"I haven't made up my mind just yet. Roku will be an

infant and will need to grow some at first. I thought, for starters, I would chart his growth statistics and measurements. Everything about his infancy care will be ground breaking."

Siscom shook his head.

"I dunno, Millie. I dunno. The best thing to do is abort Tika. Before this creates a firestorm neither of us can weather."

"I won't allow it, Gerald. I simply won't. This is my project, not yours."

"But, Millie—"

"I have had the same reservations you seem to be having," Millie said. "To understand the fear and anger evoked by chimeras, it is useful to go back in scientific history to March 1984, when an animal unlike any other ever born, or seen, adorned the cover of *Nature*, our international journal of science. The journal's audience of scientists was treated to an unforgettable photograph of an animal with a head that was mostly goat, an upper torso that was wooly sheep, with other body parts that alternated between the two species types. Its creator, a Danish embryologist, said it behaved like a goat but did not quite smell like one. It preferred the company of sheep. This first 'geep,' as the animal became christened, was physically healthy, long-lived, and even fertile. The Danish team created additional geeps over the next several years."

"But, Millie, those were all animals. Primates. No human DNA was involved."

Millie continued as if she had not heard him. "The geep is an alluring example of a laboratory-created chimera, named by scientists in honor of the creature from Greek mythology with the head of a lion, the torso of a goat, and a tail sprouting the head of a venomous snake. Like other mythological species composites, the chimera was imagined as a monster because it violated a perceived natural order in which each species is divinely created as a separate and unique category. Indeed, a chimera's potential violation of nature was so profound that rational thinkers have always assumed it couldn't possibly exist, and the word chimera has become a metaphor for a wishful idea without any basis in reality."

"Millie, I really don't want—"

She held up a hand.

"Please, Gerald," she said. "Let me finish. The Danish scientist, unlike most scientists, was unwilling to accept the natural limitations imposed by traditional beliefs. 'The role of the biological scientist,' he said, 'is to break the laws of nature, rather than to establish, let alone accept, them.' With this spark of irreverence, the man created not only geeps but also other species composites, including a cow-sheep creature that he cooked and ate after completing his analysis. The same refusal to accept conventional wisdom provided him with the confidence to bypass fertilization in the invention of the cloning technology used to create Dolly and thousands of other subsequently cloned animals. Building upon his pioneering work, other scientists combined even more distant species, creating chicken-turtle and chicken-mouse fetuses, for example. In all of these instances, chimeras were used as models to study basic biological processes."

Siscom thought for a minute. He sat staring at the ultrasound photograph. He felt himself wavering under Millie's persuasive arguments. "I must admit I am curious to see what your experiment will produce. However, I still believe we need to tell Radner and Dr. Olson the truth. Harry was wanting to come and see for himself the results, and it wouldn't be right to have him find out only after he arrived."

"I suppose not," Millie said. "But it's a risk I don't think we should take."

"She's going to deliver any day now. In fact, this fetus will be too large for a normal birth. Tika will require a Cesarean." Siscom knew he sounded insistent.

"I know, I know."

He could see the tears in Millie's eyes. Her face was flushed. She sat wringing her hands.

"Okay," he said. "We'll do it your way, for now. Maybe after Roku is here, Harry will be elated, who knows?"

"Gerald, do you know anything about Dr. Olson and this investigation of his?"

"Only what the rumor mill churns out. The paper hasn't had any news lately, so I don't really know anything. Do you?"

"No, nothing. It seems such a shame that he has to endure such a thing. He has been so good to me."

"To all of us," Siscom agreed.

"I wish there was something we could do that would sway those trustees in his favor."

"I doubt if there is."

⁊ↄ⁊ↄ

A few days later, Tika went into labor. Siscom moved her to a different area after selecting two trusted technicians to assist him. The area was off limits to the rest of the facility personnel. Standing by was a Vega 200 neonatal intensive care incubator that had been modified for primate use. It contained a double wall canopy, to reduce heat loss; unique side doors, opening from both sides; built-in weighing scale; servo humidity and servo oxygen controls; a color touch screen with trend display for temperature, humidity, and oxygen saturation; and motorized bed tilting and rotation.

Tika's labor was difficult as Roku was much larger than the average chimp fetus. After several hours of the chimp not making much progress, Siscom decided to intervene.

"The last ultrasound showed Roku weighing approximately twelve pounds so I doubt if Tika can give birth naturally. I'm going to attempt an extraction," he said. "We need to get her in the squeeze cage."

"I thought you were going to do a Caesarean," Millie said.

"This is a last ditch effort to avoid an operation," Siscom said in a worried tone. "If I can't get Roku out this way, I'll have to operate, but I'd rather not if I can help it."

Millie must have looked at the veterinarian oddly for the man said, "We're not a hospital here, Millie."

She watched as Siscom directed the technicians to roll the cage into the exam room and lift Tika into it. The chimp appeared to be in obvious pain for her eyes darted between Millie, Siscom, and the technicians.

Once they had Tika loaded in the squeeze cage and immobilized, Siscom inserted a catheter into a neck vein connected to a bag of saline. He turned it on, and it began running into Tika. "We don't have forceps like in humans," he said, donning a gown and gloves. "We use the old fashion method—our hands."

Siscom spent the good part of an hour trying to get his hands around Roku's arm and pull him further down the birth canal. But the fetus wouldn't budge. Siscom tried every trick in the book, but it was to no avail. Sweat poured off his face and through his gown. Amniotic fluid and blood soaked the cage.

Finally, he backed away.

"It's no use," he said. "We'll need to do a Caesarean."

Siscom used a stethoscope and listened to Roku's heartbeat.

"Are they all right, Gerald?" Millie said.

"Fine. We just need to get Roku out pretty quick."

He barked a few orders to the technicians who began preparing Tika for the surgery. Drapes, instruments, and sponges were laid out on a table while Siscom injected Tika with an anesthetic. Her eyes closed, and she began slow, deep breathing. While the technicians prepared for the operation, Siscom changed his gown and gloves. Millie was at his side. One of the technicians scrubbed the chimp's abdomen with antiseptic solution then arranged the surgical drapes over the operative field.

"Tika won't die because of this, will she?" she said.

"Not if I can help it," Siscom replied.

"I'm afraid this is going to be a long evening and night."

"I suspect so. Well, here we go."

It had been a few years since Siscom had performed a Caesarean operation and never on a chimp. But the anatomy wasn't complicated. As he worked, the technicians stood by the incubator waiting for the delivery. Millie turned away.

"I can't stand to watch," she said. "Tell me when you've delivered Roku."

Siscom labored through the abdominal wall and found the uterus, making a low transverse incision in it. The wound suddenly filled with amniotic fluid, and Roku slithered out.

Siscom was stunned. He had never seen anything like Roku. The ultrasound had not prepared him for the grotesque little creature. He quickly gathered the infant up in a towel and carried it to the incubator.

One of the technicians hissed. The other gasped.

Millie rushed to the side of the incubator.

"Oh my God!" she said. "I never dreamed."

Chapter 11

Harry was in his office working on administrative chores when his secretary announced that Dr. Pauling was in the outer office wanting to speak with him. His heart lurched into his throat.

"Show him in," he said, pushing a pile of papers to one side.

Pauling strode in and took the chair Harry indicated.

"Coffee?" Harry said. "Or water?"

"Nothing, Harry. Thanks. This isn't a social call I'm afraid."

"Yes?" Harry leaned forward in his chair, elbows on his desk.

"The news isn't good. The board of trustees has voted unanimously to issue you a formal letter of reprimand. I'm sorry. I did what I could on your behalf."

"I know you did, and I certainly appreciate it. Not one dissenting vote?"

"Not one, unfortunately."

"So, my friend, what's next?"

Pauling shifted in his chair and toyed with his tie.

"I am to prepare the letter, outlining your infractions, and you are to sign it. It will be placed in your personnel file."

"I suppose I have Bernard Wickingham to thank for this," Harry said. He thought he could detect a slight tremble in his voice.

"Who else?" Pauling said. "But really, Harry, this shouldn't change much. You are still a valued member of our university and, as such, I don't want you to take this too hard. You'll continue doing your work as you always have."

"With one huge difference—I've been wounded. Like a bird with a broken wing. I won't be able to fly very well. My reputation—"

"Hogwash," Pauling said. "People who know you won't change their opinion because of this. I don't want this to get you down."

"I can thank that creep Wickingham for this," Harry said, slumping deep in his chair.

"Don't know anything for sure, but it stands to reason. Who else would have the information to give to the paper?"

"Dixie thought he was a creep for sure," Harry said. "He kept staring at her breasts."

"He's one I'll live to regret."

"I may resign. It would save you a lot of grief."

"You do that, Harry, and I'll never speak to you again. Our friendship would be over."

"Dixie thinks I should quit."

Pauling looked at him through narrowed eyes. Harry could see the tense jaw muscles twitching. "You tell that wife of yours to lay off. The rest of the faculty and myself are pleased you are a part of the university. We are behind you one hundred percent. And you know that goes for Dixie as well."

Harry shot Pauling a weak smile.

"I appreciate that, Dr. Pauling. It means a lot. Thank you for the kind words at the meeting with the trustees."

Pauling stood and adjusted his tie. "Just don't let this get you down. It's a small penalty, like in a football game. Keep up the good work."

After Pauling left, Harry sat for a while. The revelation made it difficult getting back to work. However, he didn't feel as bad as he anticipated he might. The reprimand didn't carry that much weight with Pauling, so maybe he should just let it rest. Not make any hasty decisions.

But he knew his wife, and she was going to be madder than hell.

There was a knock on his door, and Dixie breezed in. *What great timing the woman possesses.*

"I saw Pauling leave your office," she said. She plopped in a chair and sighed. "What's the news?"

"What I expected. The board voted unanimously to give me a reprimand. Pauling will deliver the letter for me to sign in the next few days."

"Unanimous?"

"That's what the man said. Not a single dissenting vote."

"What are you going to do?" she said.

"I dunno. Wait, I guess."

"I vote we leave. Teach these weasels a lesson. That they can't treat a seasoned professor like this."

"Tsk, tsk, honey. I know exactly how you feel. And I appreciate you coming to my defense, I really do. We can always leave after the current term, if that is what we want to do. Let's think about it before we decide."

"They're all a bunch of morons," Dixie said.

"Pauling isn't to blame. As I listened to his passionate speech in my favor at the board meeting, I realized how much I admire the man. He went out on a limb for me. That's something I won't soon forget."

"Well, okay he's not a moron," Dixie said, the corners

of her mouth curving upward in a slight smile. "But he's the only one."

"Leaving in the middle of a term is never a good idea," Harry said. "It leaves the university in a lurch, and someone has to cover the faculty member's classes. Word of that gets around, and you're really a pariah. If we want, we can spend the time looking around at possibilities and, later, when we have cooled down a bit, make a reasoned decision."

"If I had my way, honey, I'd give the entire board a piece of my mind."

Harry had to chuckle. "It's why I love you, Dixie."

༺༻

Millie kept herself busy taking care of Roku with Siscom's assistance. Each morning, she would weigh and measure the infant, marveling how, at only two months of age, he was growing so rapidly. She became accustomed to his grotesque appearance and, in addition to entries into her notes, she photographed Roku and stored the pictures on her computer.

Roku was unlike what she envisioned an infant Yeti should look like. But, in fact, he wasn't a complete Yeti, only part. For one thing, he was completely hairless without a speck of fur anywhere on its brown body. For another, Roku had a small head and brown eyes unusually large for his head that sported a prominent frontal ridge and oversized ears.

At first, Millie thought Roku a revolting-looking creature, and it took weeks before she was comfortable looking at him. She kept him in diapers made for human infants.

In most ways Roku seemed almost human, he cried when he was hungry or needed his diaper changed, took a bottle of specially prepared formula four times each day, a milk formula concocted by Siscom.

During the first two months of his life, Roku had doubled his birth weight and was no longer confined to the incubator but was allowed in the large cage with Tika. The chimp seemed to care for Roku as her own, a fact that pleased Millie.

As Millie finished entering Roku's data into her computer, Siscom strode into the Animal Care Unit and into her work cubicle. She noticed he wasn't wearing his usual smile. He appeared to plod into the area.

"Good morning, Gerald," she said. "Nice morning."

Siscom nodded.

"I suppose," he said. "We need to talk."

"Sure. Go ahead. About what?"

"Have you finished doing the DNA testing on your friend there? Roku? You said you planned to sequence its genome as soon as it was born."

"Most of it, yes. Why?"

"And the results?"

Millie thought she detected a hint of impatience in his voice.

"Most of what I have recovered and analyzed turns out to identical to nucleotide sequences found in my own DNA and Sasha's. Just what I would expect to find. And hoped would happen."

"So Roku has your DNA?"

"So far, yes."

"Well—"

"What do you think of him, Gerald," Millie said, turning off her computer. "Isn't he beautiful?"

"Are you kidding? How can you say that, Millie? The thing is hideous to look at."

"Don't say that, please. He responds to the tone of your voice and your body language. Listen, Roku is carrying my genes. Understand? Roku is part me. He is part human."

"And what is the other part, Millie? Answer me that. The hideous part. What is that?"

Siscom's voice was rising in amplitude with a hint of sarcasm.

"Yeti, of course. Roku is half me and half Yeti. It's a good thing we still have kept this mostly a secret from Radner and Dr. Olson. You've been a big help keeping them outa here."

"I haven't been happy, Millie, telling Radner we need-ed to keep this project under wraps for the time being. But he's getting anxious to come and have a look for himself."

"No!" Millie said. "Not yet. I'm not ready."

"Actually, that is what I came to tell you. It's too late. Dr. Olson will be here this afternoon, and he and Radner will expect a full briefing and will want to have a look at Roku. I just came to warn you and give you a few hours to prepare."

"Oh no. It's way too early, Gerald. You have to stall them. Keep them out of here."

"Too late. They will be here at two o'clock.

All of a sudden, Millie was near panic. She couldn't believe what Siscom told her. It was too early for them to know the truth.

She had intended to prepare a defense of her actions, to plead her case, but this news caught her unprepared. It was premature for Radner and Dr. Olson to discover the truth this afternoon.

"You have to help me," she pleaded. "Tell them any-thing, just don't let them see Roku. Not yet."

"I can't do anything," he said. "I'm sorry."

૯൲ல

And at two o'clock, Radner, along with Harry and Dixie, strolled into where Millie was sitting in the Animal Care Unit. With them was Siscom. The veterinarian bore a somber expression on his face.

"Good afternoon, Dr. Harbaum," Radner said, smiling. "I've brought two guests with me today. I believe you know the Drs. Olson, Harry and Dixie? You were together, I believe, on the search for the escaped Yeti."

Harry stepped forward and extended his hand.

"Of course. And we chatted over a video conference call a few months ago. How are you Millie?" he said.

"Just fine, Dr. Olson." Millie couldn't bear to look her chairman in the eye.

"Millie," Dixie said, "we've come to see and observe first hand your Yeti IVF project. We understand we have a small Yeti now."

Millie shot a glance toward Siscom who shrugged his shoulders.

"Well—" Millie stammered. "It's not exactly as I originally described."

"Sure, I understand," Harry said. "Things rarely go as planned. Things always are subject to change in the middle of a project. Let's—"

"Let's see the little fella," Dixie interjected. "I understand he's a male."

"That he is," Millie said.

"Well?" Radner said.

The bottom fell out of Millie's stomach, and her head felt dizzy. *I'm not sure I can go through with this*, she thought.

"This way," she said, after noting that each and every eye was on her. Waiting.

She led them to the small examination room where Roku was sitting in a far corner, his back to the front of the cage. At the sound of their approach, he turned and half ambled-half crawled toward them. When he reached the front of the cage, Dixie let out a gasp. Harry, without uttering a sound, approached Roku and stared at the creature for a moment then turned to Millie.

"Millie," he said. "What is this? Is this Roku?"

Millie nodded, tears forming in her eyes.

Radner stepped to the cage and shook his head.

"What happened? Some sort of a mutation?"

Millie shook her head, the tears now running down her cheeks.

"Then what?" Dixie said. "Something went wrong, didn't it?"

"No, Dixie, nothing went wrong," Millie said. She wiped her eyes with the sleeve of her lab coat.

Siscom stepped forward.

"I think we need to adjourn to my office where we can talk," he said and led the group down the hallway through the airlock to his office. Their footsteps clicked on the tiled floor. Once there, they all took chairs except for Millie who continued to stand.

"Millie," Siscom said, softly, "I think it's time to come clean. Take your lumps now."

"Come clean?" Radner said, his voice taking a dark tone. "What's this all about?"

"I'll explain," Millie said, wringing her hands and voice trembling. "When I remembered we had stored frozen sperm and ovum from our adult Yeti, Bentu and Sasha, the idea formed that we could birth another Yeti right here through the process of IVF. I approached Dr. Siscom for his assistance, and he assured me we had the equipment and the technology to accomplish the feat. It would be wonderful, I thought, to be able to replace the Yeti we lost with one or however many we chose."

Millie glanced furtively about the room. She had the group's undivided attention.

"That's what I originally intended to do. But along the way, I had another idea. Why not inject my own DNA into Sasha's ovum prior to fertilization? And create a human-Yeti mixture, a chimera. So, unbeknownst to Dr. Siscom, I extracted a sample of my DNA and, late one night, injected it as I just described. The resulting embryo was kept in the incubator for several days until we implanted it into Tika, the female chimp. When Dr. Siscom did the IVF procedure, he was unaware that the fertilized ovum he used contained my genome, my complete genome. The subsequent fertilization was successful, and the pregnancy was carried to near term when Dr. Siscom delivered Roku by Caesarean section, due to the fact that Roku was too large to be delivered normally. He only became aware of what I had done after Roku's birth, and, since that time I have refused to destroy him. So this is where we are at present."

There were several minutes of silence as everyone contemplated Millie's words. Finally, Radner spoke.

"Damn you, Dr. Harbaum," he said, venom in his voice. "How could you do this thing?"

Millie said nothing, just stood, wishing she were dead.

"Let me get this straight," Dixie finally said. "Roku is a chimera. Half his genes and DNA are of a Yeti and the other half are from you. Correct?"

"Yes," Millie said.

"So is it an animal or a human?" Harry said.

"Neither and both," Siscom said.

Radner let out a long sigh and coughed. "Well, it has to be destroyed," he said.

"Please, no," Millie said. "We can study it, learn from it."

Radner shook his head. "This crossed that ethical and moral line that should never be crossed. Animal hybrids are bad enough. But human chimeras? No. Never."

Millie began weeping. She noticed Harry shaking his head.

"I'm afraid I have to agree with Dr. Radner," he said. "You and Gerald will have to destroy it. And quickly. The sooner, the better."

Chapter 12

Harry and Dixie returned to Radner's office where they continued an animated discussion of Roku and Millie's sudden disclosure. They had Dr. Pauling on the videoconferencing monitor. Radner was still disturbed by her keeping everyone in the dark until after Roku's birth.

"What should we do with her?" he said, as they settled into the leather chairs. "I can't believe this."

"Her?" Harry said. "I'd say our immediate problem is what to do with Roku."

Radner retrieved small bottles of water from a fridge and handed them to Harry and Dixie then returned to his desk chair.

"We decided that back in the animal unit," Dixie said. "He's to be destroyed."

"Then Miles is right," Harry said. "What about Millie?"

"Termination," Radner said. "It's the only appropriate course of action."

"Her career will be over," Dixie said. "Ruined."

"She chose this path, Dixie," Radner said. "This course of action. No one forced her to do this."

Harry and Dixie both nodded in agreement.

"I have to agree," Dixie added. "But let me add this to the discussion. Something for everyone to consider. Isn't destroying Roku tantamount to murder? After all, it has human genes, Millie's DNA, as its foundation."

"Jessums, honey," Harry said in an exasperated tone, holding his hand in the air, "the thing doesn't look human. It's a freak. How can you suggest it's human?"

"Because it has human DNA," Dixie continued. "Do you have to look human to be human?"

Radner took a gulp of water before speaking. "How much human DNA makes one human? A hundred percent? Seventy percent? Fifty percent? Who decides? I just know the thing needs to be destroyed, the sooner, the better," he repeated.

Harry shook his head in disbelief.

"Millie crossed a line no scientist has been willing to cross for decades," he said. "But listen to me, this changes everything. A reputed humanzee, or human/chimp hybrid, called Oliver was DNA tested and found to be a chimpanzee, albeit one which slightly differed genetically from the more familiar chimps in being bipedal and having a smaller head. Oliver may have been a mutant or represent an unknown species of ape. It is currently believed that he represents a geographical subspecies of chimpanzee. He did not associate with other chimps in captivity and was sexually attracted to human women instead.

"This meant he was never bred. Oliver's habitual bipedal gait is now believed to be a result of early training and habit, although he mastered it to a greater degree than most trained chimps. It's worth remembering that evolution is a never-ending process and that it's possible for bipedalism to develop in other apes. In a publicity event, a woman declared her willingness to be inseminated by Oliver and even to have the mating filmed for scientific purposes, but this offended public sensibilities and did not happen. Had Oliver been a genuine hybrid, then like most male hybrids, he would probably have been sterile anyway."

"Thanks for the information, Harry," Radner said, "but I hardly see how that applies to our present situation.

Harry sighed. "Soviet dictator Joseph Stalin wanted to rebuild the Red Army, in the mid-1920s, with *Planet-of-the-Apes*-style troops by crossing humans with apes. Stalin is said to have told Ivanov, his scientist, that he wanted a new invincible human being, insensitive to pain, resilient, and indifferent about the quality of food they eat. Their only legitimate source for the claim comes from a 2002 paper in the academic journal *Science in Context*, by the Russian historian of science, Kirill Rossiianov. Rossiianov's study follows the ill-fated attempt by the Russian physiologist Il'ya Ivanov to crossbreed humans with anthropoid apes. His research offers an important warning about the ethical abuses that can occur when proper standards are not enforced, but Rossiianov's paper clearly demonstrates that creating super-warriors had no part in Ivanov's work. The alleged quote from Stalin is not found in the paper, and there is no evidence that Stalin ever made such a statement."

"I don't see the point," Radner said, obviously exasperated. "We all know Millie crossed a line and breached a moral no-no. As I see it the solution for the creature is simple. The question is what should we do with her?"

Pauling, who had remained quiet during the discussion, finally spoke. Harry could tell the man was visibly disturbed.

"Folks," he said. "I can't say enough how bad this is. It's bad. The trustees will never tolerate Millie remaining on the faculty once they learn of this. And I cannot keep this from them. They have to be informed. She's in your department, Harry. You'll have to tell her."

"Tell her to destroy Roku and that she's fired all in one day," Harry said. "What a great job I have."

'I'll go with you," Dixie said. "I have a certain rapport with her."

But when they returned to the Animal Care Unit, Millie wasn't there. They found Siscom in the small lab, working.

"How'd it go with Dr. Pauling?" he said after they entered the lab.

Harry ignored the question. "Where's Millie, Gerald? Have you seen her?" he demanded, his tone terse, his spine stiff.

"Not since you all left here earlier. She may have gone to say goodbye to Roku. She had become very close to that creature. I was going to euthanize it later this afternoon. Funny thing though, I feel I'd be killing Millie in the process. It carries her genome."

"Millie's been terminated, Gerald. As of now. I need to tell her. You have no idea where she is?"

"Like I said she might be at Tika's cage saying goodbye to Roku. Let's go see. I'd like to be with her when you tell her."

"Fine," Harry said, and the trio walked to the cage area.

Millie wasn't there.

Neither was Roku.

"Okay, Gerald," Harry said, irritation rising in his voice. "Where is she? She's gone and taken the chimera with her."

"I have no idea, Harry, honest."

Harry strode through the Animal Care Unit, searching the area. "Gerald," he continued, "it won't look good on your record if I learn you have abetted her in this travesty and in taking Roku."

They stopped at the airlock.

"Harry, I swear I knew nothing of Millie's plan until shortly before delivery, and, by then, it was too late. She never took me into her confidence prior to that. You've got to believe me."

"We do," Dixie said. "Harry's just upset. This is a lot to fathom in one afternoon."

"And deal with," Harry added.

Satisfied that neither Millie nor Roku were in the Animal Care Unit, Harry and Dixie returned to Radner's office. Siscom followed. After learning that Millie could not be found, Radner exploded. Harry had never seen the man in such a rage.

"I'll find her," he said in a loud voice. "She hasn't had time to leave the facility grounds." He picked up the phone and dialed a number.

"Bruce," he said into the phone, nearly shouting, "I want you to search the facility for Dr. Harbaum. When you find her, bring her to my office. Get all available security personnel on this...What?...Just find her. She may have a little creature with her. If she does, take it to the animal unit. Now get on it."

He hung up the phone, stared at Harry.

"Bruce Drayton and his men will find her. She couldn't have gone far."

"Yes," Dixie said. "I remember Bruce, your security chief. Good man."

"Since the Yeti's escape," Radner said, "Bruce has really beefed up security here. Millie can't go far."

Harry nodded. "He was a go-to guy on that search, for sure."

"I need to go to the security office and check on this, Harry," Radner said. "I'm sorry for blowing up like that. This is unbelievable, simply unbelievable. Why don't you and Dixie relax in the conference room here? I think you'll be more comfortable. I'll have some coffee and sandwiches brought in."

"Oh, that would be great, Miles," Dixie said. "I'm starved. We haven't eaten since breakfast."

"Good. I'll stop by the kitchen on my way out. Make yourselves at home."

After Radner exited, leaving Harry, Dixie, and Siscom sitting in the overstuffed chairs in the conference room, Harry smiled at his wife.

"Just another day in paradise, sweetheart," he said. "The hits keep coming."

"Stop it, Harry," she said. "These things come with the territory, that's all. Departmental chairmen deal with these sorts of things all the time."

"Chimeras? Human-animal hybrid creations by their staff? I doubt it."

"Nowadays, it is possible for a couple of university students to concoct new life forms in the comfort of their own basement. Regrettably so, our laws have not been able to keep up with the pace that scientists have made with their creations."

"Society has always lagged behind," Siscom said.

"In turn, the entities being created are not at all illegal but certainly could pose a risk to society, by and large," Dixie continued. "There is no telling what may happen if these life forms are allowed to mate, if they can. Still, eagerness can be seen in the eyes and minds of scientists on a global level just waiting to unleash their next creation to the world. That all seemed liked fantasy just a short time ago."

"Yes," Harry said. "It can create a huge problem. Look at Roku."

"To give a concrete example, scientists have made mice with an artificial human chromosome in every cell of their bodies. Such an act is being praised as a breakthrough that may lead to different cures for a wide scope of diseases. Researchers have had much success by transferring cells from human embryos into the brains of mice. These very cells began to grow, and, in time, made the mice more intelligent. The mice showed that they were able to solve a simple maze and learn conditioning signals at a more enhanced level than if compared to before their transformation. I've read that critics are quick to question whether a practice of injecting parts of humans in animals carries more benefits than risks."

"Yes," Siscom said. "Even now, it is apparent that growing human organs inside of animals is not science fiction, but pure reality. Japanese scientists have started using pigs to grow human organs inside of them. The entire growth process takes up to twelve months to complete."

Dixie shot him a somber, frustrated look. "What should be the guideline for this type of research? I don't think anyone has figured it out."

Harry shook his head.

"As you said, the science is way ahead of the theologians and philosophers. They better catch up and fast before we have a nightmare on our hands."

ↄ෨ↄ෨

Dr. Bernard Wickingham sat in the opulent office of the president of the University of California, Merced. He had no idea why he had been called to this meeting.

He thought his Biology 101 class was going well. As far as he knew, there were no complaints.

He sat across an antique polished teak desk with ivory-looking inlays around its edges, obviously a high dollar item. Pictures and sculpture decorated the office.

John Ingersoll, university president, strode boldly into

his office and nodded at Wickingham. He was a tall man with rugged features, in his fifties, tanned, and thick glasses perched on a hawk-like nose. He sat at his desk and opened a folder in front of him. Wickingham's heart started to pound.

"I'll make this short, Dr. Wickingham. I have a letter here from the president of your former employer, Cal Pacific University."

"Yes?" Wickingham's heart fluttered, skipped a beat.

"In this letter, he outlines the reasons for your termination from Cal Pacific, something you failed to mention in your application here." He pointed to a paper on his desk. "You never mentioned you were terminated. I know Reginald Pauling, so I thought I would give him a call since we seemed to know nothing about you. You just dropped into our laps one day, so to speak. Anyway, what I learned came as a great surprise, and Dr. Pauling outlines the facts here in his letter. It seems you were terminated for trying to extort lab and office space from your departmental chairman by threatening to divulge certain embarrassing facts about the man. What these facts were are not outlined here and not pertinent to this discussion. But the overall charge is apparently supported by a witness."

"Doctor, I—"

Ingersoll held up a hand.

"It belies common sense that you figured no one would ever discover these sordid events, but they have finally caught up with you."

"Doctor, please—"

"You will not speak further," Ingersoll said. "You are here to listen.

Wickingham slumped farther into his chair, eyes toward the floor.

"In view of these facts, Dr. Wickingham," Ingersoll

said, "and in view if the fact that you were not forthcoming on your application or during your interview, I have no choice but to terminate your employment with UC-Merced. I'm sorry. But a man in your position needs to realize that honesty is, after all, the best policy. I will not entertain questions or comments at this time. Your final paycheck will be mailed to you. Good day, sir."

Ingersoll stood and strolled out of the room, leaving Wickingham's brain reeling and his stomach churning.

Chapter 13

Later that afternoon, Radner, along with Bruce Drayton, found Harry and Dixie sipping their coffee in his conference room. Harry jumped up as they entered the room.

"Well," Radner said, "neither Millie nor the creature is on the facility grounds."

"We've made a thorough search," Drayton said. "She's not here." He took a seat in one of the empty chairs.

"You search her room?" Harry said.

"Not there," Drayton said. "And it looks like she took her clothes with her."

"Plus, her car is missing," Radner said. "Apparently, she's driven off the mountain and taken that *thing* with her, Harry."

Radner had stopped calling the chimera by the name Millie gave it, choosing, instead, to call it *the thing* or *the creature*.

"She couldn't have traveled far," Dixie said. "She hasn't been gone that long."

"Long enough," Drayton said. "Dr. Radner, I suggest we notify the authorities right away."

"Of course, Bruce. Why don't you do that now? You can use the phone in my office."

Drayton left, and Radner continued.

"Harry, we've got to find her before the authorities do. We need to destroy that creature before word of any of this leaks to the press. Any ideas where she could have gone?"

"As far as I know she doesn't have many friends outside the facility here," he said. "Dixie?"

"She didn't confide in me."

"So what if the authorities find Roku?" Dixie said. "They'll just kill him."

"I believe her parents are living back East," Harry said. "I'll see if my secretary can round up a number. If she can, I'll call them."

"Yes," Dixie said. "She might try and contact them."

"Use the phone when Bruce is through," Radner said.

After Harry left Dixie chatted with Radner. Her face was contorted into a deeply furrowed frown.

"Miles, the board of trustees voted to reprimand Harry. Pauling will give him the letter to sign in the next few days."

"Gosh, Dixie, I'm sorry. I heard some rumblings of such a possibility. It's hard to believe."

"We're trying to decide what to do now."

"What do you mean?"

"If we want to stay or leave."

Radner raised his eyebrows, blinked, and adjusted his glasses. "Leave? But why?"

"I don't think Harry should work for a place that puts more value in the almighty dollar than their employees' good work. That is what it boils down to."

"But we need him, Dixie. Listen, after the Yeti escaped, I offered my resignation. Your husband wouldn't hear of it. He has my undying gratitude. And respect."

"You know, Miles," Dixie said, chuckling softly, "early on I thought you a dork. But during that crisis, you redeemed yourself in my eyes. Harry's as well. I know Harry is glad you're the facility director. I'm just sorry that Millie has done this thing."

"You're very kind. I'm so sorry for Harry. But, please—don't leave. I think I can speak for the entire department when I say that. We need and want you both."

"Thanks, Miles. That means a lot, believe me. I know Harry feels the same."

Together, they waited until Harry and Drayton returned.

❧❧❧

There was a fear in the multitudes, in society. It was one that was rarely talked about or discussed at the workplace water cooler or in churches across the land. It wasn't argued in the hallowed halls of Congress. But the fear existed, nonetheless.

The fear was that, if one started putting very large numbers of human brain cells into the brains of primates, suddenly you might transform the primate into something that had some of the capacities that were regarded as distinctively human—like speech—or other ways of being able to manipulate or relate to humans. It was these possibilities that were, at the moment, largely explored in fiction or movies that society as a whole refuses to take seriously.

There were two different aspects of research that were relevant to the warning. A creation referred to as a chimera, where full DNA was used from two separate and individual species of animals to create a new one, and a hybrid, where genetic parents of the same animal species each contributed half of the genes.

The word chimera had its origins in Greek mythology, the name of a fire-breathing creature described by Homer in the Iliad as being lion-fronted and snake behind, a goat in the middle. In Medieval art, although the chimera of antiquity was forgotten, chimerical figures appear as embodiments of the deceptive, even satanic forces of raw nature.

However, science lauded the first modern chimera in 1984, when scientists from the Institute of Animal Physiology in England created one from a sheep and a goat. Then, Chinese scientists at the Shanghai Second Medical University in 2003 successfully fused human cells with rabbit eggs. The embryos were reportedly the first human-animal chimeras successfully created. They were allowed to develop for several days in a laboratory dish before the scientists destroyed the embryos to harvest their stem cells.

One didn't have to be religious or into animal rights to think this didn't make sense. It was the scientists who wanted to do this. They'd now gone over the edge into the pathological domain.

ꞔꞁꞔꞁ

Millie woke and rubbed her eyes. Had she been dreaming? Where was she? Oh, yes, now she remembered. She was in a cheap motel on the outskirts of North Las Vegas off Interstate 15.

Driving away from the Primate Research Facility, she stopped at an ATM, got cash, fueled her car, and headed here. Around midnight, she pulled into the motel because she was too exhausted to drive farther. Besides, she didn't know where she was going, didn't have a plan. She decided she would stay here until she figured it out.

She shot a glance on the bed next to her. Roku was

asleep in his travel cage. But soon he would be awake and hungry, so she was going to have to venture to a grocer for milk.

Had Radner discovered her missing? Surely, by now, he knew she was gone. Had they called the police? Probably. Once they discovered she had taken her car, they would be combing the country looking for her and Roku. She had managed to throw a few clothes into a bag before getting in her car and driving away from Cinder Mountain.

Millie showered and changed into clean clothes, jeans, and a faded blouse. Roku was awake and fumbling with his cage. She looked at him, touched one of his small fingers.

"I need to find you some milk, Roku," she said, cooing at the creature. "I'm going to leave you here in the room, so don't be bad."

Roku looked at her with his large eyes as if he somehow understood. Millie marveled at his growth rate and how intelligent he seemed. She grabbed her purse, locked the motel room door, and left.

She located a neighborhood grocery store and bought some milk and some food for herself that she could eat in her room. Chips and sandwich stuff. Back in her motel room, she fixed Roku's bottle and herself a sandwich that she ate during the evening local news on television. So far, there was nothing about her or Roku.

Then she remembered her father's cabin in Arizona. Where it was, she couldn't remember. He bought it while she was in graduate school, but she had never been there. The Superstition Mountains sounded familiar. Maybe she could stay there a while till things calmed down.

She picked up her cell phone and dialed her parent's number in Toledo. Her mother answered.

"Mom," she said. "It's Millie. How are you and Dad?"

"We're fine, honey. You okay?" Her mother sounded happy to hear from her.

"That's great," Millie said. "Oh, I'm fine. Listen, Mom, is Dad there? I need to ask him something."

"He is, honey. Let me fetch him to the phone."

Millie waited a long moment until she heard her father's voice.

"Millie," he said, "good to hear from you. Working hard up there at the facility?"

"Yes, I'm still working, still doing my research. Listen, Dad, I wanted to ask you—do you still have that cabin in Arizona?"

"Of course, Millie. Why?"

Millie's pulse quickened. "You do? Great. I want to know if I could stay there for a few days?"

"Need some time away from the old grind, honey?" Her father's voice sounded silky smooth, a quality she always liked.

"Yes, a little vacation."

"But, of course, you can use the place, Millie. I don't think you've ever been there, however. Let me give you directions.

"I can? Oh fine. Just a minute, let me get a pen."

Millie scribbled the directions on a motel pad as her father gave them to her. They were involved as the cabin was far from anything civilized.

"What, Dad? I should buy groceries before I get there? Yes, I will."

Millie continued to write as her father talked.

"The key is where? Great, fine."

She chatted for a few minutes, hanging up, even though her mother seemed to want to talk. *Okay, I'll need to get a map. It's east of Phoenix, which is an easy day's drive southeast of Vegas.* So instead of staying here, she could try to make the cabin by morning. She would hide

out at the cabin and figure out how to deal with the current situation. And sooner or later, she was going to need
money.

She set the alarm on her phone for midnight and lay
down to get some sleep.

ઈન્ઈન

Bernard Wickingham sat in the dark of his small
apartment, downing a bottle of bourbon. He was about
two-thirds finished. He had replayed the afternoon meeting with Ingersoll over in his mind a hundred times, and
each time, it turned out the same. He had no job. And after this, no career. The thought of unloading fish for the
rest of his life made him sick to his stomach. He looked
at the bottle of sleeping pills in his hand and chuckled.
What a waste, he thought. What a waste.

Once, he had a brilliant career with a future where only the sky was the limit. Now he had nothing. No job, no
career, no prospects, and no one to hold close. All his
life, he never was close to anyone. After leaving home,
his life was working on his doctorate, followed by finding
a job. Relationships were a luxury, especially ones with
the opposite sex. He realized, of course, the fault was entirely his. There was something about his confident manner that rubbed people the wrong way, especially women.
Dixie Olson and Millie for example. Neither seemed to
ever warm to him, a fact that depressed him. The sad
thing, he thought, was that there was no longer any hope
for those warm, comforting relationships with members
of the opposite sex. His life, as he knew it, was over.
There was no longer any point in going on.

He downed the rest of the bourbon leaving a couple of
swallows for the pills. He opened the bottle and looked at
them—big red ones. He swallowed half of them with a

gulp of the liquor then finished them off with the last of the bourbon.

He thought of his mother, the only woman in his life. When he was a young boy, she told him he could be whatever he wanted to become and encouraged his pursuits. She was his rock, his anchor, always being there when he was down or needed a kind word. When she died, part of him died with her. No one ever was able to take her place.

Wickingham lay on his bed, let the darkness of the room engulf him. His head swirled. He thought back on his life, his lost opportunities, his failures, his very few successes, trying to do a balance sheet, but his brain was fuzzy. However, it seemed to add up to a huge minus.

His breathing slowed, and he relaxed.

The room became darker.

Then faded to black.

ﻌﻌﻌ

Millie woke with the alarm and showered again. Roku was asleep. After dressing, she brewed a cup of coffee in the room's small coffeepot. She carried the small cage containing Roku to the back seat of her car, poured the coffee into a Styrofoam cup, and left.

To the south, the lights of the Las Vegas Strip sparkled and flashed. Overhead, the sky was clear and inky, without a moon. The night desert air was cool and crisp.

Millie drove through the city and pulled her car onto Interstate 515, heading southeast toward Boulder City and Lake Mead. After midnight, the traffic was light, only a few eighteen-wheelers plowing up and down the highway. She stopped at a travel mart near Henderson and got gas and another cup of coffee. She felt refreshed, invigorated by the fact she was dealing with her situation.

No longer powerless in the face of daunting circumstances. For the present, she managed to put the worries over what might happen in the future out of her mind and concentrate on the tasks at hand.

As the highway curved back to the northeast, she noticed the eastern horizon getting lighter, a dull gray instead of black. She glanced at her watch. Three thirty-five a.m.

Up ahead was a dark expanse of nothingness, like a black hole in space. She knew it to be Lake Mead. The countryside here was flat, and the road fell away in front of her headlights in a monotonous straightaway. Dark ridges on the horizon, Millie knew, were the distant mountains of the Lake Mead area.

Turning back southeast, the road became Highway 93 and was a straight shot into first Kingman, then Phoenix. She turned on the radio to see if she could pick up any music and found a station playing soft rock. Roku slept and the miles rolled by.

By the time she reached the outskirts of Phoenix, the sun was peeking over the eastern mountains. Millie turned onto Highway 60 and sped east out of town. The traffic was light, so she made good time. Once beyond the city limits, she stopped for gas and breakfast, and to feed and change Roku. She withdrew the rest of her money from an ATM.

Arriving at Apache Junction, she bought groceries and milk. It was the last of civilization before entering the Superstition Mountains. Continuing on, she turned onto a narrow asphalt road and headed northeast. There were no cars on the road, only a few roadrunners and rabbits off in the distance. The sun, now higher, beat down with a new ferocity not experienced at the primate facility. But the air was just as dry, so she rolled her window down and enjoyed the fresh air. The road paralleled Salt River but soon turned in a more easterly direction where eventually it ended. To her right was a narrow, grass-covered lane that wound up into the mountains.

Following the directions given her by her father, Millie drover her car deep into the Superstition Mountains. She was alone, not another car or human did she see. A pack of coyotes dashed in front of her car. She braked and watched them disappear into the brush. After an hour of bumping up and down and following numerous twists and turns, she arrived at a clearing in the piñon forest where a small cabin sat at its edge. It was a rustic affair, just the kind her dad would love. And it was far away from any civilization. In short, the location was perfect.

There was a small covered porch, and Millie parked her car at the front of it. The cabin was as rustic on the inside as it looked from the outside. A few wooden beds with dusty thin mattresses, a wood stove, and several worn chairs occupied the single large room.

Millie unloaded her car, set Roku's cage on the small hand carved table, fed and changed him, and collapsed in one of the beds.

She was soon asleep.

Chapter 14

Harry and Dixie were having after dinner coffee on the patio of their San Mateo home. As the sun set in the west, it left deepening shadows across the water along with a chill in the air. Autumn was approaching, and the trees were beginning to lose their leaves. A gentle breeze wafted over the patio.

Five months had transpired since they'd last heard or seen Millie, and there was no trace of Roku. While they sipped their coffee, they chatted about the current state of affairs.

"So the authorities haven't found a trace of them, eh?" Dixie said.

"Not according to Pauling," Harry said. "He stopped me in the hall this morning to give me an update."

"I can't believe they just up and vanished. In this day and age, it seems so unlikely. She has never contacted her parents?"

"When I called Dr. Harbaum he said he hadn't heard from her."

"Dr. Harbaum?"

"He's a dentist in Toledo. I left him my number in case she did call him. I might try and call him again just to let him know we are still searching for her."

"Does he know why?"

"I couldn't bring myself to tell him the complete story, didn't tell him we didn't know where she was. I didn't want to worry him."

Dixie sounded surprised. "So, exactly what did you tell them if you didn't say she had gone missing?"

Harry squirmed in his chair, set his cup down. "Well," he said, "I said that I called the facility, but they told me they hadn't seen her for several days. I said she might be taking a short vacation. I don't think I alarmed Mr. Harbaum."

"And her father said he hadn't heard from her?"

"Now that you mention it," Harry said, "it was peculiar. Almost as if Dr. Harbaum didn't want to confide in me for some reason."

"So he possibly *had* heard from his daughter."

"I guess it's possible."

"Well, I think you should call him again," Dixie said. "For all the Harbaums know, she's not wanted by the authorities. They should know that she's gone missing and why."

"Maybe they do. Maybe the police have already told them." He took another pull on the coffee.

"I still think you should call. If I were a parent, I certainly would appreciate it. As her department chairman, you should make the call."

"You're right, of course. Roku would be about seven months old about now," Harry said, setting his coffee mug down. He stood, paced the patio. "I wonder how he is doing?"

"We'll probably never know. I don't have a good feeling about this."

"I know. I'll go call now."

✑✑✑

Deep within the Superstition Mountains, the sun peeked over the ridge of peaks to the east forming an orange glow in the sky. Brown-crested flycatchers, Gila woodpeckers, and gilded flickers greeted the morning with their eager calls. In the meadow beyond the cabin, California ragweed, goldeneye, and desert marigolds dotted the landscape edged with fir and Joshua trees. Gullies, washes, arroyos, buttes, and canyons punctuated the rugged terrain. The air was fresh and pungent with the aroma of wild sage, and each day filled Millie with awe. In the distance to the northeast, the famous landmark, Weaver's Needle, pierced the sky like an ancient obelisk. A thousand foot column of rock, it played a significant role in the stories of the Lost Dutchman's Gold Mine. The Needle's shadow reportedly indicated the location of a rich vein of gold, and many treasure hunters had ventured into the surrounding hills in search of it. Hundreds of people, driven by their lust for gold, prospected around Weaver's Needle.

Millie stepped out onto the cabin's porch and filled her lungs with the mountain air. Since arriving at her father's cabin, she had built a small playpen of rocks in front of the small porch where she could watch Roku play while she read or patched her clothes.

Today she was going to have to drive into Apache Junction for groceries, so she decided to allow Roku to play outside until she was ready to leave. As she fixed breakfast, Millie thought over what new words she would teach Roku. The child chimera had been learning sign language words at a phenomenal rate for the past month. And he was beginning to put the words together into simple sentences. Roku had grown much faster than his human counterparts as well. At seven months of age, he weighed nearly eighty pounds and was walking as well as an adult.

Observing the two Yeti at the facility, Millie was accustomed to the animals spending most of their time on two legs.

Occasionally, however, they would fall on all fours to lumber about their cages. Roku was different—he always walked upright.

Millie ate and went outside to the large playpen in which Roku was playing. He looked up when he heard her at the rock wall and ambled over to face her. His large lips formed a faint smile.

"Time for your '*lesson*,'" Millie said.

She signed the word *lesson*. Roku nodded and repeated the sign. She pointed to the cabin. "House," she said and signed the word "*house*." Once more Roku smiled, nodded, and again signed the word in return.

The exercise continued for another half hour until Roku appeared to tire of it. Millie took Roku into the cabin, changed his clothes, and placed him in the rear seat of her car while she drove to Apache Junction.

෴

Harry called Millie's father, John Harbaum, in Toledo. When the man answered, Harry identified himself.

"Good evening, Dr. Harbaum, this is Harry Olson, Millie's chairman at Cal Pacific University. I talked to you a few weeks ago."

"Yes, Dr. Olson. I remember. Millie has spoken of you often. She really admires you."

"I'm calling to ask if you or your wife have heard from your daughter lately."

Harry listened as John answered in the negative.

"No," Dr. Harbaum said, "it has been a number of months since either my wife or I has talked with her."

"We are concerned, John," Harry continued, "because

Millie has disappeared from the Primate Research Facility where she worked."

"Disappeared? How?" Harbaum's voice turned dark, concerned. "Have the authorities been notified?"

"Yes, of course. They were called almost immediately when we determined that she had used her car to leave with a valuable scientific specimen."

"I'm not following. Exactly what has Millie done?"

"It appears she took an animal she was using in a research project." Harry tried to sound emphatic but caring.

"And you're saying she has left and taken this animal with her? How did it happen?"

"I'm sorry, John, I can't divulge any more than I have. By so doing, however, she placed herself serious jeopardy with the authorities. If you hear from her, you need to call me as soon as possible. The animal with her could be dangerous to her as well as the public."

"Well…"

"Please, John," Harry said imploringly. "If you know anything about Millie's whereabouts, do her a favor and tell me."

"She called here about a week ago," Harbaum said. Harry sensed he was reluctant to reveal the information.

Harry listened as Harbaum described Millie's phone call a number of months earlier when she asked if she could use the family cabin in Arizona. He assumed it was for a short vacation.

"When was this exactly, John?" Harry said.

"About five months ago," Harbaum said. "Millie isn't the best at keeping in touch with her family. We just assumed she returned to the research facility to continue her work."

"I see. Can you give me the directions to the cabin? We'll need to check it out."

"Surely, she wouldn't still be there, Dr. Olson. The cabin is out in the middle of nowhere."

"We need to check all possibilities, John."

Harry took a pad and wrote out the directions given him by Dr. Harbaum. Finished, he was about to hang up when the man continued talking.

"Do my wife and I need to come to the university, Dr. Olson? We'll gladly do whatever is necessary to find Millie." The man sounded worried. And confused.

"Well, John, that's up to you. I'm happy to meet with you here at the university as I'm sure is Dr. Pauling, our president. Yes, whenever you and your wife can make it out just let me know."

"I think her mother will insist on us coming. Maybe to the primate facility."

"Of course, John. We'll keep in touch. If anything turns up regarding Millie, I assure you I'll call."

After hanging up, Dixie handed Harry a beer, and two moved back to the patio.

"So what did Millie's father had to say?" she asked Harry.

Harry took a long gulp and swallowed.

"He and his wife want to come out, so I said fine. They're upset, naturally. He did mention that shortly after Millie disappeared that she called him and asked directions to the family cabin in the Superstition Mountains. I'll need to notify the authorities."

"Yes, of course, you will. This isn't looking good for Millie."

"Not at all," Harry said. "I wish she had confided in me months ago. I might have been able to help."

"On the other hand, she was a woman obsessed with her project. And you would have nixed it out of hand. I don't think anything you could have said or done would have changed what happened. She was bent on creating a chimera, and nothing was going to stop her. I'm surprised she used her own DNA, however."

"Yes, I would have thought she would have used DNA from another animal or alien DNA."

"Alien DNA?" Dixie said.

"Yes, I read about it earlier in the year. Creating alien bases is not a new concept, and a team added modified cytosine and guanine into DNA molecules. They hardly looked like the originals. Obviously, not the same cytosine and guanine that is normally found in DNA. In test tubes, the team was able to get the foreign base pair to copy itself, but the real challenge was to get a cell to accept this alien DNA. To do that they used a complicated method to feed foreign DNA to a specifically engineered E. coli bacterium. The bacterium accepted the alien DNA, and when it ran out of alien nucleotides, the bacterium replaced them with natural ones. Foreign base pairs like these could also be used to create new proteins—which, among other things, could be used in creating new drugs or treatments for diseases. Not really alien in the usual sense but a completely made up strand of DNA."

"Interesting. You know, Harry, genetics is not one of my strong suits. Far from it."

"That's for sure," he said and laughed.

"Hard to believe how far we've come from that first expedition to Mongolia. Who knew when we uncovered that crashed Russian plane it would eventually lead to this?"

"What was the man's name who tried to kill everyone?"

"Eastwood. Rutherford Eastwood."

"I wonder what happened to him?"

"Probably rotting away in a Mongolian prison. At least, I sure hope so."

"Yeah, me too. Still bothered by the nightmares?"

"Not so much anymore. I rarely think about the cave and those Yeti. Thank heavens. Do you think of that time?"

"Now and then, I relive being in the cave-in and wondering if we were going to make it out alive. I figured we were all going to die. That was the most scared I've been in my life. We barely got outa there with our lives."

"Have you thought any more about whether you want to stay at Cal Pacific or leave?"

"Not really. I want to see this thing with Millie through first, then we'll talk it over. I do feel better now that I've had time to think about everything. I don't want to make a hasty decision that I would regret later."

"I know these past months have been extremely stressful for you, honey, and my heart goes out to you. I love you so much that I hate to see you so worried. Let's go to bed, and I'll try and help you forget for a while."

Harry smiled and followed Dixie inside and to their bedroom. She was such a beautiful woman, and he knew he was lucky to be married to her. Later, after their love-making, he lay and tried to put his mind at rest. Soon he was floating, dreaming.

He and Dixie were back at the monastery in Tenduk, high in the Altai Mountains of Mongolia. They had traveled there to examine a skull supposedly belonging to a Yeti. He had gone to her room because he couldn't sleep, and she welcomed him with a wide smile. It was there he confessed his forgery of the data that appeared in his journal article. It was then she placed her hand on his, and, on impulse, he kissed her.

And from that moment his life was different.

Chapter 15

Harry finished his lecture to his graduate class in Field Techniques and Analysis, walked out of the Science Building, and was immediately greeted by a young man in a gray suit.

"Dr. Olson?" the man inquired. He looked to be in his thirties; was tanned; and sported blond, close-cropped hair.

"Yes," Harry said, not bothering to stop his walking. The young man fell into step beside him.

"I'm Special Agent Hank Jacoby with the FBI. I'd like a word with you if you can spare the time. It's in regards to this Millie Harbaum, whom your university reported as having disappeared with a valuable scientific specimen."

The man held out his identification while Harry paused to study it,

"Yes," Harry said. "She has left our primate facility in Nevada. Her parents are naturally worried." Harry continued walking until he came to a bench under a large oak tree. He stopped and indicated the bench. "We can talk here if you wish."

"Fine," Jacoby said, sitting. He pointed to some construction along the walkway back toward the Science Building. "University is expanding?"

"Oh, that. There will be a life-sized sculpture of one of our highly esteemed faculty placed there. Dr. Julius Kesler. He was nationally known in his field."

"I see. Doctor," Jacoby said, after taking a notebook from his suit pocket. "Now about this Miss Harbaum—"

"Dr. Harbaum," Harry interrupted. "She was on our faculty here—a recent addition after completing her doctorate."

"Yes, all right. Your president, Dr. Pauling, mentioned that her father thought she might be in Arizona at a family cabin. Is that correct? I understand you talked with him."

"Agent Jacoby, I don't understand why the FBI is involved. The reason?"

"Mainly because of the possibility that, after the theft, this Dr. Harbaum crossed a state line. That makes it a federal case. That and the fact that public safety is at stake. Now, Dr. Olson, about where she might have fled."

"Public safety?" Harry said, confused.

"Your president mentioned something about the woman leaving with a scientifically created monster or the like. Now you were going to tell me something, Doctor?"

"I did speak with father the other night. He told me that a few months ago she called him, asking permission to use the family cabin in Arizona."

"Did he say where?"

"The Superstition Mountains. He gave me the directions. I then called Dr. Pauling, and I assume he called the authorities."

"He called the SFPD and, when they learned that this case might involve interstate travel, they notified us. We are coordinating the efforts of them and the Nevada State Police. I will need the directions to the cabin from you, Dr. Olson. We'll send a team of agents there and arrest her. That is, if she is still there."

"Of course," Harry said. "Come to my office, and I'll get it for you. I want to be there when you confront her."

"I dunno, Doctor."

"That's my condition on giving you the directions." They walked up the steps of the administration building and weaved their way among students coming and going.

"I could get a court order forcing you to hand over the information," Jacoby said, following Harry into his office.

"Agent Jacoby, don't threaten me. We're on the same side here. I can conveniently forget where I put the directions. I may have misplaced them. And, for the record, Mr. Jacoby, Dr. Harbaum didn't create a monster."

"All right, Dr. Olson, have it your way. We will meet at the Phoenix field office then and proceed from there."

Harry fumbled in his desk and produced a paper with the necessary directions to the Harbaum cabin. He handed it to Jacoby who studied it for a few minutes.

"Agent Jacoby, I would like for Dr. Pauling to know you are here and are speaking with me. If you don't mind, I'd like to phone him."

"Of course," the agent said.

After a brief phone call, Harry hung up and smiled at Jacoby.

"He wants to drop by and touch base with you in person. No problem, I hope. I told him we would wait for him here."

Jacoby nodded his assent and continued to study the directions.

Soon, Pauling was sitting across from Harry and the agent. The man seemed conspicuously ill at ease.

"Well," he said after smoothing his tie and crossing his legs, "everything settled here?"

"I believe so," Jacoby said. "I need to know exactly what this scientific specimen was that Dr. Harbaum allegedly stole."

He waited as Harry and Pauling exchanged awkward glances.

"Well, Special Agent," Pauling said after a moment, "it's rather peculiar. Huh...Harry, would you care to enlighten the man?"

Jacoby leaned forward in his chair and frowned. "Not going to endanger the public, is it?"

"We don't really know," Harry said.

The agent reached for his notebook.

"Go on," he said.

"Dr. Harbaum," Harry began, "initiated an experiment on her own and used deception to see it through. It's a rather involved story, but the short of it is that the Primate Research Facility in Nevada had stored frozen sperm and ova, or eggs, from two Yeti that had been housed there. You may have heard of the creatures and their transport there from Mongolia."

The agent nodded as he wrote in his notebook. "Yes," he said. "I remember reading something about them."

"Millie decided to create another Yeti, using that sperm and eggs. Using the technique of in vitro fertilization, she successfully formed an embryo and, with the help of the facility veterinarian, transferred that embryo into one of the chimps housed there."

Jacoby continued to write quickly.

"However, unknown to all concerned, Millie transferred her own DNA into the egg she used to create the embryo. Later, when the chimp delivered, she delivered a creature that was half Yeti and half human."

Jacoby stopped writing, looked up, and stared at Harry.

"What?"

"It's called a chimera," Harry said. Pauling nodded.

"Okay," Jacoby said.

"A chimera is an animal that has half its DNA contributed by one species and the other half by another," Harry continued. "They've become somewhat common in animal research—that is animal chimeras. But never before has anyone created an animal that has half its genome contributed by a human."

"What does this…thing…look like?"

"Hairless, large eyes, small head. Humanoid in a lot of ways."

"Wow," Jacoby said. "This is amazing. I never dreamed."

⊱⊰

After Special Agent Hank Jacoby left Harry's office, Pauling remained behind. He seemed nervous, fidgeted in his chair, toyed with his tie.

"What's the matter, Reginald? You don't seem like your old self."

"Harry, I feel horrible. I just feel horrible."

"What is it? You ill or something?" Harry felt his pulse rising, a familiar sour taste forming in his mouth.

Pauling rose, crossed the room, and closed his office door. He paced as he talked. "Believe me, Harry, I would sooner die than tell you this—"

"For Christ's sake," Harry said, irritation clear in his voice. "Spill it."

"I have been told by the board of trustees to terminate your contract with the university. Effective immediately."

Harry fell back into his chair, numb. Here it was at last. He was fired. What he had worried about, thought about, was now a reality.

"I'm so sorry, Harry. I tried to change their minds, but it was to no avail. They would have none of it. If you ever need a recommendation—"

"Never mind, Reginald. It's no use. You did everything you could."

"The board recommended that Dixie be allowed to stay on, of course. Her actions were not questioned."

"Yeah?"

"Your termination is directly due to your handling of the Harbaum affair. Coming so close on the heels of the newspaper article and the Yeti escape, they felt they had to act. The board felt that if you could not control your staff, that—"

"Control my staff? Are you nuts, Reginald? These people are professionals, after all. One doesn't constantly ride herd on them."

"I'm sorry, Harry. I truly am."

Pauling stood and ambled toward the office door. He stopped short and turned toward Harry. "You're to vacate your office by the end of the month. Again, I'm sorry."

After Pauling left, Harry opened the credenza, retrieved a bottle of scotch, and poured a generous amount into a glass.

As he sipped the amber liquid, he wondered what Dixie's reaction would be at the news. Elated, most likely. She was ready to leave Cal Pacific after his formal reprimand.

Finishing the scotch, he replaced the bottle and strolled across the campus where he found his wife in her office grading test papers. She grinned when he entered.

"Hi," she said, setting down her pen and leaning back in her chair. "You don't look well."

"It finally happened, sweetheart. It's done. Pauling just came by to inform me that the board of trustees, that group of distinguished men who run our university, have terminated me. I am to leave by the end of the month."

"Why now?" Dixie said.

"Due to my negligent handing of Millie and her experiment. He said if I couldn't control my staff, then I wasn't needed here. Or words to that effect."

"I told you, honey. They're a group of spineless bastards. Every last one of them."

"He said you were still welcome at Cal Pacific. They still want you."

"Fat chance of that happening," Dixie said. "Didn't they consider I wouldn't stay without you?"

"I dunno. Haven't really thought about it yet."

"Anything else?"

"An FBI agent came by and wanted to know the directions to the Harbaum cabin. He wanted to know the specifics of Millie's project."

"How did he take it?"

"Confused and stunned, as you would expect. I'm going with him when they assault the cabin. He was reluctant, but I managed to convince him otherwise. They plan to meet at their Phoenix field office, and I'll meet up with him there."

"I'm going too," Dixie said.

"But you have duties here. Your class."

"I'm heading to Pauling's office to turn in my resignation as soon as you leave here. We can find work together elsewhere. He can find someone to finish up my class. So, I'm going with you."

Harry smiled at this wife. When Dixie got something in her head, it was useless to try and change her. It was one of her more attractive assets, but it could make her difficult at times. "It might be dangerous," he said.

"Like Mongolia and hunting for Bentu and Sash wasn't?" she said. "You can object all you want, but it won't change anything. I'm going."

Harry resigned himself to the inevitable and smiled at her.

"Okay, dear. You're going."

"By the way," she said, "did you see the paper today? No? Well, there was an article on page thirty-three. It seems they found Dr. Wickingham dead in his apartment in Merced. An apparent suicide."

"No kidding? How?"

"Overdose, it seems. He had just been fired from his teaching position at UC-Merced. The reasons weren't disclosed."

"Such a shame. He showed great promise, but he wasn't willing to play the academic game."

"I, for one, am not particularly sad," Dixie said. "The man would gawk at my breasts every time he was around me. Such a creep. Not to mention extortion."

"I assume Pauling will find someone to take over my class, so I'm going to start packing up my stuff here later today and bring a box home tonight. Might as well get started."

"I'll go see Pauling right now," Dixie said. "I can't wait to see his face. When will you hear from the FBI agent?"

"Soon, I think."

✿✿✿

Dr. Pauling was stunned by Dixie's resignation. No amount of pleading changed her mind. He thought he could detect a certain amount of bitterness in her voice and a twinkle of triumph in her flashing green eyes. There weren't many women faculty in the Science Department at Cal Pacific, and Pauling held Dixie up as an example to prospective applicants that the university was one of widening opportunities.

He would miss her brilliant mind, her quick wit, and her pleasant features. Harry could count himself lucky.

Pauling was becoming exasperated with the board of

trustees and their sudden demanding deportment. It was one thing, he thought, to act as an advisor to the university president, but when they began dictating a course of action for him to follow…well, that crossed the line. Forester's condescending manner irritated Pauling, and his influence with the board had cost the university two brilliant young professors. If Forester continued at the present pace, the science department would soon be nonexistent.

Maybe Pauling would begin investigating his own options in the wake of current events.

Chapter 16

Millie noticed something wasn't right with Roku. He lay on his bed, still and listless, and staring at her with his large round eyes. They were sunken deep into his head. She crossed the room and touched his forehead. He was burning with fever. She retrieved a bottle of water from the small ice chest and brought it to him. Lifting his head with one arm, she attempted to get him to drink, but the water just dribbled from his lips onto the bed.

He didn't move.

She felt for a pulse and found it was thin and rapid.

"Roku," she said. "What's the matter?"

Roku made not a sound, just continued to stare at her through vacant eyes.

Millie found a small cloth, dampened it with water from the bottle, and started bathing the chimera's face with it. She attempted again to get him to drink, but it was no use.

She was in a panic. Roku was obviously ill, but from what? She had no idea. After undressing him, she inspected his entire torso for clues, but none were forthcoming. His body felt hot all over.

She wrung out the cloth, rewet it, and sponged Roku's

body with it, hoping to bring his fever down. What else would work? As a child, she remembered her mother rubbing alcohol on her back for fevers, but Millie thought that practice was frowned upon now. She had some aspirin in her purse but did not know if it would be safe for him.

As she labored with the damp cloth, Roku lay motionless on the bed, his eyes fixed on her as if imploring her to help him.

"I'm trying, Roku," she said in a whisper. "I'm trying."

Mille sat on the bed next to Roku, wondering what could be ailing him. Just a few hours earlier he seemed fine. Now he was deathly ill. Was it a virus? An infection of some sort? A disease of primates of which she knew nothing? From his sunken eyes, she figured he was dehydrated from the fever but getting fluids into him seemed impossible. Roku wouldn't drink. He was too weak.

She rose from the bed and crossed the small room to the front window looking out on the Superstition Mountains. In the distance, a lone wolf bounded into the trees while the setting sun cast deepening shadows across the sage covered landscape. The locusts, whose trilling was so prominent earlier, were quieting. After assuring herself that they were still alone at the cabin, she paced the room, giving Roku an occasional worried glance.

It didn't look good for the little fella. He was ill and getting sicker with each passing hour. If she didn't get help soon, Roku might die. She wasn't going to do all this work, only to have him expire in the mountains.

But where could she take him for medical help? A hospital emergency room was out of the question. They'd have been contacted to be on the lookout for her and Roku, in all likelihood. A medical clinic? A veterinarian's office? Hardly.

Roku needed a veterinarian, and he needed one as soon as she could locate one. There might be one in Apache Junction, but she didn't notice as she drove through. Phoenix was her best bet, but she feared it was too populated.

Then her mind settled on Siscom.

Did she dare chance a call to Gerald?

⋐⋑⋐⋑

At the primate facility, Gerald Siscom sat alone in his room, reading a veterinary journal. He found it difficult to concentrate because Millie was on his mind. The last time he had seen her, she was in the Animal Care Unit with Harry and Dixie confessing how she created Roku and explaining to them exactly what the creature was. Since that time, he learned that she had left the facility, taking Roku with her. Her whereabouts were unknown, and he had not heard from her.

He set his journal aside, stood, stretched his legs. He strolled downstairs to the dormitory kitchen and fixed himself a sandwich. Returning to his room, he grabbed a beer from his small fridge then plopped back into the chair. He thumbed nonchalantly through the journal while he munched his sandwich but put the magazine down in frustration. He took a long gulp of his beer and tried to relax.

His mind returned to Millie.

Their collaboration on her Roku project had brought them close, and he had been beginning to feel as if something might develop in their new relationship. Their several dates managed to bring him out of his shell. He was actually interested in something besides work.

Millie captivated his imagination in a way other women never had, leaving him wanting more...more what, he wasn't exactly sure, but he knew he longed to see her again.

But her disappearance put a glitch in that prospect.

He finished his beer and returned to the journal. Since beginning his work with Millie, he had grown fond of her. No, more than fond. It was much deeper. She was ten years his junior, but that didn't seem to mater to either of them. She was so radically different than his first wife, involved with her work and not self-absorbed as Jennifer. His ex was preoccupied with material things, fashion, jewelry, things that didn't interest Millie in the least. Their few dates were spent in easy conversation, her eyes sparkling, her lovely face smiling as if she was pleased with his company.

His cell phone squawked.

It was Millie, and, by her harried tone, he knew something was wrong.

"Millie," he said, panicked by the sudden intrusion. "Where are you? What's going on?"

"Please, Gerald," Millie said in a pleading voice.

Siscom's stomach suddenly turned into a tight knot. He instinctively knew something was terribly wrong.

"I need your help. You've got to help me."

"Calm down, Millie," he said. "What's wrong?"

"It's Roku," she said. "He's ill. Very ill. I'm afraid if you don't see him soon, he might die. Can I meet you somewhere?"

"What's wrong with him?" Siscom was still reeling from Millie's call from out of the blue.

"He has a high fever. And he's listless, just lies in bed, not moving. He just looks at me, Gerald. An imploring sort of look. His eyes are sunken into his head."

"Probably dehydrated," Siscom said. "Have you given him any water?"

"I tried, but he won't take any. Just lies there, looking at me with a sad expression."

Siscom's mind raced as he thought of the possibilities. Primates were susceptible to a host of diseases. Although humans had always shared habitats with nonhuman primates, the dynamics of human-primate interactions were changing radically. Within the last several decades, humans had been responsible for massive, irrevocable changes to primate habitats. Most primates today lived in anthropogenically disturbed habitat—mosaics of farmland, human settlements, forest fragments, and isolated protected areas. As anthropogenic habitat change forced humans and primates into closer and more frequent contact, the risks of interspecific disease transmission increased.

The importance of these issues was readily apparent from the many diseases that nonhuman primates and humans presently shared. For example, monkeys were reservoirs for the yellow fever virus, an arbovirus of critical importance to human health in Africa and South America. Other important human viruses stemming from nonhuman primates included herpesvirus B, SV40 polyomavirus, and various simian retroviruses. Among bacterial parasites, the causal agent of tuberculosis could be transmitted zoonotically, both in captivity and in the wild.

Most of these diseases didn't apply to Roku, but what it could be was impossible to diagnose over the phone. He needed to examine the chimera. And soon.

"Listen, Millie," he said. "Of course, I'll help, but I need to examine Roku, the sooner, the better. Where are you?"

"I can't say, Gerald. But I can meet you somewhere."

"Millie, come to the facility with Roku and turn yourself in. We can care for Roku here where he'll get the best care possible. Don't make this worse for both you and him."

"Not now, Gerald. I can't. Please, just meet us somewhere."

Against Siscom's better judgment he relented. "Okay," he said. "Where?"

"Can you drive to Phoenix?"

"Christ, Millie, that's a six hour drive."

"There's a park with a lake on the northeast side of town. It has an RV park. I can meet you there."

"That's an awfully long way away, Millie. I dunno."

"Please, Gerald. You're my only hope, at this point— I'm begging."

Millie's voice faltered, and Siscom's heart softened. "All right," he said. "I'll start right away. Should be there by midnight or so."

"And Gerald," Millie said. "Please don't say anything to anyone. Please don't bring anyone with you. I trust you."

"Not to worry, honey," Siscom said. "You can count on me."

He listened while Millie gave him directions to the RV park outside of Phoenix. He jotted them on a notepad.

After hanging up, he gathered a few things, hurried to the Animal Care Unit where he retrieved his medical bag and several syringes of antibiotics. He grabbed a bag of intravenous fluid and its tubing then ran to his car.

What am I doing? he thought, as he steered his car off Cinder Mountain.

એએએ

Siscom knew he was abetting a fugitive from justice. Radner had told everyone as much when he announced the FBI was looking for Millie. The thought churned his stomach and pumped bile into his throat.

Wouldn't it be better if he stopped the car, called Radner, and told him everything? Told him that Millie called and he was going to meet her and Roku? That way the FBI could arrest her or do whatever they intended to do. Take her to jail? He had no idea.

But he'd told Millie he would help, and he wouldn't betray her trust, no matter how much it cost him. And it might just cost him dearly. He wondered if he could be held as an accomplice in her flight from the authorities. Probably. They usually did whatever they wanted to do. But there was a bond between him and Millie, a bond sealed when he held her in his arms and kissed her.

He drove through the night on a southeast heading, speeding toward Phoenix. Arriving at Kingman at the I-40 junction he stopped for gas and coffee, stretched his legs. It was a balmy night, the stars were out, with only a slight breeze blowing from the south. After a brief break, he climbed back in his car and continued on.

As he approached the outskirts of Phoenix and his cutoff to the park, his pulse quickened. It would be good to see Millie again.

He hoped he wouldn't be too late for Roku.

Chapter 17

I can't believe you really resigned," Harry said to Dixie. "What did Pauling have to say?"

"Nothing much. What could he say? I do believe he
was shocked."

Harry followed his wife from the kitchen, where they
just finished with dinner, into the living room. Each held
a mug of steaming coffee.

"Now we are both unemployed," he said. "You
needn't have done it. This was all my doing, nothing for
you to worry about. I always felt that man Forester had it
in for me from the beginning, something about his condescending attitude."

"Wealth has a way of doing that to people," Dixie
said, taking a sip of her coffee. "I could cite you dozens
of examples."

Harry nodded. "However, I believe the man took
pleasure in forcing my termination. My only vindication
is that Chloe Rawlings and a number of other faculty ob-
jected to Pauling in strenuous fashion."

"I like that Dr. Rawlings. She's okay in my book."

"Didn't do much good. But you're right—she's a
standup woman."

"Where do you think Millie went? What could she

have planned for a chimera that is only months old?"

"I think she's hiding out with him somewhere. But where I haven't a clue. Sooner or later, however, she's going to need money. That means finding a job. She's got to surface sometime."

"I hope Roku is all right," Dixie said.

"It's got to be hard taking care of him. Harder than caring for an infant."

She nodded. "I'm sure it is. Why do you think she did it?"

"Did what?"

"Created him in the first place. She must have known you, Radner, and Pauling would object in the strongest of terms. And make her destroy it. Why did she do it, honey?"

Harry thought for a moment, reflected back on his own motivation for falsifying the data that eventually got him into trouble. No one outside the academic world understood what tremendous pressures were on the shoulders of young faculty members trying to rise up in tenure and also achieve recognition in their respective fields. There was only one avenue, one that so many of Harry's predecessors had traveled. Publication. It was "publish or perish" in plain simple language. One either made a discovery or published a stack of papers. The road to academic promotion was through publication in professional journals. There was no shortcut.

"I suspect," he said at length, "for the same reasons we all are tempted to push the boundaries of what is considered ethical. She wanted a name for herself. She wanted fame and notoriety, much like Bernard Wickingham. And myself. We are tempted by what we see as a shortcut, but, in reality, there is no such thing."

"I suppose," Dixie said.

She gathered their mugs and replenished their coffee then returned to the living room.

"I wish she hadn't done it," she said. "Have you heard from the FBI agent?"

"Jacoby? No. I doubt I will until we get to Phoenix when they storm the family cabin."

"You've used that word *storm* again. I hope they don't harm her or Roku."

∾∾∾

Millie sat in the RV parking lot, waiting for Siscom to arrive. Roku was in the back seat covered with heavy blankets. It was close to midnight. Even in the dark, she saw that he continued to shiver. She had tried unsuccessfully to get him to drink water before they left the cabin but it was no use—he just let the water dribble from his parched lips. He seemed weaker now. The poor fellow hardly moved. Millie's heart went out to him.

Please, God, don't let him die. I don't care what happens to me if only he survives.

The RV park contained only a few motor homes, and all were dark. The nearby lake appeared as a black void off in the distance. Only the occasional croaking frog or howling wolf could be heard. The park was otherwise eerily silent. She sat huddled in her car, listening to Roku's labored breathing, and waited for Siscom to arrive.

She glanced at her watch. Twelve-twenty a.m. *Please, Gerald, hurry*, she said to herself.

In the distance, a pair of headlights approached. The car turned off the main road and into the RV park. Millie followed the car's slow progress until it came to a stop next to her. When the door opened, she saw that it was Siscom. She leaped from her car.

"Oh, Gerald," she said. "Thank heaven. I feared you might have had second thoughts."

Millie fell into Siscom's arms. He held her for a brief moment and kissed her on the forehead.

"There, there," he said. "Where is Roku?"

"Here in my backseat." She opened the rear door and allowed Siscom to peer in.

"Millie, get my bag and flashlight out of my car, please." He scrambled into the car's rear compartment, kneeling beside Roku.

Millie did as requested and soon was shining a light into Roku's fevered face. She watched while Siscom took the chimera's pulse, blood pressure, and temperature. He then listened to his heart and lungs with his stethoscope, pushed around on his abdomen.

"Well," Millie said, eager for his opinion. "What do you think?"

Siscom looked at her and shook his head. The glow from the flashlight made his expression even more frightening.

"Temp is one hundred five. Pulse is rapid and weak, blood pressure dangerously low. He's severely dehydrated, Millie, just as I feared. I'm sure it's an infection of some kind."

"Like what?" she asked, her heart pounding in her head.

"Can't tell here without blood tests. Bacterial, most likely."

"What can you do, Gerald? I can't lose him."

Millie knew she sounded close to hysterical, but she couldn't help it. Her life revolved around Roku at this point.

"Need to rehydrate him first," Siscom said. "I brought a couple of bags of saline. Help me get this IV into his arm. "Then I'll pump some antibiotics into him, and we'll just have to hope for the best."

Millie watched Siscom as he worked quickly, getting the tourniquet around an arm, and pushed the catheter into a vein. She held the bag while he connected the tubing and began running the fluid into Roku's body. She marveled at Siscom's dexterity and efficiency at working in less than ideal circumstances. After wrapping the IV site, he searched his medical bag, produced a syringe."

"Chloramphenicol," he said. "It will kill anything."

"I hope so, Gerald. I hope so."

Siscom unscrewed the cap on the syringe, attached a needle, and injected its contents into the tubing. He and Millie watched the antibiotic, a slightly yellow color, flow into Roku. Finished, Siscom gathered his equipment and returned them to his bag.

"I brought two liters of saline," he said. "It should be enough."

"I'll pray that it is. What's there to do now?"

"Nothing but wait and hope for the best. I'll give him another dose of antibiotic in two hours. I need to stretch. My legs are cramping."

The two exited Millie's car, and Siscom paced around it for several minutes. The night was black as ink, no stars shining. No moon. The breeze that blew over them from the lake brought fresh scents into the RV park. Millie breathed deeply in the fresh air, allowing it to rejuvenate her. She watched Siscom pace around the car and wondered what he was thinking. She was glad he hadn't brought the authorities with him, for it would have been disastrous if he had.

They sat in the front seat of Millie's car while Siscom periodically checked on Roku's condition. Millie reached over and touched his arm.

"I can't tell you how much your coming has meant to

me, Gerald," she said. "I worried that you might call the police."

"Millie, I'm your friend. I hope I'm more than a friend. I was glad to help."

"You think Roku has a chance?"

"Well, you waited almost too late. Another few hours Roku would have been history. We can only hope the antibiotic will bring him around. We'll know in a few hours if his fever is down."

"How are Dr. Olson and Dixie?" Millie said.

"Worried about you, my dear. Extremely worried. I heard that Harry called your father and mother. Radner is concerned about you as well."

"It pained me to see how I hurt them. I never realized how my actions would disappoint the one man I respect more than anything. Besides you, of course. I'm sure I hurt you also, Gerald."

Siscom shifted his weight in the car seat.

"I must admit that, at first, my feelings were hurt. During our work together we had become so close. I felt you betrayed my confidence, my trust in you. But after thinking long and hard about it, I realized I might have done the same as you if I were in your place. Sometimes, Millie, the only way science makes progress is through the courage of its scientists willing to walk where no one dared before. I can't be upset with someone I care deeply about."

He reached out and touched her cheek. Millie's heart skipped a beat.

"Gerald—I—I—"

"Yes?"

"Do you ever think of your ex-wife?"

"I used to," he said. "Mostly about how much I had not been able to please her. Initially, I thought the fault lay with me, and it tore me down. A real man would have been able to keep her. At least, that's what I told myself. But after landing the job at the facility and working there a year, my feelings began to change. I saw things in a different light. One day I had an epiphany—she was at fault, not me. And it changed my life. I was free, whole again.

"Then you came into my life during our hunt for the escaped Yeti. You turned my comfortable existence upside down."

"I'm sorry," Millie said. "I didn't intend to."

"And for that, my dear, you have my undying gratitude."

After that revelation, they dozed fitfully for an hour. Siscom's cell phone alarm chirped, and he climbed into the back seat to check on Roku and to administer his next dose of antibiotic. Millie stirred, turned, watched him work.

"How is he?" she asked.

"Fever is down to one hundred. Pulse stronger and blood pressure higher. Doesn't appear as dehydrated as he did earlier. I'd say he's improved."

Siscom retrieved another antibiotic syringe from his bag and injected its contents into Roku's intravenous line.

"There," he said. "That's the antibiotic. He's had enough Chloramphenicol to kill every bug in his system. Let's hope my diagnosis was correct."

He climbed back into the front seat and patted Millie's hand.

"What if you're wrong?" Millie asked.

"I won't lie to you," Siscom said, softly. "If Roku doesn't respond to this antibiotic, his chances are slim to none. He will die. But I think he's responding. He appears a little better."

"I hope so."

"I'll check him again at dawn," he said. "If he continues to improve, I'll leave the both of you and return to the facility. I wish you would reconsider and come back with me."

"Gerald, it just isn't possible, I'm sorry." Millie felt her eyes well with tears. "You've been so kind. I'll never forget it."

Chapter 18

Millie woke with a start. The eastern sky was a dull gray, dawn an hour away. She gazed at the figure in the seat next to her, caught her breath in a quiet gasp. Siscom was sleeping quietly. She couldn't believe her good fortune in his coming to her aid. He had done so without the slightest hesitation or complaint.

His treatment of Roku seemed to be working. When he last checked, he pronounced him much improved and the crisis over. She mumbled a quiet prayer of thanks.

Siscom stirred, looked around. "Getting light," he said. "I need to be going. No one at the facility knows I left. I'll need to phone when I'm back on the road."

Millie retrieved two bottles of water from the center console and handed one to Siscom.

"I wish I had some breakfast for you," she said. "It's the least I could do. You must be starved."

"I can get something along the way." He yawned and stretched his arms. "I'm not used to sleeping in cars."

"Gerald, I can't begin to thank you enough—"

"Forget it," he interrupted. "I was glad to help. Like I said before, I just wish I could convince you to go back with me."

"I can't, I'm sorry."

"Where will you go?"

"Back to where I was. And please don't follow. You don't need to involve yourself any further."

"All right," he said. He took several large gulps of the water.

"Will this get you in trouble?"

"I dunno. I will try and hide my involvement here for as long as possible. But I can't lie to the authorities, Millie."

She reached out and touched his cheek. "I understand. I hope this doesn't cost you your job or anything."

Millie sat and stared out the car's windshield, not wanting Siscom to leave. He had become her rock, someone she could lean on, confide in. She heard Siscom continuing to talk.

"...can I tell your folks you're all right? Harry? Dixie?"

"No, Gerald, you promised. No one. Understand?"

He nodded, finished the water.

"Well," he said, "I need to be going."

He checked on Roku one last time, assured Millie he was sleeping peacefully and out of danger, then let himself out of the car. She followed him to where he stood by the door of his vehicle. A slight breeze had blown up across the lake that she could now see in the distance to the North. A few people were milling around the RV park.

Siscom looked at her with soulful eyes, took her in his arms, kissed her hard on the lips.

"Take care of yourself, Millie," he said.

Then he hopped in his car and was gone.

Millie stood for a long time, gazing at his car as it disappeared over a hill. *That's it*, she thought. *I'll never see him again.* Tears streamed down her cheeks. She brushed them away with a sleeve then turned and got back in her car. She glanced at the back seat where Roku was still sleeping. *Thank God he's better. I nearly lost him.*

She started her car, glanced again at Roku, then eased out of the RV park and onto the road. An orange glow was now on the eastern horizon, casting rays of brilliant color into a gray sky. Hunger gnawed at her ribs. She would get breakfast at Apache Junction.

As she skirted the northern edge of Phoenix, her thoughts were still on Siscom. Coming to her aid, she knew, took courage, for she realized he was a man of integrity. She loathed herself for causing him to betray his own code of ethics. But she loved him, and nothing could change that fact.

Were they destined to never be together? Two star-crossed lovers passing in the night? Only time would tell, but Millie didn't see a way out of the difficulty she created for herself.

She glanced in the rearview mirror and noticed Roku sitting up, looking around. She cooed to him softly.

"There you are," she said. "Feeling better? You look so much better. Dr. Siscom sure fixed you up."

Keeping one eye on the road but continuing to glance at Roku, she saw him lay back down. But not before he reached out and touched the back of her head.

"You're such a good boy," she cooed again. "Rest, Roku. You need rest."

On the eastern edge of Phoenix, she pushed the accelerator down and sped toward Apache Junction.

❦❦❦

Chloe Rawlings was at her desk when her phone rang. It was Radner, and he sounded excited. She turned her attention away from her computer and listened.

"Have you heard about Bernard Wickingham?" he said. "Our old faculty colleague?"

"No," she said. "What about him?"

"Police found him dead in his apartment. They think it was a suicide."

"My gosh, Miles. I wonder why?"

"He was living in Merced," Radner said. "He apparently had found work at the university there. According to a friend of mine, he was recently fired."

"Just like he was here. Hard for a leopard to change its spots, isn't it? Any other details?"

"Nothing really. They found an empty bottle of pills and liquor next to his body."

"He leave a note?"

"Not that the authorities have released. I thought you would want to know."

"He was a pompous ass. After what he tried to do to Harry, Pauling was right to fire him. I'm sorry he took his own life, but the man had no honor. Does Harry know?"

"I dunno," Radner replied. "I just got word that Pauling has terminated his contract. He's been fired, Chloe."

"What? You're kidding? How come?" Chloe was on the edge of her seat, yelling into the phone.

"Seems the trustees didn't approve of his handling of the Harbaum affair. That and the Yeti escape and needless carnage that occurred as a result."

"Not only is that not fair, Miles, it's simply not right. Both Harry and Dixie have been good for our university. Brought in a ton of money, increased our prestige. What more could they want? Damn them all!"

"My sentiments exactly, Chloe. But it's done, and I don't see how we can change it."

"Really, Miles? Really? We'll just see about that."

After hanging up, Chloe sat at her desk fuming over what Radner told her. She didn't care about Wickingham.

The man did himself in. But Harry? That was a different story. She knew there was something she could do.

She called Pauling's office and when his secretary answered she tried to speak in a controlled voice. "This is Dr. Rawlings. I need a short meeting with Dr. Pauling. As soon as possible."

‿ↄↄↄ

Back at the cabin, Millie was pleased to see Roku acting like his old self. She hummed as she prepared their dinner. Seeing the chimera well was worth the pain of Siscom's parting. It was difficult to not return with him to the facility. Nagging thoughts of how they were going to survive kept plaguing her. She knew it would be difficult, for soon her money would run out, and she would have to get a job. Doing what? She didn't know.

She only knew that keeping Roku safe was her primary goal, safe at all costs. Her hopes of future scientific papers and recognition were dashed when she fled the facility with him. Now her only thoughts were of his safety.

Millie shot Roku a glance. He was playing with a few blocks on the floor. She turned and signed to him. "*Dinner is almost ready. Are you hungry? I hope so. You need to eat and regain your strength.*"

She finished with her cooking, placed Roku in a chair, and sat next to him. As he shoveled the food into his mouth with his bare hands, she wondered how well the signing lessons were going with him. Did he understand? He seemed to, but it was difficult to judge as he could be just parroting her words. But some of his responses did seem to make sense.

Only time would tell.

Chapter 19

Gerald Siscom sat in the small office of the Primate Research Facility's security chief, Bruce Drayton. Through a window, he noticed low dark thunderclouds looming off to the north of Cinder Mountain, bringing the promise of rain later in the day. A cool breeze swept through the compound.

Sipping their morning coffee together the two men reflected upon the current situation with Millie Harbaum and Roku.

"Radner told me the FBI is going to storm the Harbaum cabin any day now," Siscom said. "Supposedly, she may be holed up there with Roku."

"Hope it doesn't turn out to be another Waco scenario," Drayton said, blowing steam off his coffee.

"I doubt it. Millie's not the violent type. I've heard now that Harry and Dixie are fired, they are going along. It all seems to be spinning out of control."

"What the hell happened? I always thought those two were an asset to the university and the facility. Harry wasn't a micromanager. He let Radner run the place here."

"I dunno, Bruce," Siscom said. Out the office's one window, he noticed a light drizzle was falling. "When

you anger the political bosses, you're going down. Radner said the board of trustees weren't happy with they
way he handled this situation, so he had to go."

"So Dixie is going with him?" Drayton said.

"That's about the size of it."

"And Millie? Any word of her?"

Drayton poured them each another mug of coffee and
returned to his chair.

"Not that I'm aware of," Siscom said.

"You helped with her experiment didn't you?"

"Part of it, yes. But I didn't know about the DNA
transfer. She kept that a secret until the very last."

"You know her very well, Gerald. Did you ever think
she was capable of something like this?"

"To be honest, Bruce, I found myself deeply attracted
to her. Enchanted, I guess. We had a few dates. So, yes, I
thought I knew her better than most. But, no, I never expected this. And, in some ways, I still don't. I can't explain it."

"I hope the bad publicity won't force the university to
close our facility," Drayton said. He drained his coffee
and set the cup on his desk. The rain beat against the
window like Morse code.

"Me either, but anything is possible with this board, it
seems. I'm worried about Millie. I hope she's not harmed
when they catch up with her."

"What will happen to the creature?"

"They'll destroy it, of course.

"It's almost a year old now."

"I know, but it won't make a difference. Cal Pacific
can't have a chimera running around being an ever-
present example of science run amuck. Instead of studying it, gleaning whatever information can be obtained for
man's benefit, they'll kill it off. Political sentiment, being
what it is in this country, our leaders will bend to the anti-

science fever sweeping the land. You know, Bruce, the idea that belief, however misguided or unfounded, trumps scientific progress. Even if it benefits mankind."

Drayton nodded his understanding. "But we all have beliefs of one sort or another," he said. "There's nothing inherently wrong with a belief system."

"I would agree, up to a point," Siscom said. "But when beliefs fly in the face of fact, what then? How does one reconcile a belief then?"

"You pose a great question, Gerald. But doesn't everyone think their own personal beliefs are the correct ones?"

"Down through the ages, beliefs have been proven wrong. The world was once thought of as being flat, then Magellan sailed around it and proved otherwise. Man used to believe in a three-tiered universe, but now we know different. Just to name a few. Beliefs have always been modified by facts and scientific discoveries. At least for most reasonable men."

"What will it do to Millie if her creature is destroyed?"

"I don't know, Bruce. Good question. But I worry it will destroy her too."

е/эе/э

Located in a multi-story concrete building on the north side of Phoenix and surrounded by a tall wrought iron fence, the FBI field office stood as a megalith in the hot desert sun. The distant mountains appeared as purple teeth that jutted skyward from a brown, desolate landscape. Heat waves rippled off the surface of the desert causing objects in the distance to undulate.

After hearing from Agent Jacoby, Harry and Dixie packed a bag and drove to Phoenix. Taking two days to make the trip, they stopped overnight along the way on the tri-state border of California, Nevada, and Arizona. Even though it was early fall in San Francisco, summer was a fighting a delaying action in the Arizona city. With the temperature hovering in the middle nineties late into the afternoon, Harry was grateful for the field office air-conditioning.

Jacoby greeted them, and, after introducing Dixie, Harry followed the agent down a carpeted hallway to a conference room where a half dozen men dressed in black fatigues were gathered. Jacoby appeared more tanned and rugged than at the university when they talked. He offered Harry and Dixie chairs at the table and took a place at its head. He cleared his throat.

"All right, let's get started. First, I want you all to meet Dr. Harry Olson and his wife, Dixie, the other Dr. Olson." He waited for the nodding to stop before he continued. "They will be accompanying us on the raid. Harry is Dr. Harbaum's supervisor. Now about the operation. Bill, what's the latest?"

A man in his forties nodded and looked at a pad in front of him.

"The vehicles are ready and parked out back. The helicopter is waiting at Apache Junction. We will rendezvous there, make our way to where the road veers away from the Salt River, and queue up. The plan is to arrive at the cabin after dark, surround it, then move in at midnight. The chopper will provide illumination and cover from above. If she's there, we should take her into custody without much trouble."

"Very good, Bill," Jacoby said. "After she's cuffed, Dr. Olson wishes to speak with her before you take her to jail for booking. There's one other item." Jacoby's frown deepened. "Dr. Harbaum probably has an animal or some sort of creature in her possession. What it is exactly is difficult to explain, but it's of great scientific value. We need to take this animal alive if at all possible."

There were looks of confusion about the table.

"But, under no circumstances, are you to endanger your own life. Shoot to kill if necessary."

There was a soft murmuring among the agents, each one shooting glance at Harry.

"Anything else?" Jacoby said.

A young man with close-cropped dark hair raised an arm. "What is this creature, sir? Can you not say what it is?"

Jacoby shook his head and looked at Harry. "Dr. Olson," he said, "care to try and enlighten us? These men ought to know what they might encounter at the cabin."

Harry cleared his throat and glanced around the table. "Yes," he said, speaking slowly. "Dr. Harbaum has created what is called a chimera. This is an animal with the genes of two different animal species—in this instant, animal genes mixed with human genes. We don't really know at this point what its characteristics or capabilities are. My advice would be to be prepared for anything. There was a small travel cage missing from the facility, so it probably is confined in it."

There was slight murmuring around the table.

"Any other questions? If not, then let's move out."

The group of FBI agents loaded into three black Humvees and began the journey to the Superstition Mountains. They drove south through Scottsdale then took a diagonal shortcut eastward toward the mountains and Apache Junction. Finally, they left the haze of Phoenix behind, and Harry breathed the clean air, refreshed by it. At the rendezvous, Harry noticed the helicopter sitting idly in a vacant parking lot.

"I guess we're here," he said softly to Dixie.

"Won't be long now," she said.

"I don't have a good feeling about this," he said. "Too

much firepower. They need to let me go to the cabin by myself."

"Now that everyone's gathered here, you'll never convince them. It's a military operation."

"Sure looks like it," Harry said.

After making sure his agents were all synchronized with the plan, Jacoby and his men found the narrow road along the Salt River. The driver of Harry and Dixie's Humvee veered right and left in a vain attempt to avoid the large potholes that were numerous, some as large as their vehicle.

Off to their right, Harry marveled at the deep gullies and ravines filled with small puddles and dotted with flowers, Joshua trees, and cactus plants. The sun was low on the horizon, and, with the elevation gain, the temperatures dropped, leaving the promise of a cool evening. The eastern sky was turning a deep shade of purple. In the far distance, the dull outline of Webster Mountain, almost six thousand feet in elevation, was plainly visible.

As dusk evolved into night, they came to the place where the road turned away from Salt River and became a rutted, grass-covered lane. The Humvee convoy stopped. Jacoby passed MREs around, and the men and Dixie ate a hurried meal. When they were finished eating, they gathered around Jacoby's vehicle, his flashlight illuminating the map he spread out on the hood.

"According to Dr. Olson's directions and the map," he said, "this road meanders along a ravine for several miles and ends at the cabin. There is a prominent mound to the south of the cabin where we can set up surveillance. When ready, we'll call for the chopper, and it will flood the area with its searchlight. Then we'll move."

Harry and Dixie climbed back into their Humvee, and the convoy crept toward the cabin. Harry felt his pulse quicken. Dixie placed her hand in his and squeezed. In the dim light of the vehicle's console, he could tell her face bore a gaunt expression. Harry wished it had not come to this. How could he have been so wrong about Millie? As a graduate student, she was the ideal scientist—hard working, curious, diligent. Although he never considered her overtly personable, Dixie managed to develop a friendship with her and always found her willing to chat. Never standoffish. So what happened?

He knew full well the pressures of the academic life, the stress of having to publish in order to get ahead, to become recognized in one's field. Was that it? Had Millie become so involved with getting ahead that she lost sight of her morals, her character? As he had once done? Or was it a matter of simple curiosity borne out of that inquisitive mind of hers?

It no longer mattered, of course. The authorities now wanted her, and Cal Pacific's Board would nail her to a tree.

The lane wound first to the north then back to the east and, at times, Harry thought they were traveling in circles. At last, however, the convoy halted. It was dark, no moon, while a few wisps of clouds obscured a good portion of the stars. The only sounds were from the crickets and tree frogs. An occasional coyote howled in the distance.

The agents exited their vehicles, along with Harry and Dixie. Harry saw that the promontory Jacoby mentioned was a short hike farther to the east. He and Dixie fell into line behind the men as they trudged up the hill and took up a position behind a large group of boulders. By the time they stopped, Harry was breathing hard. Dixie was panting.

Harry scrambled to a point behind an outcropping and peered over the top.

Below, in a small clearing, was the cabin.

Alone. Dark.

Dixie crawled beside him to have a look. "There's no car down there, Harry," she said. "She's not there. Gone."

"Maybe she hid the car behind the cabin or elsewhere. But you're right. It doesn't look like she's there."

Jacoby scrambled to Harry's side. "What do you think?" he said in a low whisper.

"Looks like she's not there," Harry said.

"We'll know soon enough."

"What time is it?"

Jacoby looked at his watch. "Eleven fifty-two."

The men waited in the dark, talking only in hushed tones. The minutes ticked by. Harry prayed it would go well and end safely for Millie. If she was in the cabin.

Jacoby looked at his watch again. "Any minute now," he said.

As if on cue, Harry heard the distant drone of a helicopter moving closer from the west. At its sound, the agents readied their weapons and began the trek toward the cabin.

Chapter 20

When Millie woke that morning, she knew it was the day she had to leave. She didn't know why she knew, couldn't put her finger on it, but she knew nonetheless. A brief rain shower had moved over the mountains during the night, leaving the desert morning cool, fragrant, refreshed. Overnight, desert willow, catclaw acacia, and evening primrose burst into bloom, flooding the cabin area with color. The perfumed air tickled Millie's nose while she loaded her car.

She led Roku to the car and put him in the back seat. He signed to her, *"Going for ride?"*

"Yes, Roku," she signed back, *"we're going for a ride. Going to live somewhere else."*

Roku continued to sign. *"I'm hungry. Can we eat?"*

"I'm sorry. We'll get something to eat on the road. We just need to get away from here."

More signing. *"Why? Is anything wrong?"*

"Why? I don't know. I just have a feeling we need to leave. Now stay in the back seat and settle down."

Millie returned to the cabin to gather the last of their belongings. After stowing them in the trunk, she climbed behind the wheel and started her car. During the process of packing, the idea came to her that San Francisco was the place to hide out—she was familiar with the city, and it was large enough that they should not be recognized—if she could find a place for Roku and her to stay.

A weak sun peeked over the hills behind her as Millie headed toward Apache Junction. Clouds from the previous night's storm still lingered low, in scattered billows, and the air was cool and crisp. Her car, an ancient Ford with worn tires, bumped over the rutted dirt road, causing her to worry what she would do in the event of a flat. She glanced in the rear view mirror and noticed Weaver's Needle behind her. Roku soon fell asleep in the back seat, his heavy breathing slow and regular. She returned her attention to dodging the numerous ruts and small boulders that lined the narrow roadway.

San Francisco, that was where she would go. She made a quick mental calculation and figured she could be there by nightfall, pending any unnecessary delays. Once at Apache Junction, she would be able to drive much faster and, from Phoenix, it would be interstate all the way, skirting the northern edge of Los Angeles. At Pasadena, she would turn northwest, travel through the San Joaquin Valley into San Francisco. At least that was how she remembered it. She would have to consult her map later when she stopped for lunch.

The road that paralleled the Salt River was wider but more tortuous. The sun was directly in her rear view mirror, making it difficult to see the road, but soon it curved southwest, and she stopped squinting. She hated to leave the quiet peace of her father's cabin, for she felt it offered a certain isolation and security she wouldn't find anywhere else, but she had an uneasy feeling about remaining another day. She thought about calling her father from Apache Junction but decided to wait until she was closer to San Francisco. She struggled with whether she should tell him what was happening with her and Roku.

Hopefully, all he knew was what she told him— that she was on a much-needed vacation from her work at the primate facility—unless the police were already looking for her and had called him. Her stay in the Superstition Mountains with Roku was enjoyable, with her managing to increase his vocabulary and signing ability. He was actually able to sign in simple sentences. The mountains were a peaceful respite from the stress of her job at the primate facility, but it was work taking care of the little chimera. But never far from her mind was the unsettling knowledge that they were running from the university and the law.

She had stolen Roku. He was university property.

So when she awoke that morning with an uneasy feeling that, if they didn't leave the cabin, they would be apprehended, she would wind up in jail—and who knew what would happen to Roku?—it was an easy decision to pack up and leave but one she hoped she wouldn't regret down the line. He father might be a different story. Would he understand when he heard the complete story from her? She hoped so. Her mother, she knew, would be in her corner, but her father was much more pragmatic and not given to hasty or emotional conclusions. It might require a face-to-face meeting to win him over.

At Apache Junction, the road turned to asphalt, and Millie pushed the accelerator to the floor. As she sped toward Phoenix, Roku stirred, and she shot a quick glance at him signing from the rear seat.

"Yes, Roku," she said, "we'll stop for breakfast in a little while."

"*Where are we going?*" he signed.

"*To California. San Francisco.*" She knew he wouldn't understand the concepts of cities and states.

"*Why?*"

Millie gave up trying to sign and drive at the same

time. "So you won't be taken back and put in that cage," she said, trying to keep one eye on the road and the other on Roku and his signing.

"*I'm hungry. I want to stop.*"

"We can't stop right now, it isn't safe. I promise, Roku, we'll stop very soon." Millie was losing patience with Roku's infantile insistence. In spite of the fact that the chimera now weighed close to a hundred pounds, he still possessed an immature personality. During the past month, Millie realized that although Roku's brain was advanced and possessed human intelligence, he was, in many ways, still a primate. His baser tendencies were definitely in the animal realm, and her primary focus, besides developing his language skills, had been an attempt to modify Roku's instinctual behavior. So far, she wasn't sure she was making progress.

"*But I want to stop. I want to stop and eat.*"

Millie slowed and signed. "*Roku, sit down and be quiet. We will stop and eat soon.*"

"Now be quiet!" she yelled. With her voice raised, Millie almost drove off the road. Roku was beginning to get under her skin. She was going to have to feed him or risk an accident.

⁊⁊⁊

Harry looked at his watch. Twelve-oh-one a.m. Below the small promontory, he saw a column of FBI agents running single file toward the cabin, their weapons at the ready. He nudged Dixie who was crouched beside him.

"Let's go," he said.

The two scrambled from their position and hurried to catch up with the agents who fanned out as they got closer to the dark cabin. The drone of the helicopter grew louder, suddenly appearing over a ridge, and descended to a clearing behind the cabin. Harry had Dixie's hand in his, and soon they were both panting hard. The ground was uneven, and Dixie had trouble keeping up. She stumbled several times, forcing Harry to wait while she regained her footing. The cabin loomed ahead, quiet and dark.

In a matter of seconds, the agents stormed the cabin. They bolted onto the small porch and, with a loud crash, burst through the door. Suddenly, the cabin was filled with light and FBI agents. As Harry led Dixie to the porch, they met Jacoby coming from inside.

"Not here," Jacoby said. "Gone. And by the emptiness of the cabin, they won't be returning. Damn."

Special Agent Jacoby returned his .40 caliber pistol to his shoulder holster and ambled to the other agents of the strike team who had assembled at the far end of the cabin, their headlamps casting eerie shafts of light through the darkness. Harry and Dixie stood alone to one side of the group. Harry wondered what the next plan was to be. Dixie put an arm around his. He felt its warmth.

"What do you think?" she said, giving his arm a gentle squeeze.

"I dunno. She's gone, obviously. But where?"

"And why? Why would she take off like this?"

"To save Roku's life, Dixie. She ran to save its life."

Harry led his wife back up the hill to the promontory where the FBI vehicles were parked. As they returned to the Phoenix field office, Dixie wasn't satisfied with Harry's explanation.

"Not just to save its life, Harry," she said as they rode through the darkness. "The creature has her DNA in it. It is part Millie Harbaum."

"This is too confusing," Harry said. "Hard to wrap my brain around it."

"I used the term creature," Dixie said, "but it is really

a chimera, part animal, part human. It is an earth-shattering accomplishment and one Millie wants the world to acknowledge."

"She's after fame?"

"No, I don't believe so. Few women are motivated by personal fame or fortune. I think it is much deeper, a sincere desire to advance mankind's knowledge."

"Why do you say that?" Harry glanced out the Humvee's window and watched the dark shadows of the Superstition Mountains recede behind them.

"I got to know Millie after our Yeti escaped and during the search for them. She was devastated by their deaths. She was deeply committed to her work at the facility. With her, it was all about the science."

"Do you think this chimera should be destroyed?" Harry said.

"Roku is its name," Dixie said. "I don't know. I have a moral dilemma where that is concerned. Lots of people would say Millie was tinkering with something best left alone. Playing God and all that. On the other hand, Roku is part human. So doesn't that make it in possession of certain rights? After all, if certain unborn fetuses have the right to live, why not Roku? One could argue that half its genetic makeup is human."

"So, where do you come down on whether or not it should be destroyed?" Dixie had the unnerving habit of dancing around a question.

"I think, right now, until we have more information, I would opt for allowing it to live."

"The cause of science trumps morality?"

"Not necessarily. But, for now, I don't think we should rush in and kill it just because we don't understand everything or have all the moral or ethical answers. We can always do it later."

"Later would make it harder. And how do we know

Millie doesn't have other genetically engineered fetuses frozen somewhere at the facility? There could be more chimeras just waiting to be thawed and implanted in a chimp. How do we know what she was planning?"

Dixie put her hand in Harry's.

"All the more reason to find her," she said. "And we need to do it before these law enforcement goons find her, don't you think?"

Harry nodded. In the distance, he could make out the vague shadows of eastern Phoenix. Behind them, the sky turned an inky gray. Dawn wasn't far off.

"We should talk with her parents," he said. "In person. Her father seemed reasonable when I called him earlier."

"As a dentist, he should understand the science involved."

"Since I am no longer employed by the university, I think we should fly to Toledo and speak to Millie's parents. They might have an idea where she could be heading. She might have called them after leaving the cabin."

"Good idea," Dixie said. "I still can't believe Cal Pacific just up and terminated you. Those bastards. After all you have done for the university. They're nothing more than a bunch of slimy lowlifes. I hope they get what's coming to them."

Harry chuckled and patted Dixie's hand.

"Bastards," he said. "Your favorite word for them."

"Can I help it if that's what they are?"

"Now, now, honey. They did what they thought they had to do. But, I admit, it was a shock. We're free. We've got some money saved. Let's find Millie."

"And if, and when, we do? What then?"

"We'll cross that bridge when we get there."

The eastern sky was a smear of orange and red when they arrived at the Phoenix FBI field office. Harry and Dixie shook hands with Jacoby and drove to the airport.

After parking their car in the long-term lot, they carried their bags into the Sky Harbor International Airport and purchased tickets to Toledo. Once they were airborne, Harry looked at Dixie who proffered weak smile. He settled back in his seat and watched the stewardesses begin their rounds.

What was he doing? He was without a job, had a wife to support, and had no idea where or when his next paycheck was coming. His career was all but finished, and his professional reputation would soon be ruined.

He didn't know it, but things would get much worse.

Chapter 21

Toledo, Ohio, was situated on the western end of Lake Erie, possessing a border with the state of Michigan. The city was founded in 1833, on the west bank of the Maumee River. Since those early days, Toledo grew quickly as a result of the Miami and Erie Canal and its position on the railway line between New York and Chicago.

After renting a car at the Toledo Express Airport, Harry and Dixie drove to Dr. and Mrs. Harbaum's home, located on the city's east side in the upscale neighborhood of Northwood. The traffic was heavy on the Interstate but thinned somewhat after they crossed the Maumee River and turned north. Northwood was a housing addition set among tall, stately trees and the homes were on large well-manicured lots. Upon arriving in Toledo, Harry had phoned Dr. Harbaum and told him of their desire to discuss his daughter and the dentist was more than accommodating. He would leave his practice early and await their arrival with his wife.

Dixie gave directions while Harry drove and when they pulled up the house Harry's mouth dropped open. A serpentine drive led the way to the two-story brick and stone home and was bordered by a well-trimmed hedge.

Towering oaks provided shade, and the entire massive home was edged with flowering shrubs Harry could not identify. A sunroom with large windows was at one end of the home. Harry parked the car, and he and Dixie walked to the front door.

Before he could ring the doorbell, the door opened, and a tall, gray-haired man greeted them in his fifties. He wore a gray cardigan sweater and a smile. "Dr. Olson?" he said. "Please come in. And Mrs—Dr. Olson. Gosh," he stammered, "I've never met a husband and wife doctor team before."

Harbaum ushered Harry and Dixie into a large library just beyond the marbled entry where a woman rose from a leather sofa.

"This is my wife, Harriet," Harbaum said.

"And please," Harry said, "call me Harry and my wife is Dixie."

"Very nice to meet you both," Mrs. Harbaum said. "May I offer you some refreshment? Coffee, soda, something a little harder, perhaps?"

"Diet soda would be nice," Dixie said.

Harbaum crossed the room and opened a large cabinet revealing a bar complete with sink, icemaker, and glassware.

"I was just about to fix myself a drink, Harry. Name your poison."

"Scotch is fine. With a little water, please," he said.

While Harbaum mixed the drinks, his wife poured Dixie's soda into a crystal old-fashioned glass and handed it to her. When everyone was seated and sipping their drinks, Harbaum spoke.

"So, Harry, this visit concerns our daughter, Millie. Correct? I pray she is not in any trouble."

Harry noticed that, at the word trouble, Mrs. Harbaum winced. The library was an oak -paneled room lined with books. In a far corner stood an antique desk with a laptop sitting on it. The walls were decorated with numerous paintings, Harry assumed were original works, and a few photographs of what he assumed were of the Harbaum family.

"I'm afraid, sir, she is. I wanted to chat with you before the authorities came calling." He took a sip of his scotch and waited for his words to sink in before continuing. The Harbaums sat silent, attentive. "As you know, I am Millie's advisor and major professor, which means I am responsible for her work at Cal Pacific. At least, I was."

"Was?" Harbaum interrupted.

"Yes. I'll get to that shortly. John, may I call you John? Fine. John and Harriet, your daughter created an organism when she was working at the Primate Research Facility in Nevada."

"Yes, we know," Mrs. Harbaum said. "She wrote us of her work there. My husband and I are both very proud of her."

"And rightly so," Harry continued. "However, this organism Millie created...well, nothing like it has ever been done before. Objections to it have arisen purely because of ethical and moral reasons. Millie, unbeknownst to me or anyone at the facility, created a chimera. It is an organism that contains both animal and human DNA. The animal DNA came from the Yeti that had been housed at the facility who escaped and were killed. The human DNA came from Millie herself."

Harry paused. Harbaum's face had turned dour, the lines in his face much deeper.

"From our daughter?" he said.

Harry nodded. "She implanted the embryo into one of our chimps, and earlier this year the chimera was born. We didn't know what it was until Millie confessed a few months ago and admitted to what she had done. Her experiment crossed all present moral and ethical boundaries in doing scientific research, and it was our president's and my decision to destroy the chimera."

The Harbaums sat, as if stunned by the news. Mrs. Harbaum was rigid, her hands folded in her lap.

"I believe Millie panicked upon learning this, for she disappeared and has taken the chimera with her."

"So that is what she was doing at our cabin in Arizona," Mrs. Harbaum said. "Hiding out?"

"Yes," Harry said. He took a gulp of his scotch and set the glass on the table next to him. "Dixie and I were with the FBI when they raided your cabin and discovered she was not there. She was gone. To where, no one knows."

"That is why we have come to you," Dixie said, speaking for the first time. "We want to find her before the authorities do. If we can, maybe we can spare her a lot of unpleasantness."

"I see," Harbaum said, nodding.

"If you have any idea where she could have gone or have heard from her, I would appreciate the information," Harry continued. "I care for Millie and feel responsible for her."

Mrs. Harbaum stood and refreshed Dixie's drink. She looked as if she had aged ten years in the past half hour. Her eyes had dark circles around them, and Harry noticed they were glistening. *Tears*, he thought.

"You said you were responsible for her work, Dr. Olson," she said.

"Yes," Harry said.

"If you were responsible," Mrs. Harbaum said, "why is it that you knew nothing of her work?" Her tone sounded to take a defensive one.

"I suppose I should have, ma'am," Harry said. "But I am not one to micromanage my staff and Millie was a full-fledged faculty member. I trusted her. Simply put, she betrayed that trust."

"I see," Mrs. Harbaum said and sat back in her chair.

"As a result of this travesty, I am no longer employed by the university. My position there was terminated a few days ago. My wife quit her position as well."

"On account of Millie's actions?" Harbaum said. "This chimera thing?"

"Partly. But it's a long story, one that need not be repeated here. Suffice it to say, Dixie and I want to find her. The sooner, the better."

Harbaum rose and refreshed his drink.

"Neither my wife nor I have heard from Millie," he said, "since she called asking if she could stay at the cabin. I believe you are sincere, Harry, and wish to help our daughter. If we knew anything, we would tell you. Please believe me."

"I do, John, I do. Now, Dixie and I must return to San Francisco, as we have to clear our belongings from the university. I will give you our cell phone numbers, and I want you to call either of us if you hear from Millie. And I'll be checking in with you from time to time as well. When the FBI talk to you just tell them the truth."

"Should I mention your visit today?"

"Of course. Everyone wants Millie found safe and unharmed."

After leaving the Harbaums, Harry and Dixie took the redeye flight to Phoenix then drove back home to San Mateo.

Arriving at dawn, they both collapsed into bed, and soon Dixie was asleep. But Harry was troubled. If he could find Millie and Roku, maybe he could save his job and salvage his career.

❦❦❦

Dr. Miles Radner pushed through the airlock and strolled into the Animal Care Unit. It was early in the morning, and only a few technicians were at work cleaning the numerous cages and other housing facilities. He found Millie's small office at the end of the hall and clicked on her computer. After entering his administrator's password, he navigated to the facility's web page and entered Millie's password. A list of files appeared on the screen. Radner found the one entitled, Project Tika and attempted to open it. However, it was encrypted, and the file would not open. He scanned her other files, and all seemed in order, dedicated to her work on the Yeti genome.

Frustrated with his inability to get into the Project Tika file, Radner wandered through the unit in search of Gerald Siscom. The veterinarian might have an idea about how to get into and read the file.

He found the man sitting behind a mound of papers in his small, cluttered office. Siscom smiled when he looked up and noticed Radner in the doorway.

"Come in, Miles," he said. "I just made some coffee. Care for some?"

"Not right now, Gerald," Radner said, still standing in the doorway. "I have been trying to gain access to Millie's computer files on her chimera project, but it seems to be encrypted. I hoped you might be of help."

"I do have the encryption password here, somewhere. Let me find it." Siscom began rummaging through a desk drawer. "Millie wanted her notes kept a secret, even from me, but she trusted me with the password. I never looked into her computer."

"Well, the FBI is dropping by later, and I want to cover all bases before I meet with them. Since she has disappeared, I don't see the harm. Besides, her work and her computer are the property of Cal Pacific." Radner entered the office and took a seat opposite the veterinarian.

"I understand," Siscom said. He retrieved a small notebook and thumbed through it. "Ah, here it is."

Radner led the way back to Millie's computer whereupon Siscom entered the password, and Project Tika sprang onto the screen.

As he read through Millie's private notes, Radner felt like a voyeur, but now that the authorities wanted her, it was necessary. When Special Agent Hank Jacoby arrived, he needed to have as much information as possible.

"Any of this make sense to you, Gerald?" Radner said.

Siscom looked over his shoulder while he thumbed through the file. "Most of it looks like background information. Plus a lot of her scientific musing."

Radner continued perusing the file until he came upon a section different from the previous one.

"Look here, Gerald. Now she has information on how to inject DNA into a cell, how to freeze and keep embryos, articles on in vitro fertilization."

"She's getting more serious now," Siscom said. "She's beginning to formulate an idea."

"Yeah, she's starting to develop the specifics."

"Look at the date on those files, Miles. Two years ago. Wow."

Looking closer, Radner saw that Siscom was right. The files, he noticed, were dated almost two years previous, which meant Millie was thinking of this experiment soon after her arrival at the facility.

"Good grief," he said, his voice showing a surprised tone. "So, all during the time of the Yeti research and subsequent escape and annihilation she was plotting her chimera project. It's hard to believe."

Siscom took a chair next to Radner, not uttering a word.

"Did you know any of this, Gerald? You worked with her on the fertilization of the chimp. How did she assemble all this specialized equipment in order to accomplish the DNA insertion?"

"Most of this equipment is all part of a general genetics lab, Miles. So the stuff was already here, like the reverse phase microscope, the injectors, micropipettes, and the like. And I thought she was using IVF to form a Yeti embryo. At least that was what she led me to believe. Until I saw an ultrasound of Tika's fetus late in the pregnancy."

"Go on."

"When I saw that ultrasound, I knew I wasn't looking at a normal Yeti pregnancy, so I confronted Millie about it. She admitted that she had used her own DNA in the implanted Yeti egg. She begged me to remain silent about it until after Roku's delivery. After the chimera's birth, Harry, you, and Dr. Pauling became aware of what she had done."

Radner fell back in his chair. He felt betrayed. How could he have been so naive? How could he have allowed this to happen? Why hadn't he more closely supervised the new scientist?

"We should have destroyed it straight away," Radner said. "By not doing so, we allowed this unfortunate situation to escalate. We now find ourselves involved in a nationwide search for a criminal and a beastly creature mankind is ill prepared to confront or contemplate."

Chapter 22

D r. Reginald Pauling looked across his massive desk into the flashing blue eyes of Dr. Chloe Rawlings, director of Cal Pacific's DNA laboratory. The woman's striking beauty always took him off his guard and left him fumbling for words. Her blonde hair fell in soft curls over her shoulders, and she wore a white lab coat over her khaki slacks and a blue blouse that matched her eyes. He picked up a pen and toyed with it.

"I am always glad to see you, Dr. Rawlings," he said, fidgeting with the pen. He swallowed and realized his mouth was dry, so he took a swallow of coffee.

"I am here to protest Dr. Olson's firing," Reginald," she said, using his first name. "You caved under the trustee's pressure when you should have had more backbone. I am disappointed in you."

"Believe me, Dr. Rawlings," Pauling said after choking down his irritation, "there was nothing I could do. I appealed to their better judgment, but it was not enough. Trust me, I am as sick as you are over this state of affairs."

"State of affairs, Reginald? Is that what you call it—a state of affairs? I would call it a travesty. You lost two brilliant scientists because of what? A stupid secret experiment by a young, inexperienced faculty member, the result of which no one could foretell? Where no one on Cal Pacific's staff bothered to act as a mentor and help with her transition to the faculty. Cal Pacific University is much the worse today because you refused to back your faculty. I can assure you that fact is not lost on those of us who remain."

Pauling's head pounded and a vein in his neck throbbed. He was near to losing his temper, but he took a deep breath and calmed himself. Through the window behind him, a bright sun caused the waves on San Francisco Bay to sparkle like tiny diamonds on a dark blue cloth. How he wished he were fishing.

"Dr. Rawlings," he said finally, more under control, "I appreciate your sentiment, I truly do. And I understand your and other's frustration with the way things have gone with the Olsons. Once again, there was nothing more I could have done."

"Well, Reginald," Chloe said, her blue eyes flashing, her brow knitted. "There is something I can do. I can find work anywhere, I know that. And I can take my million-dollar NIH grant with me. I'm sure my grad students would follow as well. That's what I can do in protest. And who knows? There might be others who feel as I do."

"I—I—" Pauling stammered. "Please—"

"I must return to my lab," Chloe said, standing. "I hope you will spend some time to reflect on what the Olsons mean to our university and reconsider. Good day."

Dr. Rawlings abruptly turned and left the office, leaving behind the vague hint of her perfume. Pauling tossed the pen he had been toying with onto his desk and stood. He paced the office, dazed by Dr. Rawlings's aggressive posture. Had she threatened him with her resignation? Not really but the implication was there, nonetheless. He couldn't have a mass resignation on his hands. What would the trustees think of his leadership?

ℰↃℰↃ

Chinatown was part of San Francisco's cultural history, dating its origin to the middle 1800s. It was the oldest Chinatown in North America and the largest outside Asia. Millie found a small walkup one-room apartment for rent around the corner from her place of employment, Mr. Ling Wu, Chinese acupuncturist. Finding a cheap place to live had been difficult, and Chinatown had the only apartment she thought she could afford. She had answered an ad by Mr. Wu who had been impressed by her intelligence and hired her on the spot. He knew of the walkup apartment around the corner, introduced her to the landlord living below, and she rented it. She kept Roku in the car out of sight until she had been given the key.

The apartment was furnished with what Millie called dilapidated Americana. It had a ragged sofa, chrome and linoleum kitchen table, and an antique gas stove. The sofa pulled out into a bed, and a sink stood in a far corner. The landlord provided a few dishes and cooking implements that allowed Millie to cook their meals most evenings.

Each morning, she would fix Roku and herself breakfast before walking the two blocks to work. She left him alone in the apartment with food and water. In the evening, when she returned, she cooked their dinner and, after dark, took Roku for a walk. She kept to the alleyways and the nearby park in order to remain out of sight. It wouldn't do for anyone to spot the chimera.

Millie dyed her hair a different color and wore no

makeup in an attempt to disguise her looks. She bought a newspaper each afternoon and studied it for headlines about her and Roku, but none appeared. Each day became a boring routine with helping Mr. Wu in his acupuncture practice and looking after Roku in the evenings where she continued to work on his language skills. Roku could sign in longer sentences and could read Millie's sign language. She was amazed at how quickly his vocabulary increased. She wondered if he would ever be able to speak. He was well over a hundred pounds, and no longer could she physically discipline him.

✿✿✿

Harry and Dixie were sitting on their patio and enjoying the sunset. They were discussing where they both might find employment and Millie's disappearance when Harry's cell phone rang.

"Harry, it's Miles Radner," the voice on the other end railed.

"Miles," Harry said. "I didn't expect to hear from you."

"We haven't talked since Millie and the creature went missing. I'm calling to offer my condolences for what has happened to you and Dixie. I couldn't believe it when I heard. It's ungrateful is what it is. Pauling should have his head examined."

"I appreciate the sentiment, Miles. So does Dixie. It's just one of those things. I wasn't able to deal effectively with one of our young faculty members, mainly Millie. First, a graduate assistant is killed at your facility, and then Millie goes and does something like this. Failed leadership on my part."

"Hogwash," Radner exclaimed. "I told Pauling as much. And so did Chloe Rawlings. I understand she really let him have it with both barrels. Threatened to quit and take her grant money with her."

Harry let out a low whistle.

"So you see, you may have lost the battle, but the war is not over, not by a long shot."

"Thanks for the kind words, Miles. And thank Chloe for Dixie and me. She was always a true friend. She and Dr. Kesler were very close before he died."

"We could do with his calm leadership right now," Radner said. "He had a way that could sway the most obstinate trustee."

"He did indeed."

"Harry, the reason I called is Gerald Siscom and I were going through Millie's computer files, and we found something interesting. She listed a Stanley Eagleton as someone who provided much needed expertise in DNA transplantation. He's a professor at Harvard Medical School in Boston. Ever heard of him?"

"No," Harry replied. "Can't say that I have."

"You might give this Dr. Eagleton a call. He might shed some light on Millie's whereabouts. Who knows? His number was in her computer."

Harry jotted the number down while Radner continued to chat.

"I don't get many chances to leave the mountain," he said, "so you and Dixie need to come out here and visit. You both are always welcome."

"Thanks, Miles. Your call has meant a lot."

After hanging up, Dixie came and stood by his side.

"What did he want?" she said.

"To say he was sorry for what happened and that he told Pauling he had made a mistake. So did Chloe Rawlings, by the way."

"Good for her."

"Radner said she threatened to leave and take her grant

with her."

"That's telling him. Think she'll do it?"

"Who knows? He also gave me a lead on someone who knew what Millie was planning, was a consultant, apparently. Gave me his phone number."

"Who is it?"

"Dr. Stanley Eagleton. He's at Harvard Medical School."

"Never heard of him."

"Neither have I, but I thought I would call him in the morning."

In the morning after breakfast, Harry managed to get Eagleton on the phone and the two men talked a long while. After he finished, Dixie peppered him with questions.

"Well, what did he have to say?"

"Not a whole lot."

"What do you mean? You two chatted for a half hour. What did you learn?"

"That we need to go see the man. He couldn't or wouldn't relay anything over the phone, but he said he had been worried about Millie for quite a while. He could tell us more about it in person. I told him we'd be there the day after tomorrow."

"This isn't sounding good," Dixie said. "I'll go throw some things together in our bags if you want to call for airline tickets. No, this doesn't sound good at all."

Dixie disappeared into the house and left Harry on the patio. In the dark, he could just make out the phosphorescent waves on the bay. A weak moon was up, and the bay itself looked dark and foreboding.

He had spent the morning on the phone calling a number of colleagues and inquiring about faculty positions. Fortunately, his reputation with the Yeti was one that other universities coveted, and his call had yielded a few promising leads. Maybe finding work would be easier than he thought. It was Dixie he was really worried about. Finding a position for her alongside him might prove difficult, especially in hard financial times, such as the present.

Radner's call had been a surprise. Although the man was somewhat of a jerk, he was a benign jerk. His offer to resign as Director of the Primate Research Facility when the Yeti escaped proved he possessed a sense of honor and integrity. Harry had torn up the man's resignation letter and his show of support now that Harry was down was encouraging.

Millie, of course, was a different story. She could be anywhere with Roku. But then again, where does one go with a chimera? How was the creature acting? Could it speak? Interact with humans? Calculate? He wondered. If Roku possessed these faculties, didn't that entitle him to be considered as part human? But how human? What determined if an organism was human? Part human? Just because an organism had forty-six chromosomes did that make it human? What percentage of human DNA would make one human? Harry knew the partial answer.

If human and chimp DNA was ninety-eight-point-eight percent the same, why were humans so different? Numbers told part of the story. Each human cell contained roughly three billion base pairs, or bits of information. Just one-point-two percent of that equaled about thirty-five million differences. Some of these had a big impact, others didn't. And even two identical stretches of DNA could work differently—they could be activated in different amounts, in different places, or at different times.

Although humans and chimps had many identical genes, they often used them in different ways. A gene's activity, or expression, could be turned up or down like the volume on a radio. So the same gene could be turned up high in humans, but very low in chimps.

The same genes were expressed in the same brain regions in humans, chimps, and gorillas, but in different amounts. Thousands or millions of differences like these affected brain development and function and helped explain why the human brain was larger and smarter.

The chimpanzee immune system was surprisingly similar to human. Most viruses that caused diseases like AIDS and hepatitis could also infect chimpanzees. But the malaria parasite *Plasmodium falciparum*, which a mosquito transmitted through its bite into human blood, didn't infect chimps. A small DNA difference made human red blood cells vulnerable to this parasite, while chimp blood cells were resistant.

If the chimera were captured alive, it would necessarily have to be left to the courts to decide how much human it was and what to do with it. Exterminate it or allow it to live. He knew one thing.

He couldn't decide.

Chapter 23

Harvard Medical School was located between the Mission Hill district of Boston and the Charles River to the north. Harry and Dixie rode a Metro Cab taxi from Logan Airport to the medical school. As they sped along Huntington Avenue, they chatted idly in the rear seat until the driver veered off the freeway and onto a crowded side street.

He stopped on Shattuck Street opposite the lawn in front of the medical school building. The 1906 Beaux Arts complex comprised five imposing structures on a twenty-six acre site, with one building for administration and four for laboratories, grouped in a U-shaped quadrangle around a long open-ended court. The complex's white Dorset marble exterior was said to have been intended for the New York Public Library. The medical school building proper was a three-story marble and granite affair with six Greek columns in its facade.

They crossed the tree-lined quadrangle, entered the building, and quickly found Dr. Stanley Eagleton's office. He was head of Harvard's Human Disease Genome Project, dedicated to sequencing the genome of patient's with heritable disorders and building a database available to all medical practitioners.

They waited in a cramped office so typical of professionals engaged in academic pursuits. Next door was Eagleton's lab and the sounds of various machines humming made Harry think of Chloe Rawlings's laboratory. A short, squat secretary typed on a computer terminal and now and then the woman shot Harry a look and smiled.

A tall, thin man breezed into the office, glanced at the secretary, and approached Harry and Dixie. He was young, in his thirties, wore an open-necked shirt over a rumpled lab coat. Coming closer, he extended his hand.

"Dr. Olson, I presume," he said in a deep graveled voice. "I'm Stanley Eagleton."

Harry stood and shook hands.

"Nice to meet you," he said. "And this is my wife, Dr. Dixie Olson. We are pleased you were able to meet with us."

Eagleton took Dixie's hand and held it for a moment.

"Married doctors, eh?" he said with a chuckle. "Rare in our business. Please come into my office." Directing his attention to the secretary, he said, "Mary, bring us some coffee, please."

Eagleton ushered Harry and Dixie into his office, the usual space filled with books, journals, computer, microscope, and a large screen television. Mary followed carrying three cups of coffee that she set on the desk.

The Harvard doctor ambled to a chair behind his desk while Harry and Dixie seated themselves in wooden chairs opposite him. Once they were seated, Eagleton lit a pipe.

"My only remaining vice," he said between puffs, "besides good bourbon. Now, on the phone, you mentioned Millie Harbaum. She was working for you, correct?"

Harry cleared his throat and leaned forward in his chair. "*Was* is the operative word, Dr. Eagleton."

Eagleton held up a hand in protest.

"Please," he said. "Can we not be on first names here? Call me Stanley."

"Thank you, Stanley," Harry said. "As I mentioned on the phone, I am—or was—the chairman of the anthropology department at California Pacific University. Millie was the associate director of our Primate Research Facility located in Nevada. Originally, as a graduate student, she worked to sequence the genomes of a pair of Yeti we had brought from Mongolia."

"Yes," Eagleton said. "It was in all the journals. Quite an accomplishment." He turned to Dixie. "And you were part of this project, Dixie?"

"I was a member of the two expeditions that discovered the Yeti and brought them to the States," she said. "But Millie was working on her own project after obtaining her doctorate."

"She was under my responsibility," Harry said, after a sip of his coffee. "Millie was a new faculty member. As such, ultimately she was my responsibility."

"You keep using the word was Harry. The past tense."

"I am no longer employed by Cal Pacific."

"Because of Millie's actions?"

"Partly. It's a long story."

"My husband has been unfairly terminated," Dixie said, placing a hand on Harry's arm. "I resigned in protest. We need to locate Millie and her chimera. For Harry's sake as well as her own."

"Stanley," Harry said, "what can you tell us about Millie? On the phone you mentioned you communicated with her." He hoped for something, anything the man could tell them that might shed light on Millie's whereabouts.

"Yes, we talked a number of times, emailed each other also. She wanted information on the techniques of inserting DNA material into cells and cultivating the resulting embryos. The simplest way bacteria can take up foreign DNA is through transformation, a technique used very frequently in molecular biology labs. In this technique, bacteria take up purified DNA through chemical and heat shock. Bacterial cell walls do not normally allow DNA in and must be made competent to take up DNA. Treating bacteria with calcium chloride makes them take up water and DNA, and a subsequent heat shock activates genes that help bacteria recover from the calcium chloride treatment."

"It's not the only possibility, I take it," Harry said.

Eagleton shifted in his chair, puffed on his pipe a few tomes. "No, in the process of bacterial conjugation, bacteria transfer native plasmids, small circular pieces of DNA, to other bacteria. This technique can be harnessed in the molecular biology laboratory to insert a DNA sequence of interest into bacteria. Like animal cells, bacteria have viruses that can infect them. Bacterial viruses are called bacteriophages. The life cycle of a bacteriophage involves the insertion of the bacteriophage's DNA into the host cell DNA, followed by removal of the bacteriophage DNA when the phage is ready to reproduce itself. Bacteriophage insertion is known as transduction. Generalized transduction is used to insert foreign DNA into bacterial cells in laboratories.

"Finally, mammalian cells can be made to take up foreign DNA through two methods, both of which are called transfection. Chemical transfection involves treating cells with a chemical like calcium phosphate, which allows them to take up DNA by a mechanism that isn't understood. Another method involves using viruses to insert foreign DNA in a manner similar to bacterial transduction. This method is called virus-mediated transfection, or simply transduction."

"Very complicated," Dixie said. "Millie was interested in all of this?"

"She was primarily interested in the microinjection method. She said her facility had an inverted phase contrast microscope and monitor and she was able to find the autoinjector for use with micropipettes. I gave her some pointers on using the very small micropipettes to physically puncture a cell and inject the DNA material into it. During microinjection, DNA is injected directly into the cell, or even into the cell nucleus via an inserted cannula. The process is observed on a monitor and controlled with the microscope. The technique is easy once learned but does take some practice as one is working with small single cells. The DNA is then integrated into the animal genome during the cell's own DNA repair processes."

"Is it a common procedure?" Harry said.

"More and more it is, yes. The beauty is that not a lot of expensive equipment is needed in order to be successful. All one needs is a microscope, a micromanipulator, micropipettes, and a microinjector. Which, I learned, was available at her facility. Bingo, after some practice, you can make all the DNA transfers you want. Assuming you have a purified DNA solution."

"We have a complete DNA sequencing lab at the primate facility, so Millie was well versed in genetic research techniques." Harry leaned forward again and gulped his remaining coffee. "I'm not surprised that she was able to develop the technique by herself in a short period of time. She's a very talented scientist."

"Dr. Eagleton, Stanley, I'm sorry," Dixie said, "do you have any idea where Millie might have gone?"

"So she actually created a chimera, did she? Your Yeti DNA and who else's?"

"Her own," Harry said.

Eagleton set his pipe in an ashtray and stood. He

strolled around his desk and paced the small office.

"You mean there's a chimera out there somewhere that is part Yeti and part Millie?"

"I'm afraid so," Harry said.

"Why, it's outlandish." Eagleton stared at Harry, his mouth open. It was as if the full impact of what Millie had done finally hit him. "I don't believe it. I refuse to believe it. I can't believe it."

"It's true," Dixie said in a voice barely above a whisper.

The Harvard doctor returned to his chair and fell into it, silent for a while.

"She had a boyfriend once," he said finally. "She left him cause he roughed her up. I believe it was when she worked for the State of California in Sacramento a long time ago. Name of George…let me see…I don't remember his last name. George…Trench, that's it. George Trench. But he may no longer reside in Sacramento. Could be anywhere."

Harry stood, and Dixie followed. He held out his hand.

"Thanks, Stanley," he said, shaking Eagleton's hand. "We'll be going. Thanks for your time and information."

"My pleasure, Harry. You and Dixie come back soon and let me give you the grand tour. And I hope you find Millie soon."

∽∾∽∾

Back in San Mateo Harry hurriedly answered a few emails regarding inquiries he made about employment. The most intriguing was a positive response from the Institute for American Antiquities, a nonprofit concern who underwrote archeological expeditions around the globe. Their director recently retired, and they were searching for her replacement. Harry scribbled a quick reply, sending his resume, while Dixie busied herself with household chores.

As he listened to Dixie's humming in the next room, Harry searched the Internet for a George Trench in Sacramento. He found several listed. When his wife returned, he closed his laptop.

"I found several people named George Trench living in Sacramento, honey. Tomorrow we should drive up there and check them out."

"How do we know if they are still living there?" she asked. "The Internet is notorious for not having up-to-date information."

"It's all we have to go on at present. We might get lucky."

"How many years ago did Millie know this man?" Dixie said.

"Well, Eagleton did say it had been quite a while. It may turn out to be a wild goose chase."

"I'm starved," Dixie said. "Let's go get a hamburger and we can talk about it while we eat. What do you say?"

"I am hungry at that. Okay, I'm with you. That place down by the Bay?"

Chapter 24

F BI Special Agent Hank Jacoby sat chewing the short stub of a cigar in the agency's San Francisco field office. He looked out of the twelfth floor window that overlooked Civic Center Plaza south of Golden Gate Avenue. To the north from his lofty vantage point, he could just make out the faint outline of Alcatraz as if it was hovering in the haze. With him were agents Sam Prescott and Lenny Baudelaire, and the three men sat around a conference table discussing the Millie Harbaum situation.

"I don't know if she was tipped that we were coming or what," Jacoby said. He removed the cigar from his mouth and sat toying with it. "But she was gone."

"You think the other doctors might have warned her?" Prescott said. He was a balding man with thick ruddy jowls and large ears.

"The Doctors Olson?" Jacoby said. "I doubt it. They seem to be as anxious as anybody in locating her and that thing."

"What is that thing, exactly?" Baudelaire said. He was the youngest of the three men and possessed a full head of blond curly hair.

"Hell if I know for sure," Jacoby said. "A monster of

some sort. A human and animal mixture. Don't ask any more 'cuz I don't have the foggiest clue otherwise."

"Is it a threat to the community?" Prescott said.

"Like I said, I just don't know. According to the folks at Cal Pacific and the Primate Research Facility, they don't know exactly what to expect. However, it gets bigger and older with each passing day. The sooner we find it along with the Harbaum woman, the better."

"Hank, any idea where she might have gone?" Baudelaire took out a pen and notebook and set them on the table.

"The crime scene technicians are finishing up at the cabin today," Jacoby said, "so we should have some information later. That is, of course, if they're able to come with anything."

"What did her parent's have to say?" Prescott rubbed his balding head, seemingly frustrated with their lack of leads.

"Not much. Dr. Olson has been there asking the same questions. Her father told the sheriff that he hasn't had any contact with her for months. So, she could be anywhere."

Jacoby didn't like not having a single lead. It bothered him, causing his stomach to rebel. His frustration level was at an all-time high, and he needed some answers— soon.

Whatever the monster was, and he had no idea what the scientists were talking about, but whatever it was, it didn't sound as though they could allow it to remain at large indefinitely.

Olson and his fellow scientists said it was some sort of hybrid, part human, part animal. And the animal part was something from the distant past. None of it made any sense. Which added to his stress. The pressure was on to find the Harbaum girl and the thing —whatever it was.

CRSCRS

The morning dawned cool and overcast as Harry and Dixie drove toward Sacramento. After crossing the seven-mile San Mateo-Hayward Bridge, Harry guided their car onto the expressway and headed north toward Walnut Creek. Lunchtime found them at the Carquinez Strait at Benicia, and they located a quaint diner near the water that served clam chowder. Harry was thankful for the break and a chance to stretch his legs. While he spooned up mouthfuls of the soup, Dixie chatted.

"I've been thinking, Harry," she said. "Millie has to eat and find a place to stay. She can't work as a scientist, at least not yet. But she does have to work."

Harry munched a mouthful of oyster crackers and swallowed.

"What's your point?" he said. "You have an idea where she might be?"

Dixie placed her spoon on the table and looked out over the water, a dark gray mass that formed small eddies near the shoreline. Gulls and storm petrels circled lazily overhead then dove into the swift current.

"She can't go home to her parent's, the police would have the place under surveillance," she said. "She knows Frisco. It's a big city. She did most of her undergraduate work at Cal Pacific, so why not? She would certainly know her way around."

"It's a possibility," Harry said.

"Any responses on the leads about a job?" Dixie said as she returned to eating her chowder.

"Nothing," he said. "I'd love to have that position with the IAA, but I doubt my inquiry will amount to anything. I'm pretty down about it."

"Honey, listen to me." Dixie's voice was soft and re-assuring. "The reasons Cal Pacific let you go were entirely political and had nothing to do with your professional competency. For that reason, you'll be able to find something, I just know it. Your anthropology skills are second to none. People in the field know that."

"Maybe. I never thought this would happen to me, to us. When we brought those Yeti back to the facility, I felt as if I was on top of the world. I knew the Professor would be proud of me. That I had finally measured up in his eyes."

"Darling," Dixie said, reaching across the table and touching his arm, "I know the Professor loved you. He told me so many times. Why do you have such a hard time accepting that?"

"I dunno. Maybe it's because once I disappointed him so."

Harry noticed the gulls were soaring lazily farther out over the water.

"That, my dear, is all ancient history. You must let it go."

"I suppose," he said.

Dixie thought their trip to Sacramento to try and locate George Trench would not amount to anything—a wild goose chase—and she had said as much. But her husband seemed determined, so here she was, riding beside him and hoping for the best. And who knew? Maybe they would get lucky, find Trench, and he would know where Millie was hiding.

But it was a long shot. The odds that, even if they found the man, he would remember Millie or know where she was, were astronomically stacked against them. But Harry felt he had to do something, anything, to try and track down his former graduate student.

During their brief marriage, Dixie had come to admire Harry's deep commitment to Cal Pacific University, its anthropology program, and, most important, his students.

Millie Harbaum was a rising star among them. And Harry had responded to her intellect, her curiosity, her hard work in the same manner had he had done with Dixie—with a warm and helpful attitude aimed at furthering her career.

And Millie betrayed his loyalty and helpfulness with her deceit and treachery. She took Harry's support and used it for her own selfish purpose, without first confiding in him or asking his opinion. She knew Harry would have stopped her chimera project so, instead of trusting his judgment, she proceeded on her own, in violation of university policy.

And yet, here was Harry, trying to locate her to help her salvage her career.

Dixie was not feeling generous now as she and Harry ate their lunch.

Later, as they passed through the outskirts of Sacramento, they crossed the river and exited the expressway into downtown. The first address on Dixie's list turned out to be a flophouse in a rundown neighborhood, and the two men they questioned were covered with tattoos and had long greasy hair.

Neither had heard of George Trench, and they shot malicious glances at Dixie. Her heart pounded, and she tugged on Harry's sleeve, signaling him with her eyes that she wanted to leave. He finally relented, and the two of them returned to their car and sped away.

"Whose next on the list?" Harry said.

"Didn't you see they way those goons were eyeing me?" she said, her voice rising in pitch. "They looked as if they could assault us any moment."

"They were probably hoping you had drugs on you," Harry said. "I don't think they found you attractive," he added, laughing.

"What?" The hurt was obvious in Dixie's voice.

"Naw, you were way too clean and well-groomed for those two." He continued to chuckle, and Dixie punched him in the arm.

The next address for a George Trench was in an East Sacramento office building overlooking the American River. The directory in the building's foyer showed that there was a George Trench, Investment Counselor, who had an office on the third floor. As they rode the elevator, Dixie's palms felt moist.

"This is beginning to look like a waste of time, honey," she said. "I will be surprised if this guy is any help."

"Then we'll be on our way back home in a short time. This office is certainly upscale. Didn't Eagleton mention this Trench and Millie were friends at one time?"

"More than friends, Harry. More like lovers. Eagleton thought she left him because he roughed her up a couple of times."

"And now he's an investment counselor?" Harry said, incredulity showing in his voice. "I doubt if it's the same guy."

The elevator door opened onto a carpeted hallway lined with several office doors. Harry led Dixie to Trench's. The two of them entered and were greeted by a smiling, redheaded secretary seated behind a desk. She peered at them over large glasses.

"May I help you?" she said in a mousy voice.

"We would like to see Mr. Trench," Harry said, "if we could."

"Do you have an appointment?" the redhead said, her demeanor changing to a formal tone.

"No," Harry said. "But it's important."

"Are you clients of his? I don't remember you."

"No, we are not," Harry said. Dixie squeezed his arm and he continued. "We are—"

"Well, I'm sorry," the secretary said. "But Mr. Trench

isn't taking on any new clients at this time. If you care to—"

Dixie's impatience got the better of her, and she interrupted.

"Please," she said in an imploring tone. "We're university professors in San Francisco and are looking for one of my husband's faculty members who has disappeared. We think your boss may have known her in the past and we're hoping we could have a few short minutes of his time." Dixie tried to put on her most forlorn expression and smiled weakly at the secretary.

"Well…"

At that moment a door opened, and a tall, well-dressed man in his thirties came to stand next to the secretary's desk. She looked at him with a sad face.

"Miss Dalrymple, what is all this?" the man said.

"Mr. Trench, these two came in wanting to see you. They don't have an appointment and are not clients. I told them—"

"That's fine," Trench said. He looked at Dixie and Harry and smiled. He was dressed in a tailored gray suit and sported a maroon tie. His dark hair was combed straight back, and he gazed at them with hazel eyes. A tanned complexion completed the successful look.

Too much tennis, Dixie thought.

"As my wife was telling this young lady," Harry said, "we are looking for a colleague. We're professors at Cal Pacific University in Frisco, and one of our faculty has turned up missing. We were hoping you might be of help."

Trench's eyes narrowed, and a frown appeared on his ruddy face. "Me? How?"

"The girl's name is Millie Harbaum," Harry said. "We understand she dated or lived with a man named George Trench. Is it possible you are him?"

Trench hesitated and shifted his weight. Dixie thought he was suddenly uncomfortable and the air of superiority had dissipated.

"Well, I don't know," he said. "Are the police involved?"

"They are," Harry said. "As well as the FBI. We just want to find her. She could be in danger."

"I dunno—"

"Look, Mr. Trench," Dixie said. "We need to find her, and soon. It's extremely important. If you can help us—"

Harry stepped closer to Trench. "If you are the man who knew her, the authorities will be here sooner or later, and you will have to tell them what you know. We just want to locate her before something bad happens to her."

"Has she broken the law?" Trench said.

"Not really," Harry said.

"But she's in danger?"

"She could be, yes," Dixie said. "That's why it's imperative that we locate her as soon as possible. Please, if you know anything."

Trench exhaled, and Dixie noticed his shoulders relax.

"We can talk in my office." Placing a hand on Miss Dalrymple's shoulder, he said, "Bring us some coffee, please."

And he led Dixie and Harry into his opulent office.

Chapter 25

Millie walked the two blocks to Ling Wu's acupuncture clinic after feeding Roku his breakfast and signing to him that he needed to remain quiet until she returned. The day was overcast, and a cold wind blew off the Pacific Ocean and into her face, reminding her she needed to purchase a sweater. When she was offered the position at the Primate Research Facility in Nevada, she packed up her meager belongings in her efficiency apartment and took them with her to the Cinder Mountain facility. Most of her clothes and a few household items, along with her cooking utensils, were still back in Nevada, and there they would have to remain.

The acupuncture clinic was a small, cluttered affair fronting a side street in San Francisco's Chinatown. Traffic was light, and only a few children were out, hurrying along the cracked sidewalk to the school, one block over. The smells of Chinese cooking wafted down the neighborhood as she made her way to the clinic.

She opened the door and was greeted by Mr. Wu, who approached her, smiling.

"Good morning, Millie," he said, in his Asian accent. "You have breakfast?"

"Yes, Mr. Wu, I already ate, thank you. You need me to sterilize the needles from yesterday?"

"No, Millie. I already put them in the sterilizer. But I do need you to prepare Mrs. Ong for her treatment. She is in the exam room."

"I will, Mr. Wu."

Millie strolled past her boss, entered the examination room, and began her day. As she worked, the hours melted away, for her thoughts were back in the small apartment with Roku. The creature was getting much too large for her to manage alone. When he wanted to be obstinate, she had to physically encourage him to do what she wanted, and, occasionally, Roku would growl at her in protest. It was those times that she realized that soon something would have to be done with him, but she didn't know what. She was toying with the idea of going back to Cal Pacific and returning him, on the condition that they use him for study and not exterminate him. She knew she was most likely in trouble and might be arrested at any moment if her whereabouts were discovered, so she needed to find a safe place for Roku. But where?

In retrospect, she harbored deep feelings of guilt over what she had done. She knew that, in creating Roku, she had crossed an invisible moral and ethical line, but she would do it over again, given the opportunity. Which now would be never. The important thing to her was that she had created Roku, used her expertise in genetics and created him, and now science needed to study him, not destroy him. It didn't matter what happened to her, as long as Roku lived.

The patients came and went with Millie assisting Wu with his acupuncture treatments. In acupuncture, very thin needles, slightly thicker than a human hair, were inserted into acupuncture points. The objective of acupuncture as explained by Mr. Wu was to regulate and normalize the flow of the Chi, so that the Yin and the Yang re-turned to a state of dynamic equilibrium. Acupuncture aimed to relieve symptoms by curing the disease. The choice of acupuncture points to be used was the most crucial part of the treatment. The acupuncturist must know the function of each acupuncture point and its interaction with other acupuncture points. Mr. Wu then planned the treatment to eliminate obstructions in the flow of Chi and to balance the Yin and Yang. After Mr. Wu had examined the patient and reached a diagnosis, he decided how the patient should be treated.

Millie learned that an experienced acupuncturist used as few needles as possible to balance the energy flows. In contrast, a novice might use many needles and still be unable to balance the energy flows. Most patients needed ten to fifteen acupuncture needles for each treatment, but sometimes only a single needle might be enough. While treating a frozen shoulder, Mr. Wu inserted a single needle into the leg and then twirled it in his fingers. In a few minutes, a shoulder that had been immobile for up to three months moved freely and without pain.

Her day ended, and, after saying goodbye to Mr. Wu, she returned home and fixed her and Roku's dinner. Afterward, she worked with him on his language and signing skills. He was now a large creature with a large head and penetrating eyes. Short, brown-yellow fur covered his body and, while he walked upright, he had a decided willingness to move about using his arms. Above everything, Millie was amazed at Roku's intelligence. The chimera had an unusual ability to learn things quickly, a faculty that led her to teach Roku simple math using toothpicks. He was able to solve almost any puzzle that Millie brought home.

As she undressed for bed, she wondered what the future held for them. Would Roku live to make history? Or would he be destroyed, his life ended in infamy? And what about her? Would she be destined to spend the rest of her life in a dead-end meaningless job working for peanuts?

She glanced at Roku lying on the floor and signed, *You're a good boy. I love you.*

And Roku signed back. *I love Mommy. Mommy is very pretty.*

Millie lay in the dark until a fitful dreamless sleep overtook her.

eↄeↄ

Harry took the offered cup of coffee and settled into a luxurious chair around a walnut table as Dixie followed suit.

Trench settled into a chair opposite the couple, put his elbows on the table, and sighed. His gray eyes flashed.

"What do you want to know?" he said.

Harry noticed a line of tiny beads of sweat on the man's brow. He swallowed some coffee.

"Mr. Trench, I am Harry Olson, and I was Millie Harbaum's departmental chairman at Cal Pacific University. This is my wife, Dixie." Trench nodded without saying a word. "As I mentioned earlier," Harry continued, "we were both Millie's professors and responsible for her graduate work at the university."

Trench smiled weakly.

"You say, were, as in the past tense. Why is that?" Trench took a handkerchief from his pocket and dabbed his forehead.

"Dixie," Harry began, "and I are no longer employed with the university. I was terminated after Millie disappeared and Dixie resigned."

"Disappeared?" Trench said, eyebrows raised.

Harry hesitated, not wanting to divulge the chimera's existence. Not knowing Trench, Harry wasn't sure if the man could be trusted to not divulge a confidence. In fact, lately Harry's trust in the people he knew had been severely strained, if not down right betrayed, so he wasn't eager to tell this stranger everything he knew. From the board of trustees down to Siscom at the research facility, the people he thought he could count on had let him down. He heard Dixie saying something and her voice brought him back to reality.

"You might as well tell him everything, honey," she said. "He's gonna hear it, sooner or later."

At Dixie's remark, Trench sat up straight and set his cup on the table. Harry thought he looked more interested than stressed.

"I guess," Harry said. "Millie, as a faculty member, was doing research at our Primate Research Facility in Nevada, Mr. Trench. Dixie and I had brought back to the States a pair of primitive animals—human ancestors still living in the mountains of Mongolia. They were Yeti. We brought them back and placed them it the facility where they would be protected, and we could study them. Millie was involved in the research. She was an expert in paleogenetics."

"Paleo- what?" Trench said.

"Paleogenetics. Using genetics to determine relationships among previous living animals."

"It is the study of the past through the examination of preserved genetic material from the remains of ancient organisms," Dixie said. "The physical chemist Linus Pauling introduced the term in 1963, in reference to the examination of possible applications in the reconstruction of past polypeptide sequences. The first sequence of an ancient DNA, isolated from a museum specimen of an extinct zebra, was published in 1984."

"I see," Trench said, half wincing at Dixie's description. "So Millie was working for you on this project?"

"Yes," Harry continued. "Unbeknownst to me or other university officials, Millie created a chimera. She created an organism whose genetic makeup was half from the Yeti and half her own."

"A hybrid?"

"Sort of, but not exactly. Scientifically, we call it a chimera. Millie implanted the fertilized egg with the different DNA into a chimpanzee, and, several months later, the chimera was born."

"Let me get this straight, Professor," Trench said, after a big gulp of his coffee. "This creature, or whatever it is, is half this Yeti animal and half human. Correct?" Harry nodded. "If you don't mind me asking, what does the damn thing look like?"

Harry chuckled.

"Like a short-haired chimp," he said. "But getting bigger each day. Millie knew she had crossed a line, so she took the chimera and left the research facility. Disappeared. We're looking for her."

"And you thought I could help?" Trench said. He got up, removed his suit coat, and ambled over to his desk. On it was a picture of a woman and two small children.

"We understand you knew her," Dixie said. "You did, didn't you?"

A pregnant silence ensued, as if Trench was contemplating his options. Harry shot his wife a glance that said, "We've wasted our time."

After some length, Trench returned to the table, sat, extended his hands, palms up. "I did, yes," he said. His face bore a sorrowful expression. "It was a long time ago."

"Mr. Trench," Harry said, "we don't wish to involve ourselves in your past affairs. All we desire is that if you are in possession of where Millie might be, we would appreciate the information. If not, we will leave you alone."

The investment counselor shook his head.

"Millie and I were a thing a number of years ago. In love, you might say. But one night I was drunk and hit her a few times. She moved out the next day. It wasn't my best moment, one I'm not proud of. I have a great wife and family now, and the remembrance of what I did is extremely painful and embarrassing. But, I'm sorry, I have no idea where she might be."

"I figured it was a long shot," Harry said. "I'm sorry we bothered you."

"It's hard to believe that the woman I lived with for a while is now doing research in paleo…paleo…"

"Paleogenetics," Harry said. "And I might add that she has a brilliant mind. It's too bad that she used it for something like this."

"What will happen to her when you catch up with her?" Trench said.

"To Millie," Dixie said, "we hope nothing. The chimera in all likelihood will be destroyed."

"Oh wow," Trench exclaimed.

Harry stood.

"Well, Mr. Trench, we appreciate your candor and thanks for your time."

Trench stood. Harry and Dixed left his office. As they passed the redheaded secretary, she smiled and waved. Once in their car and headed back to the freeway, Dixie was exasperated.

"You think he was telling the truth, honey?" she said as Harry steered the car around slower moving traffic. "He looked rather sleazy to me."

"It doesn't matter," he said. "He wasn't going to give us any information, one way or the other. He did admit to knowing her. Stands to reason that after all these years, he wouldn't have any knowledge of her whereabouts. Especially if he worked her over. What woman would stay in contact with a jerk like that?"

"I know I wouldn't. He'd be lucky to be alive."

Harry laughed, for he knew his wife was speaking the truth.

"So we are back where we started," she said. "Now what?"

"I'd like to check in with Special Agent Jacoby and see if he has turned up anything. If not, then I need to start looking for a job."

"I can call the folks at the facility and check with them," Dixie said. "Who was it you said had expressed an interest in you?"

"The Institute for American Antiquities."

"Oh, yes. They fund expeditions, don't they? You could get back to doing what you really love, which is field work. I could travel with you."

"It might be able to work."

"I know I keep asking, Harry, but what will happen if they find Roku? Will he be destroyed?"

"Like you told Trench, it's hard to say. It would depend on how much influence I still have with Pauling and Cal Pacific."

"And how much public outcry there is?" Dixie gazed out her window at the passing countryside. The freeway traffic had lightened considerably.

"Exactly. Most people don't know anything about genetics and bioengineering. What they don't understand, they fear, regardless of any scientific merit. And if science should dare threaten the pillars of religion, then watch out 'cause it's all-out war."

"That doesn't bode well for Roku's survival, does it?"

"Not at all."

They drove a ways in silence with Harry in deep

thought. As the sun faded behind the western horizon and left them in a gray dusk, they sped down the peninsula toward San Mateo. He knew if Roku was found, and Harry couldn't convince Pauling and the trustees to remand him to the research facility, the chimera would die. And it would break Dixie's heart.

It was something he could not dare to contemplate.

Chapter 26

Reginald Pauling felt horrible. His stomach was in knots, his head pounded, and his favorite scotch tasted like week-old bilge water. He replaced his pipe in the ashtray and leaned back in his chair, feet on the desk. His office was draped in shadows as the setting sun had long since dipped into the ocean. The university's business was done for the day, and only an occasional student could be seen strolling across campus.

His recent meetings with Chloe Rawlings and Alistair Forester left him mentally and physically drained. Forester's objections to Harry's continued employment mattered little to Pauling as the man was a pompous ass. But Dr. Rawling's complaint was a different story. It wasn't just that she was right about being able to find work elsewhere and take her grant with her. Deep in his heart, Pauling knew she was right about Harry's termination. That it had not been the correct thing to do. It was all politics. Pauling tried to assuage his conscience by telling himself it was all dirty academic politics, and he had been compelled to comply with the board of trustees. Either that or lose his job.

Facing the truth about himself wasn't easy for him to do. He hadn't the guts to stand up to the man when a friend's career was on the line. Not so with Chloe Rawl-ings. The woman marched in and gave him an ultimatum, just like that. She had guts, he had to admit. The one thing he lacked, a beautiful woman possessed in spades. It seemed he had been given everything—a high-paying position, a beautiful office, a great career, fine clothes, vintage scotch—everything except guts. His self-esteem couldn't get much lower.

Pauling massaged his temples, hoping to relieve the pain between his eyes. He was exhausted and needed a long rest. The dimness of his office matched his mood, and, as the shadows settled around him, his depression deepened. Maybe he wasn't cut out for this kind of work. Maybe it was time to move on.

He picked up the phone and dialed Miles Radner's cell phone. The man's somber tone matched his own.

"Miles, this is Reginald Pauling. Am I calling at a bad time?"

"Not at all," was Radner's curt reply. "How can I help you?"

"Needed to chat with you for a while, Miles. About this Harbaum affair. That is if you can spare the time."

"Look, Dr. Pauling, if you are calling to give me my walking papers, out with it. God knows I feel bad enough about it as is. It's probably what I deserve."

Pauling was taken aback by Radner's sharp abrasive tone but decided to let it pass, given all that had happened at his facility.

"No, Miles, that's not why I called. To tell you the truth, I just needed to hear a friendly voice. I'm not well thought of by my faculty at this moment. How about you? You taking Harry's side in this?"

Pauling sensed a hesitation in Radner's voice, which became more conciliatory.

"Somewhat," Radner said. "But I understand why you acted as you did."

"But you feel I acted hastily? Bowed under pressure from the trustees?"

"Sir, I believe I have told you this before. Originally, when Harry was named our departmental chairman, I was puzzled and angry. I believed the appointment should have gone to myself. Not only was I disappointed, but I was envious as well. I hoped he would fail. When the Yetis escaped from my facility, Harry did not berate, criticize, or recommend my dismissal. When I volunteered my resignation, he refused to accept it. In fact, he tore it up. With that, my opinion of the man changed, and I have been a supporter of him ever since. So you see, Dr. Pauling, I'm not the most objective person where Harry is concerned."

"I understand."

"However, I have been in academic circles long enough to realize that politics can make or break a career. Not scientific achievement or publications, but dirty old politics. Envy, jealousy, and fear raise their ugly heads and careers are ruined. If you are asking my opinion, the board of trustees is a group of spineless men who are fearful of public opinion that has not even formed as yet. They are running from something that hasn't happened. And they are ruining a couple of good people's careers for the sake of nonexistent publicity. I find that reprehensible."

"Well, Miles. Thanks for your honest opinion."

"Finally, Dr. Pauling, I do not envy your position. I would hate to sit where you do. It's bad enough from where I sit. In the end, I must believe you have made your decision in the best interests of the university. That's what you get paid to do."

Pauling noted the sincerity in Radner's comments.

"The crazy thing, Miles, is that I feel exactly as you do. I guess it's why I feel horrible about everything. I honestly felt sorry for Harry. I did not relish terminating him, and I want you to know that."

"Hell, I know that. You've always been fair and square with us faculty. But in this, Dr. Pauling, I want you to know that I think you're wrong. You've made a mistake, and the university will suffer for it."

"Dr. Rawlings said basically the same thing. I'm not very well liked by the faculty right now."

"Chloe Rawlings? Yes, I know her. She speaks her mind, for sure. I'm actually surprised I had the courage to speak to you this way. I hope you didn't take offense."

Pauling again noted the hesitation in Radner's tone, and it made him smile to himself. Knowing Miles Radner as he did, Pauling didn't doubt it took a great deal of courage.

"None taken, Miles. If we cannot be frank with other then—well, what are friends for. I count your counsel as invaluable. I won't take any more of your time. We'll talk again."

After hanging up with Radner, Pauling took another gulp of scotch and noticed it tasted better. The chat had lightened his spirits.

❧❧❧

Millie came home to find her apartment in shambles. Roku had apparently gone wild while she was at work and ransacked the place, ripping clothes from the dresser, spilling and scattering broken dishes and pans all over the small apartment. He had clawed a hole in one of the cushions from the sofa and strewn its stuffing throughout the room. He had never done anything like this before.

She was stunned.

She found him huddled in a corner of the tiny kitchen where he had opened the refrigerator, eaten all the food, and scattered the remainder of its contents on the floor. He stared at her with yellow-slitted eyes.

She approached him, intending to give him a scolding, but when she was close, he snarled at her.

His lips curled back and revealed his white fangs. He had never done that before.

She stopped for a second then walked toward him again.

He snarled.

She signed, *"What's the matter, Roku?"*

The chimera just sat huddled in the corner, staring at her.

"Why have you done this?"

Roku shifted his body and looked about the apartment.

Millie continued to sign. *"Roku, are you sick? Do you not feel well? What is the matter? Why did you do this?"*

Roku tilted his head, hissed, and signed back. *"Who am I?"*

At first, Millie didn't think she understood his signing. *"What was that?"* she signed.

This time Roku lowered his head. *"Who am I?"*

No, she thought, she had gotten it correct the first time. *"Roku, I don't understand. What do you mean?"*

"I am not like you. Why?"

Millie was confused. She couldn't comprehend or account for Roku's sudden change. He didn't appear to be ill. Why this line of questions? He continued to sign.

"You taught me what mother is. But you do not look like me. You cannot be my mother. Why?"

She sat on the floor in front of Roku, and he seemed less stressed. Why these new questions, now? Roku had never acted this way before, and he had never asked these types of questions before. She reached out to take his hand, but he retreated farther into the corner. She signed to him.

"Roku, mother means many things." Millie struggled with what to say. *"I brought you into this world. I created you. Do you understand?"*

The chimera sat with a blank expression, his gaze firmly fixed on Millie. *"What am I?"*

Millie sat transfixed by the question.

"Please, Mother. What am I? Where did I come from?"

Finally, it dawned on Millie what was happening. It was Roku's first experience with self-awareness, and it was frightening. For the first time in his life, Roku was wondering about himself, who he was, what were his origins. How was she to answer him so he could understand? Oh, she wished they were back in the lab at the research facility where she could test his intelligence.

She knew that self-awareness was one of the first components of the self-concept to emerge. While self-awareness was something that was central to each and every one of us, it was not something that we were acutely aware of at every moment of every day. Instead, self-awareness became woven into the fabric of who we were and emerged at different points depending upon the situation and our personality. Humans were not born with self-awareness.

Researchers believed that an area of the brain known as the anterior cingulate, a region of the frontal lobe, played an important role in the development of self-awareness. Experiments indicated that self-awareness began to emerge in children around the age of eighteen months, an age that coincided with the rapid growth of spindle cells in the anterior cingulate. Researchers had also used brain imaging to show that this region became activated in adults who were self-aware.

Consciousness, most scientists would argue, was not a shared property of all matter in the universe. Rather, consciousness was restricted to a subset of animals with relatively complex brains. The more scientists studied animal behavior and brain anatomy, however, the more universal consciousness seemed to be. A brain as complex as a human's was definitely not necessary for consciousness.

Humans were more than just conscious—they were also self-aware. Scientists differed on how they distinguished between consciousness and self-awareness, but here was one common distinction: consciousness was awareness of your body and your environment, self-awareness was recognition of that consciousness—not only understanding that you existed but further comprehending that you were aware of your existence.

Presumably, human infants were conscious. They perceived and responded to people and things around them, but they were not yet self-aware. In their first years of life, children developed a sense of self, learning to recognize themselves in the mirror and to distinguish between their own point of view and the perspectives of other people.

Could this be what Roku was struggling with? She signed again.

"You are part me and part animal. Part of you is human, like me. Part of you is not."

Roku sat up straight, his yellow eyes now flashing red. *"Why? Why? Why?"*

Chapter 27

Harry spent the day on the phone chatting with a number of people with the Institute for American Antiquities regarding his possible employment. Dixie had taken the car to Cal Pacific to clean out her desk, and, later, Harry planned to contact Special Agent Jacoby to see if he had any updates on Millie's whereabouts.

Dr. John Brock at the IAA was eager to discuss Harry's potential employment. The salary would be considerably more that what he was making at Cal Pacific, and the organization was looking for someone of Harry's stature to lead an expedition to Nepal. A follow-up on the Denisova bone fragment that had been found a few years earlier. The bone preserved just enough anatomy for the paleontologist to identify it as a chip from a primate fingertip—specifically the part that faces the last joint in the pinkie. Since there was no evidence for primates other than humans in Siberia 30,000 to 50,000 years ago—no apes or monkeys—the fossil was presumably from some kind of human. Judging by the incompletely fused joint surface, the human in question had died young, perhaps as young as eight years old. And Dr. Brock wanted Harry to continue the search for more specimens.

It was near the region where Harry had discovered the Yeti, and there was always the possibility of finding more of the creature he had invested so much of his time and passion in.

"John," he said trying to keep his voice level, "it sounds like a dream job. I want it, that's for sure, but I'd like a few days to talk it over with Dixie. That possible?"

"Of course, Harry," was Brock's sympathetic reply. "We're not in a hurry, so we will continue to vet you. We want the right person, and I believe that person is you. With your experience in the region and in leading many similar expeditions, you are a perfect fit. You would have a free hand in organizing the group."

"Including my wife, Dixie?"

"Whomever you desire. It would be your show?"

"You have a timetable?" Harry wondered how soon he would have to be ready.

"We'd like the expedition to have boots on the ground a year from now."

"All right, John, let me discuss this with Dixie."

"Fine, Harry. And like I said, the vetting process may take another few days, but I want you to know I think you're our man. I'll call you when everything is settled on our end."

The Denisova hominid and a chance to find another Yeti. How lucky could a guy get? Harry couldn't wait for Dixie to return so he could share his good fortune.

It would complicate things, however. He still needed to locate Millie and arrange a safe place for the chimera to be housed and studied. It was the only way to salvage his somewhat tarnished reputation. At least at Cal Pacific. He didn't want to leave with such a shroud of irresponsibility hanging over him. His old and dear Professor Kesler would understand, God rest his soul.

He heard Dixie come in and jumped up to greet her.

She carried a large box of books and journals. He took them from her and carried them into the study.

"I didn't realize I had accumulated so much stuff," she complained, slumping into a chair. She brushed a lock of blonde hair from her eyes and smiled.

"Guess what?" Harry said. "I've got great news."

"Oh yeah, what?" Dixie said, her green eyes flashing sparkles.

"Dr. Brock with the Institute for American Antiquities offered me a position."

"When?"

"Just a while ago. I talked to him while you were out."

Dixie sat up straight.

"Just like that?" she said. "He offered you a job just like that?"

Harry waved his arms in an animated fashion and giggled.

"Yeah, honey, just like that. I need to go through the usual vetting process, but Dr. Brock believes I am their man. His exact words. Of course, he knew of my work with the Yeti, and he was a close friend of the Professor's. He said I was a natural fit."

"Wow," Dixie said, slumping back in her chair. "I guess I'll be needing to find work now."

"There's more. The IAA is mounting an expedition to Nepal to continue investigations into the Denisova hominids, and he wants me to lead it. Wants to be in country in a year. And the best part is I can take you. You can be a part of the team.

Dixie looked flabbergasted. She stared at her husband for a few moments then burst out laughing.

"It's wonderful, honey. I'm excited."

After her outburst, Dixie turned somber, a frown appeared on her tanned face.

"But what about Millie?" she said. "What do we do about her?"

"We'll just have to find her. And soon. I'm going to phone Jacoby and see if he has any new information."

"The Denisova hominid," Dixie said, as she stared out the window.

"Scientists extracted the finger bone's mitochondrial DNA, a small bit of the genome that living cells have hundreds of copies of and that is, therefore, easier to find in ancient bone." Harry tried to not sound excited, but it was difficult to contain his elation. "They compared the DNA sequence with those of living humans and Neanderthals. Then they repeated the analysis because they couldn't believe the results they'd gotten the first time around. On a Friday afternoon, the lab staff gathered and the lead investigator challenged anyone to come up with a different explanation for what he was seeing. The man still recalls that Friday as scientifically the most exciting day of his life. The tiny chip of a finger bone, it seemed, was not from a modern human at all. But it wasn't from a Neanderthal either. It belonged to a new kind of human being, never before seen."

"I remember discussing this find when I was a graduate student," Dixie said.

"The mtDNA analysis further suggested this new hominid species was the result of an early migration out of Africa, distinct from the later out-of-Africa migrations associated with Neanderthals and modern humans. Some argue it could be a relic of the earlier African exodus of Homo erectus, because of the tooth size, although this has not been proved. The conclusions of both the excavations and the sequencing are still debatable because the evidence shows that all three human forms have occupied the Denisova Cave."

"I remember that this specimen has complicated the picture in Asian evolution."

"For now," Harry continued, "the population to which these two fossils belonged is being called Denisovans. A decision on how to classify them will probably be deferred until we know more of their anatomy. The fact that Denisovans and Neanderthals both interbred with humans does not necessarily mean they are one species—there are many cases of modern species able to interbreed. Animal species are more usually defined by whether they ordinarily form a single interbreeding population, rather than by whether they are merely capable of interbreeding. This is obviously a fuzzy criterion, but the fact that the Neanderthal and Denisovan contributions to the human genome appear to have been limited events means these hominids could still end up being classified as three species."

"I didn't realize you were such an expert, Dr. Olson," Dixie said, sporting a broad grin.

"It's the extent of my knowledge, for sure. But you needn't be so jocular about it,"

Harry pulled Dixie from the chair, put his arms around her, and kissed her hard on the lips.

"At least," he said, after pulling away out of breath, "we'll be able to remain working together. I'm happy about that."

Later, he phoned the San Francisco FBI office and left a message to have Jacoby call him. As he waited for the special agent to return his phone call, he attempted to devise a plan by which he and Dixie could locate Millie. Maybe they could search her room at the facility. But then she probably did not leave anything incriminating behind. Or possibly Radner had already accomplished that task. He could call the man. He remembered Gerald Siscom was sweet on Millie so maybe he could offer a clue as to where she might have gone. Dixie thought she was in the Bay Area, and that might be right. The fact that her parents had no idea where she was wasn't very comforting. But, then again, she might contact them in the future.

That Millie had been a graduate student then a faculty member in his charge weighed heavily on his conscience. He couldn't just give up searching for her. But the fact that he had been summarily discharged without much of a hearing made him angry. At first, he was astonished then bewildered and confused. Those emotions had been followed by a certain depression, one that had settled deep in his soul and left him drained. But with this new job opportunity came a sense of anger. Anger that the university, to which he had been loyal to a fault, would give him up so easily. Surely, as a tenured professor, they had violated his rights.

"I feel like such a failure," he said to Dixie who was busy unpacking the box from her office. "When I was growing up, failure presented itself as something extremely clear. You failed an exam, your team lost a game. And in the grown-up world, it was the same. Marriages failed, you failed to get that promotion. Later, I realized that failure could also be private and hidden. That there was emotional, moral, sexual failure. The failure to understand another person, to make friends, to say what you meant. But even in those areas, the binary system applied—win or lose, pass or fail."

Dixie stopped her unpacking and gave Harry a hug.

"Honey, in the long run, we are all dead, and none of us is God. You must recognize that failure is, in large part, emotion, and the fact that we are haunted by it matters not at all in the long run. The Zen of it is that success and failure are both an illusion, and these illusions will keep you from your work. They will spoil your talent, they will eat away at your life, your sleep, and the way you speak to the people you love."

She smiled and squeezed his arm.

"You're too hard on yourself," she added. "Not everything in life can be reduced to a win or a loss."

"I know you mean well, but the problem with this spiritual argument," he said, "is that success and failure are also real. You can finish a real experiment, and its results can be published or not, be reviewed or not. Each one of these real events makes it easier or harder to do one's job. If you keep going and stay on the right side of all this, you can be offered honors and awards, you can be recognized on the street, you can be recognized in the streets of several countries, some of which do not have English as a native language. And all this can happen, by the way, whether or not your work is actually good, or still good. Success may be material but is also an emotion. One that is felt, not only by you, but also by the crowd. This is why we yearn for it, and cannot have it. It is not ours to hold."

"Once you get settled in your new work," Dixie said, "all these worries will fade away. You will forget these torments. I'm sure of it, sweetheart."

"I'm sure you're right," he said. "Getting back is the hardest thing to do after you have been knocked to the ground. It takes a certain mental toughness. I want to think I possess that toughness."

"You do," Dixie said. "It just takes a little time after you have the breath knocked out of you. I'm not worried."

Jacoby called and didn't sound promising.

"Don't have anything new to report," he said. "We have checked all the doctor's offices, emergency rooms, the morgue, without any luck. Animal control hasn't picked up any strange looking animals. The fact is, Doctor Olson, she could be anywhere. And I mean anywhere."

"Well, Dixie and I are going to keep looking for her," Harry said, disappointment clearly in his voice. He had hoped that the agent would have stumbled onto something they could use.

"Good luck," Jacoby said. "If we turn up anything, I'll let you know."

ᏟᏏᏟᏏᏞ

Millie spent the evening putting the apartment back in order while Roku sulked in the corner. He refused his food and water, causing Millie to become somewhat concerned. Since her earlier discussion with Roku, she worried that he was developing into something that would soon be impossible for her to handle. The chimera obviously had an intellect surpassing the Yeti she had studied at the primate facility and was developing a self-awareness that was definitely human. Actually, his language skills and his intellectual skills were far ahead of any human child of the same chronological age. It was impossible to judge where it was all headed.

The belief that humans were exceptional by virtue of their existence and were the most intelligent species on Earth might not be true, and animals could be intelligent in their own unique ways. The idea that humans were superior to all other life forms probably emerged about 10,000 years ago when humans decided to take up farming. The feeling of superiority went up a notch with the arrival of organized religion, which niftily put humans, especially men, at the center of Life and Universe.

The belief of human cognitive superiority became entrenched in human philosophy and sciences. Even Aristotle, probably the most influential of all thinkers, argued that humans were superior to other animals, due to their exclusive ability to reason.

Animals offered different kinds of intelligences that had been under-rated due to humans' fixation on language and technology. These included social and kinesthetic intelligence. Some mammals, like gibbons, could produce a large number of varied sounds. Over twenty different sounds with clearly different meanings allowed these arboreal primates to communicate across tropical forest canopies. The fact that they did not build houses was irrelevant to the gibbons.

Tool use had been reported many times in both wild and captive primates, particularly the great apes. The use of tools by primates was varied and included hunting fish; collecting honey; processing foods, such as nuts; and collecting water, weapons, and, shelter.

Chimpanzees in the Fongoli Savannah sharpened sticks to use as spears when hunting, which was considered the first evidence of systematic use of weapons in a species other than humans. Several species of birds, including parrots and owls, had been recorded as using tools in the wild.

One species examined extensively under laboratory conditions was the New Caledonian crow. One individual, called Betty, spontaneously made a wire tool to solve a novel problem in the laboratory. Millie was aware of all these facts, but the knowledge didn't cause her to feel any better.

She was tired of him sulking in the corner. She stood in front of him, sporting a stern expression, and signed, *"Roku, get up and go sit in your chair."* No response. She signed again, *"I am tired of this behavior. Now, I said get up and go sit in your chair. Right now."*

Roku continued to sit silently. His loud breathing in the form of wheezes.

She reached down to take a hold of his arm, and, when she did, he jumped to his feet, let out a loud shriek, and grabbed both of Millie's arms. He pushed her backward out of the kitchen and into the living room. She fell onto her back and hit her head on the floor.

Roku was on her, teeth bared, snarling. His eyes, now red, glowed as if they were on fire.

"Roku, stop this," she screamed, suddenly aware of the chimera's tremendous strength. Where did it come from? "Get off me, this instant!"

Instead of obeying, Roku continued his assault. He shook Millie by her shoulders, and she began to fight back, but it only provoked a more intense response from him. She felt her head being pounded into the hard floor, again and again. Roku's eyes were fixed on some far away place, as if he was not aware of what he was doing.

"Roku, get off me," Millie pleaded. "Please, Roku."

But the chimera did not stop.

Or get off Millie.

He continued bashing her head into the hard floor.

Over and over.

She felt she was close to losing consciousness. But, still, Roku did not stop his assault. The apartment began to fade, darkness closing around her.

She knew Roku was going to kill her.

"Please," she said in a weak exhalation.

Then everything went black.

Chapter 28

Gerald Siscom sat alone in his small apartment at the Primate Research Facility atop Cinder Mountain in northern Nevada. He had retired to his living quarters after finishing his end-of-day rounds in the Animal Care Unit and assuring himself that everything was satisfactory with the animals. Dinner wasn't for another hour, so he used the time to get caught up on his emails and journal reading.

He had gone about his work all day, trying to remain focused on the tasks at hand, but found it difficult. Thoughts of Millie's kiss haunted his waking moments and as he drifted off to sleep at night. He had hoped that their new relationship might bud into something more meaningful, for they had a lot in common.

But suddenly she was gone.

He was heartbroken for he felt sure she returned his feelings in kind. He had been unaware of her original plan, but when the ultrasound revealed Roku's true nature, he became complicit in her deception. It was a decision he regretted, and he had told Radner as much. He knew what he should have done—gone straight to Radner or Harry and exposed her project.

But he found himself caring for her in an unexpected

way and just couldn't bring himself to betray her trust.

He had an idea he was in love with her.

In fact, he began to hope that there might be a life for both of them at the facility now that Millie was a full-fledged faculty member. Dr. Olson had given her the position as associate director and Radner's right arm shortly after the Yeti had been killed. And when Harry spoke of a possible return to Mongolia for more Yeti specimens, Siscom hoped to be a part of the expedition along with Millie. But that was impossible now. Millie had disappeared with Roku and the university no longer employed Harry. Life was messed up all around.

Siscom thought back on when the pair of Yeti escaped from the research facility and Harry, along with its security chief, Bruce Drayton, led the search for them. Siscom had been a part of that party along with Dixie and Millie. They tracked the Yeti to a high mountain location but, unfortunately, were too late to save them. A law enforcement helicopter swooped in and cut them down, killing them both. Although it deeply grieved each and every person who worked with the animals, the experience had brought them closer together as colleagues at the facility. It was during their time together on the search that Siscom gained a new level of affection for Millie and admired her loving respect for the Yeti.

Earlier in the day, he sauntered down to her workspace in the unit and sat in her chair, thinking. He was heartbroken over her disappearance and felt like crawling into a hole and dying. His stomach rolled, his head pounded. Running away seemed like the only way to put her memory behind him. The thought of leaving Cinder Mountain and returning to private practice was something he now considered, even though it would mean starting over. Again. His experience at the facility might even qualify him for a faculty appointment at a veterinary school. Sitting at her workspace, he switched on her computer and thumbed through her files, the ones associated with the DNA transfer project. As he reread the files that he and Radner read earlier, the thought again struck him that the woman he thought he was in love with was deceitful from the very start. How could he have been so mistaken about her?

≈≈≈

When Millie did not show up for work, Ling Wu called her apartment, but there was no answer. Since he knew she lived right around the corner, he decided to walk the short distance and see if she was ill. He didn't like the fact that she didn't answer the phone.

From the bottom of the stairs to her walkup, he noticed the front door was ajar and his heart fluttered. It didn't look good. He thought about returning to his office and calling the police, but instead decided to investigate.

Climbing the rickety steps, he whispered an ancient Chinese prayer for Millie's well being. As he approached the door, he heard a moaning emanating from inside the apartment. He hurried to the opening and peered in. Millie sat on the floor, her head in her hands.

He sprang to her side in an instant, kneeling beside her. She looked at him with a vacant stare.

"Miss Millie," he said, shaking her gently. "You hurt? It is Ling Wu. Your door was open. What happened here?"

Millie looked about the apartment, still with vacant, glassy eyes.

"Mr. Wu?" she said.

"Miss Millie, you look terrible. What happen? You hurt?" Wu's voice was insistent.

Millie started to get up, but Wu cautioned her.

"Please," he said. "Do not get up. Rest first. Tell Ling what happened here."

"I—I" Millie stammered.

"You rest, Miss Millie. Ling called ambulance."

Wu jumped to his feet, found the telephone, and dialed nine-one-one. In excited tones, he told the operator the situation then hung up and redirected his attention toward Millie. He found her bruised and bloodied with a huge knot on the back of her head. Blood was caked dry. He watched her eyes attempt to focus on him.

"Mr. Wu?" she said. "What are you doing here?"

"I come find you. You were not at work, so I come find you. What happened?"

Millie looked around, tried to stand, but Wu kept her sitting on the floor.

"Where's Roku?" she said. "Roku! Roku!"

"Calm yourself, Miss Millie. The ambulance is on the way."

"Roku is gone," Millie said in a panicked tone. "Roku is gone!"

She struggled to get to her feet, but Wu kept her on the floor. Then he heard the wail of a siren in the distance and relaxed. The paramedics would soon be here.

When they finally did arrive, Millie argued that she didn't need to go to the hospital, but Wu convinced her that it was best. She had a large gash on the back of her head and numerous scratches over her bruised body. He didn't understand her repeating something about Roku. She was obviously worried about the fact that, whoever Roku was, he or she was not in the apartment. The name sounded as if it belonged to a pet.

He followed the ambulance to the emergency room and, after she was bandaged and released, gave her a ride back to her apartment. Along the way, Wu still worried about his employee.

"Miss Millie, doctor say you must rest. Please take all the time you need."

"That's very kind of you, Mr. Wu," Millie said. Wu thought she looked a little fuzzy with her head bandaged. The multiple cuts and abrasions on her face and neck gave her the look of a prizefighter.

"You kept saying something about a Roku, Miss Millie. What is…Roku?"

Wu noticed that Millie hesitated once again at the mention of the word. Why? he thought.

"I can't say at the moment, Mr. Wu. Or, I'd rather not."

Wu escorted her up the stairs and saw her settled into a chair. Since coming to work for him, Millie had performed her duties diligently, always with a professional attitude. She seemed genuinely concerned about his patients, giving each a kind word and a soft touch. But there was something about Millie he didn't understand. She didn't smile much and, rarely, if ever, laughed. She often stayed after the clinic closed to help him clean up and sterilize the needles that were used that day. He tried on numerous occasions to make a joke with her in the hopes of seeing her smile, but his efforts were fruitless. But he enjoyed her quiet, efficient manner and decided that, whatever were her demons, she had a right to bear them in silence.

He decided to not press the issue about Roku, who or whatever it was, and left her alone in her apartment. He was now dependent on her help in the office. When she returned, he would invite her to his home for dinner to meet his family.

ဆဈဆ

The rest Millie was ordered to get by the emergency

room physician never materialized for she spent the next three days searching for Roku, and the energy it took sapped her strength further.

She ate very little and worried incessantly. Her days were filled with endless hours of treading the nearby neighborhoods in the hope of spotting him. But each afternoon, she returned to her tiny apartment, weary and unsuccessful. Her futile efforts seemed ineffectual to the required task as Roku had apparently disappeared for good. Slowly, her physical wounds healed but the inward antipathy she felt for herself drove her deeper into depression.

She watched television and searched the Chinatown newspaper for any news of Roku's sighting or being picked up by animal control but there was none. Roku was not used to foraging for himself for food or water. That fact decreased the likelihood of his survival. The chimera could have even strayed beyond Chinatown, and there was always the possibility the creature could make it to Fisherman's Wharf or the Embarcadero, in which case he would most certainly be found. Even killed.

She recognized her duplicity toward the university and those she cared about—the Drs. Olson, Dr. Radner, Gerald Siscom. It didn't help her mood any, realizing her actions were against prevailing societal norms. An Occam's Razor approach meant her views would never become popular, at least not in her lifetime. She had become closer to Gerald, and she felt some guilt for not revealing her true intent from the outset. The few dates they had were pleasant enough.

But now, because of Roku, she had left all that behind. And she would never recapture what she lost. Maybe that was what pained her. The fact that she had let so many people down, including herself, and, in the process, lost something valuable in Gerald's concern for her.

One day there would be a reckoning with the university, the law, her friends, her parents.

Most of all, Gerald.

Chapter 29

Special Agent Hank Jacoby studied the detective report sent over by the SF Police Department. After scanning the pages, he glanced out the window onto the wind-swept streets below the FBI offices and wondered if rain was imminent. He took a large gulp of cold coffee and returned to the report.

A woman in eastern Chinatown had been brutally murdered while she was out walking her dog. According to the medical examiner, the woman's face was torn completely away. No, the examiner said, more like it was chewed or gnawed away. One could easily mistake the wound as being the result of a vicious animal attack, if it were not for a witness who saw the perp run from the scene. It was dark, the man did not observe the attack, but he noticed an upright figure running, more like scampering, from the spot where the woman was attacked. The man was horrified by what he encountered and called the police.

The police report went on to mention that when the witness, an elderly man out walking his dog, arrived at the woman's side, the perp was long gone, having disappeared into a dark alleyway. The man was unable to give a clear description of the assailant, except for the fact that the man was stooped over with his arms almost touching the ground. It was dark, so he couldn't see more.

Jacoby lit the end of a short cigar, pushed the intercom on his desk, and asked Sam Prescott to come in. When the agent was ensconced in a chair, Jacoby tossed the police file toward him and puffed the cigar while the man read. Finished, Sam laid the report back on Jacoby's desk.

"What do you think, Sam," Jacoby said, snubbing the cigar in an ashtray.

"Another Chinatown murder," Prescott said. "Why do you have the file? It's a police case."

"The bizarre nature of the crime, I guess. Face ripped off, shredded I'd say. Unlike anything seen recently."

"Looks more like an animal did it," Prescott said. "Those photographs are pretty grisly. What are you going to do?"

"Nothing. We have this Harbaum case we need to close as soon as possible. Anything new?"

Jacoby picked up the cigar, twirled it in his hands, looked at it for a moment, then tossed it back into the ashtray, making a face. Prescott smiled.

"Hank," he said, chuckling, "why do you continue smoking those things? You know the doc told you to quit. They're gonna kill you one of these days."

Jacoby shook his head.

"Hell if I know, Sam. It's a nasty habit. Don't you ever start."

"Trust me, boss, I won't. Just the smell is enough to drive me away. And you stick the thing in your mouth."

The two men laughed, and Jacoby nodded.

"You're right, as always," he said. "When is Lenny returning from the girl's parents? I want to talk to him as soon as he gets back."

"He's on a return flight as we speak. Should be landing at International in about an hour. I'm going to pick him up."

"You two come directly here," Jacoby said. "He can fill me in then."

ᕔᕔᕔ

Roku woke with a start. Darkness enveloped him like the comforting blanket Mother placed around him when she went to bed. Where was he? He had no idea and couldn't remember how he had come to this place. Where was Mother? He was hungry.

Sitting upright, he realized he was at the bottom of a crevasse located deep within a dense copse of trees and brush. How had he arrived here? He couldn't remember.

Roku heard a soft noise in the underbrush and scanned the area, his red eyes narrowed, his large ears alert. In the dark beyond, there was a small animal moving quietly, but Roku didn't know what it was. Mother hadn't taught him the word. He watched, transfixed by the animal's presence, as it skulked its way past. Something deep within his marrow urged him to pounce on the small critter and devour it, but he hesitated—Mother would find him soon and feed him.

He was thirsty. He knew that word, and he knew he needed to find water. Mother got it for him out of something called a faucet, but there was no faucet nearby. He could see that. He pushed his bulky frame to his feet and lumbered out of the gully, slashing his way through the forest of vines and shrubs. The only sounds he heard now were the tree frogs and crickets.

It was starting to get light, which made it easier for Roku to find his way. The dim outline of a path came into sharp relief, so he scooted along it hoping to find water. A shallow depression alongside the path had water in it, and he drank. It didn't taste like the water Mother gave him. Where was she? Why hadn't she come to get him?

He continued to stumble over the path. Suddenly, a car horn honked and he jumped. He was at the edge of the forest and cars were going every which way. One almost ran him down, its driver shouting words Roku didn't understand. He jumped back into the safety of the trees, his heart pounding.

Roku scurried back into the forest, deeper into the dim world of trees and brush. He fought his way through tangles and briars, thorns tearing at his flesh, snagging his short, fine fur. Frustration mounted in his brain, part human, and part animal. The emotion he didn't understand, but some force drove him to seek safety. He was operating at some primal level, a level he sought to understand, but Mother never could explain.

He was tormented by a single question—who or what was he? His thought processes were far advanced of his ability to communicate them, and it made him angry. It was obvious he was different from Mother and others like her. Adding to his frustration was the fact that he had never seen another like himself. Not one. He knew he was different but why? He pleaded with Mother for answers, but none were ever forthcoming. Why? Was he so different that it defied explanation?

He knew the answer. Of course, he was.

Mother spoke strange words that came out of her mouth. He was only able to grunt and growl. Why couldn't he make sounds and words like Mother? He even looked different. His head was huge while his eyes were red, not green like hers. His skin had longer hair, his ears were much larger, and his nose protruded much more than hers. And his arms were much longer.

Roku stumbled onto an opening and, upon further investigation, found it was a concrete portal that led underground. Covered by thick brush it had almost gone unnoticed. But a shaft of sunlight glinted off its surface and attracted his attention. Pushing the limbs of a shrub aside, Roku gazed into the dark beyond. It appeared to be a long tunnel. He ducked his head, lumbered a few meters into the shaft, stopped, and listened. Nothing, no sounds. All was quiet.

Roku sat and thought.

Where was he?

He was confused.

And angry.

ೲ

Dixie was worried about her husband. It had been several days since Harry talked with Dr. Brock with the Institute of American Antiquities and still no word on the job offer from them. Dr. Brock had told Harry the vetting process would take several days, but he had not called with an offer. What was taking them so long? Harry became sullen and morose, retreating to the study to read or listen to music. Dixie humored him the best she could, saying everything would work out, that the IAA was just being slow, and that sooner or later he would get the call he wanted. But he just looked at her with a doleful expression and nodded.

She fixed a sandwich and a glass of milk and took it into him. He sat in his chair, the one that belonged to the Professor, staring out the window. As she entered, he turned around.

"Here, honey," she said, smiling, "I brought you a snack. I thought you might be hungry."

Harry didn't return her smile. She set the tray on the desk and placed a hand on his shoulder.

"Don't be so depressed, sweetheart," she said. "I know everything will work out for the best."

"Yeah?" Harry said, looking back out the window. "What makes you so sure?"

Dixie's heart sank. Why had he lost the faith he had only a few days earlier? She hated to see him like this. Harry, for all the years she'd known him, always possessed a survivalist attitude about his work. When Professor Kesler died unexpectedly, Harry took the reins of the department and continued in the man's tradition. And with excellence, she might add. When Dr. Wickingham threatened to cause trouble with the university over Harry's past mistakes, he didn't fold up and become depressed. She couldn't explain it.

"I just have faith, that's all," she said.

Harry turned back to face her and said in a very low tone, "Faith doesn't put food on the table."

His demeanor shocked her. How could she console him? She put her arms around his shoulders and kissed the back of his neck. She felt him stiffen and tears welled in her eyes.

"Harry, you can't be like this," she said. "You are stronger than this. The man I married can conquer anything. And has. We have each other, and we will face this together. If it get's too much, I can always go back to Cal Pacific. I'm sure Dr. Pauling would take me back. Eating a little crow wouldn't bother me."

"But it would me," Harry said, still gazing out the window.

"Oh, hogwash. You can get unemployment for a while, and I can go back to the university. We can make out till you find something. We'll just eat beans more often." She laughed at that remark. "Come on, honey. Cheer up."

Harry turned back to her and shook his head. "Just

leave me alone right now, Dixie. I want to be alone."

She left him in the study and returned to the kitchen, where she sat and sipped her coffee. Harry's mood unnerved her, and she couldn't fathom the reason. Could it be the fact that he was now unemployed? Millions of people went through unemployment all the time. Or could it go deeper, something she hadn't thought much about? Something professional people had? A tremendous amount of pride. Harry had accomplished a lot in his short career, had risen to a height few men of his age were able to. Along with that, came an ego, and Harry certainly had one. But maybe it was even deeper than all that.

Being a paleoanthropologist was who he was. It wasn't just a job with Harry. It wasn't something he did for fun. It was who he was as a person. She knew it gave him a tremendous sense of self-worth. To be summarily dismissed for things beyond his control was not only premature but also grossly unfair.

Dixie wondered how long she should allow him to remain alone with his thoughts. She feared the longer he stewed over his dismissal and inability to find another position, the deeper into depression he might sink. She decided she would take him on a drive to the San Bruno Mountain State Park for a picnic dinner where they would stare at the bay while the sun set. She put together cold chicken, pate, smoked oysters, and wine and packed it all in a basket. When she was ready, she returned to the study, sat in Harry's lap, and demanded he go with her.

He smiled and followed her to the car.

Chapter 30

Andrew Daisuke locked the door to his Chinatown diner and began the six-block walk to his apartment on California Street, not far from Old St. Mary's Cathedral. It being close to midnight, there was no one on the sidewalk, and only an occasional car sped by. His diner, The Golden Spoon, served a variety of Asian and American fast foods and had been busier than usual for a weekday evening. Andrew spent an hour after the last customer left, making out his grocery list to give his vendor in the morning.

The night air was cool and crisp, and, as he ambled along, he marveled at a large yellow moon that had risen over the Bay. Passing the cathedral, he remembered his daughter's catechism class held earlier that evening. He would have to get the particulars from his wife, May, when he got home. It was gratifying to have the family cathedral in the neighborhood, so convenient for Mass and other activities. Especially bingo. Andrew loved bingo.

At the intersection, he turned the corner and headed east toward the Bay. Passing a dark alleyway, he paused, for something caught his eye—a brief movement in the darkness. The sidewalk was empty, and only a few lights glowed from apartment windows that overlooked the street. He stood for a moment, pulse rising, searching the dark alley. Seeing nothing, he continued his walk but, again, a muffled sound stopped him. He turned and peered into the alley.

"Who's there?" he said. The hairs on his neck stiffened, his skin prickled.

Nothing.

Andrew took a step into the alleyway and scanned its depths. It was difficult to see into the darkness, but he satisfied himself that there was nothing there. Must have been a cat, he thought.

Just as he directed his attention back to the sidewalk, he was grabbed from behind and jerked into the dark recess of the alley. Something had him by his neck and shoulder, and its hot breath blew past his head. He struggled against the powerful grip on his neck and shoulders, to no avail.

"What the hell?" he shouted. "Who are you? What d'ya want?"

There was no answer. Andrew continued to struggle.

"Stop it, dammit! For Christ's sake! Lemme go!"

He twisted his arm up and managed to get a hold on one of the hands that gripped him. Good god, it felt different, like fur or something. From behind him came a growling, grunting sound, one that sounded like something from another world. Like a large animal. The grip he had on the hand felt cold and wet. Strong.

He tried to wrestle free, but it was no use. The more he struggled, the tighter was the grip on his neck and shoulders. He felt an arm move around his neck into a chokehold and squeeze. He couldn't breathe.

The growling was louder, and he fought to get a breath. His heart pounded, and he felt as if he was going to vomit.

"Turn me loose, dammit!" he shouted, inhaling enough air to speak.

Andrew fought with all the force he could muster, but he felt himself fading, his strength waning. The other arm of whoever was attacking him wrapped around his head, forcing him down.

Then everything went black.

෴

FBI Special Agent Hank Jacoby strolled into the San Francisco morgue located in the office of the medical examiner in the Hall of Justice. A pert secretary whose black glasses were too large for her face greeted him. After peering at his identification, she led him down a long, brightly lit hallway and ushered him into a cramped office.

"I'll tell Dr. Brathwaite you are here, sir," she said. She left him standing next to a small window that overlooked the Bryant Street parking lot below. A fresh wind blew leaves into small whirlwinds while people scurried about their daily activities.

A young man in scrub attire entered the office. He smiled through a neatly trimmed beard and extended a hand.

"Special Agent Jacoby," he said, eyeing the agent through wire-framed glasses. "I was apprised that your office wished to be notified if any victims arrived exhibiting a manner of death similar to the woman of a week ago."

"Yes, yes, Doctor," Jacoby said. "What do you have?"

Brathwaite picked up a file off the desk and handed it to Jacoby, who took it and began thumbing through it.

"This victim was brought in early this morning," the doctor said. "Our office picked him up over in Chinatown. As you can see by the photographs, the man was the victim of a vicious attack by person or persons unknown."

The doctor picked up a Styrofoam cup half filled with cold coffee and gulped it down. He waited while Jacoby looked at the crime scene photos before continuing.

"I called because the man's wounds are similar to the woman's from last week. I was just getting ready to do the man's autopsy. Would you care to join me? You can see first hand what you are dealing with."

Jacoby's stomach twisted. He hated postmortems, but they were a necessary part of the job. He was glad all he had for breakfast was a roll and coffee.

"Sure," he said. "When do we start?"

"Let's get you into some scrubs first. Follow me."

Jacoby followed the young pathologist through a maze of sterile hallways before finally reaching large room whose sign on the door read, *MEDICAL STAFF LOUNGE*. The room contained several sofas and chairs, a television, a cabinet with coffeepot resting on its surface along with a platter of doughnuts and rolls. A microwave completed the appointments.

Brathwaite led the agent through the lounge and into a smaller locker room. He pulled a set of scrubs from a shelf, handed them to Jacoby, and pointed to the bathroom behind the bank of lockers.

"Find yourself an empty locker, and you can use the bathroom if you need to. I'll wait in the lounge."

Jacoby changed into the scrubs and joined Brathwaite. The doctor led him to the autopsy room, where the lifeless body of the victim lay naked on a stainless steel table. A surgical light shone brightly on the corpse. Brathwaite moved to one side, and a technician took up a position on the opposite side of the table. Jacoby stood at the doctor's elbow.

Talking both into a microphone and to Jacoby, Brathwaite's voice was soft but firm. "The victim is Andrew Daisuke, a fifty-two year old Asian male."

With that introduction, the doctor began the methodical routine of the autopsy. First, he examined the surface of the body in minute detail, even using a magnifying glass at times. Jacoby could see for himself that the victim had met with a horrific and violent end. Similar to the woman of the previous week, the face had been destroyed, the skull crushed. There were numerous gaping wounds on the arms and torso of the victim. Dried blood covered the body. Jacoby fought the urge to leave. His stomach churned.

Brathwaite continued his dictation. "The face has been totally destroyed," he said. "The edges of the wounds are ragged in nature, indicating a macerating type of injury. The posterior skull is crushed, numerous cranial fractures are evident, and brain matter is both exposed and missing. There is a crush injury of the larynx, indicating a chokehold or garrote. The victim may have died as a result of suffocation."

Jacoby peered over the pathologist's shoulder to gain a better view. The swollen, blue gray neck had a reddish mark over the Adam's apple. The victim was choked, he surmised.

"Moving to the skin," Brathwaite continued, "there are numerous gaping wounds over the entire body resulting in a tremendous loss of blood. Most notably, there are large bite marks over the entire back, large areas on the anterior torso where skin and muscle are missing. The left arm has been dislocated and nearly torn away from the shoulder."

The technician turned the corpse over. Brathwaite took a set of calipers and began measuring the marks on the victim's back. He methodically went from wound to wound, and Jacoby noticed he was intimately engaged in his work. The pathologist seemed unaware of the agent's presence. "Wounds on the back have the appearance of bite marks," Brathwaite said into the microphone. "There are numerous abrasions and avulsions of the skin and, in many areas, deep lacerations."

As Brathwaite worked his way over the body, the technician charted each one by a simple sketch with measurements. At one point, Brathwaite stopped his work and turned to Jacoby.

"The shape of the mouth arch on the arch width on some of these wounds is puzzling," he said. "There are some wounds here that still show definite bite mark characteristics. You can see them here." He pointed, and Jacoby nodded. "And here and here."

Again, Jacoby nodded. "You said they are puzzling, Doctor. How so?"

"Well, for starters, the measurements are outside the range of most human bites."

"What do you mean?"

"Bite mark injuries and suspect teeth possess pertinent physical characteristics, which are amenable to digital measurement. The most obvious are the distance from cuspid to cuspid, the shape of the mouth arch, the evidence of a tooth out of alignment, the width and thickness, spacing between teeth or missing teeth, the curves of biting edges, the arch width, and the labiolingual position."

Jacoby didn't need a bunch of medical double talk. He needed the young pathologist to get to the point. Holding back his irritation, he smiled and nodded as if he understood. "So what are you saying, Doctor?"

"I don't believe these wounds came from a person," Brathwaite said. "Most likely came from an animal of some sort."

"I don't quite understand."

"Each person has a unique dental arrangement, and these unique features are sufficiently replicated in a bite mark to identify an individual to the exclusion of all others. The marks left by the teeth of a person may be used to identify the individual. A human bite mark is usually described as an elliptical or circular injury. That is not evident in these wounds. The differences in size and shape of teeth can sometimes be easily noticed, especially when teeth are missing or prominent. However, a bite mark is not always an accurate representation of the teeth. It depends on the jaw movement and use of the tongue. The lower jaw is moveable and gives the most biting force. The upper jaw is usually stationery and holds and stretches the skin."

"Please, Doctor," Jacoby said, now losing patience with the science, "just cut to the chase here. You said these bite marks weren't made by a human, right?"

"That is my initial opinion, yes. You see, it's the shape of the arch and its measurements that lead me to that conclusion. But let's finish the post, shall we?"

The rest of the autopsy failed to yield any surprises and ended in a routine fashion. Jacoby felt like leaving but stayed to the bitter end. As he sat in the locker room and changed back into his suit, Brathwaite brought him a cup of coffee.

Jacoby accepted it with gratitude, took a sip of the coffee, and shrugged. "Sorry if I was short in there, Doctor. I don't handle medical speak very well."

Dr. Brathwaite sat and cleaned his glasses. "Not to worry," he said. "It comes second nature to me, and I sometimes forget that not everyone gets as excited as I do. You're going to have your hands full with this one, I'm afraid."

"Doctor," Jacoby said as he tied his tie. "I would like you to do something for me."

"Sure, if I can."

"I would like it very much if you could go back to the autopsy on the woman of last week and take another look at her injuries. I would be interested to know if they are in any way similar to today's victim. See if she had any bite marks and, if she did, if they were similar to this victim's. Can you do that?"

"Certainly," Brathwaite said. "I didn't do her postmortem, but I can review the findings and let you know. Would later this afternoon be satisfactory?"

Jacoby nodded. "Fine, just fine," he said.

Chapter 31

Rupert Innes crawled on his hands and knees along an underground passage. Pieces of rock, dirt, and cement fragments pressed into his palms and kneecaps, keeping them from staying in one place too long. The air was stagnant and thick with dust and age. He had moved far enough that no one would hear if he got into trouble and called for help. Every few feet or so, he moved wires or scrap metal out of his way. In the distance, a lantern had been forgotten, or perhaps abandoned. The path was littered with plastic caps, trash, and decaying insects.

Shit, he thought, surprised. *What was that? The largest cockroach I have ever seen!*

In an instant, everything went dark. The top of the flashlight came off and lay in pieces in the dirt. As he fumbled to assemble it, he stopped and peered into the darkness. He could hear something moving toward him. He was underground, alone, and blind. In the darkness, it was as if every sound was amplified. Finally, he managed to get the light on again and continued to the end of the passage.

The tip he'd gotten from another junkie that there were remnants of a secret tunnel, leading to something cool and hidden, turned out to be a forgotten staircase that led nowhere.

Almost everyone had heard something about the secret tunnels under San Francisco. And while some might say they were an urban legend and didn't exist, Rupert knew for sure they did. They were his home, a safe haven from, thieves, murderers, and other addicts strung out so far they would kill for the smallest bit of smack. There weren't many still alive that were willing to share what they knew. The younger generation had only heard rumors or whispers about the tunnels and the ones who did know never admitted it to a stranger. If there were any of these secret locations still undiscovered, they were surely being used for things that were illegal or profitable, and, therefore, private.

Many had stories or experiences that proved, at one time or another, that there were plenty of tunnels that connected different locations. After years of building, expansions, and earthquake retrofitting, the number of these passageways was dwindling. There might be a few tunnels left, but the misfits who ruled them were not quick to advertise their whereabouts.

San Francisco had a relatively short history, compared to other great cities of the world. But in its brief existence, it had had a sordid past. Everyone agreed that Chinese immigration, brothels, and speakeasies ran rampant in this city, at one time or another.

Rupert's previous home was a tunnel that had been located in 1940 by city engineers who were starting construction for a new Nob Hill hotel. The entrance was discovered in the foundation of a mansion that belonged to a prominent family. Engineers followed the tunnel, well below street level for fifty yards. It was nine feet wide and nearly the same height, the ceiling was bricked in an arch shape. It had possibly been lit by lanterns or torches at one time. The tunnel stretched straight and long under California Street and ended at another mansion.

Rupert and his friend, Dink—he never knew his real name—were run out of there shortly before Dink died of an overdose. The tunnel was closed by the city. Rupert had no idea what purpose the tunnel originally served. Rumors spread that it was built because someone was having an affair and used it to more easily visit his mistress. Others said that sort of elaborate passageway could only have been built for something illegal. However, all ideas were only speculation, and the true secrets remain buried in the tunnel.

Rupert shined his flashlight about his new home. It was more like a concrete bunker. Asian graffiti lined its stained walls. *Damn these panda trainers and butter heads*, he thought. *They all should be run out of Chinatown.* He lit a small candle he'd found in a dump and doused his flashlight. He worried about the unseen killer of living underground—gas. Methane and hydrogen-sulfide gas were produced by decaying organic garbage and were a constant threat to anyone in the tunnels for an extended period. The hydrogen sulfide smelled like rotten eggs. He had known of people who went to sleep in a tunnel and never woke up. Not from their drugs. The gas killed them.

A sound came from the entrance of the tunnel, the way he came in. It was a shuffling sound. Someone or something was moving through the trash-strewn passageway.

Moving toward him.

He needed a fix soon and had brought the stuff with him. But the sound coming closer worried him. If it was another druggie, Rupert would either have to fight or share, and he didn't have a weapon. There was no place to go, for he was at the end of the tunnel. He shined his light around and noticed what looked like a manhole in the ceiling at the far end. He had no idea where it led, but if he could climb up there, he might be able to wait until whoever was coming left.

He crawled below the manhole and, holding his flashlight in his mouth, pushed on the cover. It didn't move. *Rusted shut*, he thought.

The cover had three holes in it just large enough to allow his fingers. He gripped the cover once more and, with much effort, attempted to jerk it free. The shuffling sound was louder, and he thought he heard grunting. *Raccoon?* he thought. Those varmints were all over Chinatown. *They must like fortune cookies*.

Rupert tried again to loosen the manhole cover but was unsuccessful. He turned around to confront whatever was coming down the tunnel—and stared into the face of the unworldliest thing he had ever encountered.

ഏഃ

Harry sat at the breakfast table, drinking coffee and reading the morning paper. He thought about looking through the want ads to see if there were any interesting jobs listed but decided against it. He was still waiting for the IAA to call. Hopefully, it would be today.

Dixie ambled into the kitchen and poured herself a cup of coffee. She sat and smiled at him. "Good morning, sweetie."

"What's so good about it?" he said. He didn't feel like having a cheerful conversation at the moment.

"Look outside," she said. "It's a beautiful day."

"I really don't care."

"Come on, honey, cheer up. Things will look up soon enough."

He threw the paper on the table and poured himself another cup of coffee. Why was it when a man wished to be alone with his own thoughts and misery a woman always tried to cheer him up? He could tell her it was useless, but it would be to no avail, for he had done exactly that several times in the past few days. He gazed at her bright eyes, her dimpled cheeks. How could she be so naive? He was no good unless he could get his career back. "When?" he said.

"When what?"

"You said things would look up soon enough. I want to know when."

"How should I know? Listen, Harry, I don't wish to be a nag, but you've got to get a grip on yourself. You're letting this thing get you down, depressed, and it's just not worth it."

"Yeah? How should you know? You weren't the one fired from his job."

"Honey, I understand that depression, anxiety, and malaise aren't just a case of the blues to snap out of. I know these things will sap your confidence and impact your ability to think and act, making it difficult to sell yourself as the best and brightest candidate for a job. Trust me, I understand."

"Do you realize how long it's been since I interviewed for a job?" he said through narrowed eyes. "I'm out of practice."

"Well, I could practice with you," Dixie said, still smiling over her cup of coffee.

"Not the same," he replied in a monotone. He didn't make eye contact with her now.

She set her cup down and got up.

"I've got laundry to do," she said. "Let me know if you change your mind."

She disappeared, and he heard her bustling about in the laundry room. Soon he heard the washing machine begin its cycle.

He returned to the newspaper and thumbed through its back pages. Buried among the articles was one that caught his attention. A homeless heroin addict had been found murdered in a Chinatown tunnel. Boys playing in the area had been drawn to a foul odor and discovered the tunnel. A city sanitation crew entered the tunnel and found the body of Rupert Innes who had been viciously murdered. His face was torn away by some savage force, and his skull was crushed. So sad, thought Harry.

As he read farther, the article stated that the method of Innes's murder matched two others in Chinatown in the past two weeks. They too had their faces torn away and their skulls crushed. All victims had multiple gaping wounds over their entire bodies and bore bite marks that did not appear human—as if a monstrous animal had done the dastardly deeds.

Those two words caught his attention.

Monstrous animal.

Three murders in a short period of time, all with the same method of killing, as if a monstrous animal had been the attacker.

Harry's mind was in a whirl. He took the paper into the next room where Dixie was working.

"Look at this article," he said, handing her the newspaper. He pointed to the one and waited while she read it.

Finished, she looked up. "Who would do such a thing?" she said.

"I draw your attention to those words *monstrous animal* the article referred. Sound like anything?"

She looked at him, shook her head.

"How about our chimera, Millie's chimera?"

"Roku?" she said.

"Why not? He certainly would be capable by now. Big enough. Part of him is a Yeti, remember. And we don't have a clue as to his whereabouts."

Dixie's eyes widened. Her jaw dropped.

"My lord," she said. "It certainly is possible, I guess."

"And all these murders occurred in Chinatown," Harry said, now animated. "Roku could be hiding somewhere in Chinatown. We don't know where Millie is or even if Roku is still with her."

"If he had escaped her care, he could be lurking, hiding in the various parks in Chinatown," Dixie said, "and only coming out when he was hungry in search of food."

"And he fed on these poor victims. Don't you see, honey? It does make sense. It is possible."

"You—you—called me honey."

"What?"

"You haven't called me that in many days," she said. She put her arms around his neck. "What now?"

"I'm calling Jacoby. I want to give him this lead."

Later, when he had the agent on the phone, Harry's spirits rose again.

"I just talked to the Medical Examiner," Jacoby said. "He performed all sorts of measurements on the latest victim's wounds and bite marks and compared them with the other Chinatown autopsy results. It is his expert opinion that the wounds were not caused by a human but by some sort of animal, whom they are now trying to identify. But here's the kicker, Dr. Olson. There was saliva on the last victim, Mr. Innes, and the DNA analysis was inconclusive."

Harry sat back in his chair.

"What do you mean, inconclusive?" he said.

"I mean there were some human DNA elements in the saliva. There were also some elements that could not be identified. Some DNA in the saliva was not human."

"That's him, Agent Jacoby. That's our chimera, Roku," Harry said. He jumped up, pacing the house while he talked.

"That's what I thought," Jacoby said. "We are making up fliers with a description of it along with Miss Harbaum's picture and will distribute them throughout Chinatown and the surrounding neighborhoods. Maybe we'll get lucky. Maybe someone has seen them."

"Anything I can do?"

"Right now you can hope for the best."

Harry hung up and returned to his chair. *If they find them,* he thought, *Roku is as good as dead.*

Chapter 32

Roku rambled back to the tunnel. The gray early dawn arrived with the quiet chirping of birds and the rustle of small animals returning to their holes, while the rich loamy fragrance of the forest filled the air with a sweet perfume. After spending several days and nights in the safety of the concrete enclosure, Roku returned late one afternoon only to find someone in it. The man, dressed in strange looking clothes, became a ready meal for him. It was easy to overpower the invader, but, after eating his fill Roku fled, unnerved by what he had done. When he returned the next day, the tunnel was surrounded by a crowd of people, most in strange looking clothes. *Uniforms* he thought, *Mother called them uniforms*. It wasn't until two days later that the tunnel was empty, and he felt comfortable using it again.

Roku was confused. Since losing Mother—and he didn't know or remember what happened to her or why she had left him—he wandered around the city, frightened of the traffic, crowds of people, and the noise. Mother wasn't there to feed him and care for him. He couldn't understand why she abandoned him. He didn't know what to do.

He wondered about many things, mostly who he was

and why he looked so different from all the others on the street. He didn't understand why he could not make the sounds Mother made and could only communicate by signing. Feeding on others like Mother, wandering around in the cold night, and hiding out in the tunnel during the day, didn't seem like such a good life to Roku. He didn't understand it all.

Who was he?

What was going on?

Where was Mother?

Not having the answers, he took refuge in the tunnel and searched for food at night.

෧෮෧

The alarm clock on her bedside table sounded. Millie, groggy from little sleep, turned it off and stumbled out of bed. She had not gone to bed until after midnight, worrying over Roku's disappearance. It had been a week since he attacked her and left the apartment in shambles, and she spent many sleepless hours trying to figure where he might have gone. She would much rather search Chinatown than go to work, but Mr. Wu had been so nice and thoughtful, she felt it imperative to show up.

Millie strolled into her cluttered kitchen and made coffee and, while it was perking, took a shower. After dressing, she sipped her coffee and wondered where in Chinatown she would look for Roku after work. Two days earlier, she had started at the neighborhood's north end and gradually worked her way south. She drove around in her car, and, if she spotted a possible area, she parked and searched on foot, figuring the numerous parks were the most likely candidates in which Roku would hide. Those she gave a closer inspection. To date, she had been unsuccessful.

Finished with her coffee, she fixed her hair and put on her makeup. The bruises and scratches were healed, but there remained a scar on her psyche. Still unnerved by Roku's violent attack, Millie wasn't looking forward to a reunion with her creation. Satisfied with the way she looked, she placed the coffee mug in the sink with the other dirty dishes and walked out the door.

She had a strong desire to call Gerald Siscom, to apologize for her deception because she genuinely cared for him. She felt she owed him that much. But there was a certain danger in calling Gerald. He would want to know where she was, would want to see her. Could she afford the risk? Would she dare divulge her whereabouts?

While at work, the idea of making contact with Siscom weighed heavy on Millie's mind, filling her thoughts and preventing her from devoting her complete attention to her work. Several times during the day, Mr. Wu asked her if she was all right and needed to go home, but she told him she was fine, just a little tired. All the same, she continued to fret over contacting Gerald. There were a number of things she wanted to get straight with him, even apologize for. First and foremost, she wanted to apologize for deceiving him by not telling him the true nature of her experiment. Her only defense was she knew he would not help her if he knew the truth. So, she decided to keep it from him, a big mistake. Then she wanted him to know that she missed him terribly. Her heart ached not seeing his smiling face each day and hearing his cheerful voice. Finally, she wanted to see him, but only if he promised not to go to the authorities. Maybe they could meet somewhere between Cinder Mountain and Frisco. Somewhere she could feel safe.

The day dragged on until, finally, Wu closed and locked the front door. She said goodbye to him and walked the short distance to her apartment. On the way, she stopped at an Asian diner and bought some egg rolls and stir-fry for her dinner. Once changed into jogging clothes and ensconced on her sofa, she opened the egg rolls and stir-fry. She picked up her cell phone and dialed Gerald's number. She had ditched her old phone and only recently purchased a new one, so she didn't know if he or anyone else had ever tried to reach her. It was better to not know.

Sitcom answered on the first ring.

"Hello," he said in a low voice. He obviously didn't recognize the number.

"Gerald," Millie said, hesitating. "It's me. Millie."

She waited for a response on the other end and eventually it came.

"Millie," Sitcom said, his tone suddenly loud and animated. "Where the hell are you? Are you okay?"

"I'm fine, Gerald," she said, holding back tears. "But I can't tell you where I am, sorry."

"Millie, for Christ's sake. Everyone, and I do mean everyone, is out looking for you. Harry and Dixie. Even the cops. The damned FBI has been here asking questions about you. Are you sure you are all right?"

"Yes, I'm fine."

"My, this is a surprise. I had given up hope of ever hearing from you." Siscom had calmed down and now sounded like his old self. Millie's heart skipped a beat. "I tried numerous times to call you, but you never answered. I was heartbroken."

"Oh, Gerald," Millie said, her mouth suddenly dry. "I'm so sorry. I got rid of my phone. I was afraid they could trace where I was with it. I've wanted to call you so many times but was afraid. I—I have missed you very much."

"Our times together meant a lot to me as well. What are you doing now? Can you tell me where you are? I'll come. I want to see you, Millie." His words were short and clipped, she could hear the concern in his voice.

"I'm so sorry that all this has happened and fallen back on you and the university. I'm especially sorry for not confiding in you about my plans. I just didn't think you would understand. It wasn't that I didn't trust you, it was…well, I guess I didn't trust you to understand. I'm sorry. I should have known better. But, at the time, every-thing seemed all confused and was moving too fast. I didn't allow myself to trust you."

"I wish you had told me everything," Sitcom said. "Sure, I would have tried to talk you out of creating that chimera and implanting the embryo. Because the stakes were so high, Millie. But I would have never betrayed a confidence, never."

"Even if I had refused to abort my experiment, Ger-ald? Even then?"

"Well…I—"

"See, you're hesitating. And I just couldn't take that chance. I know you are an honest, forthright man, Gerald. You have honor and integrity. I doubt you would have allowed me to proceed, knowing what I was doing. You would have gone to Radner or Dr. Olson. I don't fault you for that."

She heard Siscom's long sigh, as if a weight had been lifted off his shoulders.

"How is Roku?" he asked.

"Roku has disappeared," she said, with tears again welling in her eyes. The remembrance of the attack was unbearable.

"You mean, as in gone?"

"Yes. He attacked me last week and took off. I don't know where he is."

"He attacked you? How?"

"He physically attacked me and hurt me. I would never have believed he would do such a thing. After all, I raised him. I have no idea where he is."

There was a long silence, as if Siscom was trying to comprehend what she said. Finally, he spoke. "My God, how badly were you hurt? I was afraid something like this might happen."

"I was taken to the hospital, but they patched me up. I'm doing okay now. Back working."

"Where, Millie?"

She ignored the question. "For all I know, Roku is starving somewhere. He's never had to forage for himself. He'll be cold and afraid. He might hurt someone else. If I had known it would come to this, I don't think I would have created Roku. It's all been a nightmare, Gerald. I can no longer take care of Roku myself. He's gotten too large. His Yeti DNA now controls a large part of his behavior."

"Any human signs of intelligence?"

"Oh, Gerald, he is extremely intelligent. Of course, he cannot speak words, but he has a several-thousand-word language using sign. We communicate nicely. He even puts short sentences together in complete thoughts. Just the other day, he was asking questions about himself. Who or what he was, where he came from. That's when he became frustrated and attacked me. It seemed as if he was becoming aware of himself as a distinct being. And he recognized that he was different. I think it frightened him."

"Well, self-awareness is a trait of higher intelligence, Millie. Obviously, the human portion of his genome. I have to ask this question—didn't you think through the ramifications of what you were about to do? I mean, didn't the ethical questions about this sort of genetic engineering trouble you? Scientists all over the world are on record as not supporting this type of experimentation.

You've not only put your friends and the university in a pickle, you've placed all of genetic science on the firing line. There is genuine public outrage over this. You're a smart woman. You should have been able to predict the firestorm that has erupted." He sighed. "My heart goes out to you."

"To be quite honest, I thought only of the positive side, Gerald. I was so intent on being the first to create a human-Yeti chimera and what would be the result that I didn't allow thoughts of restraint to enter my head. Call it naiveté or sheer stubbornness. In retrospect, I just refused to weigh all the possible outcomes. For doing so, I am eternally sorry and will have to live with what I have done. I hope God can forgive me."

"Can I see you?"

"I dunno. Right now I need to find Roku and make sure he is all right."

"Millie, I need to see you. I—I'm in love with you. Please."

She was stunned at his revelation. Her feelings toward him were similar, but she had not sorted them all out. But she needed to see him.

"Millie, where are you? I'll come to you. Tell me where you are."

Her mind was in a whirl, jumbled thoughts spinning about her brain. She felt suddenly drained of all strength.

"I need a little more time, Gerald," she said. Her hands felt clammy and her knees weak. "Maybe in a few days, we could meet somewhere. Let me think about it and get back to you."

"You don't want to see me, is that it?" His voice broke when he asked the question.

"No, I do want to see you. Gerald, *all* of me needs to see you. Is that plain enough? Let me think about where

I'll feel safe in meeting you, and I'll call you. Please, it has to be this way."

After hanging up, Millie slouched on the sofa and cried. Tears of guilt, sadness, and relief rolled own her cheeks. Besides her father, Gerald was the only man who ever mattered to her. She heard the disapproval in his voice and, knowing she had besmirched his naive assistance, made her guilt that much harder to bear.

When there were no more tears, she went into the bathroom; took a long, hot shower; and fell into bed. As she tried to relax, visions of Gerald flashed through her brain, his wonderful smile, the touch of his kiss.

She tossed and turned most of the night.

Chapter 33

Gerald sat in his darkened dormitory room at the Primate Research Facility. The phone call from Millie both thrilled and worried him. He was delighted to hear from her but worried about her safety. She was on the run from the police and FBI, and that made her unpredictable. He opened a bottle of water, took several long gulps, then returned to the veterinary journal he was reading before her call. Absentmindedly thumbing through the pages of the journal, he couldn't process what was written on the pages. After a few minutes of struggling with his concentration, he tossed the journal aside and slouched farther into his chair. His heart ached to see Millie.

If he could just talk to her, he was sure he could convince her to give herself up and join the hunt for Roku. He didn't believe she had broken any laws. Maybe she was guilty of stealing university property, Roku, but that was about all. And he knew he could convince Radner to talk to Pauling and not have the school press charges. It was all an unfortunate state of affairs brought on by distressed egos, managerial hubris, and a gullible desire for fame and notoriety.

Everyone involved in the fiasco shared in the blame

for the current situation from the university officials down to Millie herself.

Should he notify the FBI that she had contacted him? Harry? If Millie agreed to see him would he dare bring Harry and Dixie along? Even though they were no longer with the university, they would certainly be concerned and interested in Millie's welfare. They would help her. But she might view their presence as a betrayal of her trust in him.

He agonized as to what was the best thing to do.

∽ↄ∾

The FBI fliers did their job. The day after they were distributed in Chinatown an elderly woman by the name of Maureen Shen called Jacoby's office and reported that she had seen a strange shadow lurking near her apartment. She wasn't sure what it was, for it was dark when she took her garbage out, just that it wasn't anything she had ever encountered. Five feet tall, long arms, very large head, stooped stature, it scurried down the dark street like a monkey. She thought something had escaped from the zoo, but when she saw the flier, she decided to call and report what she saw. "Creepy," she said. "Very creepy."

Jacoby jotted the woman's address on a notepad, found Lenny Baudelaire, and the two men drove out to interview Mrs. Shen. She lived near the Baptist Chinese Church close to the Willie "Woo Woo" Wong Playground.

Mrs. Shen greeted them with a firm handshake and a toothless smile. After ushering them into the small apartment, they sat on vintage worn chairs as the woman talked.

"When I saw this paper," she said, retrieving the flier describing Roku, "I knew I must call. It was after dark when I took my garbage to the curb that I noticed it lurking across the street in the shadows."

"What was it doing?" Baudelaire said.

"Just prowling around. Like it was searching for something," the woman said.

"Probably food," Baudelaire said. "Can you describe it any better, ma'am?"

"Not really. Like I said, it was dark. Whatever it was looked like a large monkey but not really. It had long arms, an extremely large head, and prowled around in sort of a shuffling gait. Oh yes, and it had red eyes."

Jacoby placed a quick cell phone call and then turned back to the woman. "Red eyes?"

"Yes," the woman said. "It looked at me once from across the street, and I noticed its eyes. Glowing red."

"Interesting," Baudelaire said.

"It wasn't an animal from the zoo then?"

Jacoby cleared his throat and shifted in his chair.

"No, not from the zoo. It escaped from a research project, and it's important that we recover it as soon as possible."

He noticed out Mrs. Shen's front window that a number of patrol cars had arrived on the scene and uniformed officers were searching the area. *Quick response from my phone call.*

His cell phone rang. He answered it, listened for a while, then hung up.

"Come on," he said to Baudelaire. "They found another body across the street."

As the headed for the door, Mrs. Shen sat in her chair, a concerned look on her face.

"Oh, dear," Jacoby heard her say as he closed the door behind them.

෴

The corpse lay amongst trash barrels, and a dumpster in a cramped alleyway on the west side of the playground and by the looks of the wounds was at least eight to twelve hours old. The wounds had the same appearance of the other recent Chinatown homicides with a large amount of blood on the ground and the victim's skull crushed. Flies circled the body. The medical examiner had yet to arrive on the scene.

"Same MO has all the others," Baudelaire said, rising from his stooped position over the body. Has to be that monster."

"The scientists would take offense at your use of that term, Lenny," Jacoby said.

"Well, whatever the hell it is," Baudelaire said, "it's a monster to me. When those educated folks from the university can't explain in plain English what we're dealing with, I call it a monster. Some sort of half man, half animal. To me, that's a monster. And it's starting to get on my nerves."

"You want Prescott to spell you?"

"Naw. I can take it. It's just creepy, that's all. I've never chased a monster before."

After the medical examiner finished looking over the body, it was loaded into an ambulance and ferried to the downtown for the required autopsy. Jacoby chose to skip this one. Instead, the two men grabbed a quick lunch at a Hunan diner before returning to their office.

Jacoby sat alone, his stomach belching fire from the spicy lunch. He chewed a handful of antacid tablets and lit the stub of a day old cigar. It tasted foul, so he snubbed it out and gulped down some bureau coffee.

The number of victims was beginning to pile up, and all he knew was the perpetrator was some sort of animal-human mixture that scientists had created, like in science fiction movies. And they were no closer to nabbing the thing than weeks ago when he first visited Dr. Olson at Cal Pacific. Since that time, he'd learned the professor had been fired, and his wife had quit. Jacoby remembered reading in a magazine how the genes for human insulin had been sliced into a bacteria's DNA and now that bacteria was a little human insulin factory, pumping out human insulin, so patients no longer needed to use animal insulin. Science was doing weird things these days.

Two years earlier, his wife died of cancer. When the doctors first discovered it in her breast, they were confident a lumpectomy followed by chemotherapy would do the trick, but within six months the cancer had spread to her bones, then to her brain. She'd had radiation therapy to her head and more chemo. She put up a valiant fight, always smiling to the end, but it was not enough. She slowly succumbed to the disease and died in her sleep one night in the middle of winter.

Jacoby was lost without her, and that first year he almost quit the Bureau. But he was assigned a complex white-color-crime case, where he spent six months investigating and living in Philadelphia, so gradually the pain of her death lessened. He still missed her, but he tried to stay busy with his career and a few hobbies.

This current case, with what Dr. Olson termed a chimera, puzzled him. He couldn't get his mind around the idea of a creature—and that was what this thing was, a creature whose genetic makeup was part animal and part human. And the animal part was something Olson called a Yeti, some sort of prehistoric animal. Jacoby knew a little about genetic engineering, and what he knew frightened him. Since he began the case, he had done some reading. The chimaera was a hybrid monster in Greek mythology, child of Typhoeus and Echidna and sibling of Cerberus and the Lernaean hydra. It had the head and body of a lion, as well as the head of a goat that was attached to its back, and a tail that ended on a head of a snake.

It had resided in Lycia, a place in Asia Minor, where it ravaged the lands with its fire breath. Assisted by Pegasus, it was killed by Bellerophon when King Iobates of Lycia asked him for help. Bellerophon rode on Pegasus's back flew overhead and shot arrows at the chimera from above. Modern day genetic chimeras were created artificially by combining genetic material from different species into a single embryo. The adult animals that developed had different populations of cells that reflected the different contributions of the species from which they were produced. Scientists had created the geep, for example, by combining genetic material from both a goat and a sheep. If this creature was man-made, what could science do next? What bizarre monster could be unleashed upon an unsuspecting public? And most of all, who was overseeing all of these experiments? Congress? The FDA?

၎၃၎၃

Dixie waited for Miles Radner to come to the phone. Harry had driven downtown to see Special Agent Jacoby, so she sat in San Mateo until she summoned the courage to call the research facility. Radner sounded cheerful when he answered.

"Sorry to keep you waiting, Dixie. I was down in the Animal Care Unit, doing a little inspection. What's up?"

"Miles," she began, a slight quiver in her voice. "I don't know where to begin. There have been a number of murders in Chinatown that seem to point to a large animal-like creature. It sounds like it could be Roku—"

"In San Francisco?" Radner butted in.

"Yes, in Chinatown. The FBI and Frisco police are investigating, but it is beginning to look like it is Roku. Where Millie is we don't know."

"Gosh, Dixie, that's not good."

"It isn't. But mostly, Miles, I am worried about Harry. He hasn't found a job as yet, and he's depressed. I don't know what you can do but…"

Dixie did her best to keep from breaking down and sobbing. But she was at her wit's end. Radner cleared his throat.

"Dixie, look, Harry means a lot to me. When Jimmy Winkleman was killed, and the Yeti escaped, I offered Harry my resignation. You know what? He just smiled and refused to accept it. I can't begin to tell you how much that meant to me. So, if there is anything I can do to help, you know I'll do it gladly. How can I help?"

"I don't know, Miles. I think he's taken it on the chin about Millie's experiments and her disappearance. On top of feeling responsible and guilty, he was terminated. He felt bad enough and then to—"

"Yes, yes," Radner interrupted. "Harry would have been well within his rights to fire me, but he didn't. To this day, it's hard for me to believe just how far out on a limb he went for me. Dixie, I always felt the trustees and Pauling acted too hastily in firing Harry. In fact, I have learned that other faculty members feel as I do."

"That's wonderful to hear," Dixie said. "It might make Harry feel somewhat better, but it won't put bread on the table as he likes to point out."

"Well, maybe there's something I can do. Along with a few others. I owe Harry that much."

"Like what, Miles?"

"You know, Dixie, all my life I've been a gamer. Always figuring the odds on any endeavor, weighing people and how they could further my career. When the Yeti escaped, your husband wasn't thinking of himself. He was thinking of his staff and protecting the public along with saving a rare scientific specimen. And everyone admired him for that. We were proud to be called his colleagues. His actions made my life up to that point seem foolish. Maybe it's time for me to do the same. Maybe it's time for me to act honorably. Maybe I can return the huge favor Harry did me."

"How, Miles?"

"I'll think of something, Dixie," he said. "I'll think of something."

Chapter 34

Roku sulked in the shadows along a row of buildings, his gaze darting furtively from the sidewalk to the street and back again. Since being alone and on his own, he'd learned that the streets during daylight hours were dangerous and were safe only after dark, when there was less traffic and fewer pedestrians. Since yesterday, however, there were many more men with uniforms driving black and white cars with lights on top. They seemed to be everywhere, and now and then, Roku saw them talking to a man or woman on the sidewalk.

In his quest for food, he'd found a small shop that had bread in the window, so he had broken the glass and taken a number of loaves back to his tunnel. He was beginning to find his way around and remember where he was and the routes to his tunnel that were safe and devoid of people, especially the men in the black uniforms.

Now he ducked into an alley and lumbered among the trashcans until he found one that smelled of food and began scavenging through its contents. Whatever it was, it smelled good, and, when he had it in his hand, he gobbled it down in several large bites. Roku found he no longer needed to kill to eat and survive. The people who lived here put food in metal containers behind their houses and stores, and he was able to scavenge enough to eat.

Still, he didn't understand many things.

Where was Mother and why had she left him alone?

Why was he different from her?

Mother and the other people could use their mouths to communicate with each other. Why was it necessary for him to use his hands to make strange shapes for Mother to understand him?

But most of all, the one thing he wondered most was—

Who was he?

Finished eating, he continued down the alley to where it emptied onto a large street. It was dark and absent of people. He looked around then started across the street.

All of a sudden, there was loud shouting.

Glancing behind him, he saw two men in black uniforms pile out of a black and white car. In the dark, he could see their faces, and they looked like Mother when he had done something bad. And they were running toward him. And shouting.

Roku turned and lumbered across the street and down the sidewalk. The shouts were still behind him. He found an alley and plunged into its darkness, but the shouts were now closer. He glanced over his shoulder and saw that the men had something in their hands.

He heard a loud explosion.

Pain shot through his shoulder. But he kept running, knocking over barrels and cans as he did.

Another loud retort.

This time there was a pain on the side of his head, and it knocked him sideways into a fire escape. He reached up, felt his head, and noticed his hand was filled with blood.

What were they doing?

They were still behind him, shouting. Their voices

sounded angry. Like Mother when he did something bad.

Still, he lumbered on, desperately looking for a way out of the alley. He dipped into a recess. Ahead was a tall wooden fence with a number of trashcans in front of it. He headed toward it.

Who are these men? Why are they after me? Where is Mother?

He jumped and crashed up onto the garbage cans. Several of them fell over and rolled away. He grabbed the top of the fence and pulled himself up.

Another *bang, bang.*

This time a knifelike shock pounded through his right leg. He felt his strength waning. Roku pulled himself up and over the fence and dropped to the ground on the opposite side. Pain caused his entire body to shudder.

Limping, he scampered into the dark recess of the alleyway and out of sight of the men pursuing him. He could no longer hear their shouting. They did not follow over the fence. He glanced at his leg and shoulder and saw a thick dark red fluid covering his thin fur. It was blood, he knew. Mother had taught him. Somehow, he and Mother both had the red stuff inside their bodies, and it was important. He knew that much.

He worked his way back to his tunnel, remaining in the dim recesses as he limped along. He ducked into the underbrush and felt safe. Scurrying through the dense vegetation, he finally made it back and collapsed into the tunnel's small confines.

കൗകൗ

After much internal debate, Millie decided to meet Gerald. She decided to drive to Reno for the weekend, and he would drive over from the research facility. He had rented a room at the Sands Regency between Interstate 80 and the Truckee River. After crossing the bay using the San Francisco-Oakland Bay Bridge, Millie continued northeast toward Sacramento on Interstate 80 through Berkley and Fairfield. The sun was bright, and the clouds were few. The two-lane road wound through the rural countryside, where the houses were few and far between. Short grasses of varying shades of greens and browns covered the treeless landscape while the low lying hills gradually gave way to flat terrain the closer to Sacramento she got.

Early evening found her on the outskirts of Reno. She steered her car off the Interstate and found the Sands without much difficulty. After parking her car, she checked into the room Siscom had reserved for her which had a commanding view of the casino's courtyard and pool area. She unpacked her bag and sat on the bed, hungry. As she was about to wander downstairs to the restaurant, there was a soft knock on her door.

It was Siscom.

She leaped into his arms with tears flowing down her cheeks and kissed him. Surprised at herself she pulled away, her face flushing.

"It's good to see you, Millie," he said. "I've missed you."

She took him by the hand and pulled him into the room, where they embraced again. Millie, embarrassed by her tears, slouched in a chair while Siscom did the same.

"Gerald," she said, "I...I...I don't know quite what to say. I'm sorry for any and all trouble I caused you because of my actions. It never was my intention to do that."

"I know," he said. "You did what you did. That's all there is to it. We just need to try and repair the damage. Any idea where Roku is?"

"No. I believe he must still be around where we were living, but I have no idea."

"Care to tell me where you are living now? You can trust me."

Millie hesitated, her stomach suddenly churning. She dreaded this part of the reunion she knew would have to be faced. She thought she could trust Siscom, but, once she told him everything, there would no longer be safety in anonymity. Gerald had never been anything but her trusted friend, and they were close to being lovers, a possibility she never thought could happen. She glanced at him sitting across from her. He looked haggard, maybe from the long drive, she thought. But, otherwise, he reclined comfortably and smiled at her. She felt relaxed in his presence, sensed his willingness to protect her.

"Not yet, Gerald. Maybe later."

He nodded as if he understood.

"I've got something to tell you," he said. "And I hope you won't feel poorly about me or become angry."

"What? What?"

She could see Siscom fidget in his chair and clasp his hands together.

"Harry and Dixie are here. Down the hall in my room."

"Oh, Gerald!" Millie cried. "How could you?" Her face went pale in the soft yellow light of the hotel room.

"Please, don't say that. They just want to help."

"No. I won't see them." She stood and grabbed her bag and opened a dresser drawer.

"Millie," Siscom said, at her side and his arms around her shoulders. "They are your friends as well. And only want to help. Honest. At least see them. Talk to them. Together, we can work all this out. I'm sure we can. Just see them. Please."

Mille shrugged his hands off her. Turning, she looked at him through narrowed eyes.

"And I trusted you, Gerald. I trusted you, and you do this to me. Without asking."

"I can assure you my heart is in the right place. I don't want to see you throw away a promising career. Ruin your life."

"My career is finished, Gerald. I know that. Don't play word games with me."

"It may not be. All I ask is you talk with Harry and Dixie. If you don't like what you hear, they'll return home."

"And not tell the cops? Ha!"

"You can trust them. But if your answer is no, I'll go tell them."

Siscom started for the door.

"Wait," Millie said. "I guess there's no harm in meeting with them and hearing them out. Okay, I'll do it." She surprised herself in relenting so easily.

Siscom smiled, nodded, and put an arm around her as they left her room. Walking down the carpeted hallway, her head began to pound, and her knees became weak.

Siscom opened his hotel room door, and she saw Dixie spring out of a chair and cross the room. Millie broke down and began sobbing and let her head fall into the woman's shoulder.

Millie stood for a while in Dixie's embrace as she wept. Dixie led her into the room and placed her on a small sofa then sat next to her, an arm still around Millie's shoulder.

She heard Dixie's soft voice soothing her. A hand smoothed her ruffled hair.

"There, there," Dixie said. "It's all right. You're among friends here."

Millie looked around and noticed Harry standing by a

window. Siscom took a seat near the door. She dried her eyes and forced a laugh.

"I must look a sight," she said.

"You look fine," Dixie said. "Don't you think, Harry?"

Harry crossed the room and stood next to her. She glanced up at him.

"Yes, she looks fine. Like our old Millie. We've missed you, young lady. Your parents have been concerned as well."

"Gerald—I mean Dr. Siscom—"

Dixie laughed at her remark. "It's okay, Millie. Gerald mentioned you two dated a few times."

"Well, Gerald told me you wanted to help, but I don't know how. I crossed the line, I realize that."

Harry strolled back to the window then turned to face her.

"You did cross a line, Millie, but it is a nebulous one. A line that other scientists have crossed down through the centuries. So, I don't think you have done irreparable harm to yourself. Especially if you can tell us where we can find Roku."

"I can't," Millie said, gazing at the floor.

"Can't or won't?" Harry said.

"Roku attacked me and disappeared," she said.

"Oh, Millie," Dixie said, alarmed. "Are you all right? Did he hurt you?"

"I'm fine. Just a few bumps and scrapes. But I don't know where he is. And haven't for the past two weeks."

"Where is that?" Harry asked.

Millie ignored the question and looked at Harry with an anxious eye. "He is so intelligent. It's hard to believe," she said.

"It would be nice to measure it," Dixie said.

"He's beginning to become aware of himself, was asking questions."

Sitcom cleared his throat and smiled.

"A definite sign of intelligence," he said. "Interpreting other people's actions and intentions involves a mutual ascription of contented mental states such that the understanding of the social world around us becomes coherent and intelligible. Our everyday understanding of others, our folk psychology, is our most fundamental resource for introducing meanings in a world of causes. Folk psychology, as a practice, has been a major topic of philosophical and psychological investigation along the overall history of thought. Recently, a new perspective on folk psychology has emerged in philosophy of mind and psychology. According to this perspective, our interpretive abilities should be viewed as a competence, a specific endowment of the human mind specialized to understand others and ourselves in terms of mental states. A new field of investigation, called Theory of Mind, is now emerging as a major issue in cognitive studies."

"I've never heard of it," Harry said. "Explain, Gerald."

"Theory of Mind is a specific cognitive ability to understand others as intentional agents, that is, to interpret their minds in terms of theoretical concepts of intentional states, such as beliefs and desires. It has been commonplace in philosophy to see this ability as intrinsically dependent upon our linguistic abilities. After all, language provides us a representational medium for meaning and intentionality. Thanks to language, we are able to describe other people's, and our own, actions in an intentional way as in, 'Ralph believes that Mary intends him to persuade George to do something.' According to this view, the intentionality of natural language—that is, its suitability for expressing meanings and thoughts—is the key to understanding the intentionality of our theory of mind.

"A major challenge to this view came from studies on primate cognition and comparative psychology. In a famous paper, 'Does the chimpanzee have a theory of mind?' the authors argued that experimental evidence of chimpanzees' understanding of human behavior could be interpreted as detection of intentions. Although other primatologists have challenged their experimental data, there is growing evidence showing that non-human primates have some intentional understanding of their social world. The presence of such a capacity in non -human and obviously non-linguistic species led to the conclusion that it was possible to investigate Theory of Mind as a biological endowment independently of language."

"Interesting," Harry said. "But, unfortunately, not relevant to the immediate problem."

"You said the line was nebulous, Dr. Olson," Millie said. "What did you mean?"

Harry sat in the remaining chair and sighed.

"We scientists have always been on the cutting edge of ethics, and our discoveries have sometimes caused public outcries. One of our tasks is to educate the public about what we do. Otherwise, what is ethical behavior to large groups of society becomes confused and ingrained in ideology."

"I don't understand," Millie said.

"There is currently an epidemic in this country that seems harder to cure every day, and it becomes the overriding force of the American dialogue, consuming all sense of reason and rationality. The concept at the core of this epidemic is that ethics and science are in polar opposition, and, in order to be an ethical human being, you need to oppose science as an idea, in and of itself, lest you be labeled an enemy by a moral majority of your peers. For example, when the news media conducts an interview with a leading geologist, discussing the current state of plate tectonics and the current prediction models for earthquake activity in our Bay Area, they almost always feel compelled to also have a guest named Joe Blow from San Diego, who believes that the earthquakes are really caused by demons celebrating the rampant homosexuality in San Francisco, and the only way to save ourselves is to embrace God. This is the level of false balance we've fallen to when discussing science in America.

"As scientists, we have the responsibility to make sure that the decision makers who control our funding and our professional careers fully understand the science behind what we do every day. When they don't understand, they make wrong decisions."

"We believe that's what happened in your case, Millie," Dixie said. "And Harry's case as well."

"Dr. Olson's case?" Millie said, surprised by the comment.

"Harry was fired from Cal Pacific, Millie," Dixie said.

"Oh, no," Millie exclaimed, putting a hand to her mouth.

"So you see," Siscom interjected, "it's important that we find Roku and get the university to reinstate you and the Olsons. And the sooner, the better."

"I—I—don't know," Millie said. "What about the police? Will I be arrested?"

"I'd have a talk with Special Agent Jacoby," Harry said. "He might have an answer."

Chapter 35

Dr. Pauling gazed across his desk at Dr. Miles Radner. The director of the Primate Research Center was in town to discuss an important matter with him, and Pauling had cleared his afternoon calendar to accommodate the man. Each held a porcelain mug of coffee.

"You wished to discuss Harry Olson's departure from the university, I understand. That's why we're here, right, Miles?"

"Yes, sir. As I mentioned on the phone, Dr. Olson's dismissal weighs heavy on my heart, and, while I in no way wish to relieve him of any responsibility in the events leading to his termination, I am here to try and negotiate his return to the university."

"Yes, Miles, I understand." Pauling rose from his desk and crossed the room to the door. "And that is why I've asked the chairman of the board of trustees to meet with us." Pauling opened the door and ushered in Alistair Forester, who took the remaining available chair. After returning to his desk, Pauling continued. "Dr. Radner, this is Alistair Forester. Mr. Forester, please meet Dr. Miles Radner, Director of our Primate Research Facility."

Forester nodded. He wore an immaculately pressed

wool suit, his silver gray hair perfectly coifed. His right ring finger bore a large diamond ring. "Yes, I have heard good things about you, Doctor," he said and held out his hand, which Radner shook.

Pauling cleared his throat. "Well, let's get right down to cases, shall we? Miles here wants us to reconsider taking Dr. Harry Olson back into his old position. I am open for discussion on the matter."

Forester frowned. "I would like to hear Dr. Radner's reasons as to why the university should reverse its decision. Please, Doctor, enlighten me."

Radner shifted his weight in his chair and smiled at the two men.

"Well, first of all, gentlemen," he said, "Dr. Olson is nationally known in his field. And this notoriety brings the university financial gain. Second, he has served Cal Pacific admirably since Professor Kessler's death. In fact, he was the Professor's choice when it came to his successor. And during that tenure, Dr. Olson performed admirably. In fact, more than admirably. I would say all of his faculty heartily approved of his leadership and counted themselves fortunate to be a member of his staff. Third, many faculty members, myself included, do not feel that the unfortunate and misguided act of a new hire should be held against the man. He wasn't responsible for Miss Harbaum's actions. Finally, the Yeti Dr. Olson's team discovered in Mongolia and brought back to our research facility has not only advanced modern anthropological science but has put Cal Pacific center stage in academic circles. The number of students seeking enrollment in the anthropology program here has increased significantly under his direction. It is for these compelling reasons that I humbly beseech the trustees to reconsider their actions and allow Dr. Olson to return to our university."

Forester looked at Pauling and then toward Radner.

"Dr. Radner," he began, "I appreciate your thoughts regarding Dr. Olson. No man had a better friend. However, even though I cannot argue with most of your comments, there is one I do take issue with. And that is that Dr. Olson could not and should not be held responsible for the actions of his students. To that, I would say that we hold our athletic coaches responsible for the actions of our student athletes. Why should the same standard not apply to our teachers? And I might point out that this was not the first instance we trustees had to question Dr. Olson. If you remember, we had a graduate student killed, and the Yeti housed at the facility escaped not too long ago. So, it's my feeling that the recommendation of the board was entirely justified. If Reginald wishes us to revisit the issue, we will, but I doubt the result would be any different."

Pauling cleared his throat again. "I feel I must interject a personal observation here," he said. He nervously adjusted his tie before continuing. "There is a groundswell of support for Dr. Olson among the faculty, and it is building each and every day. Soon, I fear, we may have a full-scale mutiny on our hands. Dr. Rawlings has already threatened to resign and take her lucrative grant with her. Others may follow her lead. Ultimately, we may not have an anthropology department."

"And one last thought for the trustees to consider, Mr. Forester," Radner said. "There is a feeling that the board acted prematurely, in advance of any public reaction. Who knows what the fallout will be? It might be miniscule. And even if there is a public outcry, there is growing sentiment in Dr. Olson's favor among the staff—that his termination was an overreaction by the board. Another reason to reconsider your decision."

∽∽∽

Harry's cell phone jingled. It was Jacoby, and Harry paced Millie's hotel room while he talked to the FBI agent. Millie and Siscom sat silent.

"Say that again, please," Harry said.

"I said we have spotted a creature that matches the description of that thing…that…"

"It's a chimera," Harry said, irritation in his voice. "Goes by the name of Roku."

At Roku's name, Millie leaned forward in her chair, alert.

"Whatever," Jacoby replied. "The Frisco police spotted it in Chinatown last night and gave chase. Fired a few shots at it, and may have wounded it."

"Wounded it? How bad?"

At that, Millie began weeping silently. Siscom put an arm around her.

"We don't know, exactly," Jacoby said. "The thing got away. But the police have the area cordoned off, and they'll find it. Only a matter of time."

Only a matter of time, Harry thought. "He's still in Chinatown?"

"Yep. And he can't go far. The police have set up a command post, and I'm headed there now."

"I know you have to capture him, Jacoby but please don't kill him. He is valuable property."

"I can't predict what will happen, Doctor. If it threatens anyone, the uniforms will shoot to kill. You need to be here. How soon can you make it down to the Chinatown command post? I'll give you directions."

"I'm out of the area at the moment, but I can be there later this evening. I'll make it as soon as I can."

Harry jotted down the address of the command post and stuck it in his pocket.

Millie wiped tears from her eyes and nodded. "The police found Roku?" she said, sniffling.

"The spotted him last night in Chinatown and gave chase. Apparently, they fired a few shots at him. Wounded him."

"How bad?" Siscom said, settling back in his chair.

"Unknown," Harry said. "But the police have the area surrounded and have a command post in the vicinity. They'll find him, it's just a matter of time."

"If they find him, they will kill him, I know it," Millie said.

"Maybe not if we're there," Harry said. "We need to get to Chinatown as soon as possible, however."

Siscom nodded.

"Millie," he said. "How about you? You can ride with me, Harry, and Dixie."

Dixie, who had been quiet during this last conversation went to Millie and gave her a hug.

"Come on, honey," she said. "I'll help you."

"It's now or never, Millie," Harry said. "You can be of help, or you can decide to run. Were you living in Chinatown?"

Millie looked at him with doleful eyes glistening with tears. She nodded slowly.

"Yes," she said. "I've been outa my mind since Roku disappeared. I never expected him to attack me like he did. I always thought he knew I cared deeply for him."

"What happened?" asked Dixie.

"He kept asking me questions about who he was, as if he finally understood he was different. Kept asking me why? It was frightening, actually. I guess he became frustrated when I didn't answer, and he lashed out. He hurt me and left, and no one has seen him since."

"Until last night," Harry said. "Well, let's get going. We've got a drive ahead of us."

c/so

The four-hour drive to San Francisco passed in relative silence for the car's occupants. With Siscom at the wheel, Dixie and Millie sat in the rear but didn't converse much. Dixie felt she wanted to be left with her private thoughts, so she sat quietly and watched the desert landscape roll by.

Halfway to San Francisco, her cell phone rang. It was Miles Radner.

"I wanted to bring you up to date on the meeting I had with Pauling and Alistair Forester."

"Yes," Dixie said. She kept her voice low, as she didn't wish Harry to learn of her request of Radner. He sat in the front seat, chatting with Siscom, seemingly unaware she was on the phone.

"Well, I gave it my best shot," he said. "But I've got to tell you, it's an uphill battle. Pauling is going to ask the board to reconsider and use my arguments, but I don't know. It's a tossup."

"I appreciate it, Miles, I really do. You are a true friend.'

She hung up, and Harry glanced back at her.

"Who was that?" he said.

"Miles Radner," she said, not wanting to say more.

"Oh, yeah? What did he want?"

"Nothing, really. He just wanted to know if we had heard anything more concerning Roku."

Harry nodded and returned to his chat with Siscom. Dixie felt a twinge of guilt in the pit of her stomach. She hated not telling Harry the truth.

⋯⋯

It was after dark when they drove into Chinatown. Fortunately, the traffic was light, and they headed to the command post without much delay. Once over the bay, they turned north to the police command post located down the street from the Ritz Carlton Hotel. Here the streets were up and down the hills for which the city was famous. Siscom negotiated the car along the narrow streets until Harry saw the SFPD trailer parked in a small parking lot. Several black and whites were parked alongside. Siscom pulled into a vacant parking space a block down the street, and the four walked the short distance back to the command post.

Harry knocked on the door, and a ruddy-faced policeman in uniform answered it.

"Yes?" he said in a burly voice, eyeing each of them with suspicion.

"I'm Dr. Harry Olson. Special Agent Jacoby of the FBI wanted to meet me and my colleagues here at the command post."

The policeman snarled and looked the three over.

"Just a minute," he said. "Who are you?"

"Harry Olson. And this," he said, pointing to Millie, "is Miss Harbaum, whom the FBI is seeking."

The policeman stepped aside, holding the trailer door open.

"Come in," he said, some of the gruffness in his voice gone. "Sit in those chairs there while I locate agent Jacoby."

There were exactly four chairs in the cramped trailer. Besides a desk and filing cabinet, there was a radio transceiver, a large map of San Francisco on a wall, and a rack of riot gear hung in the trailer's rear. Harry heard the policeman on a portable radio, requesting the whereabouts of Jacoby. The radio squawked a few times, and the man returned.

"He's on the way," he said. "Just sit tight."

The policeman sat at the desk and thumbed through a stack of papers, occasionally making a note on them.

Harry looked at Millie, who seemed as if she'd lost her last friend. Was this the right thing to do? he wondered. Suddenly, he was struck by the thought that she might not be able to get out of the jam in which she found herself, that Cal Pacific might not be willing to overlook her transgressions. If that happened, how could he ever look himself in the mirror?

He thought of the plaque with the motto that hung in his office. *Veritas et honorem.* Truth and honor. It had been his mantra ever since his own personal misstep years ago. He figured his past mistakes were forgotten until Dr. Wickingham's arrival dredged it up again. Might the same happen with Millie? Was she forever doomed to be haunted by one act of childish selfishness?

Dixie, he noticed, sat next to Millie, now and then patting an arm, smiling. His wife had an amazing ability to look, and hope, for the best in an uncertain future. Regardless of the situation and how bleak things appeared, she believed all would work out for the best. And they usually did.

Siscom sat nervously in his chair, his hands fidgeting with themselves. Harry surmised he was feeling guilty for bringing Millie back to face whatever justice there was to face. It was obvious he cared for her—the poor man was in agony.

The trailer door opened ushering in a wave of Chinatown smells. Jacoby clambered into the trailer, followed by a uniformed policeman. His suit was rumpled, as if he hadn't slept in several days, and his face sported a growth of beard.

"Good to see you, Doctor," he said extending his hand. He shot a glance at Dixie and Millie. "And one of these ladies is our missing scientist?"

Dixie stood. "I'm Dixie," she said. "Harry's wife. This is Dr. Siscom, the facility's vet. And—" She indicated

Millie with a nod if her head. Millie smiled. "—this is Millie Harbaum, our missing faculty member."

"I've met Dr. Siscom," Jacoby said, "when I toured the research facility. Now, Miss Harbaum, please tell me about this thing you created."

Chapter 36

For two days, Roku sulked in the tunnel, nursing his wounds. His head sported a deep gash, and his shoulder and leg wounds sent shock waves reeling throughout his body. He had lost a great deal of the red substance Mother called blood, making him too weak to ramble about. So he remained in the tunnel, eating only a little of the bread he had.

Now, he felt stronger, but he was thirsty, extremely thirsty. So at dark, he ventured out of the tunnel, hobbled through the vegetation a short distance to where it ended at the edge of a sidewalk that looked out onto an avenue of cars speeding right and left. He crouched behind a large shrub and peered out into the night. The loamy earth smelled sweet and luxuriant.

As usual, traffic was light, but men in black uniforms paraded along the sidewalks and sped down the street in their special cars. They seemed to be everywhere. *The same men who hurt me.*

Watching the traffic through the boughs of the shrubbery, he noticed a black uniformed man strolling on the sidewalk toward him. The man was tall and stout. In the dim streetlights, Roku saw that he carried a stick in his hands. He walked along at a leisurely pace, turning his head from side to side, as if searching for something. His cap was pulled down low over his eyes hiding his face from Roku's view. The man stopped directly in front of him, looking out over the street, his back to the shrubbery.

Roku crouched deeper within the dense vegetation, the only sounds piercing the still night were the chirping of crickets and the barking of a distant dog. He remained perfectly still, not twitching a muscle or hair, his eyes riveted on the man in front of him.

The uniformed man twirled his stick and whistled a low tune. And he continued to stand there, watching, looking.

Something deep within Roku bubbled to the surface, forcing him to clench his fists and emit a soft low growl. The man turned and stared into the shrubs where Roku was hidden. Roku huddled deeper. After staring for a moment, the man turned his attention back to the street. Roku felt a sudden rage take hold of him. He bounded out of hiding and grabbed the man from behind in a powerful grasp.

The man lurched to one side, but Roku's grasp held him tight about the neck. The man fought, trying to extricate himself from Roku's clutches but Roku only tightened his grasp on the man. The man's left hand reached up and tried to grab Roku by a shoulder, but Roku tightened his grip. When the man struggled to turn his head to face him, Roku's other powerful arm wrapped about the man's neck. While the man struggled, he only managed a soft gurgling noise. Roku pulled the man back into the reaches of the shrubbery. Concealed by the vegetation, he continued his grip on the man's throat until he collapsed. Roku dragged the man through the underbrush until they arrived at the tunnel.

Then the man struggled again, soft murmuring noises

erupting from his mouth. His eyes were mere slits. Roku gnawed on the man's arm, and he let out a short, garbled shriek. The gaping wound spurted blood, and the man tried to get to his feet, but he fell back into the dark hole of the tunnel.

Roku snapped the man's neck, and he went limp.

ℰ✑ℰ✑

After questioning Millie for the better part of an hour, Special Agent Jacoby dismissed the police stenographer who had taken her statement, sat, and lit the stub of a cigar. The unpretentious command trailer felt cramped, stale. As he blew acrid smoke into the air, he surveyed the group assembled. Each person's brows were knitted into a furrow of concern and dismay.

Finally, after a long silence, Harry spoke. "So, what do you think?"

"It's not up to me, Doctor. She'll be transferred to the city jail until the court decides what to do with her case."

"Have you arrested her?" Siscom said.

"No, not yet."

"Are you going to?" asked Dixie.

"I haven't thought that far ahead," Jacoby said, puffing on the cigar.

"If you don't arrest her, then there's no need for her to go to jail, is there?" Dixie was patting Millie's arm.

"Doctor Olson, I do believe you have something," Jacoby said, smiling. "If I released her into your custody, can I rely on you and your husband to bring her in if necessary?"

"She can stay with us," Harry said. "Couldn't she, honey?"

"Of course," Dixie said, squeezing Millie's arm.

"We'll be happy to take Millie off your hands," Harry

said. "When you need her, all you have to do is call."

Jacoby frowned and shot a glance toward Millie.

"Miss Harbaum, can I rely on you to stay in the Olson's custody and not disappear again?"

Millie nodded. "Yes sir," she said, in a halting voice.

"I mean, if you ran away while the Olson's are responsible for you, it will not only be bad for you, but they would be in serious trouble."

Millie nodded her understanding.

"It's settled, then," Jacoby said. "You all are free to leave. I'll call if I need you for anything."

Siscom drove them down the peninsula to San Mateo and Harry and Dixie's home. It was after midnight when they arrived, and Dixie made coffee while they lounged in the study.

"You'll spend the night, of course, Gerald. You can drive back to the facility tomorrow," Harry said.

"Thanks," Gerald said. "I'm bushed."

As they sipped their coffee, Millie spoke of her guilt.

"It's something I don't think I can recover from," she said. "I never thought I was the sort to thumb my nose at ethics. Like your plaque reads, Dr. Olson, 'Truth and Honor.'"

"We scientist do have certain responsibilities," he said. "Ethical questions appear at the forefront of many advances in the field of human genetics. Following high-profile successes, genetic therapies have been researched for treatment of various blood diseases, metabolic disorders, and cancers. You know, the promise of groundbreaking cures entices those inside and outside the scientific community. But questions regarding science and research have come alongside ethical, religious, and political ones. Some fear the technology could be implemented for less benevolent purposes, such as artificially improving intelligence or cosmetic features."

"Parents will always desire smarter, better -looking children," Siscom interjected.

"Until recently," Harry continued, "a distinction was made between the acquisition of knowledge, science for science sake, and the application of knowledge in technologies—science for technology. While this distinction is still theoretically valuable, we must recognize that, in practice, the frontier between them is becoming increasingly blurred, because within modern societies, such domains as politics, economics, technology, and science are more and more interrelated and interdependent. Consequently, we cannot make a radical separation between pure science, which is not subject to any ethical norm, and applied sciences, which must be governed by ethical rules.

"As a general principle, any knowledge concerning the human genome or any potential technique of intervention in the human genome are ethical and, therefore, would be welcomed, provided that they respect human dignity and human rights. On the other hand, science and technology, which are potentially detrimental to individuals, as well as to populations, must be totally rejected, even if they greatly benefit science itself. This limitation is set more to guide than to stop research."

"You are correct in that assessment, Harry," Siscom said. "In science, as well as in ethics, an awareness of the elements involved in a problem is the first step toward its solution. It's also the first step toward wisdom. And humanity stands in great need of this wisdom in using science and technology when it involves the human genome. I know it sounds like preaching but it must be recognized that scientists, throughout history, have played, and will continue to play a vital social role in improving the general well-being of individuals and populations, even if some of their discoveries proved to be detrimental, as in the case of nuclear physics used for military purposes. Because of their expert knowledge, scientists are called upon to alleviate suffering and to improve the welfare of society in general. Science and technology, therefore, are needed to meet these challenges."

Dixie poured more coffee for Harry and Siscom then returned to her chair.

"Scientists involved in genome mapping and sequencing," she said, "must recognize that they occupy a pivotal position, thus far unknown in the history of science. Their field of research is not only around or outside the human being, but rather inside the very blueprint of the human being, that is to say, decoding genetic information.

"As soon as research findings and techniques involve present and future generations, they are no longer morally neutral, and ethical concerns must go hand in hand with the task of the scientist. As the saying goes, 'No science without conscience.'"

"You are making my point, I think," Millie said, yawning.

"But, in addition to responsibility, there is education of the public," Harry said. "And that is a fact that the scientific community has not taken seriously. It is the reason we find ourselves in the position we do."

"I think what Harry is trying to say, Millie," Siscom said, "is that the trustees do not truly understand what we at the primate facility are about. And even though what you did may have crossed some intangible ethical line, you did what any curious scientist would have done, given half the chance. I think I can safely say that."

"And we scientists need to come to your aid," Dixie added. "Right, Harry?"

"Couldn't have said it any better, honey," Harry said.

ജയെ

The police corporal's disappearance caused a stir within the SFPD, and the chief ordered a full-scale search for the man. Jacoby, after releasing Millie, returned to his office in the FBI field office and collapsed on a cot for a few hours. Rising shortly after dawn, he washed his face, used his electric razor, brewed coffee, and then drove back to the Chinatown command post to be appraised of the latest developments.

There was no sign of the chimera and no sign of the missing policeman. The massive search was still underway, and Jacoby wanted to be near the information center in case there was a discovery or breakthrough. So, he sat in the trailer, drank coffee, and smoked a cigar, waiting.

Near mid-morning, his cell phone rang, and it was Harry,

"Just wanted to let you know that Dr. Siscom has gone back to the primate facility. If you need him, you can reach him there."

"Thanks," Jacoby said. "Nothing new on the search for the chimera. Still looking for him. In addition, a policeman involved in the search has gone missing. There's a large dragnet in Chinatown looking for any trace of him. I hope your monster didn't drag him off. They got a couple of shots at him, you know."

"*What?*"

"Yeah. Several days ago some uniforms chased him down an alley and fired several rounds at him. They believe they hit him because they found some blood splatters around a fence he jumped over."

"Let's hope he's not hurt bad. Keep me posted, please."

"Will do."

After hanging up, Jacoby strolled down to the corner and ordered a lunch to go from the Hunan deli. Back in the trailer, he attacked his food and was half way through when a policeman burst through the door, out of breath.

"Sir," he said, panting, "there's been a discovery. A large pool of blood has been found in some bushes not far from here. And, from the looks of things, the body was dragged a ways, for there are some tracks leading into the middle of the park. The sergeant wants you to come and see for yourself. Please follow me."

Jacoby sprang from his chair and followed the policeman out into the bright sunlight.

Chapter 37

The conference room next to Pauling's office was as reserved as a church during a funeral. The men gathered there, including Alistair Forester, were in a somber mood, having been called to the meeting by Pauling the previous day.

Dressed in their dark suits of blues and grays, the four men waited patiently for Pauling to arrive and begin the meeting. Pauling's secretary quietly circled around the table offering coffee to each man as they chatted among themselves in solemn tones.

Pauling entered, a manila folder in his hands, and took his seat at the head of the polished mahogany table. He nodded at the group. "Thank you all for coming on such short notice," he said, laying the folder in front of him.

A man at the end of the table scowled. "What's the blasted emergency, Reginald?"

"Yes," exclaimed another, "what's so all-fired urgent that it couldn't wait for our regular meeting?"

"Gentlemen, gentlemen," Pauling said, holding a hand in the air. "Please indulge me. Bill and John, I appreciate your aggravation, but I believe we acted much too hastily regarding Dr. Olson's dismissal.

"Here, now," the man named Bill Hastings retorted. "I

believe we gave that man a fair hearing. I don't see why we need to relive that unfortunate affair."

"Now, Bill," Forester interjected. "Dr. Pauling and I listened to a very impassioned entreaty by Dr. Radner on the man's behalf. I agreed to this meeting. I hope we can put this matter to rest once and for all."

A resigned Hastings slumped into his chair and nodded.

"Thank you, Alistair," Pauling said, opening the folder before him. He felt a twinge of anxiety course through his body. His fingers tingled. He removed several papers from the folder and passed them around. "Dr. Radner made several very logical arguments in favor of keeping Dr. Olson. Those remarks are highlighted in the paper before you."

Pauling went through each point of Radner's reasoning while the men sat in silence. He noticed that they did give him their undivided attention, a good sign.

"As you can see," he continued, "Radner believes, and I must include myself here, that education is the key. Too often lay people don't understand exactly what science is about and the ramifications of their work. And gentlemen, with all due respect, that includes the board of trustees."

He knew he was on dangerous ground here, potentially insulting these commanding men's intelligence. But he believed in what he said. They may know law and business but not necessarily the intricacies of science and genetics.

"Please elaborate, Dr. Pauling," Forester said, a thin smile on his face.

"I'd be delighted. I'll give you several examples of what I mean. The concept of genetic modification is really the process of selecting desirable traits through gene manipulation, rather than generations of cross breeding.

It's typically a more focused method that allows for less chance of error in the end product than traditional breeding methods. The primary argument against this concept is often that it isn't natural. People have it in their minds that scientists are taking needles and injecting harmful chemicals into animals and our food, and the public, in general, is terrified of chemicals. This highlights the lack of understanding of chemicals, and that everything on earth is made of chemical compounds, as well as the whole idea of dose and dilution. There are many substances that at a certain dose can cure an illness, while at a higher dose can kill the patient. This is common knowledge amongst our educated scientific community, and it is what many scientists see as a failing of our education system where the general public is concerned.

"The same holds true with the large and deadly Ebola epidemic sweeping its way across the African Continent. There are vaccines that have been developed to combat it, but they're in the very basic testing stages. Scientists have a major choice to make as to whether to set aside standard protocol and consider the ethics of live field-testing these vaccines on patients and workers in outbreak areas. They have the potential of saving the lives of thousands. The consequences of these decisions will have far reaching effects across the globe. Looking at the state of scientific literacy in America today, I can't help but be concerned that we, as a society, aren't intellectually prepared to make decisions of this weight, and that the education system is not currently designed to prepare even the next generation to make similar decisions."

"So you see, gentlemen," Forester said, "a number of our faculty do not believe that we as a board have the necessary scientific acumen to make a fair decision where Dr. Olson is concerned."

"And I might add," Pauling said, feeling lightheaded

after Forester's blunt remark, "a number of our faculty feel as I do. And strongly, I might add. One was in my office recently, threatening to take her sizable NIH grant elsewhere."

A buzz went around the table.

"And that does not even address the fundamental issue of fairness," Pauling continued. "Although we are quick to hold Dr. Olson responsible for events that occurred under his watch, they were, after all, not under his direct control. Accidents do happen, gentlemen. People are free to pursue their own desires."

The buzz around the table continued, Bill Hastings leading the chatter.

Pauling sighed. "I don't wish to turn this into a power struggle, believe me. I have no desire to insult anyone's intelligence here. All I am asking is that we take an honest look at the situation and give Dr. Olson an impartial reevaluation. If we do that, I think we can all leave here knowing we discharged our duties to him and the university fairly and equitably."

છ·ઝ·છ·ઝ

The pool of blood lay on the ground at the base of a large bush growing near the sidewalk. The area had been taped off with yellow crime scene tape and, as he approached, Jacoby noticed a group of uniformed officers milling around, talking. As he walked up, a man in a sports coat separated himself from the crowd and grinned.

"I'm Detective Longmire," he said. "You our man with the FBI?"

"Hank Jacoby," he replied and shook the man's freckled hand. "What do you have, Detective?"

"Looks like a homicide scene," the detective said.

"This is where Patrolman Clark was standing when last seen by his partner."

"And his partner was where?" Jacoby said.

"Directly across the street," Longmire said, pointing in the general direction. "Clark's partner says he glanced up the street toward what sounded like a disturbance and, when he looked back, Clark was no longer standing here. He thought he had gone to search the vegetation but, when Clark didn't return, his partner became concerned, crossed the street, and saw all this blood. That's when he called in a ten-thirty-three."

Jacoby nodded. A ten-thirty-three meat emergency. "Go on, detective."

"There were two units on the scene in less than three minutes, and the men searched the area. They found this trail of blood here," he said, indicating splattered blood on the ground, "and followed it until it ran out down there a ways." Again, he pointed through the dense shrubbery.

Jacoby nodded and followed the blood trail a short ways, the vegetation becoming denser as he did.

"Blood type is A negative, sir, the same type as Clark's. The lab is doing DNA testing as we speak."

"No one has heard from the patrolman? He didn't get sick and go home?"

"No way, sir," Longmire said. "I know the man. He would never leave his post like that."

Again Jacoby nodded. "Your guys searching this area?"

"Half the day watch is combing the area right now. If there's something to be found, we'll find it. I just pray it's not Clark."

"I'll second that," Jacoby said.

"Sir, exactly what is this thing we have been searching for? The men who were chasing it said it was the strangest looking being they ever saw. Not at all human. Is it some sort of animal?"

"I wish I could say, exactly, Detective. Even I'm not sure I understand what it is. Some scientific experiment gone awry is about all I can say for now. The scientists at Cal Pacific are worried, however."

"The officers thought they hit it a few times when they chased into the alley but it got away. Maybe all this blood belongs to it."

"I doubt it," Jacoby said, ambling back to the sidewalk.

A patrolman hurried to where he and the detective stood. "Detective," he said. "We picked up the blood trail again. Beyond those tall trees over there."

Jacoby and Longmire followed the patrolman through the forested park to where another patrolman stood, waiting.

"It goes this way," he said, pointing. The patrolman led the way over a thick carpet of dead leaves, following the trail of blood.

The four men trudged through the forest and, every few yards, Longmire stooped and stuck a yellow flag on a thin wire into the ground, marking the blood trail. The blood splatter coursed not in a straight line but followed a serpentine fashion, as if whoever was wounded was disoriented. Jacoby's stomach rolled. Were they going to find the patrolman's mutilated body in the next few minutes?

They came to a clearing, and the trail became easier to follow. Jacoby thought the blood splatter was less, the drops farther apart. They rested in the clearing as Longmire sought to get his bearings.

"The Hilton Financial District is over that way," he said, pointing to the east. "Pretty soon we'll be out of the park."

"Whoever was bleeding," Jacoby said, "was losing

less blood by the time they got here. This isn't looking good, Detective."

"From the looks of the way the leaves are packed down around here," Longmire said, "whoever it was rested in this clearing. May have been getting weak."

They continued following the blood splatter and soon found themselves back in dense vegetation among a grove of oak trees. The blood trail ended at the base of a small mound. One of the patrolmen edged his way to the mound. The other had his nine millimeter drawn and at the ready.

"Looks like there is an entrance of some kind here," the patrolman called over his shoulder.

The other three men took positions on either side of him. The afternoon daylight was waning, making it difficult to see through the dim light of the forest. The patrolman edged closer.

"Careful," Longmire said. "What do you see?"

He took a flashlight from his belt and shined it into the dark recess. "Like I said, a tunnel or something."

The other men gathered closer, straining for a better look. Longmire had his pistol out. Jacoby felt his heart jump.

"I need to get a closer look," the patrolman said, and he inched his way nearer the opening, the light from his flashlight flickering through the vegetation in the dark distance.

The patrolman dropped to his hands and knees and crawled to the opening. Jacoby watched his light disappear as he shined it into the entrance. *Entrance to what?* Jacoby thought. The carpet of leaves made a rustling sound as the patrolman wormed his way into the darkness. The light from his flashlight flickered for a moment then reappeared, dancing through the leaves. *Hurry up getting there,* Jacoby thought. *Tell us something.*

Then the patrolman stopped his moving. His light stopped flickering. The forest was deathly quiet as the men waited for a signal from the patrolman. Jacoby's pulse quickened.

Then a sorrowful voice belched forth from the dim recess.

"Dear God, no."

Chapter 38

Patrolman Clark lay on his side, legs askew, with his skull crushed. The dark dried blood that pooled around him glistened under the flashlight's harsh glare. Jacoby eyed the body while Longmire looked over his shoulder. The small tunnel was blocked at its far end and on the floor was scattered the remains of scraps of food, empty plastic bottles, and a pair of shoes. An overwhelming stench of urine, decaying flesh, and rotten eggs filled the small enclosure.

"Someone has been living in here," Jacoby said.

"Probably a homeless person or addict," Longmire said. "They love to hide out in these tunnels."

"And that thing we've been after," the patrolman said from inside the tunnel.

Longmire stood.

"Well, let's get the crime scene folks down here pronto," he said. "And the medical examiner."

"How many of these tunnels exist?" Jacoby asked, stooping to gain a better view of the tunnel's dark interior.

"Too numerous to count," Longmire said. "They are remnants of a past history of San Francisco and Chinatown and are mostly used by the homeless or addicts like

I said. But there are a few brave souls who love to explore them. Sorta like caving. Most of them have been destroyed as the city found them or in earthquakes."

"Detective, look here!" The patrolman's voice in the tunnel sounded urgent.

Jacoby and Longmire ducked their heads into the opening and peered into the tunnel. The patrolman's flashlight flickered on the tunnel's ceiling revealing a large hole. A manhole cover and a small pile of rust lay on the floor beside the officer. He pointed his light into the hole.

"Someone or something's been up here recently," he said. He stood with his upper body extending into the manhole. "There's another tunnel up here."

Outside the tunnel's opening Jacoby stood and thought for a brief moment.

"All right," he said to Longmire. "It's logical that the chimera escaped into the tunnel complex after dragging Patrolman Clark here. It's probably gone up through the manhole. Detective, get a squad of your SWAT team together and assemble them here. We'll check it out. In the meantime, I'm returning to the command post to wait. I need to get Dr. Olson down here. Notify me when everything is ready. I'm going in with you."

"You bet," Longmire said and began barking orders into his radio.

Back at the police command post, Jacoby dialed Harry's cell phone. The man answered it on the first ring.

"Dr. Olson? It's Jacoby."

"Yes," Harry said. His voice sounded groggy, as if he hadn't slept for a while.

"I need you and the Harbaum lady down at the Chinatown command post as soon as you can get here. Is she still with you?"

"Yes, she is. Why? What's going on?"

"Don't have the time to explain, Doctor. Just get down here as soon as possible. Understand?" Jacoby's voice was gruff and official.

"Yes, sir. We're on the way."

Finished on the phone, Jacoby studied the map of Chinatown on the trailer's wall. Pins were stuck in the map, identifying the location of the homicides of the past several weeks, and he noticed they were clustered around a small area to the north of the command post. In the center of the pins, he pushed one in at the location of Patrolman Clark's body and the tunnel.

He didn't know much about San Francisco tunnels, but if Longmire was right, Chinatown was rife with them, remnants of an earlier time. And those tunnels ran for miles. Old streetcar and subway rails stretching on endlessly. If the chimera had found its way into the main tunnel system, it would take a miracle to find it.

Later, with Harry and Millie at the command post, Jacoby outlined the current situation. He noticed that Harry's wife, Dixie, was had come with them. She looked nervously from him to Harry.

"I think we've got your creature cornered," he said. "We believe he found his way into a tunnel complex at the other end of this neighborhood. We tracked a blood trail to an opening into a tunnel where we discovered a dead policeman. Same MO as with the other victims. Since we have yet to locate the beast in Chinatown, he must be below ground in the tunnels."

"You've spotted him?" Harry said.

"Not yet but I feel certain he's in there. We are going in, and I want the two of you to come along. We may need your help if we get him cornered."

"We'll do what we can. You can count on us."

"Your wife can watch our progress over the CCTV on the monitor there," Jacoby said, pointing to a flat screen sitting in the desk. "We'll be carrying shoulder cameras and microphones."

"I'm going with you," Dixie said.

Harry shot her a quizzical look that turned to a frown.

"I'm afraid not," Jacoby said. "This is not up for debate, Doctor. You may remain here and watch the search on the monitor, or I will have a police officer take you back home."

Dixie slumped in her chair with a dejected look on her face.

Jacoby thought he detected a slight pout on her lower lip. "Sorry," he said. "In this, it's my way or the highway."

Dixie nodded her understanding.

"Fine." Jacoby turned to Harry. "Now let's go."

He led the way out of the command post and drove Harry and Millie to the park that now contained a horde of uniformed police officers. As they plodded through the forest, Jacoby heard Millie gasp and groan when she stumbled over a rock or root. She and Harry followed Jacoby and the yellow flag trail until they came to a small clearing filled with policemen in black fatigues who were all highly weaponized. Each wore a small shoulder video camera with a self-contained microphone.

A member of the SWAT team approached Jacoby and handed him a camera and battery pack. "Sir," he said. "Attach the camera to your lapel and fix the battery pack to your belt. Hit the green button, and you'll be on the air—live."

Jacoby did as instructed and noticed that Harry and Millie were not given a camera. Four SWAT team members, plus Longmire and Jacoby, gave their group six cameras to be monitored back in the command post by Dixie and a patrolman.

When everyone was connected, Longmire checked in

with the officer at the command post and assured himself that everything was in working order. Satisfied, he gave the thumbs up and headed toward the tunnel entrance.

"Time to lock and load," he said. "Sergeant, lead on."

The SWAT officer tumbled into the tunnel, and everyone followed suit, with Jacoby bringing up the rear and Harry in front of him. Millie pushed her way into the cramped confines of the tunnel ahead of Harry. At the back of the tunnel, Jacoby saw the first SWAT member clamber up into the manhole and disappear. One by one, each person inched their way through the hole and into another tunnel, this one much larger. Now Jacoby was able to stand. The headlamps of the SWAT team glimmered down through the tunnel, revealing trash scattered on the floor and graffiti scrawled on the walls.

ოოო

Dixie sat alongside a patrolman, eyes trained on the monitor in front of her. The screen was divided into six small rectangles, each a view from one of the cameras inside the tunnel. The picture flickered. The patrolman adjusted a knob on the monitor, and the flickering subsided.

Entranced, she watched the team's headlights dance over the walls and ceiling of the tunnel after they climbed through the manhole. The tunnel was littered with trash, empty plastic bottles, and drug paraphernalia, while the walls were covered with graffiti, *PIGS, ARYANS FOREVER!* and *KILROY WAS HERE.*

The team walked, single file, through the dark tunnel. Only the lights of their headlamps gave any illumination.

Dixie watched the team move slowly. Her cell phone chirped, and she answered. It was Pauling. He sounded upbeat.

"Dr. Olson," he said, his voice nearly singing. "I've got good news. I've been trying to reach Harry, but he doesn't answer."

"He's on a search for Roku at the moment, Dr. Pauling. What is it?"

"After meeting with the board of trustees, the university has offered to give Harry back his old position."

"That's wonderful," Dixie said.

"There's just one caveat."

Dixie's heart sank. "Yes?"

"He will be on a year's probation," Pauling said. "Strictly a formality, I assure you. It won't really mean anything."

"Dr. Pauling, if it doesn't mean anything, what difference does it make? Why do it?"

"I understand, Doctor, I do. But it's the condition laid down by the trustees. I don't think it will be all that bad or harmful to Harry's career. Two or three years from now, no one will remember."

Dixie hesitated a few moments before continuing. He anger was boiling near the surface, threatening to spill over. She tried to calm herself. "Dr. Pauling," she said, "Harry will know. As will I. And it will be on his record."

She heard a long sigh from Pauling.

"I tried my best. I couldn't do more."

"Harry and I appreciate all you have done, we do. But I don't think your solution will be acceptable to him. I will tell him you called, but I doubt he'll go for it. The man has a great deal of pride."

"Can I count on your help in trying to convince him otherwise?"

"Absolutely not, Dr. Pauling. Whatever he decides on his own, I will support one hundred percent."

After hanging up, Dixie returned her attention to the

monitor where it appeared the team along with Millie and her husband were in a different tunnel.

⌒⌒⌒

Millie trudged along in the dark in front of Harry wondering the real reason she was accompanying the team. Harry had mentioned to her on their drive to the command post that Jacoby wanted her along in case they needed to converse with Roku. She didn't believe, at first, that they had stumbled onto Roku. It was still difficult. But on the drive into Chinatown Harry convinced her to trust the FBI agent. All logic pointed to the fact that Roku was in this complex system of underground tunnels.

It was different underground, she thought. No light, no sounds except the tramping of their feet or the occasional whisper among the men. She worried about what would transpire when they caught up with her creation. As they stumbled forward, she said a silent prayer that she would be able to save Roku's life. It really didn't matter what happened to her, but Roku should be saved for the sake of science. He should be allowed to live so others could study and learn from him.

And, besides, he was half human.

The team halted where the tunnel divided into two diverging passageways. Jacoby conferred with Longmire. Millie tried to overhear what they were saying as water dripped in a steady stream from some unknown spot above them. But it was impossible to make out their discussion. Then the men's voices rose, and she could hear clearly. The tunnel acted as a funnel, echoing their conversation.

"What do you think?" Jacoby asked the detective. "Any idea where we are now?"

"We've been heading east," Longmire said, shining

his headlamp down the tunnel to their right. "That way," he said, pointing in the direction of his light, "may wind up under the financial district. But I'm not absolutely sure."

"Sir!" came a shout from the other tunnel. "Look here!"

Millie, along with Harry and the rest of the men gathered at the entrance of the left-hand tunnel. Soon, a SWAT team member emerged from its dark depths. He wore a quizzical look on his haggard face.

"You've got to see this," he said.

He turned to reenter the tunnel, and the others followed. Millie stumbled into darkness, eyes focused on the flickering lights ahead of her.

A rush of cold air greeted them, smelling dank and oppressive. The tunnel opened into a vast void of darkness, several stories high. At least a hundred meters across, the huge room had the feeling of an enormous empty auditorium or sports arena. Water trickled down the walls, glistening in the dim light. Millie strained her eyes to see beyond the reach of the headlamps, scanning the perimeter. As her eyes became adjusted to the dark, she was able to focus on the center of the underground chamber.

She couldn't believe her eyes.

"My God," she said in a loud voice.

Chapter 39

Harry was stunned by what he saw. He rubbed his eyes and blinked. In the middle of the huge chamber was an antique San Francisco streetcar. The faded green and white car sat like a silent sentinel to a time long past. As he became accustomed to the multi-storied room, he realized there were several other faded and rusting streetcars alongside the first, most missing their wheels. The group milled around the cars, chatting in hushed tones.

"What is this place?" Harry said, marveling at the dilapidated vintage streetcars.

"I believe," Longmire said, "that it may be a central streetcar station from the early days of Chinatown. From its christening as the first major, publicly owned, land-based transit agency in the United States in December 1912, the San Francisco Municipal Railway, known the world over as Muni, has operated with a singular mission—to provide safe, accessible transportation to all of the city's diverse and disparate populations, neighborhoods, and communities. Today, Muni serves as the transit arm of the San Francisco Municipal Transportation Agency, the umbrella agency responsible for operating and managing the city's integrated surface transportation network. This multimodal network includes walking, cycling, transit, parking, traffic, and taxis."

"I see," Harry said, slowly approaching the nearest streetcar.

"Cable cars proliferated throughout the city for over thirty years until the arrival of electric streetcars around 1900. Once perfected, these electric streetcars soon became practical on most grades in hilly San Francisco, although their high capital costs relegated their development to a slow pace, and cable cars continued to dominate up until the earthquake and fire. This period also was characterized by the consolidation of many independent and competing systems into the first Market Street Railway Company in the late 1800s, and further consolidation of all but three of the remaining independents as the United Railroads around 1900."

"Seems more like a graveyard for old streetcars," Jacoby said, joining Harry and Longmire.

"I believe there used to be a streetcar substation in Chinatown back in the old days," Longmire continued. "This may be it. There's several lines of tracks over there, and I think I see a roundtable as well."

"Roundtable?" Millie said.

"A circulator of sorts," Longmire said. "It is used to turn the streetcars around in order to have them face another direction. I remember when a steel millionaire, who had ridden the car regularly as a boy, purchased the famous Car Forty-Four. He later sold the car to Western Airlines, which motorized it and used it as a rolling ambassador of good will on a hundred -thousand -mile tour of the Western US and Mexico. It is now on display in Salt Lake City."

The group continued to mill around the cars, flashing their lights into each to illuminate its interior. From the far side of the chamber, a shout rang out.

"Detective! Over here!"

The SWAT team moved rapidly to surround the officer standing next to a lone streetcar at the rear of the substation. Longmire and Harry hustled to where the team had gathered followed by Jacoby and Millie.

"What is it?" Longmire said, as he approached the young policeman.

"There's movement inside the car sir," the man said. "My light picked it up as I was scanning this area."

Harry craned his neck to get a look inside the car, but its windows were too high. He stood on his tiptoes, but it was still no use. The bank of windows along the side of the car were simply too high to get a look inside. He walked around to the front of the streetcar and peered through the windshield, but it was impossible to see anything. The car's dark interior revealed nothing.

"You sure you saw something, Sergeant?" Jacob said. "It's hard to tell anything in this dim light, and the interior of the streetcar is totally black."

The young officer straightened and glared first at Jacoby then at Longmire.

"I can't be sure what it was," he said coldly, "but something definitely moved inside the car."

Millie ran to Harry's side and grasped his arm.

"It might be Roku," she said.

The rest of the SWAT team gathered around, weapons at the ready, awaiting their next orders. Harry stood stoically, uncomfortable in the cold of the chamber and the spookiness of its contents. If Roku was hiding in the streetcar, he doubted Millie could entice him to come out.

"Get your men surrounding the streetcar," Jacoby said to Longmire.

"What's your plan?" Harry said, his mouth dry. He had a sense that this was not going to end well.

"Toss a tear gas grenade in there," Jacoby said, motioning toward the car's front door. "When the thing comes out, kill it."

"No!" Millie screamed. "Please, Harry. Don't let them do this!"

Harry turned to Jacoby. In the dim light, the agent's jaw was firm, his brow knitted in a scowl. Longmire stood by, watching.

"Millie's right, Jacoby," Harry said. "We need to preserve this thing, if we can."

"I'm not in the mood to argue, Doctor. But quickly, tell me why?"

Harry and Millie started to talk at the same time, but she deferred to her former chairman. Her arms crossed over her shoulders, she listened.

"For no other reason than for the good of science," Harry said. "For the good of humanity. Let us study it, learn from it."

"For the good of humanity, Doctor? Really? The best thing for humanity right now is to destroy that thing. Your science friends have proven security is not your strength. Am I not right? If I remember correctly, your security was sorely lacking when your Yeti escaped last year. No, doctor, society cannot trust your security."

Turning back to Longmire, Jacoby continued.

"Disperse you men, Detective. The sooner we get this over with, the better."

"Please!" Millie pleaded again. "Let me see if I can talk to him and get him to come out with me. He knows me. If I can get him to come out on his own, you could bind him, and we could take him back to the research facility. Won't you give us that chance?"

Harry noted the agony written on Millie's face and his heart sank. Tears streamed down her cheeks, and her eyes were swollen. He glanced at her and noticed her face bore a panicked expression. Jacoby was silent for a moment.

"Jacoby," Harry pleaded. "We don't have much time. At least allow her this attempt. If Roku refuses to cooperate, you can do it your way."

"All right," he said. "You can try. But if you fail, we will do it my way." His tone accentuated his determination. "I am here to protect the citizens. But I'll allow the attempt. If something goes wrong, we're going in."

Millie nodded and headed toward the streetcar's front door. It took a minute of work to pry the rusted door open. Stale, musty air greeted Millie as she boarded its steps. Harry took up a position directly behind her while the SWAT team fanned out around the car. Jacoby remained on the steps of the car's entrance.

Harry could barely make out Millie's dark shape as she made her way down the car's center aisle.

∞∞∞

Millie's heart pounded wildly in her throat. The interior of the streetcar was black, the seats barely visible from the weak light of the SWAT team's headlights. She stood motionless at the front of the car for a moment allowing her eyes to become accustomed to the dark. No sound came from the car's rear. She fought to get her racing pulse under control.

"Roku?" she said in a voice just above a whisper.

Nothing.

"Roku, it's me, Mother."

Millie knew Roku would not be able to understand her words, only that he might recognize her voice. She hoped if she spoke in a calming voice he would allow her to come near him so he could recognize her. Then, hopefully, she could lead him out. But only if she could gain his trust. Maybe he remembered the word, *Mother.*

She took a hesitating step toward the rear of the streetcar and stopped. She strained her eyes into the dark recess of the car but saw nothing. She heard nothing.

She took several more halting steps toward the back of the car.

"Roku," she said in as calm a voice as she could muster. "Don't be afraid. I'm not going to hurt you. No one is going to hurt you. It's Mother."

Nothing.

Millie continued down the aisle. When she was in the middle of the car she stopped.

There, she thought. She heard a muffled noise as if someone moved.

"Roku, it's Mother. Let me see you."

As she approached further down the aisle, a low growl erupted from the dark.

She stopped and gazed into the black.

There, she saw it.

Two red glowing eyes staring at her.

Those eyes, she thought. Once playful yellow slits when she and Roku rolled on the floor together. Happy times when he was much younger.

Now those eyes glowed red, menacing, like glowing red coals.

And those eyes now pierced her to her very core.

"Roku," Millie said. "Don't be frightened. I won't let anyone hurt you."

She saw a dim form, almost ethereal, rise out of the gloomy darkness and approach her. Its red glowing eyes were fixed upon her, unwavering. Millie reached out her hand.

"Roku, it's me. It's Mother. Remember? Come with me."

In the blink of an eye, Roku was upon her. She screamed, and the terror in her voice pierced the massive cavern. She felt Roku's hands around her throat and his teeth ripping into her flesh. The pain was unbearable.

She struggled, but his strength was overpowering. Fixed in his powerful grasp, she felt Roku's hot breath on her neck. A quick thought of her parents and Gerald flashed through her head before everything went blank.

ᴄ⁄ɔᴄ⁄ɔ

Millie's scream jolted Dixie upright in her chair, her eyes glued to the monitor. She watched in disbelief as the SWAT team bolted into the streetcar and listened in horror as gunfire erupted from within. A shock grenade exploded, and its flash momentarily caused the monitor to fade. It sounded as if a small war was declared. Muzzle flashes appeared as small strobes on the monitor, and its light filled the small trailer. Then, as quickly as it had started, the gunfire ceased, and all was quiet. Smoke poured out of the streetcar's open door.

"Oh, my God," Dixie muttered to herself. "Please God, let Millie be alive."

ᴄ⁄ɔᴄ⁄ɔ

Harry was caught off guard by Millie's scream. He clambered up the streetcar doorway steps but was pushed aside by the SWAT team rushing inside.

Suddenly, there was a tremendous explosion and flash of brilliant light. Gunfire erupted, creating an unbelievable echo inside the car. SWAT team members shouting amidst the noise added to the confusion. Harry collapsed into the driver's seat and hung his head. He was powerless to do anything but await the outcome.

He thought he felt a ricocheted bullet glance past his shoulder and crash into the car's front panel. He shot a look into the rear of the streetcar and saw members of the

SWAT team firing away until their clips were empty, muzzle flashes temporarily blinding him. He struggled to find Millie but amidst the confusion and crowded car could not locate her. A thick pool of blood ran down the aisle and circled his shoes.

Then it was over.

One by one, the SWAT team exited the streetcar, and, in the dim light, he could make out Millie's blood-stained body lying slumped in a heap on the floor. Next to her, lay the lifeless form of Roku, the chimera she created.

Harry sat for a long moment, numbed to his core. He heard Jacoby board the streetcar and the man took a seat behind him. The agent shook his dead.

"It's the only way it could have ended, Dr. Olson," he said. "Except for the young woman being killed. I never wanted that."

Harry looked at the FBI agent, his eyes glistening.

"I think we could have expected it would have ended this way," he said. "In fact, I think Millie knew it would, also. After Roku's attacking her earlier, I think she knew he would again. If she couldn't save him, then maybe she just didn't wish to live in a world that would kill her creation."

"When the ME is finished with the thing's body, the university can have custody if they wish," Jacoby said. "Like you said, they may want to study it."

"A little late now," Harry said.

"Think of the families who will sleep a little better tonight knowing we killed their loved one's murderer. If there is any justice in this world, that has to be it."

"Justice, Jacoby? I wonder."

Harry stood, stumbled out of the streetcar, and followed several of the SWAT team back to the street. He needed to see Dixie.

Chapter 40

The setting sun cast deepening shadows and rays of orange and magenta over San Francisco Bay. The view from the patio of Harry and Dixie's San Mateo home was breathtaking. Gerald Siscom, Miles Radner, and Chloe Rawlings were gathered, and, while Dixie mixed drinks, Harry stoked the barbecue grill. It was a somber occasion, not the usual lighthearted bantering that accompanied their get-togethers. Millie's death cast a pall over the group.

"She was a tremendous asset to the university," Dixie said. "A brilliant, hard-working graduate student and a promising faculty member. She will be sorely missed."

"Here, here," Harry seconded. He sipped his drink and noticed Siscom sitting quietly. "How about you, Gerald? You worked with her every day."

Siscom shifted in his seat and cleared his throat. It was obvious he was having difficulty with Millie's death.

"What is there to say?" he said. "I was in love with her. I can't believe she's gone."

"We all feel that way, Gerald," Chloe said. "She was in a class of mine. No one worked harder."

"Harry talked with her parents the other day," Dixie said.

All eyes turned to him, expecting more. He nodded.

"Yes," he said. "I spoke with her father, mainly. They are devastated, of course. There wasn't much I could say. I believe Pauling called them as well."

"We will all miss her," Dixie said.

Radner brought news.

"Harry," he said, as the group lounged on the patio, drinks in hand. "I bring tidings from Dr. Pauling." He shot a glance at Dixie and winked. "He and the board of trustees have graciously reconsidered their decision and are offering you your old position back. Isn't that wonderful?"

Chloe set her drink on a small table and smiled.

"That's wonderful, Miles," she said.

"About time," Siscom chimed in.

Radner nodded.

"You talked with Pauling?" Harry said. He ambled to the barbecue and checked the steaks that were sizzling on the grill.

"Yes," Radner said. "And he is as excited about this turn of events as well."

Chloe Rawlings wore a white pantsuit and had pulled the jacket about her shoulders to ward off the evening chill.

"It's what we have all wished for, Harry. To have you back. Business as usual."

Radner frowned and shook his head.

"Well, not quite business as usual."

"Okay, Miles," Harry said. "What's the catch? There is a catch, right?"

"Just a slight one," Radner said, trying to sound upbeat. "You'll need to be on probation for a year. But, Harry, it's only a formality. No reflection on your character or reputation."

There was a moment of silence while Harry thought this over.

"No reflection, eh? Then why?"

"Oh, Miles, How could the board..." Rawling's irritated voice trailed off when Harry held up a hand.

"Listen, everyone," he said. "I love each of you and have had a grand time working with you. But I cannot accept the position under those terms. Miles, I'm sorry. I know you must have had a hand in this, and I appreciate it. You all have been so supportive. But, please, let's not let it spoil our evening."

Harry dished up the steaks and poured the wine while Dixie passed the salad around. Gradually, the talk turned to idle chatter with Harry being as relaxed as he had ever been. Later, when Dixie poured coffee, the phone rang. It was Dr. Brock with the Institute of American Antiquities.

"We've finished the vetting process," he said, "and I am pleased to offer you a position with the Institute. As we talked before, you can write your own ticket. I am so pleased."

Harry hardly knew what to say, but he accepted. Returning to the patio, he sported a large smile that wasn't wasted on Dixie.

"Who was that?" she said.

"The Institute," he replied. "Offered me a position, which I accepted."

Dixie jumped up and hugged him. "Oh, that's just wonderful," she said.

"What will you be doing?" Siscom said, sipping his coffee.

"I dunno. I haven't thought about it much."

Chloe Rawlings, who had been silent through most of dinner, rose and stretched her legs. "Harry," she said. "Congratulations. I wish you all the best."

"As do all of us," Radner enjoined.

Chloe continued. "I have been struggling with what Millie did. On the one hand, what she accomplished was a giant scientific step forward and took a tremendous amount of courage. On the other hand, didn't she just create a monster? A monster that, in the end, society had to deal with and that took her life?"

Harry shook his head. "Well, classically, a monster is any creature, usually found in legends or horror fiction, often hideous, that produces fear or physical harm by its appearance or its actions. The word derives from the Latin monstrum, which means an aberrant occurrence, usually biological, that was taken as a sign that something was wrong within the natural order. The word usually connotes something wrong or evil. A monster is generally morally objectionable, physically or psychologically hideous, or a freak of nature. It can also be applied figuratively to a person with similar characteristics like a greedy person or a person who does horrible things."

Siscom laughed, patting Harry on a shoulder. "He sounds just like a college professor, doesn't he?"

"You can laugh about it if you want, Gerald," Chloe said. "But Roku was, in my opinion, a genetic monster."

"Nature does this all the time, Chloe," Harry said. "It's called mutation. Most of the mutations do not survive very long and die off."

"The chimera didn't look like any of us, didn't act like any of us, and, quite simply, wasn't like any of us. So what good was Millie's experiment? For what noble purpose was Roku created?"

"Are you suggesting, Chloe," Radner said, "that the work of science should be solely for society's benefit? How about knowledge for knowledge's sake?"

"Isn't that the story of the fall of man?" Dixie said. "Trying to be like God?"

Harry pursed his fingers together. It felt good to be among friends, debating serious issues.

"I think," he said, "we have this intelligence, and we should use it. Whether it was given to us or it was developed over eons, matters little to me. We have it, and to not use it would be tantamount to wasting our unique gift."

"It's such a shame to not see how Roku turned out," Dixie said. "We all might have been surprised."

Later that evening after his guests left and Dixie was asleep, Harry sat in his study. The soft light from his desk lamp illuminated what he held in his hands. Now that he had a position with the Institute of American Antiquities, he could go anywhere, do anything his heart desired. But what was that?

He stared at the tube of blood he held. It was a tube of Roku's blood he procured from the ME's office during the autopsy. Cal Pacific declined the donation of Roku's corpse, so the chimera's body was dumped in the ME incinerator and destroyed.

But within Roku's blood lay his genetic code, the secret of what made him different. Part Millie Harbaum and part Yeti.

He thought for a long while.

What could he do with Roku's blood?

Then he smiled.

About the Author

Richard Edde was born and raised in Oklahoma. After graduating from Central State College, he attended the University of Oklahoma College of Medicine, where he earned his medical degree in 1971. After spending a few years in family practice in two rural Oklahoma towns, he completed a residency in anesthesiology. Following a long career in academia and private practice, he retired to devote time to writing. His first novel, *The Photograph*, was released in 2014. Dr. Edde resides in eastern Oklahoma with his wife.